Geoducks Are for Lovers

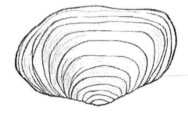

A NOVEL

Daisy Prescott

Alex—
Thanks for coming to
our tampa stopping!
xo
Daisy Prescott

ISBN: 978-0-9894387-3-5

Cover Design by ©Sarah Hansen at OkayCreations.com

Cover Photo: Smit/Shutterstock

Shell illustration: Shawn Hauserman

First Print Edition May 2013

For Shawn

ata

It is never too late to be what you might have been.

~ George Eliot

One

Geoduck (*Panopea generosa*)
(pron.: \gü-ē-ˌdək\ "gooey duck")
n. The world's largest burrowing clam
~~~~~

Do laundry.
Stop by the farmers' market and pick up the weekly produce box.
Make the beds in the guest rooms.
Find blankets for the twin beds upstairs.
Put extra towels in the downstairs bath.
Ask John for firewood.
Locate some fresh caught salmon and make a couscous salad.
Start restaurant review and article on huckleberry recipes.
Check that Bessie has gas.
Confirm Quinn's flight arrival.

As Maggie takes the shortcut through the woods she makes a mental list of everything she needs to get done today. The cool shadows of the trees are a nice break from the strong August sun. Her dog, Biscuit, dashes ahead of her after spotting a squirrel on the trail. He's an island dog through and through and loves when she cuts into the woods on their daily runs almost as much as he likes getting squirted by the clams on the tidal flat. Speaking of biscuits, Maggie makes an additional mental note:

Buy ingredients for scones.

The trees end, and she rejoins the main road. It's another perfect summer day with a cloudless sky. Turning for home, Maggie sprints down the hill to her beach cabin. It still feels strange to call it hers even after over a year of owning it outright. So much has changed over the past few years. Yet the road beneath her feet, and the view over the bay and beyond Double Bluff to the Olympic Mountains, is the same from her childhood summers.

* * *

Coffee in hand, Maggie sits at the table on her deck facing the water. A cargo ship heads north toward Admiralty Inlet and out to the Pacific Ocean. Beyond the stray piles of sun-bleached driftwood and rock-strewn beach at the foot of the stairs, the tidal flat that gives Useless Bay its name lays exposed with the ebb tide. Shallow streams and deeper pools create continents of wet sand extending for nearly a mile out to the receding water.

With her long hair pulled into a messy bun after her shower and wearing her favorite black shorts with her ancient Evergreen geoduck T-shirt, she copies down her mental to-do list to prepare for her house guests. Biscuit romps on the lawn with Babe, the yellow Lab from next door. They appear to be in a tug o'war with a piece of driftwood, and Biscuit is losing.

"Knock, knock?"

Maggie hears a voice call out and glances up from her laptop to see her neighbor, John, waving at her from the steps. He's holding a large freezer bag.

"Please tell me that is some freshly-caught salmon. You'll save me a trip to the store or having to thaw some of my frozen stash."

"It is indeed. Caught a King earlier this morning," he says, laying the bag with a large piece of gorgeous salmon on the table.

"You are the best. Can you put it in the fridge for me? And as a reward, there's coffee in the pot if you want some."

"Sounds like a fair deal. Need a refill?" John brings her cup inside.

John rents the house next door from his uncle. Their homes sit in a row of four similar modern, weathered cedar-shingled cabins on Sunlight Beach. Most of the original, more modest houses along this stretch have been razed and replaced with larger summer homes for tech elite and other wealthy Seattle weekenders.

There are worse things in the world than being a single woman of a certain age and having sweet eye candy next door who can also dispose of giant spiders and mice, and provide free crabs. Over the last several years, the two have settled into a regular routine of coffee and walks on the beach when their schedules allow. Quinn nicknamed him Paul Bunyan because of his 'lumberjack good looks,' as he calls them. Tall, with dark hair and matching beard, John does resemble the legendary lumberjack. A dog named Babe and his ever present plaid shirt only add to the similarity.

"So no walk with the dogs this morning?" he asks when he returns with their coffees.

"Sorry. Can't. Got up and took Biscuit for a run already. Must run errands, write an article, and get ready for Quinn's arrival tomorrow."

"Babe will be disappointed. I wondered why you were showered and dressed. Normally when I stop by this time of day, you're still in your pajamas. Nice T-shirt, by the way. Geoducks are for lovers, huh?" He winks at her.

Their easy-going friendship is one of the things she loves most about living on the beach year round. John's lived on the island his whole life, but moved down to the beach three years ago, right before Maggie came back. Winters are quiet and still. It's nice to have someone to play Scrabble with when the power goes out from the latest winter storm.

"Hey now, don't diss my alma mater. You know I'm a writer. Pajamas are practically a required uniform—along with yoga pants and fleece. Admit it, you love catching me wearing my PJs just so you can tease me."

John laughs. "You are fun to tease. Your feistiness is one of your best traits. But speaking of yoga pants, the new wife in the compound at the end of the road was doing yoga again in the smallest shorts ever seen. I'm pretty sure they'd be underwear for anyone else." He sits down at the table.

"Ooh, did she catch you gawking at her?" She pokes his arm.

"Nope. Was wearing my shades." He doesn't deny the ogling.

"You better behave. I heard the husband is a big deal lawyer in Seattle. We don't need you being the scandal of the week."

John has a habit of flirting with the summer wives, although he doesn't go further. He's certainly better looking than most of the husbands—and a decade or two younger. Their wives love the attention from the hot local guys and probably think it comes as part of the island lifestyle package that accompanies their enormous "cabin" on the sand.

"Mags, I only have eyes for you."

"Ha!" Maggie knows about John's little crush on her. Being ten years older than John isn't what holds her back from encouraging his pursuits. No, it's more to do with her feelings about ruining their friendship for some hanky-panky. Things would be awkward if they fooled around and didn't work out. She knows how getting physical with a friend can change everything, and frowns at the thought of repeating history.

"College gang coming up this weekend?" he asks

Her mood lifts when she thinks of seeing her old friends again and she nods. "They are. I'm excited. It's been a while since we've been together." Thoughts of her friends distract her for a moment. "Picking up Quinn tomorrow. The rest arrive Thursday."

"Is the gorgeous Selah part of the gang?" He looks a little sheepish asking about her sexy friend right after declaring his fidelity to her.

"So much for only having eyes for me. Yes, Selah drives up from Portland tomorrow. I think she's bringing a date, though, so you might not get the chance to flirt with her again."

"Flirt? Me?" He attempts to act insulted.

"Yes, you. You are the king of flirts. Certainly of this beach if not all of south Whidbey, but you've met your match in Selah."

"I need a crown, then. And a T-shirt." He finishes the last of his coffee, his eyes brightening with mirth.

"I'll start right on that," she says, laughing. "But before that, I must finish up this writing business and get going." While she loves her morning coffee and walk ritual with John, he tends to linger if he isn't working.

"Need any help before the invasion?"

"Oh, thanks for reminding me. Actually, there is something you can do for me. We want to have a beach fire Friday night and maybe Saturday. Can you get me some wood? And don't make a lewd comment about your wood."

"You're no fun. Yes, I've got firewood. I'll drop it on the beach for you on Friday morning, since I'm off island tomorrow and Thursday for some meetings. I might set the traps if I get up early enough to take the boat out Friday. You want crabs if I pull any?"

"Do I want crabs? What kind of silly question is that? Of course. Dungeness is my lobster."

He furrows his brow. "Wouldn't lobster be your lobster?"

"I meant for most people lobster is the ultimate shellfish, but for me, Dungeness crab is the best, especially fresh caught and free."

"Gotcha. I'll stop by Friday morning with wood and crabs." He snorts at his own joke.

Maggie rolls her eyes at him. "If you come over early enough, you might be able to see both Selah and me in our jammies."

John's eyes sparkle. "I'll be over early. Definitely."

She watches his backside as he walks the short distance between their houses, stepping between her overgrown flowerbeds that serve as a property line of sorts.

Biting her thumbnail, she wonders if maybe she should be brave and give in to his flirtations. It *has* been a while… for a lot more than sex.

Geoducks Are for Lovers

Two

After gathering her list and the mugs, Maggie heads inside to find her keys and bag. Biscuit comes running when she whistles for him, wagging his tail and bouncing when he sees her purse. She suspects he loves going on errands with her because he knows he'll get treats wherever they go. The two are rarely apart; he is her loyal companion and friend.

First stop on today's list of errands is picking up her weekly Community Sustained Agriculture box from the farmers' market. Her cabin's small lot means no sizable kitchen garden, so Maggie supplements with local produce. The long history of farming on the island makes her feel proud and the foodie in her loves the challenge of cooking with whatever she gets for the week.

Sally mans the CSA stand when Maggie and Biscuit arrive.

"Look who finally turned up on Tuesday."

Maggie furrows her brows. "Did I say I was coming on Saturday? It completely slipped my mind."

"Welcome to the aging brain. No worries, we redid your box fresh this morning figuring you'd turn up today."

"Sorry. I get lost in my head some days. What's in the box this week?"

"Lots of greens, more zucchini, Japanese eggplant, some cherry tomatoes, and cucumbers. I put a pint of marionberries in there, too." Sally reaches down to scratch Biscuit's head. "And a few homemade dog treats." Biscuit gives her a paw to earn his treat.

"Sounds perfect. I was going to try to pick some wild blackberries this week."

"There should be some ripe berries out there, but you better get picking before the weekenders turn up if you want the best ones."

Maggie nods in agreement. "Good point."

"Can't wait to read what you make this week. Lester and I still talk about the stinging nettle pasta you posted this spring. Who'd have thought you could make something delicious with such nasty stuff! Your blog is delightful." Sally smiles with pride.

Her mother's friend's kindness touches Maggie. "I love that you read my blog. Thanks for the support."

"You're a Whidbey Island girl now and we support our own." Sally gives her a hug. "Are you doing any baking with those berries? Boy, do we miss your mother's baking. Such a shame."

"I'll probably make scones or a pie. Or both. Some days I really miss the bakery." Maggie's eyes begin to prick with tears. "It wasn't the same without Mom, you know?"

"Oh sweetie, nothing is. You did the best you could for as long as you could. Caring for your mom and running her bakery would be too much for anyone. It was the right thing to sell. Anne's recipes live on, even if they aren't quite as good as when she or you were there."

Maggie takes in a quivering breath. One of the toughest things she did in the past year was selling her mother's share of the bakery after Anne's death. "Thanks for saying that. I was never the baker Mom was. I'm a writer, not a baker."

"You doing okay these days?" Sally strokes Maggie's arm.

"Hanging in there. Friends are coming up this weekend and this beautiful summer weather helps."

"Friends sound fun. You should have good weather all weekend. Sun trumps rain most days. Although you don't want to get spoiled and forget where you live."

Maggie gestures out over the field toward the Sound and Mount Baker in the distance. "How can we ever forget?"

The people who call this corner of the world home perpetuate the myth it rains around Seattle every day, year round. Locals attempt to protect their treasure by emphasizing the never-ending rain and damp winters while avoiding talk of long sunny, warm, but rarely hot, days lasting late into the evening hours. These summers almost balance the long, cold, dark days of winter. Almost.

Connie from the bank walks over from the parking lot. Knowing she'll get stuck in an epic gossip session if she doesn't leave now, Maggie grabs the box marked Marrion and says a quick good-bye. She waves to Connie as she passes her on the way back to the car.

A short drive later, Maggie parks on Second Street in Langley. "Another cookie?" she asks Biscuit, who bounds from her car after getting his leash attached.

An empty table in the shade outside Useless Bay Coffee waits for them. After tethering Biscuit's leash to a chair, she heads inside. Biscuit won't run off, but if he isn't tied up, he'll wander around, on the hunt for treats. "No begging," Maggie calls over her shoulder. Biscuit sighs and lies down under the table.

"Morning, Maggie," Erik greets her from behind the counter, wiping his hands on his green apron. His lanky build and floppy blonde hair remind her of Quinn in college. Or a golden retriever puppy.

"Hey there," she says, eyeing the pastry case.

"Regular? Or are you in a fancy mood today?"

"Nah, I'll have an *au lait* in a bucket. I need to get some writing done this morning."

"Bucket *au lait*. Got it." The espresso machine whirs to life as Erik starts to make her drink. "What's today's article about?"

"Huckleberries. Not sure what I'm doing with it. Every time I go to write it I get distracted by Huckleberry Hound and Mark Twain. Then the cartoon dog starts quoting Twain, and well... I need more coffee." She shakes her head and chuckles at her own rambling.

"Maybe you need less coffee. My grandmother makes the best huckleberry jam and syrup. She cans them and we use it over everything."

"Hmmm..." Maggie's mind begins to spiral. "I think you might be on to something. I've been so focused on fresh, I hadn't considered canning them. My grandmother made huckleberry syrup and I bet I have her recipe. Erik, you're a genius."

The twenty-something grins and his cheeks pink at her praise. Maggie feels a little bit like Mrs. Robinson. He's so young. No flirting with young boys, she reminds herself.

"Huckleberry syrup it is." She begins plotting her article in her head as she waits for her drink.

"Pastry?" he asks.

"Nah." She waves off his offer. "Just the coffee."

"Here's something for Biscuit." Erik hands her a homemade dog cookie.

She thanks him, pays and then heads outside to find Biscuit on his back, getting his belly rubbed by a man in cycling gear.

"Gorgeous dog. Yours?" he asks Maggie as she puts her coffee and bag down on the table.

"He is. Although sometimes I think he'll be anyone's for the right treat."

At the word 'treat', Biscuit rolls over and sits up, brown eyes focused on Maggie. She breaks the cookie in half.

"Interesting looking dog. What kind is he?" The stranger asks, standing. He looks like a typical summer visitor over for a day of cycling. He's clearly built up a sweat riding around the island. Maggie pegs him as a Web 2.0 kind of guy after eyeing his expensive looking gear. He easily could be one of her seasonal neighbors down at the beach.

"He's a rescue dog. I'm not really sure. Most people think English Setter, maybe Border Collie, mutt. Something black, white, and freckled."

Biscuit proffers his paw to the stranger.

"Biscuit, no begging," Maggie admonishes, but hands the second half of the treat to the cyclist.

"Good boy." Cyclist guy pats the dog on the head. "I'll leave you to your day. Have a good one."

He grabs his helmet off an adjoining table and straps on his gear before giving them a wave and riding away.

Biscuit stares at Maggie. Seeing she has no more cookies, he sighs and lies back down near her feet.

"Flirt," she chastises him before scratching his head, laughing at her companion.

After taking her Macbook out of her bag, she sips her coffee as her blog opens, and ponders the many uses for huckleberry syrup—buckwheat pancakes, crepes, ice cream, cocktails, Pavlovas... her stomach grumbles. Maybe she should have grabbed a pastry from Erik. Writing about food on an empty stomach is torture.

A half hour later she has the bones of her article finished as well as her coffee. Life as a food blogger means she can work from anywhere and at any time as long as she meets her deadlines. A few trips to Seattle a month to review restaurants, bakeries, and the latest foodie store suits her better than doing a daily commute and worrying about magazine layoffs. She checks her blog stats and reviews her advertising revenue. Freelance writing doesn't pay what it used to, but she wouldn't trade her current flexibility or beach cabin for a big byline.

She thinks about her life today while gazing up at the cloudless sky. The battles of the last few years linger in her mind as she looks out at the water and Camano Island in the distance. Her view is the same one her mother saw every day from her bakery down the street. Everything can change in a short amount of time, yet life keeps moving forward.

Biscuit stretches, yawns, and nudges her with his nose.

Shaking off her melancholy, she gathers her things. "Right. Let's go. We have stuff to do."

* * *

Maggie stretches out her arms, her shoulders protesting from hours of working on her laptop. After sending her review of a Fremont cheese shop to her editor, she adds the final photos to her article on six ways to enjoy her grandmother's huckleberry syrup before posting it to her blog.

"Done," she announces to the empty room, the quiet broken only by the music from her playlist.

From her perch at the dining table, aka her downstairs office, she surveys the state of the house. With its vaulted ceiling and a double row of large windows, the open living area is airy with a view out over the deck and water beyond. The clean house feels inviting. The beds are made upstairs. The salmon for tomorrow's dinner is in the fridge and couscous cools on the stove. Her excitement grows as she mentally checks off the last of her to-do list before Quinn's arrival tomorrow. Remembering her overgrown flowerbeds, she decides she'll pick flowers in the morning before catching the ferry.

"Ready for company?" Biscuit tilts his head, but doesn't answer. She didn't think he would. She's become used to these one-sided conversations between her and the dog.

"It won't be so quiet around here with a house full of people this weekend." Silence answers her.

Wandering around the living room, she grazes her hand over books in the bookcase in the corner. Many of her mother's favorites still line the shelves. Classic romances and a few of her grandmother's birding books are mixed together. Bronte and Austen meet the birds of the Western U.S. The lower two shelves hold some of her parents', and maybe even grandparents', record albums from the sixties, seventies and eighties.

The cabin has been passed down through the women of her family, from grandmother to mother, and now to Maggie, not because of any formal declaration, but solely because the women have outlived the men. She recalls her grandmother survived her grandpa by five years; her mother outlived her father by nine.

Inhaling deeply, she breathes in the scent of ocean, old books, and decades of fires in the wood-stove– the history and constancy of this home make her smile. The cabin is winterized, thanks to her parents wanting a year-round retreat, but the wood-stove is her favorite way to heat the house on chilly nights. Icy storms and windy winter rains are still a few months away, she reminds herself.

Randomly pulling out an album, she mutes her playlist, walks over to the credenza under the window, and turns on the stereo. Joni Mitchell's voice croons from the speakers when she puts the needle down on the turntable and cranks up the volume.

As Joni sings about dancing and taking chances, Maggie joins in on harmony—so many memories hidden in these albums. Happier times with her parents here in this room mix with the longing she rarely lets herself feel to have one more day with either of them.

Her father called Whidbey his briar patch back when the long sunny summers were all about salmon fishing and telling tales about the latest catch after a round of golf at the club. Her mother spent summers growing giant dahlias and baking pies that would win best of show ribbons at the Island County Fair.

Wondering if her mom listened to Joni when alone and nostalgic, Maggie runs her hands over the cool white marble surface of the kitchen island and hears her mother's voice expounding about coldness of stone being good for working with butter doughs and crusts. The luxurious stone is incongruous with the simple modern kitchen, but the scratches and stains of years of use fit right in with the vintage style of the cabin.

Her mother's countless homemade pies lead to the opening of the bakery. Anne's pride and joy became much more than a side project to keep Anne busy after the death of Maggie's father. Anne went from running the bakery six days a week to being sick and dying over two short years.

Joni makes her melancholy, so she takes *Blue* off the turntable. Maggie looks at the next record over on the shelf: *Avalon* by Roxy Music. She had the same album in high school and college. Turning it over, she searches for her initials. Small uppercase M's are carefully written on the back. She doesn't remember bringing the record to the cabin, but here it is.

With the first notes of "More than This," the ghosts scatter as other memories take over– 1988 and a road trip with a beautiful boy with shaggy, brown hair. Maggie hums and smiles at the image of her eighteen-year-old self on the road with new college friends. The first big adventure of her newly-found freedom was driving down to the coast to hear a band in concert and staying on a stranger's floor. Some of those friends from that road trip will be arriving tomorrow. Biting the side of her thumb, she remembers the beautiful boy and wonders if he ever thinks of her when he hears this album.

Her reflection greets her in the window when she looks out at the dark, summer night sky. If she squints, she can almost see her college self —hair is different, body is different, but something of her former self is still in there somewhere.

"I'm a sentimental fool, Biscuit." She glances over at the dog. "You could disagree with me just once, you know." Biscuit gets up and walks over to the door out to the deck. It's his way of saying 'time for bed'.

The night outside is inky. A few of the other houses down the beach are illuminated, but the water beyond is black. Sparse lights twinkle on the far shore. Stars, so seldom seen in the city, sparkle above. After three years, Maggie is still getting used to the quiet darkness. She shudders and wraps her sweater around her in the cool night air. No more sweltering, summer nights in the concrete jungle of New York. The chill and quiet remind her of her solitude. Calling out to the dog, she gratefully returns to the warmth of her cozy living room.

Geoducks Are for Lovers

Three

Finding her garden clippers in the garage, Maggie walks out to the neglected flowerbed the next morning. She deadheads some of the flowers and cuts others for vases in the guest rooms. The tangled mess of dahlias, cosmos and zinnias begins to look less like a jungle and more like a proper lady's garden. Her mother and grandmother started the flower gardens on the lot, and guilt, rather than a green thumb, compels her to replant them every summer. On her list of things she loves about the cabin, weeding and tending to the beds are toward the bottom.

Admitting to herself she likes the idea of free flowers as much as free crabs and fish, Maggie finishes the task, giving a small thanks to the island and its abundance. As a kid she didn't appreciate the simplicity of being here, but years of living in the city have taught her the value of dirt under her nails and sand between her toes.

Back inside, flowers are bunched and in their new homes on bedside tables, in the bathroom, and even in a slim blue glass bottle on the ledge above the kitchen sink. Their bright colors make her happy.

* * *

After changing into a navy cotton shirt dress and green sandals, Maggie puts Biscuit into his crate. "I know you want to come with me to lick Quinn upon arrival, but Bessie only has two seats, and not enough room for both you and Quinn. Try not to pine."

Biscuit whines like he understands he is missing out, then curls up with a sigh. Maggie swears he's pouting, so she gives in and hands him another cookie.

"Spoiled dog."

Maggie grabs the keys to Bessie along with two faded Mariners caps from the hooks by the front door, finds her purse, and heads to the garage. Taking off the tarp, she reveals her prized possession—a 1972 MG Midget convertible. Like the cabin, Bessie has been handed down from mother to daughter. The convertible is the perfect summer car. She isn't in pristine condition, but Steve the mechanic loves the MG as much as Maggie does, and keeps it in top shape. All the locals recognize her hunter green finish and white racing stripes.

Anne hated Maggie nicknaming her car Bessie. She laughs and rolls her eyes at her mother's name for the car, Queen Elizabeth the Second, or QE II. Unfortunately, Bessie's customized license plate still bears the more pretentious QE II name. As much as she dislikes the vanity plate, she can't bring herself to get rid of it.

The convertible can only be driven in good weather because the top leaks and the heating is temperamental at best. Given its tiny size, the car rarely leaves the island to face the big highways over in 'town,' a term the islanders call everything on the other side of the water.

Picking up Quinn for a weekend of old friends and ghost stories from the past officially counts as a special occasion deserving of Bessie.

Baseball cap on her head to tame her hair and protect her nose from the sun, she starts up the car and backs out of the garage. The drive down to the ferry takes about fifteen minutes, and given it's mid-morning during the week, there shouldn't be a long wait.

Maggie smiles when she counts only a dozen or so cars on the dock as she heads down the hill from Clinton. Looking across the water toward Mukilteo, she calculates the ferry is a few minutes from docking. Perfect timing.

No articles to be done, a good run in the woods, and now an afternoon with one of her best friends—this is turning out to be a great day. Maggie grins as she pulls into the ferry lot.

When she pays, the woman in the ticket booth hands her the fall ferry schedule. Once the summer craziness fades with the passing of Labor Day, the ferries drops a few runs as the island quiets down for the long, gray winter.

"Is it bad I look forward to the fall schedule and not having to work my life around ferry waits?" Maggie asks.

"If you didn't, you wouldn't be an islander. I think we all cheer the coming of fall and getting our island back."

Maggie beams at being called an islander. To be accepted here as a local isn't an easy transition—she'll take the compliment.

"Lane three. Have a good day." She waves Maggie through to the waiting area on the dock.

Bert loads the cars on to the ferry as she pulls forward. He's an old friend of her mom's and she can't remember a time when she didn't know Bert. He gives her the prime spot in the middle at the front of the ferry—first to be loaded off the boat. Maggie takes this as a good omen.

"I see you're taking Bessie to town," Bert says as she gets out of the car to head up top. "What's the special occasion?"

"College friends coming up for the weekend. We're having a pre-reunion reunion before the actual one in September. Figured nostalgic times called for nostalgic transportation."

"Reunion? How long has it been?"

"Twenty years."

"Sweet lord. Twenty years? That's hard to believe. If you're that old, well, I must be ancient."

Maggie looks at Bert. His lined and weathered face makes her think of the expression 'salty dog', but she resists the urge to point out the facts.

"I can tell you're thinking about telling me I'm old. Just you wait. Time flies even more on the back side of the slope. Is that a gray hair?" He reaches out toward her strawberry blonde hair. Thanks to her colorist, she doesn't have any gray hairs.

"Don't remind me. Some days I feel like I'm still twenty-two."

"Me too," he says, then smiles, showing gaps in his teeth. "You kids have fun. I'll be looking for you in the paper next week."

The weekly police report in the local paper is a favorite of island residents, summer people, and tourists. Most of the reports feature sheep in the road or a stolen crab trap. The typical crimes reported are petty theft or car accidents. Darker, more sinister crimes tend to stay out of the paper or make the front page if a scandal is involved.

"The last time I was in the police report was a long time ago. And there's still no proof I left Bessie on the baseball diamond at Maxwelton."

"Sure, but we all know the truth." Bert taps his nose as he walks toward the back of the boat.

Upstairs on the passenger deck, she sits at a table by the window and watches the water as the ferry makes its quick crossing back to the real world. Maggie wouldn't trade living on Whidbey. This island and all its quirks is truly her home. When she first moved here full time, it surprised her how Connie at the bank was informed so quickly about her life, hours or days after things happened. Maggie suspects Connie, Sally, and Sandy at the grocery store, are part of an old fashioned telephone tree. News travels fast around here. By the time she gets back with Quinn, she bets those women will know all about her guests for the weekend. Sandy might even happen to stop by with a loaf of zucchini bread, claiming to be overrun with squash again.

Four

The little MG holds its own amongst the traffic and intimidating trucks on the I-5 through the heart of downtown Seattle.

Arriving at SeaTac, Maggie spies Quinn in his aviators and 'Legalize Gay Cupcakes' T-shirt on the curb of Arrivals. It would be hard to miss his tall, lean form, and blond hair even if he wasn't wearing a pink and white shirt.

He seems more excited to see Bessie than he does Maggie. She thinks he even kisses Bessie's hood when she hops out to open the trunk. He's always been obsessed with the MG.

"Maggie!" He folds her up in a hug, which ends in a spin. "I've missed you, woman!"

"I've missed you, Q. How was the flight?"

Boyfriends, girlfriends, husbands, jobs, and parents may all go, but her anchor remains Quinn. Living in the same city, they'd never let more than a week or two pass without seeing each other, but that's changed since she left him behind in New York.

"Good, better now that you've brought my one true love, Elizabeth the Second. Can I drive her?" Quinn looks at Maggie expectantly, though they both know she'll never let him drive Bessie.

"You two can get reacquainted from the passenger seat." Throwing his weekend bag in the trunk, they pile into the car, and she hands him the other baseball cap, which he refuses, brushing over his short hair to show he doesn't need the hat.

As they head back north to Mukilteo to catch the ferry home, Quinn reaches into the glove box to pick out a mix tape. Maggie has never updated Bessie's sound system—it's either a cassette tape or the radio. Her tapes from the 80s and 90s are a perfect soundtrack for the weekend ahead. Over the angst of Nirvana and the noise of the road, Quinn shouts, "When does everyone get here?"

"You're the first. Ben and Jo arrive tomorrow. They're driving down from Vancouver after his meetings end. Selah said she'll get in tomorrow tonight as well. She's coming with a date. Any idea who the mystery man might be?" She raises her voice to be heard over the wind.

Silence greets her. Glancing over at him to make sure he heard her, she sees Quinn looking like he swallowed the cat who ate the canary.

"Who is it? Oh, he's not that horrible guy she was dating, is he? The one from the dating website who wrote her an email as Mr. Rochester? Please tell me it isn't him. Please?"

"Nope. Guess again." He seems delighted about Selah's mystery guest.

"New lover?"

"No, not a lover. Not so new." Quinn smirks.

It must be someone he knows. Maybe she knows Selah's guest, too.

"Someone I know?"

"Yes, someone you know." He bites the inside of his cheek to stop himself from saying more.

"Will this person be at the Greener reunion?" She gets a sinking feeling.

"Yep."

"No." *It can't be.* The sinking feeling in her stomach begins to resemble the Titanic.

"Yep."

"Could you please stop saying yep?" She gives him a sidelong look.

"Yep."

She smacks Quinn on his shoulder and his oh-too-happy self. Brown eyes and shaggy hair flash in her mind.

"It's Gil, isn't it? And don't say yep again!"

"It is indeed Gil."

"Oh."

"That's it? That's all you have? 'Oh?' I thought I might get more than 'oh'." Quinn crosses his arms in disappointment.

"She mentioned bringing someone with her when we started talking about everyone coming to visit before the reunion, but since she was vague, I figured it was Mr. Rochester and she didn't want the judging. So. Gil, huh?"

"Yep."

She smacks him again.

"What was that for?" Rubbing his shoulder where she hit him, he leans as far away from her as he can in the tiny car.

"The yep and not telling me before about Gil."

Gil. At my house. Tomorrow. Her mind races.

"You knew this all along, didn't you? Does everyone know?"

"I may have had conversations with Selah about said matter, yes. You know she's the optimistic romantic in this group. I think she's always had a soft spot for you and Gil. In her mind, if the French Incident hadn't happened, it was only a matter of time before you two realized you both felt the same way and acted on it. Now you're both divorced, and she's back to drawing your initials on her notebook. No pressure or anything." He laughs and ducks from another slap which doesn't come.

"Yeah, no pressure. Gil and I are friends. Just like the rest of us. It'll be nice to see him again."

"Uh, huh. Friends. And 'nice to see him again.' Keep telling yourself that, Magpie."

If only Quinn and Selah knew the truth. Gil and Maggie had acted on their feelings. And despite her hoping for a different outcome back then, they had remained just friends—friends, but no longer best friends.

* * *

When they pull into the ferry waiting lot in Mukilteo, she's ready for a cocktail. They are far enough back in line to have one drink at Ivar's Clam Bar before the next ferry loads. It's tradition to get a drink, a cup of chowder, or soft serve ice cream at Ivar's, depending on the time of day and the ferry wait. Today might be both a cocktail and ice cream day given Quinn's revelation about the unexpected guest.

Quinn excuses himself to the bathroom, leaving her at the bar with her thoughts. She stares at the water and ferry dock, not seeing either as her mind and heart try to wrap themselves around his revelation.

Gil's coming to the island.

Of all the friends in the group from college, Gil and Maggie have been the worst at keeping in touch. Neither one believes in Facebook, so they don't get the constant updates, snarky online cards, and pictures of children and pets of each other's lives. Forced to rely on the old school methods of leading questions to mutual friends, vague and infrequent updates disappoint. Because Selah and Gil both live in Portland, she's the best source of information. Selah's the one who told Maggie Gil and Judith got divorced three years ago. She also told Gil when Maggie's mom died and he sent a card. Maggie wonders if she should have sent a card when he got divorced. Do they make cards for divorces? She makes a mental note to ask Pam at Island Hallmark. She'd know.

Quinn comes back and eyes the shrimp in his Bloody Mary.

"Shrimp for your thoughts." He waves the speared prawn at her.

"Just wondering what it'll be like to have everyone together again. It's been, what? Five years? Since we've all been together? I see you and Selah often, and Ben when he comes through Vancouver on business, but Lizzy's funeral was the last time we were all together."

"So you haven't seen Gil since he had the Judithectomy?"

Maggie laughs. "Judithectomy? She wasn't that bad."

He gives her a look. "Yes she was and you know it."

"Okay, okay. Judith was horrible. How did he ever marry her?"

"Maybe she was a conciliation prize because the one he wanted got away."

"Ha! Well, at least he came to his senses." She sighs. "Gil is coming." The disbelief in her voice matches the look on her face.

"You're overthinking. We're going to have a blast. It will be like *The Big Chill* without Kevin Costner and with better music."

"Did you make your 'Lost Youth' playlist? Lots of Hole and music inspired by boys in flannel?"

"I did. I also made an old skool with a 'k' Hip Hop mix. Cause we used to own that shit."

Maggie laughs at his statement. Quinn never owned Hip Hop back in the day. His long hair and hippie style in college earned him the nickname Aslan from *The Narnia Chronicles*.

"Listen, Aslan, you were never going back to Cali, so don't even start. You were much more Bryan Ferry than LL Cool J."

"True. Remember Lizzy dragging us all on that road trip to see Bryan Ferry at the Greek in Berkeley?" That road trip was the beginning of her closest friendships.

"I do. I found my old vinyl copy of *Avalon* the other night."

"Maybe it's a good sign. Happy memories then, happy times now."

She quirks an eyebrow at him.

"Hey, I know you're freaking out about seeing Gil. I can see it and that poor napkin can feel it... what's left of it."

She looks down at the shreds of what used to be a cocktail napkin.

"You're both adults and old friends. Don't let the what-ifs of the past get in the way of enjoying this weekend. We could all use a little fun in our lives."

He's right. Quinn is her conscience—a pervy, gay, conscience.

"Speaking of lives, how's Ryan? Still in the honeymoon phase?"

"Dr. Gooding is dandy. Who would've thought I'd be the one to marry the dreamy dermatologist? I mean, did you ever think? Dr. and Mr.?"

"I am happy for you, but there are plenty of women doctors out there—lots of doctors and their misters. However, I never thought we'd see the day we'd have Mr. and Mr. in this country."

"Right you are. How sexist of me. Lots of mister-misters now."

Laughing at his word play, she says, "The wedding was amazing."

"The wedding was perfect, wasn't it? Cape Cod in the summer. Sublime. Can't believe it's been two years already." Quinn gets a dreamy look on his face.

"Your wedding was one of the few bright spots in my life over the past three years. Is Ryan still coming out this weekend?"

"He'll be here Saturday morning, and he's really been looking forward to seeing you. We have some news to share with everyone."

"News? Care to give me a hint?"

"No hints for you. Everyone will hear it when we're all together."

Maggie pouts and wonders what his news could be.

"Fine, as long as you promise it's good news. I need more good news in my life."

"It's great news. I promise. Maybe not as good as Gil crashing the weekend, but it's right up there." He winks at her. "You'll just have to wait until Saturday."

"You are a mean one, Mr. Dayton."

Quinn laughs at her, ignoring her pout.

"I hope we have good weather this weekend. I plan to introduce Ryan to the entertainment of the geoduck hunt."

"Somehow I suspect he's already acquainted with your geoduck." She laughs at the old island euphemism.

"The man knows a thing or two about geoducks."

"Strange given he's a dermatologist and not a marine biologist."

"Or a urologist. Thank god." After making a sour face, he sucks the last of his drink through his straw.

Outside the ferry pulls into the dock. "Time to go, funny man."

* * *

After getting Quinn settled in his room upstairs, they head out to the deck. The tallest buildings of Seattle sparkle to the south like the Emerald City of its nickname. The high tide is still hours away.

"Home, sweet home," Quinn says, taking a big inhale of salty air. "Now that's island fresh." He coughs, then laughs. "Yeah, tidal flat on a hot, sunny day must be an acquired taste."

Beyond the beach, kids are building mound of wet sand taller than a man, more mountain than castle. A game of king of the hill ensues. All of their hard work will be washed away once the tide comes back later in the day, but they don't seem to mind.

Sitting on lounge chairs on the deck with tall glasses of iced tea, Quinn and Maggie catch up about the little things going on in their lives. They Skype, Facetime, text or chat nearly every day, but it's different talking in person.

What seems like minutes later, Maggie realizes the tide is in and the time is later than she thought.

"We should eat. I have salmon to grill and a couscous salad in the fridge. Sound good? Plus, both white and red wines, and a Spanish Rosé." She turns on the propane on the gas grill sitting in the far corner of the deck.

"Sounds great. Especially the wine part."

"I'd hate for you to dehydrate."

"Is Rosé a fancy way of saying White Zinfandel?"

"Shh. Maybe. Pretty label and doesn't give you the hangover like the stuff we drank in college."

"Speak for yourself. I never drank White Zin. I'm not that much of a gay stereotype."

"Right, you preferred 'Mountain Rhine'. I can still see the jugs in the fridge."

"Mountain sounded masculine. Manly mountain men who drink wine in Germany. Kind of hot, as hot as you can be in lederhosen."

"Way to avoid stereotypes, Q."

Her phone chirps with a text. Looking at the screen she sees Selah's name.

Decided to come up tonight. On the ferry now. Surprise! Don't hate me. All good. xoxo

Quinn's phone chirps.

"Don't bother. It's Benedict Selah. She and Gil are on the ferry. Don't suppose you knew this?"

"I didn't. Swear. Should I open the wine? Or do you need something stronger?"

"Wine will be fine. Wanna keep my wits about me." Maggie nods to herself.

Shit.

Five

"White or red?" Quinn's voice carries upstairs.

With sunny days turning to cool summer nights on the beach, Maggie decides to change clothes. Normally she'd throw on a pair of skinny jeans and a hoodie, but Gil will be arriving at her house in less than a half hour. This information throws her into a dilemma. Gil. Probably still hot Gil is coming over. *Probably still hot?* Ha. It hasn't been that long. He's definitely still hot.

"How about the Rosé?" She shouts down to Quinn

"Glass or bucket?"

"A glass to start. I'll save the bucket for later."

"Wear your jeans and a hoodie, Magpie. This isn't a formal occasion."

Maggie laughs, Quinn knows her so well. She grabs her favorite dark jeans and a blue hoodie. She brushes her hair out of its tangled bun and even bothers with lipgloss and mascara. Sitting on the deck all afternoon means her face shows some color and her hair is wavy from the bun. Looking in the mirror she thinks she looks pretty good for forty-one.

"You don't look a day over twenty-five," he says as he hands her a large glass of chilled Rosé. "Your ass hasn't aged a day."

"If only it was true. I miss my twenty-something ass. I didn't appreciate it while I had it."

"We never appreciate what we have at the time."

Letting the deeper meaning of his words sink in, she sips her wine, and surveys the house. Everything appears to be in place. From the wall of windows in the living room, she notices the sun starting to dip towards the horizon. Sunset won't be for a few hours.

"I turned off the grill. Figured we should wait for Selah and Gil to get here, then all eat together. Knowing you, you made more than enough for four, let alone two."

Quinn is right. Inheriting her mother's gift for hosting, she is more than prepared for extra guests.

"I'm going to make some snacks. Nuts? Olives? Cheese straws? Everyone loves cheese straws, right?" she says as she heads into the open kitchen.

Quinn pulls up a barstool at the end of the island. "Everyone but the lactose and gluten intolerant."

Maggie gives him a dirty look.

"Fine. As far as I know neither of our dinner guests is either. Relax, drink your wine. It'll all be fine."

She organizes a tray with spiced pecans, cheese straws, olives, and a roll of salami.

"Q, will you take this out to the table while I grab the wine and an ice bucket?"

They make their way out to the deck. Biscuit joins them and lays at Quinn's feet, looking up at him adoringly. With the high tide the boats in the bay bob in the water once again and small waves lap the shore.

"You and Biscuit are having a fine romance. Are you sure you didn't line your pockets in bacon? Bacon cologne? I hear they make such a thing now."

"Biscuit is an excellent judge of character. No other explanation."

She raises her glass. "To good characters."

He clinks her glass with his own.

"I can't believe you two didn't wait for us to start drinking!" Selah's voice carries over from the stairs leading down to the side lawn.

"Showtime!" Quinn says with a little too much enthusiasm for Maggie's liking. She finishes her glass of wine and stands to face the new arrivals.

"Hi!" she greets Selah, matching Quinn's exuberance.

Selah wears one of her typical flowing skirts and tank top accessorized with a huge necklace, which draws attention to her large chest. Oversized sunglasses hold her dark bob away from her face.

More distracting than even Selah's breasts is the tousled brown hair of the man behind her. A few steps behind Selah stands Gilliam Morrow. Maggie's heart flips at the sight of him.

Biscuit barks out a greeting at the new guests and scampers over to sniff them. He's the world's most friendly dog and more apt to lick than bite.

Selah walks over to hug Quinn, giving Maggie a clear view of the man walking up the stairs. His brown hair is shorter, and it might be sprinkled with a little more gray. The face shows a few more lines around his warm brown eyes than the last time she saw it, but it's still a handsome composition of angles. Wearing khaki shorts and a faded Jane's Addiction T-shirt, he is a mix of old friend and stranger.

Gil makes eye contact with Maggie and smiles. He runs his hand through his hair, and gives her a small wave.

"Who's this fine beast?" Gil asks.

Biscuit sniffs around the newcomers. Gil scratches the dog's head, and from the way Biscuit leans into him, the two of them will be fast friends.

"That's Biscuit. He's a manwhore," Quinn answers for Maggie who stands quietly staring at Gil.

"Hi, Maggie." Gil strides over to her and gives her a friendly peck on the cheek.

"Hi," she says as she hugs him. It is a hug of two strangers who used to be friends, who used to be more. Gil's tall frame towers over hers —she barely comes up to his shoulder. She inhales his clean scent with hints of sunscreen and salt. He smells like summer.

"Hi," he says again and then laughs at himself. "I guess I already said that."

"Hi." She laughs along with him.

"Sorry to crash the weekend. Hope you don't mind." His deep voice is soft with genuine feeling.

"Of course not. It wouldn't be the whole gang if you weren't here." She hopes she sounds cooler than she feels.

Selah comes over and saves them from the awkwardness. She steps between Maggie and Gil, and hugs Maggie. Gil walks over to shake Quinn's hand.

"Forgive me?" Selah whispers in her ear.

"We'll see," Maggie whispers back.

Louder Maggie says, "How was the ferry? Where are your bags? Do you want wine? There's a Rosé open. Or beer. You probably want a beer, Gil. I have beer. Or iced tea. You don't have to drink."

The word vomit seems unstoppable until Selah touches her arm.

"The ferry was good. Quick once we got onto the boat. Bags are in the car. Why don't we all sit, have a drink, enjoy the view, and then you can give us a tour," Selah says, rubbing Maggie's arms.

"Sounds good to me," Gil answers.

"Beer or wine?" Quinn asks as he steps toward the door to the living room.

"Wine for me," Selah responds.

"Beer's fine. I'll come with you," Gil says, following Quinn inside.

With only the screen door closed, the guys' voices carry outside. Knowing they can be overheard as well, Maggie walks Selah over to the table in the far corner of the deck.

"Want to explain what you're up to?"

Selah puts on a knowing smile. "Exactly what you fear and hope I'm doing. I'm putting you and Gil in the same place at the same time again. Only this time you're both single and no dead body to drag down the mood."

"Nice. I'm sure Lizzy appreciates that. What about his girlfriend?"

"What girlfriend?" Selah smirks.

"What do you mean 'what girlfriend'? The one you told me he's been seeing for ages."

"Hmmm. Doesn't ring a bell." Selah winks.

Maggie is stunned by Selah's revelation. She's assumed Gil had a girlfriend for the past year based on cryptic responses Selah gave her whenever she asked about him. She gives Selah a dirty look.

"Oh, come on. There's always been something between you and Gil. Stewing, brewing, steeping, fermenting between the two of you, but the timing was never right. Now the time is right. Plus, I'm bored of playing telephone for you two Luddites, so I figure why not put you in the same place before the reunion, and get all the awkward out of the way."

She pauses to take a sip of Rosé and plops a nut in her mouth. "And now that Gil's here, this weekend will be a mini-reunion of all my favorite Greeners from college. Call me selfish." Selah eats another pecan and pulls out one of the teak deck chairs. "Sit, and let's enjoy our wine. Tell me what you've been up to this past week. If you are good I'll tell you about Jeremy."

"Jeremy? New lover?"

"Perhaps. I haven't decided yet."

"Sounds more like you've decided, but haven't fucked him yet."

"Who hasn't fucked who, yet?" Quinn asks as he and Gil return.

"Technically it is 'who hasn't fucked whom," Selah corrects him.

"Whom schmoom, let's get to the fucking." Quinn sits next to Maggie at the table, leaving the chair opposite her empty for Gil.

"Crass much, Q?" Gil asks. "Some things never change."

"Sue me. I'm an old married man now. I need the vicarious thrills and intrigue from my single friends."

"Selah was telling me about a new prospectus, Jeremy."

"Jeremy. Sounds like a grad student. Or is he an undergrad?" Quinn asks.

"I don't sleep with undergrads. Such a cliché, Quinn, and sadly frowned upon by the powers that be these days."

"Gil, have you ever fucked one of your students?" Quinn enquires.

Gil looks stricken. "No, never." He visibly shudders. "I stay the same age and they get younger and younger. They hold no appeal for me."

"Funny. I would think that would be some of the appeal of being an academic." Quinn tosses an olive in his mouth.

"I haven't been with an undergraduate since I was one," Gil replies, glancing at Maggie briefly.

"So anyhoo..." Maggie interjects to avoid the growing awkwardness. "I have salmon and salad for dinner. I thought it was going to be Q and me, but I we can make everything work. Anyone starving?"

"Sounds perfect," Gil says. "The salmon local caught?"

"Very. My neighbor caught it this morning," Maggie says with pride.

"Paul Bunyan fishes too?" Quinn asks as he walks over to relight the grill.

"Your neighbor's name is Paul Bunyan? Like the lumberjack?"

"No, his name is John Day. Quinn calls him that because he works in timber."

"And wears plaid, and has a beard, and is tall, dark, and handsome..." Quinn practically salivates.

"And his dog's named Babe," Selah interjects.

Surprised by this, Maggie gives her a look.

"What? He and I are Facebook friends." Selah defends.

"John is on Facebook? And since when are you friends?" Selah and John being online friends makes his questions about Selah yesterday make more sense now.

"We exchanged info after your mom's funeral last year. Good way to keep an eye on you. Plus, he's hot."

"Maggie, everyone, but you and Gil, is on Facebook," Quinn says.

"I hate Facebook," Gil says.

"Me too," Maggie agrees.

"See? You two still have so much in common!" Selah claps her hands together in mock enthusiasm.

Maggie rolls her eyes.

"Q, can you handle the grill? I'll bring out the salmon, and Selah and I will finish the salad."

"Yes, ma'am." Quinn salutes. "More beer. Gil, you want another?"

"Sure, I can grab one and bring out the fish," Gil offers and follows the women inside.

In the kitchen there's a shuffle to get the fish and beer out of the fridge as well as the couscous. Gil brushes against Maggie more than once. She wonders if it may or may not be intentional on his part, seeing his smile each time they touch. Maggie's skin tingles in a way she may or may not admit to liking. She does know being close to him makes her want more wine.

"Gil, will you grab the other bottle of Rosé from the door?"

Gil's hand brushes hers when he hands her the wine.

Yes, there's definitely a tingle.

"Hey, you never gave Gil the full tour. I can dress the salad and Q will man the grill while you show Gil the rest of the house and where to put our bags." Selah says.

Maggie gives her a look.

"Okay. I can help with the bags."

"Nah, I'll run out and grab them. Do you mind if I use the bathroom first?" Gil asks.

"Of course not! I'm such a bad host. First door on the right as you head toward the front door."

After Gil walks away Selah comes over and hugs her. "Magpie, relax. It's only Gil. One of your best friends. He won't bite. Unless you ask him to, and I suspect you aren't into the whole vampire fetish."

Maggie hugs Selah back and exhales. "I'm being weird. Does everyone know I'm being weird? Why am I being so weird? It's weird that I'm being weird, isn't it?"

Selah pats her arm.

"It is a little weird. The word vomit is so not like you. Why are you nervous around him?"

"I guess it's been a long time. Plus, he's gorgeous. I think I forgot how gorgeous he is."

They hear the bathroom door open and Gil's footsteps in the hall.

"I'll grab the bags from the car and be right back," Gil calls from the front door.

Selah gives her another half hug, and says, "You're gorgeous, too."

Six

When Gil comes back, Maggie makes a sweeping gesture, and says, "I'll give you the tour. You've seen the kitchen, dining area, living room, and hall bath."

She loves that neither of her parents ever updated the house other than to replace the avocado kitchen appliances with stainless. A few coats of paint on walls, cupboards, and floors upstairs, new furniture mixed with the old, and the removal of the aged wall-to-wall carpet that was more sand than carpet—these are Maggie's main additions to the cabin.

"Down here is a bedroom that's a TV-room-slash-den with a fold-out sofa. Selah will be in this room tonight. When I thought you were Selah's date, I figured I'd put you both in here, giving Ben and Jo the upstairs room with the twin beds. But now I'm going to have to shuffle people around."

"I feel guilty for causing any inconvenience."

"Don't worry about it. At all. I'm glad you showed up." She gives him a genuine smile. "Do you and Selah mind sharing a room tomorrow night?"

Maggie walks toward the door on the left, across from the bathroom.

"I'm happy to sleep with Gil," Selah calls from the kitchen. Something in her tone is teasing, but also has an undercurrent of double entendre that makes Maggie feel possessive of Gil.

"I'm fine sharing with Selah. She snores like a bear. I might need ear plugs."

"I heard that, and I do not snore!"

"She so does," they both say at the same time, and then laugh.

"I'll find ear plugs for you."

Gil brushes past her and drops Selah's bags in the den. "This is cozy. I didn't notice a TV in the living room and thought you became one of those anti-TV recluse types for a minute." He teases her.

"Lord no! I'm addicted to horrible, embarrassing television. I like to hide my shame from company," Maggie explains.

"So, this is where you watch porn?" Gil gestures around.

He's flirting with her. Or at least she thinks he is. Two can play at this.

"No, silly. I watch my porn online in my bedroom like most people." She winks at him.

Apparently momentarily stunned by the thought of her watching porn in her bedroom, in her bed, Gil takes a few seconds to react. She chuckles that she stunned him into silence. His shocked expression pleases her.

"Your room is upstairs next to Quinn's. Ryan arrives Saturday, so you're in the room with the two twin beds. Hope you don't mind."

Maggie walks up the stairs with Gil following behind her. She swears she senses his eyes on her but she's afraid to look back. Instead, she adds a little extra swing in case he's looking.

Gil pauses on the landing and picks up a rock on the windowsill. "Why do all these rocks have white lines around them? I saw some downstairs, too."

"They're wishing rocks."

He quirks an eyebrow at her. "Wishing rocks? Like magical rocks?"

"Sure, mock the island traditions. You find a rock with an unbroken white ring, make a wish, and throw it into the water."

"Do the mermaids and Selkies grant your wishes?"

"Ha ha. Not sure either are in the Sound. Wishing rocks are something my grandmother taught me."

"They're cool. Definitely." Gil strokes his finger over the ring. "If you throw them in the water to make your wish, why do you have so many here? Hoarding wishes?"

She tugs on the sleeve of his ancient concert T-shirt. "You're one to talk about holding onto things. I collect the rocks. You never know when you'll need a little extra hope and faith. Plus, they're pretty. I love how nature creates something perfect."

He leans against the wall and nods at her words. "We'll have to find you more tomorrow," he says softly, watching her face.

"They're everywhere if you keep your eyes open."

"Kind of like wishes," he says.

"Maybe." She smiles at him before continuing up the stairs.

At the top of the stairs, she points to the left. "My room's down that way. Two bedrooms on the hall share a bathroom. Your room is here." She gestures to her immediate right. "Quinn and Ryan have the room closer to me."

Gil walks into the small, gray-painted bedroom. The room's eclectic style is all Maggie. The pair of white twin beds are made up with white linens and folded Hudson Bay striped blankets lay over the footboards. A collection of sand dollars and beach rocks line the window. Above the beds hangs a group of amateur paintings of the island. He drops his bag on the navy wingback chair in the corner next to a small dresser.

"I hope the bed isn't too short for you. These were my grandmother's and I think those older beds were smaller since people were shorter." Maggie babbles.

"I'll be fine. It's only for a few nights and I'd happily sleep on a sofa. I like the room, it has character."

"Thanks. Okay, let me show you the bathroom."

Maggie walks out of the room and down the hall to the door on the left. "Your basic bathroom."

Inside is more beach flotsam and island decor. White tiles and walls are accented with a driftwood frame around the mirror and sea glass in a large jar on the counter. The Magpie's collection of natural treasures matches the style of the guest room.

"Nice," he says.

She moves down the hall to the other guest room.

He pokes his head into the room. "Nice."

'Quinn's room' is another airy space with white walls and a queen bed in pale blue sheets and a white coverlet. A large piece of driftwood hangs on the wall above the bed. Under the window sits a small desk holding a spyglass and a collection of old books.

"And finally my room." Maggie's voice sounds nervous.

"Perfect."

The early evening sun streams in through the oversized picture windows facing the water and bluff, giving the room a golden glow. A king bed in white linens faces the view. The floors are white-painted wood covered with a few small, vintage rugs. Another vintage desk, similar to the one in Quinn's room, sits below a picture window, and a telescope stands next to it. The pile of papers and the comfortable chair make it obvious this is a place where Maggie does some of her writing. An old love seat with a Biscuit-shaped indent in the cushion sits below the other window. Through a door behind the wall with the bed is another bathroom.

"Great set up. I love the rugs. These are kilims, right?"

His knowledge of the kilims surprises her. Then again, he has traveled everywhere and teaches history. Figures he knows Turkish rugs.

"They are. My mother bought them in Seattle years ago. I love how sun-bleached and faded they are now."

"Me too. I love things that show their age. It only makes them more beautiful."

Maggie smiles at his words. "Says the history professor."

Gil laughs. "Good point. Do you use the telescope to spy on the neighbors?"

She wonders why he frowns when he mentions her neighbors. "Tempting, but no. The telescope is perfect for star gazing, whale watching, and following the container ships in the Sound. I like to imagine what's in all those containers."

Gil walks over and looks out the telescope that is, in fact, pointed at the shipping channel. "What do you imagine inside them?"

"Sometimes random stuff. If the ship is bound for port in Seattle, then I assume it's something from Asia like squid flavored candies or Apple products. Outbound ships are probably filled with Starbucks and geoducks."

"Do they even ship their coffee from Seattle?"

"Good point. I don't know."

"Where are the geoducks going?"

"Japan and China, of course. They're an expensive delicacy in Asia and thought to improve male virility." Maggie scrunches up her nose.

"Not a fan of the giant clam?" Gil says, clearly amused by her reaction. "Geoducks are resolutely phallic."

"Visually, not so much. They're pornographic." Maggie laughs at the fact she's standing in her bedroom talking about phallic bivalves with Gil.

"You have a dirty mind, Maggie May. They're our alma mater's mascot." He points at the stuffed Speedy the Geoduck on her desk.

"Hmm." She hums. "No one has called me Maggie May since college. Actually, no one but you has ever called me that." Her cheeks warm at the familiarity and small thrill she has from the name.

"That makes me happy to hear." Gil turns and faces her with a small smile tugging at his lips.

His familiar smile stirs something in Maggie. It's the same smile nineteen-year-old Gil used to give her. Part shy, part stunning... it was irresistible then and it's pretty irresistible now. She smiles back at him.

"It's wonderful to hear you laugh again. I love your house. It's very *you*. Thanks for making me feel welcome and not like the crasher I am."

Maggie looks around at the room with its white-washed wood walls and simple furnishings. It *is* very her.

"Thanks. I love this room. And it's good to have you here. Like no time has passed at all." She means it as she imagines how much his absence would have been noted this weekend. Maybe the wine makes her a little more than nostalgic.

"We should make sure Quinn hasn't charred the fish."

"Charred fish sounds like one of his studio art pieces."

"It does." She laughs as they walk downstairs.

* * *

Selah pours herself a glass of wine as Gil and Maggie walk into the kitchen.

"Who needs refills?" she asks, holding up the bottle.

"I'll grab another beer," Gil says, opening the fridge.

Maggie pours another glass for herself and walks outside to check on Quinn.

Selah and Gil follow shortly after, carrying table settings, the salad, and wine.

"Dinner is served," Quinn says with a fburish toward the perfectly grilled, not charred, salmon on a cedar plank in his hand.

The rest applaud.

Once everyone serves themselves, Maggie makes a toast. Raising her glass, she says, "To old friends."

The others echo her and clink their glasses. She glances over the top of her glass at Gil, who sits opposite her. *To long lost friends found again,* she thinks. As if he could read her mind, Gil winks, and she smiles in response.

It might be the wine or the wink, but Maggie feels warm and happy, and maybe a little hopeful for the first time in ages.

An hour later, her guests compliment her about the amazing food as Maggie clears the table after telling them to sit and enjoy the sunset. She carries the plates and salad bowl into the kitchen with a promise Gil can help her wash the dishes later.

Not ready to think about dessert yet, she grabs a bottle of wine and another beer for Gil. She flips the switch for the twinkle lights hung around the railing of the deck, giving enough light outside to balance the creeping darkness. Selah lights a cigarette and moves to sit on the deck railing, with Gil's empty bottle as her ashtray.

"Quinn was nicely pointing out I'm the last person on the planet to smoke," Selah says from her perch. Thankfully she's down wind. "Back in the day, you all smoked. Quitters."

Quinn laughs. "Yes, and 'back in the day' we all thought forty was old age."

"Forty is the new thirty, don't you know?" Selah quips and blows smoke rings. "At this rate, by the time we're fifty, we'll be forever thirty and twenty will be the new fourteen."

"Ugh, don't mention fifty," Maggie moans. "We're closer to fifty than twenty."

"How did that happen?" Gil asks.

"We got boring and married, and grew paunchy." Quinn pats his belly, which is almost as flat as it was in college. "And by we, I mean all of you."

"Perpetual youthful teenager is no way to go through life, Quinn," Selah says, jokingly.

"I've made a career of pandering to the base of youth obsessed culture," Quinn replies.

Maggie sips her wine and observes the sparring between Q and Selah.

"How's the poster business, Q?" Gil asks.

"Now, now don't you start. Poster business?" Quinn laughs.

"Plastic and printable satire? What did the critics call your show earlier this year?" Selah interjects.

Maggie has to suppress a grin. That line had particularly irked Q when he read it to her over the phone.

"Hush, woman. Let it be known, I sold out most of the show before the opening. Lars was interviewing collectors to determine who was worthy to own one of my masterpieces."

Selah puts out her cigarette and snorts.

"Tiara-wearing honey bears are hardly masterpieces."

"Selah, you teach about art filled with the nakedness and nudity of the old ages. This is contemporary art, conceptual. Those bears were eighteen-carat gold-plated."

"I prefer my 'Liza Loves Me' puffy heart box from your first show," Maggie interjects.

"Art is in the eye of the beholder," Gil adds.

"Art with a big A or a little a?" Selah asks.

"Both. Look at Maggie's collection of paintings of the island. All amateur, all not very well done, but together they form a collective piece that becomes more than the sum of their parts," Gil says.

Maggie blushes over how Gil seems to understand her little collection of misfit paintings.

"Did Maggie invite you upstairs to show you her etchings?" Quinn can't stop teasing.

"Disappointingly, she didn't. She was a complete lady on the house tour."

"Disappointing indeed." Quinn does, in fact, look disappointed.

Selah joins them at the table and refills her glass. "I'm well on my way to tipsy so I'll forgive the 'nudity and nakedness' comment."

"Oh come on, Elmore," Quinn bats his eyelashes. "Think of all the young men you've lured into taking art history with the promise of boobs and bush."

"Dr. Elmore, thank you. Boobs and bush—now that's a course title. Much better than 'The depiction of the female form from Renaissance to Impressionism'."

Quinn fake yawns and Selah gives him the stink eye. Maggie knows provoking Quinn is entertaining and comfortable for Selah.

"I should invite you to give a guest lecture next time you're in the area. You can expound on the cultural relevance of poop or history of plump children in art."

Their opinions about art rarely agree, yet they both enjoy the verbal sparring. Quinn gives as good as he gets.

"Those pageant girls are living cherubim. Most of their proportions are classic Italian Renaissance."

Gil and Maggie roll their eyes at Quinn.

"I will say anything's better than 'Gary Busey is my co-pilot' sticker campaign you did right after college," Maggie says.

"Dude, Busey was epic. Had to pay respect to the man."

Selah hits her head on the table in exasperation while Gil chuckles.

"How many times did we watch *Point Break*? I used to have that movie memorized," Gil says.

"Ben will know. Remember when he had us get the dead presidents masks and go as them for Halloween?" Quinn asks.

Gil laughs. "Man, I'd forgotten about that."

"I wish I could forget about it." Selah half grumbles, half laughs. "I got so sick of the three of you always quoting that movie."

"Johnny Utah was the man. Never compromised, never worked for the man. He's my hero." Quinn raises his mostly empty glass. "To Johnny."

"To Johnny." They all toast with laughter.

Seven

Maggie starts the water for the dishes while Quinn and Selah sprawl out on the gray sectional sofa in the living room. Biscuit curls up by Quinn's feet.

"Hey now, I'm supposed to be washing dishes. I didn't contribute at all to dinner." Gil walks around the kitchen island and joins her at the sink.

"You really don't have to do the dishes, Gil. It's fine."

He takes the sponge from her hand, bumping her out of his way with his hip. "Move. I need to earn my keep."

"Okay, you can help. It's an old dishwasher—everything needs to be scraped and rinsed. You rinse and I'll load."

When Gil hands her the dishes their fingers brush together. Maggie decides his actions must be deliberate, but she can't deny the little touches affect her.

"Remember when we didn't even have a dishwasher in the house that summer? What a disaster."

Maggie laughs. "Remember Quinn insisting on paper plates during his week on dish duty?"

"The chore wheel thing was a nightmare. Who came up with that?" Gil asks.

"Jo. Had to have been. She ruled the roost with an iron fist."

"I think you're mixing your metaphors." He teases.

"I'm a little buzzed." She admits and laughs. "Now I'm imagining a chicken with an animatronic human hand."

This is easy. Like old times. They can do this. They'll be fine.

"Yeah, I'd say you're a little buzzed." Gil joins her laughter.

"Whose idea was it to burn the chore wheel in the barbecue before we all moved out?" Gil asks.

"Quinn. I think he declared the fire performance art. Jo was pissed." Maggie laughs at the memory of the charred chart.

"Right. He's a clever bastard. He gets away with everything by calling it art."

"Ahem, I can hear you two, you know," Quinn says from the living room. "I'm right here." He waves over his head and points down to himself.

"Q, don't worry, we can never forget about you. You won't let us," Gil says.

"Damn straight. I'm the gay glue holding this group together," Quinn boasts. "Selah is the heart, Maggie is the memory, and you are the brain, Pinky."

"Talk about mixed metaphors," Maggie whispers to Gil. He leans down to hear her. Their heads are close together, very close. Suddenly aware of where she is, and who she's with, she pulls back and turns off the water.

"Thank you for your help," she says to Gil rather formally.

"No problem. Happy to help." He gives her a small smile that doesn't quite reach his eyes.

Wandering over to the stereo by the dining table, he picks up a couple of albums sitting on the credenza.

"Feeling sentimental, Maggie?" He holds up the cover to *Avalon* for her to see.

"I was going through some of mom's albums the other night and discovered that shelved next to *Blue*, one of her favorites."

Maggie ignores the silly grin on Gil's face that he's trying to hide by facing the window, but she can see his reflection. Finding that album and his unexpected arrival are probably more than coincidence. She fights her own smile at the thought.

"I have dessert if anyone wants it—local gelato and cookies. Anyone?"

"Me," Selah says from the sofa where she checks her phone.

"Can you even get service?" Maggie asks. "The island is notorious for dead spots."

"If I sit here and face south, I can. I'll tap into your wi-fi later if you don't mind. I need to do a little writing this weekend."

"Academic or smutty pirates?" Quinn asks.

"Academic pirates who give up everything for one good fuck." Selah snarks.

"Really? Cause that sounds interesting. Based on anyone we know? Gil could be a pirate. Or at least he could've when he had long hair." Quinn muses.

Maggie pauses scooping the gelato, and closes her eyes, thinking about Pirate Gil and his shoulder length, shaggy hair in college a la Dave Grohl.

Gil's voice brings her back to the present.

"Every guy had long hair in college." Gil sits down on the sofa next to Quinn. Maggie watches Biscuit nudging Gil's hand with his head to be petted.

"Not Ben. Never Ben," Maggie says.

"No, never Ben. Shame. How different his life might have been had he been a long hair."

"Ben's life is just as it should be and as intended," Maggie says in an uptight voice. At times she's been jealous of Ben and Jo's seemingly perfect life.

While everyone grabs a bowl and a spoon, she sits in the available space in the corner between Gil and Selah.

"Ben's life is just as Josephine intended," Selah says. "They are the perfect American dream. Handsome, two-point-five children, golden retriever, big house, cars, and vacation home. If I didn't love them, I would hate them." Selah makes a face and eats a cookie.

"It's your worst nightmare, Selah," Gil says.

"Oh, I know." She shudders. "Not my American dream. Some of us are breeders, some of us are not. Wouldn't trade places for anything."

"You know you're not missing out. Didn't you sleep with Ben freshman year?" Quinn asks.

"I did indeed. It was nice." Selah shrugs.

"Nice?" Gil asks.

"Nice is Selah's way of saying boring," Maggie adds.

"Nice is boring," Selah says.

"Nice doesn't have to be boring," Gil defends.

"Oh sweetie, you are one of the nice guys. Never boring though." To emphasize her words, Selah nods.

"I wasn't fishing for compliments, but will take it." Gil rubs the back of his neck.

Maggie senses his awkwardness. "Why do we always go for the bad boys when we are younger, never realizing they are called bad boys for a reason? We waste so much time."

"Cause the bad ones make you appreciate the good guys when you finally open your eyes and see them," Quinn says.

"I still like bad boys." Selah surprises no one with this statement.

"And pirates," Maggie mumbles with a mouthful of ice cream.

"Arrgh," Quinn adds, and they all crack up.

Gil puts down his empty bowl and leans back into the sofa with his long legs extended and his feet resting on the edge of the ottoman. Maggie notices his shirt rides up slightly, revealing a thin slice of skin and a noticeable line of hair extending down from his navel.

Gil catches her staring, but doesn't immediately pull down his shirt. He avoids looking at her directly, but out of the corner of her eye she thinks she sees him smirk.

"Something about fresh air makes me tired," says Quinn.

"Probably the oxygen and lack of smog does you in whenever you leave the city." Maggie teases him. There are times she misses life in the big city, but can't imagine fighting the everyday battle of living there anymore.

"I could never live in New York. Too big, too many people," Gil adds.

"I couldn't go back, but I loved the city when I was there," Maggie says. "But you can lose yourself."

"Sometimes when you lose your way, you find yourself."

"Wow, Q, that was deep." Selah sounds surprised.

"I have my moments. I should probably go to bed on a high note." Quinn stands and takes the tray of empty bowls over to the sink.

"We are old if Quinn is going to bed at eleven," Gil says, craning to see the clock on the kitchen wall.

"I'm still on East Coast time. Not old."

"Yes, Peter Pan, you'll never grow old." Gil laughs. "Quinn, the perpetual teenager."

"I think I'll go to bed as well." Selah yawns and stretches. "Too much wine."

"Then there were two," Gil says, turning to lean closer to Maggie.

"Then there were two," Maggie repeats, remembering how she and Gil always tended to be the night owls of the group, hitting their second wind at midnight, and studying or drinking into the wee hours.

"Are you tired? I can go up and read in my room. I don't want to keep you up."

"I usually stay up late. Some things don't change. We can't watch television because Selah is in the only room with a TV."

"We could play cards or a game of old school Scrabble," Gil suggests, gesturing at the basket of games and cards tucked next to the bookcase in the corner.

"Deal." Maggie gets up to grab the Scrabble board. "Do you want to play at the dining table or sit on the floor here?"

"Dining table if you don't mind. You set up the board while I put the bowls in the dishwasher."

"Do you want another glass of wine?" He grabs the bottle and waves it at her.

"Are you having another beer? I don't want to be the lush."

"I'll have another one if you do."

"Sure."

He fills her glass.

She has the board and bag of tiles out and ready when he settles in the chair at the head of the table. If she stretches out her feet, she'll be touching his legs, so she keeps her legs tucked under her chair.

He pulls out a "B" tile from the bag before she reaches in and takes out a "M".

She sets up all her tiles and looks at her selection of letters: U, R, C, N, T, S, P. If they were playing dirty Scrabble, she'd have the perfect word.

As if reading her mind, Gil plays "LICKS".

Tempted but not sure she should go there, she plays "PUNTS."

She grabs five more tiles from the bag.

While he studies his tiles for a few minutes, she notes he's the same player he was in college— slow and methodical.

He plays "LEASE" off of the "L" in "LICKS," and then adds up his points on the pad of paper and sips his beer. A comfortable quiet settles over the table.

She drinks her wine and studies her new tiles before deciding to play "GLOVE" off of the last "E" in "LEASE." Looking up writing down her score, she notices Gil looks sleepy.

"Hey sleepy, you forgot to take tiles out of the bag." Maggie nudges him with her foot.

"Sorry. I think I hit the wall…" His words trail off into a yawn, his deep voice more rough with sleep.

"We can call it a night." Maggie hides her disappointment. She's been enjoying Gil's quiet company.

"Do you mind? Let's tip our tiles down and continue this tomorrow."

"That sounds like a good idea since we don't need the table for meals. I'll have to kick your butt later."

When Gil stands up and stretches, she stares at a sliver of exposed skin again. Shaking her head, she can't believe she is ogling Gil's stomach.

"Like you ever kicked my butt at Scrabble." He tugs down his shirt.

"Once I did before I grew to hate playing with you. You never let me win."

"You wouldn't have liked it if I 'let' you win and you know it."

"This is true," she says, busying herself with turning off lights around downstairs.

"You should be all set. Extra towels in the linen closet in your room and toothbrushes etc in the vanity in the bathroom."

"Thanks," he tells her as they head upstairs. "Good night, Maggie May. It's great seeing you again."

"Same." She means it.

After getting ready for bed, she stands at her bedroom window, looking out at the dark water lapping the beach. She picks up a wishing rock from the many scattered along the windowsill and sets it on her nightstand before slipping into bed.

Eight

Maggie opens her eyes to the rude light of another cloudless, deep blue sky. The bluff appears close enough to touch out the windows. Stretching, she bargains with herself to skip her morning run. Maybe she can use a house full of guests as an excuse to avoid her daily three miles. Biscuit stretches out beside her and presents his belly for a rub.

Hearing a knock at her door and before she says come in, Quinn walks in with a cup of coffee in both hands. Maggie sits up, relieved and vaguely sad it's him.

"Morning, starshine. Good morning, Mr. McGhee." Quinn dutifully scratches Biscuit's belly.

"Morning yourself," Maggie mumbles while reaching for the oversize mug of steaming coffee.

Quinn hands her the cup and sits against the headboard.

"So. What's on the agenda for today, Magpie? You better say baking a batch of those amazing scones of yours is the first thing you plan on doing. I'm giving up the giving up of carbs for some of your baked goodies this weekend."

"Scones do sound good. I have a pint of marionberries in the fridge. Will those work?"

"Perfection," says a male voice that's not Quinn's.

Gil stands in the doorway looking sleep rumpled in a pair of cargo shorts and an Evergreen State T-shirt. He walks over to the bed and sits on the edge. She's self-conscious about her spaghetti-strap, cotton nightgown. Quinn seeing her like this is no big deal. Somehow having Gil in her bedroom, sitting on her bed, while she is barely clothed feels entirely different.

"What is perfection?" she finally asks.

"Marionberry scones for breakfast," Gil answers

"If I make scones, I'm definitely going to need to go for a run."

Quinn pinches her bare arm. "Yep, you're a big squishy ball of fat. You should probably skip the scones and give your share to me."

Maggie brushes off Quinn's pinching fingers. "Be nice, Mr. Eight-Percent Body Fat."

"You run?" Gil asks from the foot of the bed. "Since when?"

"For a few years now. Needed something to beat back the clock. So I started running and practicing yoga. Biscuit and I were both starting to get paunches."

"I don't see any evidence of a paunch or wrinkles." Gil smiles at her. "I still run. What's your typical run?"

"Three miles, sometimes four. If I want to torture myself, I run on the tideland during the low tide, but usually I keep to the roads."

"I brought my running shoes. We should go for a run together," Gil suggests.

The idea of sweating and panting next to Gil gives Maggie pause.

"Okay, before you two start talking 5Ks and 13Ks and who has a 26.4 sticker on their car, let's get back to the scones," Quinn interrupts.

"Always about the food, Q. Marathons are 26.2 miles and 13Ks are not a thing, you know," Maggie says.

"Whatever. Now chop chop!" Quinn attempts to push her out of bed.

"All right, all right. I'm getting up. Run first, then scones. Can a girl have some privacy for a minute?"

"Magpie, it's nothing we haven't seen before. Hello? Topless sunbathing phase."

Maggie blushes at the memory of their tar beach summer before junior year.

"I miss those twenty-year-old boobs."

She swears she hears Gil whisper "me too" as he walks out the door. That's strange, she thinks. *All twenty-year-old boobs or my boobs specifically?*

* * *

By the time Maggie gets outside, she finds Gil stretching on the front steps, wearing running shorts and the same gray Evergreen T-shirt. His long legs are toned and tan. He looks good. Really good.

Maggie wears her typical black capri leggings and a purple running tank, her hair pulled into a high pony tail. She's forgone her iPod and earbuds in case Gil wants to talk.

"No Biscuit?"

"He's going to stay behind and make love-eyes at Quinn."

"What's our route?" Gil pulls one of his legs behind him to stretch.

"I usually run up the hill to the main road and then head out toward the bluff. It's pretty flat with a couple of gradual hills in the middle. That work for you?"

Gil makes a sweeping gesture toward the road. "After you."

"I might be a slower runner than you. Are you sure you don't want to head out on your own?"

"Nah. I'm here more for the scenery and the company. Run to your pace and I'll adjust."

His sweet words make her smile.

Maggie jogs up the hill to warm up before running to her typical pace once she hits the main road. Gil easily keeps up. He doesn't seem to be breaking a sweat. *Of course not.*

"If you ran in college, we could've run together. Think of all the fun you missed out on back then."

"Fun? You crew boys got up at the crotch of dawn. Masochists. Running now is enough masochism for my delicate soul."

"No runner's high for you? That's the best part."

"I think runner's high is an urban legend. It's torture. Every step."

"Then why do you do it? Other than the view." Gil gestures to the break in the tall pines revealing the water shimmering in the sun below the bluff.

"When my mother was sick I needed something only for me, something to help me work out some of the stress and sadness. Long walks in the woods were melancholy, so I trained for a 5K. After the first one, I kept going."

"I'm sorry about your mom. I wish I were around more when she was ill. Portland isn't very far away."

"Thanks, but you were busy with classes and Judith."

"Yeah, Judith was always a handful." Gil shrugs and stares over the field next to them.

"Sorry about the divorce. Divorces suck."

"Actually, it was pretty mutual by that point. We hadn't been good for each other for a few years. She's remarried now. Has a kid even."

"Wow. Judith as a mother." Maggie shakes her head at the thought.

"She wasn't that bad." Gil laughs. "She always wanted kids and we tried for years, but it wasn't in the cards for us. It was the beginning of the end."

"I'm sorry. I didn't know." Maggie always wondered why they didn't have a kid. Gil would make an amazing father. "You'd make a great father."

"So would you. I mean, you'd be a wonderful mother. Why didn't you and Julien have kids?"

At the mention of Maggie's ex, also known as the French Incident, her back stiffens.

"Julien and I were..." She pauses. They weren't too young for kids, so what were they? "The whole marriage was a mistake and never really had a chance. We both focused so much on our careers in our twenties, and the chef lifestyle isn't exactly pro-babies. Plus, his mother hated me." It's been over ten years since her divorce yet the thought of Madame Armand still makes her stomach sink. "There hasn't really been 'the one' since then. Mom got sick and it took over my life for a few years. Now here I am. Landowning spinster."

"You deserved better, Maggie May. You deserve everything."

Her heart skips.

"Maybe." She gives him a soft smile. Lost in his sweet words, Maggie slows to a jog next to a field full of sheep when she realizes they've missed the three mile turnaround point.

"Looks like we're doing four miles today. The sheep are two miles from the cabin. We should head back."

"You use livestock as road markers?" He laughs at her.

"Hadn't thought about it, but I guess I do. My other route has a turnaround point at some llamas." Joining him in laughter, she heads back the way they came.

"Quinn's probably passed out from starvation and Selah might even have dragged herself out of bed by now."

"My money is on her being up, but not dressed."

"Agreed." He nods, before picking up the pace.

The run back to the cabin is quiet. Both are lost in the ghosts of exes and relationships past.

When they reach the hill down to the beach, Gil yells, "Last one to home doesn't get any scones," and sprints down the hill.

Not one to be left in the dust, Maggie races behind him. She suspects he might be letting her catch him as they approach the cabin. When he stops short at the steps to the deck, she crashes into his back, which is warmed by the sun and their run. He smells of sweat and some familiar memory.

* * *

Quinn and Selah are sprawled out on the sofa in the living room with their laptops open when Gil and Maggie enter the house.

"Mind if I take a shower first?" Gil asks.

"Mind if I join you?" Quinn quips without looking up.

"Sorry, Q. Still not my type."

"Pfft. So you say. You could use the outdoor shower. I could walk by. Nature could take its course."

"Think I'll stick with the upstairs shower for right now to be safe."

Quinn glares at Maggie, and snaps his fingers. "For the love of the Queen Mother, scones, woman, scones!"

"Can I help?" Selah offers from her spot curled in the corner of the sofa. Her uncharacteristically-tousled, dark bob is barely visible above the plaid throw wrapped around her.

"You stay right there. I can make these scones with my eyes closed. In fact, there were probably many pre-dawn mornings at the bakery when I did. I'll get these in the oven and then take a quick shower when Gil is done."

"You and Gil should shower together and save water. Save the environment and all that good stuff you love." Selah sits up, her red silk robe emphasizing the devilish expression on her face.

"Or not." Maggie blushes and heads into the kitchen.

Disentangling herself from her blankets, Selah walks over to refill her mug with coffee while Maggie takes out the baking sheet and ingredients.

"How was the run?"

"Good. We chatted about ex-spouses and not having kids."

"Before breakfast? Yikes."

"I know. What was I thinking?" She swats Selah's hand as she tries to steal a marionberry.

"I'm glad you two got it out of the way. Onwards and forward. With that sage advice, I'm going outside for a cigarette." Selah steals another berry, then prances out of Maggie's swatting range.

"I think you're the last person I know who smokes. Didn't you quit?"

"I know, I know. I need to get those fancy electronic cigarettes the cool kids have. Remind me to research them."

"You'll give yourself wrinkles," Quinn pipes up from the sofa.

"Thanks for the judging." Selah flips them off before heading out to the deck with her coffee.

Maggie mixes up the scone dough and puts them in the oven. After going upstairs, she turns the corner to her room, and runs into the wet body of Gil coming out of the hall bathroom.

"We have to stop running into each other like this." Gil smiles down at her.

Speechless, she gazes down at Gil's body wrapped only in a towel around his hips.

"My eyes are up here." He laughs.

She glances up at Gil's twinkling brown eyes and sees he is barely repressing a smirk.

"Sorry." She manages to get out. His fingers softly graze hers as she shuffles past him to go to her bedroom. After shutting the door, she leans against it to collect herself. He still affects her the same way he did back in college. Gil is a friend, an old friend. He isn't the same Gil she loved from not-so-afar in college, she reminds herself.

No, he might be better.

Nine

Maggie walks into the kitchen as the egg timer sounds. Her damp hair is pulled into her typical bun and she's thrown on a pair of jean shorts and a boatneck T-shirt since she doesn't know what the plans for the day will be.

At the sound of the timer, Quinn bounds off the sofa and bounces next to her as she pulls the scones from the oven. Setting them on a cooling rack, she protects the pastries from Quinn's grabby hands.

"You'll burn your tongue off, young man," she scolds in a mocking tone.

Gil appears on Maggie's other side and reaches for a scone. He snatches his hands back after touching one.

"Damn! Those are hot."

"Did the two of you not watch me pull them out of the hot oven? We graduated from the same college, I know you aren't stupid."

"Perhaps not Dr. Morrow, but you know I skid by on my good looks." Quinn grabs a napkin to hold his hot scone, attempting to cool it by blowing on it.

"Didn't Dr. Morrow live on an island full of mutant animal-human hybrids?" Maggie asks as she retrieves butter and a jar of homemade raspberry jam from the fridge.

"Different spelling," says Gil while sucking on his burnt finger.

When she turns around and sees him, she thinks, *That's hot.* Post shower he wears a pair of flat front gray shorts with an old button down white oxford with a frayed collar and the sleeves rolled up. He's barefoot with wet hair. *Okay, he's a lot hot.*

Selah comes in from the deck and joins the huddle at the island. She puts her mug on the counter, saying "Hit me," to no one in particular. "The scones smell amazing."

Quinn moves to swat at her while Gil grabs her cup and refills her coffee. "Maggie, you want more?"

"Yes, I definitely need caffeine."

"Milky but no sugar, right?"

"You remembered? Wow. Some things never change. I still can't drink sweet coffee. Don't even get me started with the fruit-flavored coffees."

"Fruit should not be allowed to taint coffee. Ever." Gil agrees.

"What about a white chocolate raspberry mocha?" Selah asks.

Both Maggie and Gil shudder.

"That hardly even counts as coffee. Jonah at the coffee hut up the road refuses to make anything fruit-flavored or similar to 'they who shall not be named'. When I first moved here, I ordered a venti and he scolded me for five minutes. Small, medium or large only."

"Coffee hut? Like one of the huts from my game of Hut Island?" Quinn asks through a mouthful of scone.

"No, not a hut from your beloved game of Hut Island. I forget you come from the land of sidewalks and pedestrians. Jonah's place, Fellowship of the Bean, is in one of those old Photomat booths in the parking lot of the grocery store up the road. Jonah covered the exterior in cedar shingles and added a corrugated tin roof, kind of industrial style. There are a few independent roasters and coffee huts around here. We take our coffee seriously."

"I'm going to need to visit this coffee hut. Is Jonah cute?" Quinn waggles his eyebrows.

"May I remind you, you're a married man?" Maggie says.

"Doesn't mean he's dead. He can still look. Looking is half the fun anyway." Selah picks a berry off of one of the last scones.

"What's the other half?" asks Gil.

"Flirting."

"I love to flirt." Quinn sighs.

"Who doesn't?" Selah replies. "Flirting gets the juices going and that's always a good thing."

Maggie picks up her scone and slathers it with butter. As she takes a bite, melted butter dribbles down her chin. She looks up to catch Gil staring at her mouth and quickly wipes the butter away with the side of her thumb.

Gil continues to stare as she licks her thumb. She catches his eye and blushes when he winks at her.

"Maggie, if I wasn't a married man, and if I didn't already have Jonah on the side, I'd marry you for your scones." Quinn reaches for his second one. "The best things ever."

"If you're good, I'll make them again tomorrow. I was thinking Selah and I could pick more berries after lunch. Have a little girl time."

"Sounds good to me, but you know I don't believe in the charm of the whole farm/manual labor/back to the earth thing like you do."

"What if after picking berries, we go to Langley for dinner and drinks?"

"Better."

"What should Quinn and I do while you are being gatherers? Hunt something?" Gil asks with a smirk.

"Hunt? Me? I could rock an orange safety vest and goggles." Quinn laughs as he pretends to fire a gun.

"You could go hit golf balls at Holmes Harbor. Or hang out here. The water is going out, so the tide flat will be exposed mid-day. People walk their dogs, ride horses, play volleyball, and go clamming out there during the low tide," Maggie says, gesturing out at the bay extending between two bluffs.

"Sounds like a tampon commercial." Selah's face shows her disdain for outdoor activities.

Ignoring the tampon comment, Quinn pipes up with, "Or visit Jonah."

"Leave Jonah alone." Maggie throws a berry at Quinn, which he catches in his mouth.

"Speaking of flirting with the natives, where's your hunky neighbor?" Selah turns toward John's house as if he will miraculously appear.

"Probably working. He said he'd drop off the firewood for a beach fire tomorrow morning."

"Did he ask about me?" Quinn asks.

"Actually, he asked about Selah. She made an impression on him at the funeral."

"Lucky bitch." Quinn scowls at Selah.

"Paul Bunyan is the hunkiest of hunky neighbors. Probably much hotter than even Jonah." Quinn dramatically sighs.

Maggie laughs. "You've never seen Jonah, Quinn. I guess John is hunky." She tries to nonchalantly shrug off John's hotness. There's no denying it.

"I wonder if he'll pose for one of my book covers." Selah muses out loud.

"I thought you wrote about smutty pirates, not sexy lumberjacks, Ms. Suzette Marquis?" Maggie asks, using Selah's pen name.

"Maybe I should start a new series on lumberjacks. Think of all the wood euphemisms!"

"I'd like to saw Paul Bunyan's wood."

Maggie scowls at Quinn.

"If I were single. Please. Like I'd ever cheat on Dr. Gooding?"

"I know you love him, Quinn. You're lucky to find your person." Maggie sighs.

"Some of us aren't meant to be lobsters, Maggie. Lots of fishes and lots of seas, but you need to have your hook in the water to fish," Selah says.

"You sound like Bert on the ferry with the fishing references. Although, the hook reminds me of Captain Hook. Didn't one of your pirates have a hook?" Maggie asks

"Am I the only one who doesn't read Selah's smut?" Gil asks as he pours the last of the coffee into his mug.

"Erotica, not smut. Erotica. I'm crushed you never read my books." Selah attempts to look crestfallen.

"I don't think I'm your target audience. Pirates aren't my thing."

"Gil, You don't celebrate International Talk Like a Pirate Day?" Quinn asks.

"There is such a thing?"

"Yep, in September, matey. Might want to try to keep up with what the young folks are doing these days, Captain," Quinn declares in his best fake pirate voice.

"On that note, shall we get on with our day?" Still laughing, Maggie puts the dirty pan and mugs in the sink.

"Leave those and I'll do them while you're gone." Gil volunteers.

"Really? Last night wasn't a fluke? A man who wants to wash dishes? You are the best thing ever." Maggie hugs him without thinking. His warm, summer, Gil smell is intoxicating.

"I told you I want to earn my keep around here. I figure if your coffee taste hasn't changed, neither has your abhorrence of washing dishes." Gil looks down at Maggie still hugging his arm.

At the mention of the time they all lived together between sophomore and junior years, Maggie drops Gil's arm and steps back. She tries to quell her reaction to Gil mentioning that summer and walks past him to let Biscuit out on the deck. "Selah, you going berry picking in a robe or are you getting dressed? And be sure to wear long sleeves to protect your arms from the thorns."

Selah dashes to her room down the hall. "I'll be ready in ten minutes," she calls out.

Maggie follows the dog outside and starts deadheading some flowers in the boxes around the deck with her fingers. She needs to get away from Gil and his intoxicating self.

"That was interesting." Quinn coughs, and then laughs as he bites into the last scone. "Very interesting indeed."

Gil still stands at the sink. Things went from fun and light to uncomfortable in a few seconds after the infamous summer was brought up. Wondering if she still regrets what happened, he turns on the hot water to distract himself from Maggie's reaction.

Quinn walks over to the counter with his mug.

"I'm not one to pry—" He stops when Gil raises his eyebrow in doubt. "Okay I am, but we all know something went down between you and Maggie before she left for France. I have my suspicions, which I'll keep to myself. But if there's still that thing between you two that's always been a thing between you two, now is the time, dear man. Plastics and all."

"Plastics?"

"It's the advice Mr. Robinson gave Benjamin in *The Graduate*. I think it's code for seize the day and fuck my wife. Not sure though."

"Pretty sure it wasn't code for 'fuck my wife', Q."

"In any case, the carpe diem part is what I'm getting at here. Don't let her shut you out again. Life is short."

"Are you giving me love advice?"

"Maybe I am."

"Huh. Never expected that."

"Maybe if I'd opened my mouth instead of playing along twenty-two years ago things would have worked out differently and you wouldn't be a weekend guest here. Think about it."

"If you only knew," is all Gil can manage.

* * *

Maggie and Selah take Bessie down the road to the cafe at Bayview Corner. They snag a table outside after ordering at the counter.

"I love this place," Selah comments. "It's like an extension of your living room."

"Me too. It's a great place to come and write. They'll let me stay for hours if they aren't busy. Sometimes Biscuit and I walk down here together. He's notorious at every cafe around here for being a cookie mooch."

"I'm glad you got him. I worry about you being on an island all year by yourself."

"Don't forget there's a bridge over Deception Pass, so we aren't completely cut off from the mainland, even in the worst of weather. I'm not up in the San Juans, where they lose power for days or weeks, and only get off the island by boat."

"For a city girl like me, who can walk to four coffee places, this is remote." Selah takes a sip of her coffee. "But the coffee is better."

"Everything is better here."

"Everything?" Selah looks skeptical. "How's your love life? Forget that. When was the last time you had sex?"

"Wow. Cut to the chase much?"

"Sex and love are not mutually inclusive. You can do each without the other. Sometimes they are better that way. Answer the question."

Maggie sighs. "Let me try to remember… I'm pretty sure it was since the millennium. Maybe even this decade."

Selah growls. "Ha ha. You are very funny. Fine, don't answer. If I were you, I'd be taking advantage of your eager neighbor next door. He seems more than willing, and able."

"John and I are friends. I don't fuck my friends," Maggie replies.

"Why not? You're both adults. Both single. Both healthy. Both gorgeous."

"I'm not like you. I need the emotional connection as well as the physical. Otherwise I'm happier taking care of things on my own."

"Thank fuck. I worry about you. I know the past three years haven't been easy and you're in mourning still, but I don't want you locking yourself away in some virtual attic."

"Like the first Mrs. Rochester in *Jane Eyre*? Nice. I'm not crazy. And I divorced my bastard of a husband more than a decade ago."

"Again, thank fuck. I get the appeal of the French Incident, but you deserve better."

"Funny, Gil said the same thing earlier today." Maggie wonders if the two of them are in cahoots.

"We were all surprised when you brought him home with you. Never imagined you'd end up marrying him. He must have been a great fuck."

"Not sure I want to go into my sex life with Julien, but yes, things in bed were always incredible with him. Well, until they weren't. But early on, yeah…"

"Thought as much. All the French pheromones and the accent had your head spinning."

Maggie sighs at the memory of young Julien seducing her. She'd never been seduced before him. It was a heady thing at the time. He wasn't her first, but he was the first of many things.

"You might be right. Unfortunately, I learned sex and chemistry a long and healthy relationship do not necessarily guarantee."

"I'm sure you don't want my opinion on the matter, but I think he is a classic hunter personality. Once he captured his prey and played with it for a while, he moved on to the next hunt."

"He never cheated on me, Selah. I know he had many flaws, but infidelity wasn't one of them. His career became more important. Chef's hours aren't conducive to a happy home life. We hardly ever saw each other."

"I'm not saying he did cheat. His crimes were taking you for granted and his despicable mother."

"You have no idea. She would send baby presents to us. Subtlety wasn't her forte." Maggie puts down her fork, completely without an appetite to finish her salad.

"Ugh. Horrible, horrible woman." Selah shakes her head, and then finishes her bagel.

"Why all the talk about Julien and Madame Armand?"

Selah picks up a caper from her plate. "I'm trying to figure out why you're cloistering yourself away. You're gorgeous, smart, successful, sexy… want me to go on?"

"Who's cloistered? I'm not cloistered. As you pointed out, I have a hot neighbor who you think is ready and able at any time. I haven't felt like myself for the last few years, so dating hasn't even occurred to me. John is a good friend, and I don't want to ruin the friendship with sex." Maggie feels they are getting dangerously close to a sensitive subject.

"I'm fine, Selah. I swear. Spinster life suits me." Maggie jokes, hoping to lighten the mood.

"But that's the thing. You aren't a spinster. You shouldn't act like one. Find someone to have sex with. Nothing better for your mind, body and spirit than an orgasm with another person."

Maggie tries to remember the last time she had sex. It was definitely before she moved back here. Or shortly after. Wait... has it been three years since she's had sex? Ugh. Selah is right, she does need to get laid, but she isn't going to admit this to her.

"I'm fine. I swear."

"Have sex. You'll feel better. Have sex with Gil. He seems willing and ready." Selah teases.

"Ha ha, now I know you are joking."

"I'm not joking. You and Gil have a great sexual energy. Always have. Well, until the French Incident. I think even after you met Julien, but you buried it under a mound of camembert."

Distracted by the image of a giant pile of cheese, she ignores Selah's point.

"All I'm saying, and I'm saying this with love, is I don't want to watch you hide your life away on the beach. Love more, laugh more."

"You sound like a greeting card."

"Shoot me now. I can give you this whole speech again sans the treacle if you want."

"Nah, it's okay. I get the point. No hiding, get laid."

"In a nutshell, yes. Ding ding ding... we have a winner." Selah fakes enthusiasm.

"With the discussion of my non-existent sex life over, how about we go pick blackberries?"

"Will said berries be turned into delicious carbs? Cause if no one is going to get laid this weekend, we might as well eat all the carbs."

* * *

When Maggie parks in the small, gravel area on the side of the narrow road, Selah's face is full of doubt.

"Is this even legal? I don't want to get arrested for stealing berries."

"Completely legal. I know the people who own the land." She hands Selah a plastic tub with a long loop of string through the top she pulled from the trunk of the car.

"What do you want me to do with this?"

"Put the string around your neck, so both hands are free to pick and eat berries." Maggie puts her tub around her neck to demonstrate.

Selah shakes her head in disbelief. "Remind me why we're doing this again?"

"Because this is a good reminder of how much work goes into picking berries. You won't complain about the price next time you buy them at Whole Foods," Maggie says, walking toward the far end of the berry bramble.

"This could get tedious fast." Selah eats a berry.

"Less eating, more picking. So, since we established I have no sex life, let's talk about who you're having sex with these days."

Selah sighs. "No one. Clearly not Mr. Rochester. And I broke things off with Tom at the end of the spring semester. He wanted me to meet his kids and I didn't envision us becoming that kind of relationship. People get locked into their lives by making lazy decisions. Then never get a second, or third, or fourth chance to get it right."

"I get it. I never figured I'd be single and starting over in my forties either."

"I know you miss your mom, but maybe this is all meant to be. Maybe this is your fresh start, your second chance."

"Maybe. I am blessed to be here. This life is a gift no matter if it's what I planned or not, since life rarely turns out the way we expect."

"Sometimes it surprises us and is more than we imagined." Selah tosses yet another berry into her mouth. "These are amazing."

"I think you've eaten more than you've picked." Maggie stares into her half-full bucket, and then peers at Selah's much emptier one.

"Isn't that the point of picking your own?" Selah eats another couple of berries. Juice dribbles down her chin and her fingers are stained purple.

"If you keep eating them, we'll be here all day, you know."

"True. So getting back to life and second chances…"

"Yes?"

"How do you think John would be in bed?"

Maggie laughs.

"Why are you laughing?"

"Because I swore you were going to mention Gil."

Selah smirks. "Funny your mind would go to Gil."

Maggie sticks out her tongue. "I never slept with John, let me remind you, so I can't comment on his lovah skills."

"Lovah skills?"

They both laugh.

"John does have big hands and big feet, and is tall. You'd think everything would be in proportion."

"You would think, but it isn't always the case. I wonder if he would be offended if I brought this up. I could say I need to know for research purposes."

"What sort of research would require you to ask him if everything is in proportion?" Maggie asks.

"Ah, you underestimate me. I do teach about the human form in art. The Classical Greeks misrepresented the penis to keep things in ideal proportions."

"So you're going to ask John about his penis following ideal proportions?" Maggie giggles. "Good luck with that. He's an island guy, Selah. You don't just start talking about penises in polite company here."

"Since when was I ever polite?" She eats another blackberry.

"True." Maggie calculates they've picked about two healthy quarts of berries. "Let's get you out of here before you turn purple like the Selah version of Violet Beauregard and the Oompa Loompas come to take you away."

Ten

"Hello," Maggie calls out as they walk into the house. Biscuit comes bounding down the hall to greet them.

"Hi, sweet boy." She scratches his head.

Selah walks ahead of her with the bucket of berries and puts them on the counter. Gil's sprawled out and sleeping on the couch with a book on his lap. Or at least he is until Biscuit hops up beside him and curls up at his side. After yawning and stretching, he scratches his jaw.

Turning away from Gil, Maggie turns on the sink to rinse the berries, then lays out a towel on the counter to dry them before she'll put them into the freezer for dessert tomorrow night.

"I guess I fell asleep." Gil yawns again.

"Hi, sleepy head," Selah greets him with a wave.

"Sorry we woke you up. Looks like Biscuit took advantage of a new guest and napped with you on the sofa." Maggie gives Biscuit a scolding look.

"Hey. Sorry about the dog on the couch. I didn't know."

"He isn't banned from the furniture, but I try not to encourage him. There's a perfectly good bed by the wood stove."

Gil scratches Biscuit's head. "Nice to have a dog around."

"You should get a dog," Selah suggests, pouring a glass of water, then joining Gil on the sofa.

"I should. I could probably even bring him to campus with me. Be the cool professor with the dog."

"Dog, bow tie, patched corduroy jacket… you'd be the hot professor fantasy come to life," Maggie says.

Gil smirks at her. "Hot professor fantasy? Want to share something?"

Maggie blushes, realizing what she's said. She reminds herself about Gil's girlfriend. *Maybe girlfriend.*

"Yeah, um. Doesn't everyone have one at some point?"

"No bow tie fantasies for me." She shakes her head.

"Me neither," Gil adds. "Now that the hipsters have claimed them, bow ties have been ruined for us stodgy, middle-aged professors anyway. Damn hipsters."

"Speaking of hipsters, where's Quinn?" Maggie asks.

"He's outside playing Peter Pan."

Maggie walks over to the screen door and spies Quinn on the beach with a group of tween and teen boys. They're building something out of driftwood.

"What are they making?" Selah asks, craning her neck from her favorite spot on the sofa.

"I'm not entirely certain. Quinn seems to be in charge and is using the kids for manual labor." Maggie steps out on the deck to get a closer look.

Quinn sits on a large driftwood log above the high water mark and directs a band of kids in constructing something from pieces of driftwood.

"Hey Q, whatcha doin'?" Maggie asks as she walks down the stairs to the beach.

"Hey, Magpie. I'm building a driftwood dog. The original design was a horse, but we had some issues with height. I should've hired taller assistants."

"Hired? Are you paying them?" Maggie sits next to Quinn. She watches the boys trying to balance a small log on top of a growing pile of logs and sticks that could possibly be a dog, if you knew it was a dog ahead of time.

"Technically, no one is getting paid."

"Hey Mr. Dayton, where should I put this one?" One of the smaller boys asks, holding a long, flat piece of wood.

"Save that one for the head."

"Mr. Dayton?" Maggie raises an eyebrow.

"He told me his mother didn't let him call adults by their first names. Can you believe it?" He leans closer to Maggie's ear and whispers, "Kiss ass."

She laughs.

"How was lunch and berry picking?"

"Both were fun. Selah ate more berries than she picked, but I enjoyed the company. How about you guys?"

"Gil and I foraged for food for lunch, then he started reading. I came out here and wrangled up a work force."

"Hey guys." Gil walks up and joins them on their log. "Are they making a crocodile?"

"It's a dog," Maggie says like it's obvious.

"A dog? Really. Are we sure? What happened to the driftwood Trojan horse, Q?"

"Overzealous design and untrained workers required some scaling back." Quinn gets up to adjust a few small pieces and places the flat piece of wood on top for the head. He steps back to admire his work.

"Do you see the dog?" Gil whispers, leaning closer to Maggie.

She can feel his warm breath on her neck and smell his clean, summer scent.

"Not at all." She turns to whisper back and realizes Gil is still leaning toward her.

"You smell like berries," he whispers, his gaze dancing across her face.

They both blink at each other for a beat longer before Maggie pulls back.

"I still think it resembles a crocodile." He stretches out his legs and digs his feet into the warm sand.

"Since Q is our very own Peter Pan, a crocodile makes more sense. We should put a clock in its mouth."

"Wasn't Hook afraid of the crocodile? Not Peter Pan? Archenemy and all?" Gil furrows his brow.

"I'm trying to remember the Barrie version of Peter Pan, but can't stop picturing Dustin Hoffman in a terrible wig." Maggie tries to recall the meaning of the clock.

"I think the whole thing was about fearing, accepting, or avoiding growing up."

"I'd say Q was in the latter category, avoidance."

"What about you? Do you fear or accept it?" Gil asks, sounding genuinely interested.

"I think I accept it now, but try to avoid being old. Growing up and growing old don't need to be the same thing. I'm not ready for the walker and eating dinner at four-thirty. What about you?"

"I think I've been old for a while now. Or at least I feel old some days. Some days I swear I'm still twenty. Or maybe twenty-five," Gil replies.

"Me too. It's weird."

"It is weird how it all works." Gil draws random shapes in the sand with a stick, then erases them.

"I feel like we're all essentially the same, with a few more battle scars and war wounds. Then I see friends' kids, and think 'how did they get so big', and it kind of freaks me out."

"Why do you freak out?"

"They've been growing and having all sorts of firsts in their lives. And my life is more of the same pretty much day in and day out."

"You went through a lot of grown-up things over the past few years, too." He stops drawing and puts his hand on her shoulder.

Gil's touch is soothing and sweet. Still, underneath Maggie feels a familiar heat where his hand touches her skin. She reaches up and covers his hand with hers, and gives it a squeeze.

"I have. We've all gone through some pretty big grown-up things in the past five years."

Gil pulls away and goes back to his drawing in the sand.

Maggie forgets all about Quinn and the Lost Boys while she and Gil are talking. Looking up, she sees they're standing around admiring their work, which now looks much more like a dog.

"It *is* a dog!"

"I told you so." Quinn acts put out. "When are you two going to believe me when I speak the truth?"

"Now the show's over, who wants a beer?" Maggie asks as she gets up from the log and dusts off the sand from her butt and legs.

"Me," says one of Quinn's workers.

"How old are you?" Gil asks him.

"Twelve."

"Nice try." Maggie laughs as she and Gil walk back up to the deck. Quinn hands out high-fives to the boys and follows behind them.

Selah sits in the shade of the table umbrella, texting on her phone. "Sounds like Ben and Jo won't get here until late. Ben says we shouldn't plan on them for dinner, but if we go out to leave them a key. They might want to crash."

"So, four for dinner? That works. We can go to Prima Bistro or Cafe Langley, then drinks at the Doghouse," Maggie suggests.

"Sounds good. Selah, you want a beer?" Gil asks as he heads inside.

"Sure, why not."

"Me too," Maggie calls out. "Quinn can drive tonight."

"I can drive where?" Quinn kicks the sand off his feet as he walks up the stairs.

"Dinner. Ben and Jo are arriving late, so just the four of us," Selah explains.

"Oh, like a double date. Or a date with two chaperons. Very formal."

"Who's going on a chaperoned date?" Gil asks as he returns with their beers.

"No one is going on a date. The four of us are going to dinner without Ben and Jo," Maggie tells him.

"Double date." Quinn smirks.

"Not my type." Selah laughs.

Maggie listens to their easy banter. A date with Gil sounds fun. Back in college they hung out in the group or sometimes off on their own, but never dated. She wonders what he'd be like on a real date, not hanging out as friends. Selah's strange reaction about his girlfriend flashes in her head, and she wonders if he is unattached.

"Let's head out at 6:30. I'm going to take a shower," Maggie says.

"Outdoor shower?" Gil teases.

"No." She laughs as she walks inside.

* * *

Waiting for the others to finish getting ready, Gil stops by the dining table and glances down at their Scrabble game. His eyes widen when he realizes more words have been added.

Quinn notices Gil gaping at the Scrabble board and goes over to look. "I can't believe you two were playing dirty Scrabble without us last night!" He theatrically huffs.

"What? We weren't playing dirty Scrabble," Maggie says. When she sees the board, she blushes. The words from last night are switched around. Only "licks" remains the same.

Selah walks inside and joins them.

"Please, love, licks, sighs, cunt, moan," Selah reads aloud. "Which one of you two played 'cunt'?" She glances between Gil and Maggie.

"I didn't play cunt," Maggie whispers the last word. "Someone's been messing with the letters." She looks pointedly at Quinn and Selah.

69

"Maggie May saying the C word." Gil laughs. "Impressive. I remember when you couldn't even say 'c-word' above a whisper. You'd whisper it like you were saying the actual dirty word. I used to think you meant cancer."

"I still don't say that out loud. I'm a lady." Maggie defends herself, but she can't keep a straight face as everyone laughs at her.

"I remember getting you drunk and promising to do your laundry for a month if you'd yell it in Red Square on campus." Selah wipes her eyes.

"I hated doing laundry more than I hated that word." Maggie laughs. "That was an easy bet to take."

"Say it again," Gil prompts. Maggie saying cunt is all sorts of dirty and hot.

"I will not! Unless Selah promises to do all my laundry again."

"I send my laundry out, so that would be a no."

"I'll wash all the dishes for the weekend if you say it." Gil offers.

Maggie considers his offer for a second. "Hey, you said you were doing the dishes anyways to earn your keep."

"Damn, true. I'm a man of my word, so yes, I'll still do the dishes even if you don't say it."

"We've apparently reached an impasse with Magpie and her cunt. Since the game has taken an interesting turn, I say let's keep going," Quinn says as he adds "ASS" to the board.

"Oh, this will be fun." Selah claps, then adds "MOIST".

"Ew." Maggie cringes.

"What's wrong with moist?" Selah taunts her.

"You know I can't stand that word."

"What? Moist?" Quinn moans "Mmm, this cake is deliciously moist."

Selah studies the board. "I wonder if I could play panties off of moist."

"Gah." Maggie flails her arms and runs away. "Stop!"

"What's wrong with moist panties? I thought wet was a good thing for girls." Quinn laughs.

He knows this teasing is more juvenile than sexual, but the thought of Maggie, panties and wet makes Gil heat up. He needs to think of something less enticing.

"Taint," Quinn says aloud as he set down the tiles.

That works. Gil gratefully exhales.

Eleven

After dinner, everyone decides to walk to Langley's historic pub, The Doghouse. The town sits above the water on a bluff. Tourist-friendly shops line the streets offering books, antiques, and art prints in addition to the mandatory sweatshirts and Orca-decorated mugs. Gil and Maggie walk behind Selah and Quinn, who are debating whale songs as music.

"The Clyde," Gil reads the marquee of the town's single screen theater. "Wow, I didn't think these old movie theaters still exist."

"The Clyde is a beloved institution around here. When they replaced the seats a few years back, people bought specific seats where they had their first dates or first kisses. Or even where they proposed."

"Island people are a sentimental bunch. You fit right in here," Gil says, while looking around for a bakery amongst the colorful storefronts. "Where was the bakery?"

"Over on Second," Maggie points south, "a block over. It's still there—just not mine anymore."

"Do you miss it?"

"Sometimes. When I sold mom's share to her business partner, she brought in her niece to help. They sell cupcakes now."

"Cupcakes are everywhere. They've taken over."

"They have. Mom did classic pies, cookies and cakes, mini loaves of banana bread, that sort of thing."

"What about scones? Or is that your thing?" Gil could eat Maggie's scones every day.

"The scones are mostly me. The one thing I can consistently bake. I'm much better writing about food than baking. Have to play to my strengths."

"Your food is amazing."

They catch up with Selah and Quinn at the entrance to the bar. As they walk in the double doors they can hear music coming from the back room.

"Ooh, live music," Selah says, delighted. "Where there's live music, there's the potential for hot rocker guys."

"It's a Thursday. On Whidbey. Highly unlikely these guys will be rock stars," Maggie argues.

"Remember when Gil was a rock star?" Quinn asks as they join the crowd at the long bar that runs the length of the right side of space.

Gil notes the pool table in the center of the room, the small tables on the left surrounded by flannel-wearing locals, pitchers and pint glasses scattered around the tabletops.

"I was never a rock star. I played bass in a college band."

"Yes, but in a college band in Olympia when Seattle was the epicenter for grunge. Plus, you were hot enough to be a rock star." Maggie smiles at him.

Gil stares at her. The wine from dinner has loosened Maggie's tongue.

"It's true. You were always much hotter than whatshisface, the lead singer of Inflammable Flannel."

"Mark. And thanks. Worst band name ever." Gil laughs.

"Right. Mark Jones. I fucked him," Selah casually says.

"You and most of the fans of Inflammable Flannel." Gil shrugs. "Mark definitely got more than his fare share."

"Personally, I always preferred the quiet bass player types in glasses." Maggie winks.

This surprises Gil, but he doesn't comment.

Pitcher and glasses acquired, they make their way through the crowd to the back room. Gil puts his hand on Maggie's lower back to help guide her down the narrow hall packed with people. His notices how his hand fits perfectly on the small of her back like it was made to be there.

A four top opens up in the corner and they grab it. Gil's leg bumps Maggie's as they squeeze into the crowded space around the table.

He catches her eye and smiles.

Quinn pours beer from the pitcher. "Cheers." He raises his glass of water. They all clink glasses.

"They're not half bad," Quinn shouts over the music.

The band is a classic four piece of a motley group of guys who look to be between mid-thirties and fifty.

"None of them are remotely hot, but they can play." Selah pouts. "Certainly not as hot as Paul Bunyan."

As if she conjured him, Selah points behind Maggie's head. "Hey, isn't that John?"

Gil's eyes follow Selah's finger to tall guy who does indeed resembles a lumberjack, or maybe the paper towel man with a full beard, leaning against the wall, drinking a dark colored pint of beer. He immediately feels territorial and drapes his arm over the back of Maggie's chair.

"We should invite John to join us." Selah nudges Maggie.

Gil catches Selah's eye, and sneers at her. She laughs and winks at him.

"Maggie, invite him over." Selah whines.

"What she said, invite the lumberjack over," Quinn says.

The room is crowded and the music too loud for John to see or hear them. Maggie attempts a small wave, but John turns his head to talk to the guy next to him.

"There's no room at our table," Gil grumbles.

"He can sit on my lap. Or I can sit on his." Selah purrs.

The band plays a blues song and a few people dance in the small area right in front of the stage.

"Hey, this is that song from that show with the old ladies?" Gil asks.

Quinn stares at him with an exaggerated shocked face. "Um, that would be *The Golden Girls*. A television classic." He looks genuinely disappointed in Gil's description. Quinn sings along with the band for a bit. "The love I have for Betty White—she's a minx."

"That sounds like a future Quinn project... Betty White as a woodland creature," Selah comments.

Quinn drums his fingers on the table. "You may be on to something, Ms. Elmore. What kind of animals are minxes? Are they where the coats come from?"

"No idea." Maggie laughs.

"None," Gil adds.

"Maggie, John's waving at you," Selah says, pointing to the far corner..

Maggie glances over her shoulder at John, who smiles and raises his beer. She does the same. He frowns, but tries to cover it when Maggie turns back to him.

Gil hears the familiar notes of "You Can Call me Al" and grins at Maggie as the band begins the song.

"Do you remember dancing in the kitchen to this song?"

Her grin tells him she does.

"Care to dance, Betty?" He gestures toward the middle of the room. Memories of laughing and dancing with her late at night flood his head, causing him to smile.

"Here? Now?" She asks, sounding shy. Selah smiles at Maggie in encouragement.

"Sure. It's no kitchen, but we can make it work." Gil stands up, and holds out his hand.

"Okay, Al." Maggie grabs Gil's hand and he pulls her to her feet.

He holds her hand as he moves through the crowd. When they reach the front of the stage, he spins her around and grabs her waist, keeping their hands linked.

Maggie laughs as they do a messy two-step in the small space. She has always been a fantastic dancer, that hasn't changed.

Gil pulls Maggie closer, shifting his thigh between her legs and moving his hand lower on her back. He threads his fingers through hers. As she sings along to the chorus, he realizes their energy has shifted. They've gone from laughing to moving closer. Gil bends her back a little.

He stares down at her beautiful face, her green eyes bright with mirth, and her cheeks pink from dancing. Her hair is as long as it was in college, dangling below her head as he dips her. He feels like he's twenty again. Transported to a beat-up kitchen in a dingy, student summer rental with perpetually-dirty linoleum underfoot, and the smell of pizza in the air—drunk on cheap beer and the girl in his arms.

Everything in the bar fades away until only they exist in a bubble, both unaware of the time or place.

The band finishes the song, and the lead singer leans into the mic. "For our last song, we're continuing the Paul Simon love-fest... our version of "Cecilia", folks."

"This has always been my favorite," Gil whispers in her ear.

He breaks away and spins her, catches her eye, and smiles down at her before pulling her back into his arms.

"Jubilation," Gil softly sings. It's both a statement and a wish.

He can feel her pulse quicken where he holds her wrist. When he tips his head down to hum in her ear, he breathes in her spicy, floral scent and it warms him. He spins her and joins in her laughter. The joy in her eyes makes the moment perfect. "Cecilia" isn't the best song for dancing, but in their silliness she doesn't seem to mind.

Gil forgets all about the others until the song ends and the band says goodnight. He's still holding Maggie's hand as she looks around for their friends. They're seated at the table, only now his seat is occupied by John. He can't decide if he's mad the lumberjack has joined them or happy because Selah's clearly in her snake-charming mode.

John moves to stand up when they approach. "I stole your seat, Mags."

Maggie waves him back into the seat. "It's okay. I'm going to go up front and grab another pitcher of beer and maybe some water." She looks flushed from dancing.

"You certainly worked up a sweat together. You two have some moves," Quinn says. "Grab me more water, will you? Designated driver is dehydrated."

Maggie blushes and Gil wonders if it is about working up a sweat with him. He's taken off his long sleeve shirt and stands in his dark blue t-shirt and faded jeans, and his hair is a little damp along the hairline. While she stares, he wipes his forehead with the back of his hand, then runs both hands through his hair. He feels a little overheated himself.

Snapping out of his Maggie-induced stupor, he realizes she is introducing him to John.

"John, this is Gil, another friend from college." She gestures at Gil standing next to her.

Gil holds back a frown at the "another friend" label, but what else can he expect? "Gil, my best friend until we had sex and I broke his heart" is a mouthful even if it is the truth.

"Hey." Gil wipes his hands on his jeans and then holds out his hand to John. He's pretty sure John sizes him up before shaking hands with an overly firm grip.

Fucking lumberjack.

"Hey, good to meet another one of the old gang." John sounds friendly enough.

Gil fights the urge to establish himself as the alpha dog because he doesn't have any claim on Maggie other than old friend.

Quinn interrupts Gil's thoughts. "With the way Selah was flirting with John here I was going to request the band play Mrs. Robinson next, but they ended their set."

Everyone laughs, even Selah. "Hardly. Wasn't she twenty years older than Benjamin?"

"True, but in reality Anne Bancroft was only older than Hoffman by a few years when they filmed," Quinn adds.

"The king of pop culture would know that." Gil grabs the empty pitcher. "I'll help you carry the beer and water."

Maggie follows him to the front of the bar. Now that the live music is over the place is clearing out. The crowd waiting for drinks thins to only one or two people deep. She stands in front of him when they get to the bar. As she leans forward to give their order, he doesn't resist the urge to check her out, and says a blessing to whoever designed skinny jeans.

Someone bumps into him and he loses his balance. Reaching out, he grabs her hips to steady himself, and she turns around to look at him. She covers one of his hands with her own.

"Don't think I didn't catch you checking out my ass," she teases as she leans back into him.

Keeping his hands on her hips, he leans forward. "It's a very fine ass, and I won't deny looking. You don't seem to mind the compliment." Gil gives her hips a squeeze. Flirting is good. Flirting with Maggie is the best.

"Thanks for not qualifying that comment with 'for a forty-something'. Me and my ass thank you."

"Your ass has only gotten better with age. Must be all the running."

"Flattery will get you everywhere, Dr. Morrow." She wiggles her butt.

He moves her hair to whisper in her ear, "Everywhere is where I want to be."

In the infinite perfect timing of the universe, the chatty bartender chooses this moment to come back over with their pitcher and four glasses of water.

Maggie is tempted to pour the water over her head to cool herself off from Gil's sexy banter. Instead, she downs one of the waters and puts the empty glass back on the bar. Gil isn't acting like he has a girlfriend and she makes a mental note to ask him about her, but not now, not tonight. Why spoil the fun with reality?

"That'll be fourteen dollars, Maggie." The bartender refills her glass.

Reaching for her wallet, she realizes she left her bag back at the table. Before she can say anything, Gil is already putting a twenty on the bar and telling the bartender to keep the change.

John's still at their table when they return, but his chair is now much closer to Selah. Gil grabs an empty chair and drags it over to the table. He drapes his arm across Maggie's chair again, and plays with a lock of her hair, twirling it around his fingers. He did this back in college —a gentle, sensual, toe curling, yet slightly teasing habit Maggie remembers.

Beers poured, they settle into friendly conversation. Maggie looks around the room, seeing a few familiar faces, but no one who qualifies as more than an acquaintance outside of the group at her table. Even though she's lived here full time for years, she hasn't established her own social network outside of John. She considers maybe she has cloistered herself away more than she admits.

Selah pulls out her phone and reads a text. "Ben and Jo are in Oak Harbor. Does this mean something?"

"It means they're about forty-five minutes away, give or take."

"They're tired and going to drive straight to the house," Selah continues.

"Should we head back and greet them?" Maggie asks the group.

"The sooner I can offend Ben, the better. I say let's go," Quinn says, partly teasing.

"See you tomorrow, John?" Selah puts her hand on his bicep, giving him a small squeeze.

John makes a fist and cracks his knuckles. "Sure, yeah. I told Maggie I'd bring over firewood for the bonfire."

"Love a man who shares his wood," Quinn jokes. Everyone laughs at the horrible euphemism.

"Let's go before you shiver his timbers." Gil puts his shirt on over his T-shirt while waiting for Maggie to stand and make her way toward the door. Once again, he walks behind her with his hand on the small of her back. The pressure and warmth from his hand are both familiar and exhilarating.

Outside, an empty street greets them. The marquee of The Clyde is dark and the quiet town resembles a stage set when the theater lights dim. She steps into the street and slowly spins with her arms out.

"Come on, Betty, you don't want to be run over." Gil grabs her hand and pulls her across to the other sidewalk.

"Al, you're so silly. This is Langley. No traffic to worry about."

"Here we go with the Al and Betty stuff again." Selah groans. "It's summer of '90 all over."

Maggie smiles at Gil while swinging their linked hands together. "That was a very good summer."

Gil winks at her. "It was, it was."

Twelve

Maggie, Quinn and Selah settle on the sectional while Gil sifts through the shelves of albums. After dancing with Maggie, he's feeling nostalgic for the summer they spent as housemates. He puts *The Graduate* soundtrack on the turntable just as the doorbell rings.

"They're here!" Maggie jumps up. Quinn races her down the hall while Selah and Gil laugh at them, following behind.

Maggie pulls open the door. "You don't need to ring the doorbell. Always so formal."

It's almost impossible for Ben and Jo to walk into the house with the crowd at the door. Hugs are given and bags are taken as they all shuffle inside.

"Come in, come in," Maggie greets them, leading everyone back to the living room.

Gil carries the bags into the den. Earlier in the day his new roommate moved her things into his room. Sharing a room with Selah is a little odd, but it won't be the first time. At least there are two beds this time instead of a king size and four friends on a road trip.

When Gil returns to the living room, he sees Ben standing by the dining table and the now dirty Scrabble game.

"You guys are playing dirty word Scrabble?" Ben shakes his head.

"Didn't start out that way, but yeah, we are now." Gil answers.

"We have a pervert amongst us, but they haven't identified themselves yet," Maggie says, joining them at the table.

Ben pulls out a handful of tiles from the bag and arranges them on the support. Looking over the board, he then plays 'PUSSY' off of 'SIGHS'. "Nicely played, Mr. Grant. Wonderful addition to the board." Gil pats him on the back and Maggie groans.

"Anyone want a drink? Water? Wine or beer? Tea?" Quinn offers from the kitchen.

"We brought clam broth." Jo sets a paper bag on the counter.

"Nothing says being in the Pacific Northwest like a steaming hot cup of clam juice." Selah snarks and wrinkles her nose.

"You like a Bloody Caesar with clam juice, Selah. How's this any different?" Gil asks.

"First, no vodka. Second, no tomato juice to hide the clam flavor. Third, warm clam broth. Do I need to go on?" She picks up a cup and smells it.

"My mom would always get a cup at Ivar's when it was cold and we had to wait in the ferry line." Maggie grabs the cup from Selah and takes a sip. "Thanks for bringing some, Jo. I'm sure I'll find some way to use it."

"I remember you talking about it at the funeral." Jo hugs her shoulders. "Sorry to bring down the mood."

"It's fine. I'm fine." Maggie gives her a watery-eyed smile.

Watching the two of them from across the kitchen island, Gil wishes he was the one to comfort Maggie. He knows he should have come up for her mom's funeral, but he wasn't sure he would have been a welcomed addition or a burden.

"What's happened so far?" Ben walks over to the fridge and grabs a beer. "Anything interesting? Other than Gil's presence and listening to music on actual vinyl records." He nods toward the turntable.

"Let's see… Maggie made scones, Quinn played Peter Pan, Gil and Maggie danced to 'You Can Call Me Al', and I was forced into manual farm labor." Selah fills them in on the highlights.

"Ah, explains the Simon & Garfunkel tunes. Ugh, I remember that song being kind of your thing when we all lived together," Jo says. "I can't hear it without thinking of the time the table got knocked over and the last two of the nice wine glasses were broken."

"I think we were better off drinking wine from plastic cups anyway. More stability." Selah gestures with her stemless wine glass.

"Speaking of wine, do you have a decent white? I can't drink chardonnay anymore," Jo asks.

"Me neither," Maggie says as she grabs a bottle of wine from the fridge. "Sav blanc okay?" she asks, reaching for a proper wine glass with a stem.

"Perfect."

"We missed the world famous scones?" Ben asks. "I was looking forward to eating carbs. Jo has put us both on another low carb diet."

"The joys of aging," Jo groans. Neither one of them appears to have anything but perfect body fat percentages and ideal BMIs. Ben's curly, brown hair has receded over the years exposing the worry lines on his forehead.

"I thought triathletes needed carbs for fuel. Isn't the whole point of doing triathlons is so you can eat whatever the fuck you want?" Quinn asks.

"I'm not in training now. Knee issues and my ortho banned me from competing until next year." Ben looks sad at this news. "Jo is running a 10K in September, though, so we still have one competitor in the house."

"Aren't the twins playing tennis anymore?" Maggie asks.

"Christopher does, but Theo got bored. He's trying out for lacrosse this year."

"Neither of them are gifted athletes. Ella did the required two years of soccer and stopped. She'd rather bury her head in a comic book," Jo explains.

"I think they are called graphic novels now," Ben says.

"Comic books, graphic novels… same thing." Jo rolls her eyes.

"I think Ella will make a fantastic goth in a few years," Quinn says. "I can picture her with striped tights and crinolines."

"Are goths even still a thing?" Maggie asks.

"Of course they are. Wherever there are emo teenagers, there are goths." Quinn rolls his eyes at Maggie.

"Oh, joy." Jo takes a big gulp of her wine. "Something to look forward to." She laughs at herself. "How did I get to be the mother of a twelve-year-old and fourteen-year-old twins? How is that even possible?"

"You don't look like the mother of teens, if it makes you feel better. Your dermatologist must be fabulous," Quinn says, looking closely at Jo's face.

Gil and Ben sprawl out on the sofa while Quinn examines Jo's face in the kitchen, Maggie and Selah observing from their perches on the bar stools at the end of the island.

"So how are you, man?" Ben asks as they drink from their bottles.

"Good. Better. I mean life is good."

"Is better sitting in the room?"

Gil laughs at his obvious transparency. "Better might be in this room."

"Good. About time." Ben tips his bottle in Gil's direction before taking a sip.

"I knew you had Botox!" Quinn's voice carries over to them.

"What happened to the music?" Selah asks no one in particular.

After walking over to the stereo, Maggie laughs. "Oops, no one turned over the record."

"What a pain in the ass," Quinn comments. "I remember having to get up and turn the television channels, all four of them."

"Ugh, can we not go down the 'We're so old do you remember blah blah' road? It's bad enough we all even remember what records are," Jo says.

"Hipsters know what records are. Vinyl is cool again," Quinn responds.

"How are you and Jo?" Gil asks Ben, ignoring the conversation about vinyl. "Where are the kids this weekend?"

"We're good. Same really. The boys are at sleep away camp and Jo's mother is staying with Ella this week."

"It seems like sleep away camp is more of an East Coast thing."

"It is. We've lived back east their entire lives, they're truly East Coast."

"Where are you guys again? Maryland? Connecticut?"

"Maryland was before Connecticut. We've been in Darien for the past three years."

"You like it?"

"It's okay. I spend most of my life in the office or on the road for meetings—it's all the same to me."

"How's business?" Gil takes a swig of his beer and lets his eyes follow Maggie across the room.

"It isn't what it was before 2008, that's for sure. I come out to Vancouver more often. At least it's nice to see Maggie now she's out here. It's a long haul trip to make once a month and I end up missing a lot of stuff at home."

"Yeah, I can't believe how many of us ended up back in the Pacific Northwest. Only you three traitors on the east coast now."

"I'd love to move back here or to Vancouver, but with kids in school it makes it more difficult to move around. After we moved to Darien, Jo said no more moves until the kids were in college." Ben puts his beer down on the floor. Biscuit flops down next to it and sniffs the bottle. Gil reaches out and rubs behind the dog's ears.

"You catch any Mariners games when you're out here?"

"Yeah, they still suck." Ben laughs. "I've gone to a couple of games when I've been in Vancouver. Easy drive down and you can get tickets on game day."

"Hey, let me know when you're in town. I'll drive up from Portland to meet you."

"Sounds great. You still in the same place you shared with Judith?"

"Nah, she insisted we sell the house in the divorce. It's fine. Too many memories. Bought a Craftsman-style place. I spent the first year stripping paint off the original woodwork." Gil is uncomfortable talking about the end of his marriage and fall out from the divorce. He stopped being in love with Judith long before the ink was dry on their legal separation, but the divorce is still a dark period in his life.

"Sounds like torture."

"It was a great way to work out some frustrations, that's for sure."

"Yeah, I can imagine. Judith was a piece of work."

"Everyone keeps reminding me." Gil's laugh holds a tinge of bitterness.

"Whatcha talking about?" Maggie walks over and joins them on the sofa, tucking her feet under herself.

"Stripping paint." He doesn't want more Judith and divorce talk to taint what has otherwise been a fun night.

"You two need another drink?" Ben asks, heading into the kitchen.

"I'm good."

"Me too," Maggie agrees. "Were you really talking about stripping paint?"

"Yeah. The woodwork was covered in layers of it when I bought the house."

"I bet it looks amazing now."

"You need to come see for yourself."

"I'd like that. Maybe after the reunion weekend?"

Walking back to the sofa, Ben mentions to the group, "Speaking of reunions, Jo and I rented a house for the weekend in Olympia."

"We figured a house would be easier than hotel rooms," Jo says as she perches on the arm of the sofa next to Ben.

With her dainty figure and perfectly blonde hair, she looks like a small, yellow bird. Maybe a goldfinch, Gil muses. Jo was the golden girl in college. The prize and perfect match for Ben, all brains and a big man on campus—at least in his mind he was.

"Sounds great. Ryan is looking forward to seeing everyone and visiting campus," Quinn says, joining them on the sectional. He scoots in next to Maggie, forcing her to sit closer to Gil.

"Will we get to see the good doctor this weekend?" Jo asks.

"He arrives Saturday morning. The more, the merrier."

"Good thing we didn't bring the kids. They'd have nowhere to sleep."

"Can always put up a tent on the lawn," Maggie suggests.

Jo looks mildly horrified by the thought of her kids sleeping on the front lawn in a tent. Quinn chuckles.

"Reunion weekend is no kids, right?" Selah asks.

"Heavens yes," Jo answers. "I'd rather protect them from stories from Auntie Selah and Uncle Quinn about their parents' adventures in college."

"You mean they don't know about how *Animal House* is tame compared to some of Ben's antics?"

"I never put a horse in anyone's office. There's no proof that goat had anything to do with me. Or anyone else I know," Ben adds, looking at Gil.

"Hey, don't look at me." Gil holds up his hands. "I'm sure I had an airtight alibi at the time."

"Yeah, what was her name? Dawn? Erika? Suzanna?" Ben asks.

Gil furrows his brow and squints. "I'm pretty sure it was Suzanna. Or maybe Suzanne. It was a long time ago."

"And you, dear sweet Gil, were a bit of a slut," Selah pipes in.

Gil laughs. "Okay, kettle."

"It was college. That's what you're supposed to do," Quinn says. "Unless you are Ben and Jo, you don't end up with your college love. It's all about experimenting, finding yourself, and heartbreak."

Maggie avoids Gil's eye at Quinn's observation. Gil bumps her leg with his a few times to get her to look at him. When she does, he gives her a soft smile, and says, "All of that is ancient history. What matters most is who we have in our lives now."

"Amen." Selah raises her glass.

"Speaking of sleeping, where are we sleeping tonight? I'm exhausted," Jo says.

"You and Ben are downstairs. Gil and Selah are upstairs in the twin beds, and Quinn is in the other guest room," Maggie explains.

"Great. I'm off to bed, then." Jo kisses Maggie on the cheek and blows a kiss to everyone else.

"Me too," Ben adds, following Jo down the hall. "Night."

"Towels are under the sink in the hall bath," Maggie calls out as they retreat down the hall.

As if on cue, she yawns. It's been a long day with many beers this evening. She snuggles more into the couch and a little bit more into Gil. Dancing with him tonight broke the ice. The wall around her heart where her feelings for Gil are kept begins to crack. He feels like home even after all these years. In many ways he is the same charming, sweet boy she met freshman year. The guy who couldn't believe she liked Roxy Music so much she had a giant Bryan Ferry poster above her bed.

"I was thinking of freshman year. Whatever happened to my freshman roommate you dated?" With her eyes closed she tilts her head in his direction.

"No idea. Can't even remember her name," Gil says.

"I think it was Jennifer." Opening one eye, she squints at him.

"Hmmm... rings a bell. I imagine she has a kid in college and a mini-van. She seemed keen on getting her M.R.S degree right from the start." He cringes.

"She might be at the reunion and we can find out. Maybe you'll see her again and remember your love for her."

Gil laughs and then looks at her. "No big interest then, no interest now."

"There was some interest then. I remember having to hang out at the library late more than one night. You never know. Maybe she's hot. Maybe she married a much older guy and he died, and left her millions, and she got a boob job." She opens her other eye to stare at him.

"Sounds like just my type."

"I knew your type was Anna Nicole Smith."

"My type has never been that. My type is more natural, less silicone." Gil traces down her arm, then pokes her in her side.

When Maggie squirms away from him with his threat of tickling, she notices Quinn and Selah are gone. "Where did everyone go?"

"Miss Observant, they left sometime between Jennifer and Anna Nicole."

Maggie realizes she didn't even hear them slip away. "We should go to bed, too. You okay sleeping with Selah?"

"I'll manage." Gil yawns and stretches out. "If she snores, I can always sleep out here. Or crawl into bed with you, like old times."

Maggie doesn't take him seriously. "The couch is really comfortable. I've fallen asleep out here many a night next to the wood stove— warmest spot in the house some nights."

"I notice you missed my overture." He winks. "I'll let Biscuit out. You should head up to bed. I think I'll stay up for a bit and read."

She blinks at him for being called out, but decides to let it pass. "That's sweet. Are you sure? He's usually pretty quick this time of night."

"No problem."

"Okay, well, goodnight." She turns toward him and gives him an awkward half hug.

"Night." He kisses the side of her head. A kiss she can feel down to her toes.

She drags herself off the sofa and up to her bed. Alone like many other nights. Only tonight her bed seems big and empty with only her.

Thirteen

The sun shining into his room wakes up Gil earlier than normal. He rolls over to see Selah still conked out in the twin bed next to his. Stretching and yawning, he remembers last night's dancing and flirting with Maggie. He doesn't stop the smile that crosses his face. Amazed how a song can transport him back in time, he hums a few notes and feels lighter, more optimistic than he has in a long time.

Maggie's door is closed when he walks by and he decides not to disturb her. Well, he does want to disturb her, but not for running. He'd like nothing more than to quietly crawl into bed with her. Unlike college, he isn't even that bold, so he decides he'll go for a run to work off some of the pent up energy and sexual tension in his body. Maggie has only been back in his life two days, he knows he needs to proceed cautiously.

* * *

The smell of coffee greets a very sweaty Gil when he walks through the front door. Heading into the kitchen, he spies Quinn and Ben by the stove, making what appears to be breakfast.

"Hey guys," he greets everyone as he walks over to the sink to fill a large glass with water.

"So that answers the 'where is Gil?' question. Selah must still be asleep," Jo says from her perch at the island. Jo has never been a morning person so an entire sentence from her is impressive.

"What wonder is this?" Maggie passes through the kitchen on her way to let Biscuit outside.

"They're attempting to make omelets," Jo answers.

"Morning to you, too," Quinn kisses Maggie's cheek and swats her bottom with a spatula when she pours herself a cup of coffee.

"Anyone else need a refill?" Maggie asks the room in general.

Jo holds up her cup.

Gil catches Maggie ogling him while she stands at the counter.

"Morning," Maggie greets him. "You look hot." She pauses.

He quirks an eyebrow at her inadvertent compliment and watches her cheeks pink.

"I mean literally. You're sweating."

"I just got back from a run." He tugs his T-shirt from his damp skin. Her eyes follow his movements.

"How far did you go?" Maggie asks, lifting her eyes to meet his.

"Not sure since I don't know the island, but I ran for about forty minutes. Five, six miles maybe. I turned back at the donkey."

"I knew you were flattering me by keeping to my pace yesterday," Maggie comments, joining Jo at the counter.

Gil gives her a sheepish smile.

"Since when do you run, Maggie?" Jo asks. "In college you'd only have run if a clown was chasing you or there was free booze."

"Ha-ha on the booze, and who wouldn't run if a clown was chasing you?" Maggie laughs.

"Why would the clown be chasing you?" Quinn joins the conversation from his sous chef position at the stove. "This is the important question. Is he a demonic clown? Maybe the clown wants to give you a gift? And you keep running away and hurting his feelings."

"Are you honestly analyzing the mindset of a clown chasing Maggie?" Gil laughs at Quinn's crazy questions.

"Can we stop talking about clowns?" Ben says.

"Still have the clown phobia, Mr. Grant? What if it was a mime with a flower instead?" Quinn asks.

Ignoring the clown talk altogether, Ben finishes chopping mushrooms for the omelet. Piled on the cutting board is a mound of grated cheese, another of ham, and now an equally impressive one of mushrooms.

"What do you want to go with your omelets? Bread? Or maybe potatoes?" Ben asks.

"Oh, Gil can make his home fries. Those were the best hangover breakfast or late night snack ever back when we didn't worry about what we ate," Jo comments.

"Gil should definitely make home fries." Maggie gets up from her stool. "I have potatoes and onions. Spices are in the drawer." She begins pulling things together.

"I'm happy to help, but need a quick shower first. Mind if I use the outdoor shower?" He gestures at his sweat dampened self.

"Like we'd ever say no to you using the outdoor shower," Quinn scoffs.

"I need a towel," Gil says, glancing at Maggie.

"I'll grab you one out of the downstairs bathroom," Maggie calls out as she walks down the hall.

When she returns, Gil thanks her for the towel and heads outside. The shower stall sits off to the left side of the house, near the kitchen window. Three teak walls create privacy, but if someone wanted to peek, there is a narrow gap between the walls and the side of the house.

Gil tosses his T-shirt and shorts over the door of the shower to keep them from getting wet. He's conscious of being naked outside and being steps away from Maggie. As he turns on the spray and adjusts the temperature, his mind wanders and his body responds to the fantasy of Maggie joining him in the shower.

* * *

Standing at the kitchen sink, Maggie tells herself she is not thinking of Gil in the outdoor shower. No, not at all.

"Ten dollars if you go outside and offer to wash his back," Quinn stage whispers to Maggie as she drinks her coffee, obviously lost in a daydream.

"Ten? I bet she would for five," Ben teases from the stove.

"Who would do what for five?" Selah asks as she walks and heads straight for the coffee maker.

"Quinn was betting Maggie ten dollars to go offer to wash Gil's back in the outdoor shower." Jo fills Selah in on the teasing.

"Gil in the outdoor shower? Mmm, nice." Selah hums as she pours her coffee.

"Have you ever had sex out there?" Quinn asks Maggie.

"That's none of your business, Q," Maggie laughs, snapping out of her daydream.

"Can Ryan and I have sex in your outdoor shower? Someone needs to. It's a shame if it's never been christened. Outdoor showers are made for sex."

"I think outdoor showers are intended to wash the sand off after being on the beach to avoid clogging the septic system, or track sand through the house," Ben explains.

Quinn frowns at Ben's literal reply. "Is he always this stiff, Jo?"

Without looking up Jo replies, "Only in the morning."

Quinn bursts into laughter. "Oh, the lady is hysterical." He high-fives Jo, who can't hide her smirk.

"You have my sympathies." Selah takes Maggie's old stool at the counter.

"Thanks. Such is the reality of middle age." Jo sounds resigned.

"Doesn't have to be. There are these delightful pills now, like *Valley of the Dolls*, only for boys," Quinn says.

"Hello? Me and my middle-aged penis are standing right here." Ben waves his spatula.

"According to Jo, the standing is the issue." Quinn continues to tease.

"Okay, let's leave Ben and Big Ben alone," Jo says.

Quinn raises an eyebrow. "And which one might Big Ben be?"

Maggie observes the visible tension shimmering between Selah and Jo—they both know the answer to the question.

"No comment."

"No complaints," Jo says.

"Okay, I think we've exhausted the conversation about Ben's genitals." Maggie laughs. "Sorry, Ben."

"No worries."

"What did I miss?" Gil walks back inside, wearing a white towel around his waist. Water drops from his wet hair making slow rivulets down his bare chest.

At the sound of his voice, Maggie turns to glance at Gil. Her mouth drops open. Looking at Selah and Jo at the bar, she sees similar expressions on their faces.

"Nothing much. Just talking about Ben's penis. Typical pre-breakfast conversation," Quinn, who is staring too, says.

"Okay. That's normal." Gil looks between everyone in the kitchen and smirks. "I'll get to work after I put on some clean clothes. I have home fries to make."

"No need to get dressed on our account," Selah suggests.

"No, no need at all," Maggie mumbles to herself, regaining the last shreds of her composure as she watches Gil's retreating back.

Hearing a knock on the door, Maggie looks up and sees John standing outside with a cooler at his feet. She waves him inside. "Morning," she greets him.

"Hiya. Hope I'm not interrupting." John smiles at the group.

"No, of course not. The guys are making breakfast. You should join us," Maggie suggests.

"Nah, I already ate."

"Are you sure? We have coffee," Selah offers, gesturing toward the coffee maker.

"I'll take a cup, but I can't stay for long. I wanted to let you know I chucked the wood down by the fire ring for you."

Quinn snorts. "Woodchuck."

Maggie, Jo, and Selah make eye contact.

"Roger." Jo stifles a laugh behind her hand.

"Are you all fourteen?" Selah asks them while pouring a cup of coffee for John.

"Sometimes, yes, yes I am." Maggie blushes at the memory of Roger and his legendary "wood chucking" skills in the freshman dorms.

Ignoring her giggling friends, Selah asks John, "How do you take your coffee?"

"Black is fine," John answers Selah. "I also have a few crabs I picked up in my traps. Thought you might like them for dinner tonight."

"Yum!" Selah claps. "Can I see them?" She hands John his coffee.

"Sure. Not much to look at, but they're in the cooler on the deck. Probably shouldn't leave them in the sun for too long."

Selah follows John outside and Maggie joins them.

"Of course the lumberjack is here," Gil says under his breath as he walks into the kitchen and sees the women now fawning over John.

"He brought over some crabs for dinner," Ben explains.

"Lumberjack and fisherman. Is there anything he can't do?" Quinn asks, sounding dreamy.

"Apparently not," Gil grumbles.

"Someone sounds jealous," Ben comments.

"I'm not jealous. Why would I be jealous?"

"Not saying you are, only that you sound jealous."

"The growling is hot, though," Quinn says

"I wasn't growling." He growls.

"If she was going to fuck John, she's had plenty of chances. Even if she did fuck him, or does fuck him, he isn't ever going to be more than that. Too young and too much of a lumberjack. Just sayin'," Quinn says.

Gil stares at Quinn like he's grown a second head. "Okay," he says slowly. "Thanks." He realizes he needs to rein in his bad attitude toward the lumberjack. He doesn't hold a claim on Maggie. Ben and

Quinn probably aren't the only ones to notice his growling, not that he admits to growling.

Gil stirs the home fries and puts on the lid. Grabbing a coffee, he joins Jo at the counter.

"What's up with you and Maggie? I'm having deja vu back to us all living together. You can cut the tension between you two with a butter knife."

"I'm not really sure to be honest." Gil shrugs. There's been enough meddling in what is brewing between he and Maggie. He doesn't need more.

"Whatever is going on, I hope you get yourselves sorted out right this time. Stupid French Incident ruined everything."

Jo's words surprise him. He wonders if everyone in the house knows what happened twenty-two years ago.

* * *

They decide to eat breakfast outside in the sun. John waves off another offer to join them, for which Gil is grateful. Maggie and Selah have been gushing over his crabs and resourcefulness while Quinn muttered sexual entendres under his breath about wood and crabs. Even cool, collected Jo seems to be under the lumberjack's spell. Gil is two seconds from rolling his eyes.

"He's just the sort of guy you'd have an affair with." Jo notes after John walks back over to his house.

"Oh, trust me, you are right about that." Selah sighs.

"You two sound like most of the women who summer on this beach." Maggie rolls her eyes, causing Gil to smile.

"Does he fuck around?" Hope twinkles in Selah's eyes.

"Not with the married women. The island is a small place, so if he were a slut, we'd all know. My guess is he's a good guy or discreet."

"Good guys can be sluts too, you know," Quinn says.

"He's a good friend. And a neighbor."

"Locationally-desirable is a bonus," Jo agrees.

"Yeah, but a little close if things got awkward. He's sweet. And where would I get free crabs if we weren't friends?"

"I am resisting making any commentary about getting crabs from John. I just want you to know that," Quinn says.

"Thank you," Maggie replies.

Ben and Gil quietly watch this exchange as they finish their breakfast.

"Since I didn't cook, and it's my house, I'll clear and do the dishes." Maggie gets up from the table and starts gathering plates. "If we want to hike Ebey's Landing, we should head out sooner rather than later."

Selah and Jo help her clear before following Maggie inside.

"Look at us being 1950s women washing dishes whilst the menfolk digest," Jo declares.

"More like the Victorians." Maggie unloads the dishwasher.

"If we were Victorian ladies, we'd have servants," Jo says as she scrapes food into the trash.

"Wait, you do have servants, don't you?" Selah asks.

"A babysitter and a housekeeper, who comes once a week. Hardly 'servants'."

"What about a gardener? Groundskeeper?" Selah continues to tease as she rinses the dishes.

"True. We do use a landscaper and someone deals with the pool during the summer. Neither Ben nor I have green thumbs. Or the time."

"These days, who does?" Selah muses. "I have a cleaning woman who comes twice a month. Otherwise it would look like meerkats shared my house."

"Are meerkats notoriously messy creatures? Don't they live underground? Do they hoard things?" Maggie asks.

"Who knows? I'm more of a magpie. I like bright shiny things and useless trinkets."

"Shiny trinkets sounds like pirate booty." Maggie chuckles.

"Speaking of pirate booty, how are those books you write doing? Still selling on Amazon?" Jo asks.

"I won't be retiring on them, but they sell surprisingly well. Apparently, I am not the only woman, or man, who has a thing for eye patches and beards."

"Johnny Depp as a pirate helps the fantasy, that's for sure." Jo loads the dishwasher.

"I wonder if eye patches will be the new hipster eyewear," Maggie says.

"Did I miss the monocle trend? I figured that was next with the whole nerdy glasses going on these days in Portland," Selah says.

"I don't think we have hipsters in Connecticut."

"No, probably not. Hipsters don't do mortgages or good school districts," Selah responds.

"I think Quinn is a hipster, we should ask him." Maggie glances out toward the deck to where the guys are hanging out.

Ben paces outside, giving instructions in some sort of code on his phone. "Marcus can't. He's busy on-boarding the new client. Have Neal handle the P&L reports, as well as the quarterly statements," Ben says.

Gil and Quinn sit at the table with their coffees, half listening.

"Do you think Ben is in charge of the TPS reports?" Quinn asks.

"He might as well be quoting *Office Space* for all I understand." Gil looks at Ben in his polo shirt and madras shorts—the picture of success.

"Once Marcus is done with the on-boarding, make sure he finishes the new CMS upload."

"See? He said TPS." Quinn chuckles and drinks the last of his coffee.

"He said CMS," Gil corrects.

"Does he ever stop working?" Quinn asks.

"I was just checking in with the office, not working," Ben answers after ending his call. "My being in Vancouver for the week means everyone will have been slacking off and getting nothing but the bare minimum done. Zero focus."

Maggie walks out on the deck. "Being the boss isn't all it's cracked up to be. Everyone secretly hates you, some less than secretly."

"Try running a studio where people are living off of your creativity. Then having 'critics'... " Quinn makes air quotes around the word. " ...ripping your genius to shreds."

"When I write a restaurant review I always try to say something complementary even when the food was horrendous and inedible. Sometimes I just focus on the decor."

"Yeah, but art and food are two different things. Food disappears in a few minutes. Art lives on for the ages."

"Bad food can kill you though," Gil says. "Bad art will only give you nightmares."

"True. Although I think one of Christo's umbrellas killed someone," Quinn says.

Ben joins them at the table. "So we're hiking today? Do I need gear?"

"Just comfortable shoes. We're not climbing Rainier or anything," Maggie says.

Selah and Jo walk outside. Selah wears Bermuda shorts and a colorful, gauzy shirt. Jo wears a pink polo and short khaki shorts, which show off her long, perfectly-tanned legs.

"We aren't doing anything strenuous, right?" Selah points down at her worn chucks.

"Everyone is dressed fine as they are. This is more of a beach walk with a big hill. Let me grab Biscuit's leash and we'll go." Maggie follows Gil over to the door.

At the word 'leash' Biscuit runs to the door as Gil opens it to head inside. Biscuit practically tackles him to get inside where his leash is kept. As Gil reaches out to steady himself, he braces himself using Maggie's arm, pinning her against the door jam.

He hears her breath hitch while his heart races, and it isn't from the adrenaline of almost face planting. Taking a moment to collect himself, he realizes they are still partially entwined.

"Someone's excited to go," he states the obvious.

"Biscuit loves going anywhere. He acts like he's a shut-in who never leaves his house." Maggie pulls away from Gil's body heat and closes the door behind her, but not before he hears Ben say, "Get a room, you two."

She rolls her eyes at Ben.

"I feel like we're twenty again around this gang. Is it just me?" she asks him.

"There is something about all being together that causes us to revert to old behaviors."

His words sting Maggie and he sees the hurt flash briefly in Maggie's eyes, or at least he thinks he does. He's not sure why she looks hurt by his words, but he wants to fix it. The two of them were always huge flirts with each other before the French Incident. "I mean some old behaviors aren't bad things at all. We wouldn't all still be friends if it was all bad. Some of the past was really good."

"It was?" She sounds insecure and unsure.

"Of course it was. Some of my fondest memories are with this group of people." Feeling bold, he adds, "Some of my best memories are with you specifically. I wouldn't change those for anything."

"Really?"

"Don't you agree? I mean, I'm not one of those types who had their glory days in high school or college, and feel like everything since then has been downhill. But everything was bigger... more, back then. Everything felt deeper, more important when we were in our twenties."

"Probably the undeveloped frontal lobe or something." Maggie jokes.

"Maybe. Some feelings become deeply ingrained and never fade, even with time." He squeezes her arm.

"Maybe," is all she can get out.

"No maybes about it for me," Gil says, looking into her eyes.

She blinks and he squeezes her arm again, then steps away from the door. The rest of the group walks in and busies themselves gathering their stuff to leave.

Unspoken words bounce around his head as they head out to the car.

Fourteen

Maggie hooks on Biscuit's leash when they pile out of Ben's rented SUV in the parking lot of the trail-head. After Selah and Gil crawl out from the back row, Maggie giggles over the thought that they all resemble clowns getting out of a tiny car.

Gil stretches his arms over his head, then tugs at Maggie's French braid. "So, island girl, where do we go?"

She points at the trail marker and starts walking in that direction. "We'll head north up the bluff first."

Gil walks beside Maggie and Biscuit leads the way up the trail through the tall grass. The rest of the group follows behind, with Selah and Jo trailing last, having an in-depth conversation about gray nail polish.

The trail narrows at the top of the hill as they approach the tree line, so they walk in a single line, with Gil following Maggie.

Wondering if his eyes are on her, she teases, "Are you looking at my ass?"

Gil laughs, knowing he's been caught. "I'm so busted. I was just admiring your strong leg muscles from running."

"Uh huh. Leg muscles." To taunt and tease him, she wiggles her ass, and peeks over her shoulder at him.

"Are you trying to kill me, Maggie May?"

"Maybe." She giggles. Flirting with him is like floating, effortless once she relaxes.

Sweat dampens her neck from the sun's strong rays. She hands Biscuit's leash to Gil, then pulls her long-sleeve shirt over her head, and feels a light breeze on her stomach and breasts. Her face warms when she realizes she's pulled both shirts over her head. "You really are trying to kill me, aren't you?" Gil softly groans as she tugs her T-shirt back down.

Her head pops back out when she finally pulls off the thermal. "Sorry about that."

When she sees Gil staring at her chest, her face heats more while she ties her thermal around her waist.

Even though he's wearing aviators, she can tell where he is looking. Her breasts are fuller now than they were in college. He rubs his neck and pushes his hand through the back of his hair. Maggie smiles at his familiar gesture that reveals his discomfort. Her eyes wander down his shirt-and-shorts covered frame, stopping when she notices a telltale bulge. *Oh my*, she thinks.

When she raises her eyes up, he waves her to face forward and continue walking. "Nothing to see here. Let's keep going."

"I wouldn't say nothing." Maggie flirts, seeing it's Gil's turn to have his face redden

"What's the hold up?" Ben asks as the rest of the group stops behind them.

"Nothing," both Maggie and Gil say at the same time.

"Then carry on." Ben suspiciously glances between them.

After hiking along the bluff, Selah wants to wander over to the old cemetery. The goth girl in her still has a thing for death and headstone epitaphs. Selah convinces Quinn to join her, and they link arms as they walk away.

The others beachcomb while Biscuit plays in the small waves. Gil finds a stick-size piece of driftwood and tries to get Biscuit to fetch. The attempt becomes a game of Biscuit watching Gil running back and forth fetching the stick, which amuses Maggie. She laughs at Gil.

Jo walks over to Maggie, who scans the beach for wishing rocks. "It's good to see you laugh again. The past few years sucked."

Maggie gives Jo a one-armed hug. "Thanks. It's amazing to laugh and feel light after so much darkness and death, like the sun is out again after a long rain." Her gaze wanders over to Gil.

"I wonder if the sun has a name."

Maggie realizes she's been staring. "I'm happy to be with all of you. Old friends are the best. No need to explain yourself, you can just be."

"Uh, huh. You don't get a dreamy expression when you look at me or anyone else." Jo nudges her with her elbow.

"Hmmm, maybe."

"What's going on with you two anyway?"

Maggie bends down to pick up a beach rock with a white circle. The ring doesn't connect on the bottom, so she tosses the rock down on the sand.

"I'm not sure. This is the first time we've seen each other in years. It's nice to hang out with him again. I'd forgotten what an amazing guy he is. So easy to be with."

"And single."

"I don't know if Gil is single. What happened to the girlfriend?"

"What girlfriend? You need to verify your information with him, since you refuse to join the world of social media world. I was surprised there isn't a rotary phone at the cabin."

"There's a rotary phone in my bedroom left over from my grandparents."

Jo laughs. "This place really is a time capsule."

One of the things she loves best about living here is the timeless beauty. Maggie stares out over the water toward the dormant volcano of Mt. Rainier in the distance. Closer, a large container ship moves out to sea with cargo destined for faraway ports.

"Slowing down and not being a slave to consumer living are good things," Maggie says.

"Cutting yourself off from the world and letting life move past you are not." Jo's words are clearly about more than the island. "You are an amazing woman. You can't hide away on an island for the rest of your life. You're young, beautiful, fit, sexy—stop trying to deny who you are."

"Aw, thank you for the compliments, but I'm not hiding away. I write reviews and articles read around the world. I'm very international. In fact, I might be up for a big magazine assignment for my former editor that could push me to the next level." She picks up a small rock with a whole circle and rubs off the sand. She holds it in her hand as they walk, gently stroking its smooth surface.

"Your work isn't hiding, but you are."

"Lumberjack John is right next door."

"Yes, but you'll never have a real relationship with him. What is he? Twenty-eight? He's a child."

"He's thirty-two, and hardly a child. It's good to flirt with someone who brings me food and wood, and can change a light bulb. What more do I need?"

"Maggie, you know I love you, but life is short. Lizzy reminds us of that. I want to see you happy and whole." Jo's exasperation comes out in her words.

"Meaning married with kids and the whole shebang? We don't all get the American dream wrapped up in a neat box with a pretty bow. Not all of us want the box or the bow."

"Sometimes the pretty box is more of a cage. I'm not saying you need the kids and the ring on your finger to be happy. Lord knows it doesn't guarantee happiness." Jo's eyes drift over to Ben. "But I think life is better when you have love. Not a friendly neighbor, or old friends kind of love either, but a love that causes your heart to race and your toes to curl."

Maggie glances back toward Biscuit and Gil playing behind them in the distance. Ben sits on a large driftwood log tapping away on his phone. They've walked further than she realized.

"Does anyone still have that kind of love at our age? Do you and Ben?"

"Some people do. Sometimes it's more a day or even an hour of happy, giddy love. Ben and I have our moments. It's hard with the kids and his career. But yeah, he can still make my heart race."

Maggie tucks her arm into Jo's as they walk. "I'm happy to hear that. You two have been together forever. I would hate to think what was once a great passion is only an ember now."

"I'll be honest, most of the time it's the ember. But every now and again the fire reignites. The trick is to keep the ember alive. You can't have a roaring fire every day."

"No, not a roaring fire. Especially not in front of the children." Maggie chuckles.

"Fires and children aside, everyone needs love in their lives. Real love between lovers. Not friend, parent, child, or even dog love."

Maggie knows what she means. She's shut that part of her heart off for so long.

"Life's messy, with no guarantees, but you still need to live and love. None of us know how long we have here."

"That's the truth. Mom's death reminded me of that and it's why I sold her share of the bakery. It wasn't my passion. But her death is also why I'm here on the island. And being here makes me happy in ways living in the city, with its paper dragon wealth chase, never did. I can live more in the moment."

The two of them reach the others gathered on the beach. Gil has joined Ben on the log. A wet and sandy Biscuit happily chews on a stick at Gil's feet.

"No more speeches from me," Jo whispers in Maggie's ear. "Know I love you and I want you to be happy. I also love Gil." Jo kisses her cheek.

Maggie is overwhelmed by her friend's love. She hadn't realized how much she misses all of them. Her eyes water with a few tears, so she looks down at the driftwood.

Stacked next to Gil are six wishing rocks. They are perfectly balanced from large to small. He sees her looking at them and smiles.

She smiles back. "You found wishing rocks?" she asks even though she knows what they are.

"Yeah, I thought we could all make a wish with them. Or you could hoard them for later." He winks.

Quinn and Selah stroll over to the group.

"No one is hoarding my wish," Quinn says and takes the top rock.

"How does this work again? Do we rub three times and a genie pops out?" Selah picks up a rock.

"Ha ha, no. You close your eyes, make a wish, and throw it into the water. Some people try skipping them if they are flat enough." Maggie grabs a rock.

"What do we wish for?" Ben eyes the rock in his hand.

"Anything you want. But you can't tell or it won't come true." Maggie walks over to the water. Her friends join her, each holding their own rock.

"Like birthday wishes?" Ben sounds skeptical as he tosses and catches his rock.

"Like all wishes you want to come true, Ben. Where's your faith?" Jo asks.

Gil throws his rock into the water first. It skips with three bounces before disappearing.

"That was quick," Ben observes.

"I know exactly what I want to come true." Gil smirks.

Maggie hears the splashes of the other rocks. She is the last to make her wish. Closing her eyes, she kisses the rock before throwing it into the cold water.

"What did you wish for, Maggie May?" Gil asks.

"Oh, I'm not telling. I want this one to come true." She winks at him.

Fifteen

Ben makes the short drive into downtown Coupeville following Maggie's directions. After parking in the shade and leaving the windows open for Biscuit, they stroll down the main street, which cannot escape being called quaint with its white clapboard storefronts. Sitting directly on Penn Cove makes this the best place for the famous mussels of the same name.

Maggie directs them to her favorite tavern. The wood walls are decorated in a medley of photographs and island trinkets. The most stunning decoration is a large bison head over the doorway to the bathrooms.

They pile into a red Naugahyde upholstered booth surrounded by picture windows overlooking the water and a rock-strewn beach below.

"Always nice to know exactly where your food comes from." Ben points out the window at the floating mussel farm.

"Unless it's a hamburger, then no thank you," Jo says.

"Seeing your steak before eating is so *The Hitchhiker's Guide to the Galaxy.*" Selah shakes her head in disgust. "Those lobster tanks always freak me out. I want to liberate them all."

"Didn't Quinn do that in college? He liberated something in the dining hall," Ben says.

"What was it? A big banner was involved, I remember." Gil says, stretching his arm behind Maggie's shoulders in the booth.

"You old people and your lack of memories. It was a Cesar Chavez project. I was protesting grapes."

"I swear lettuce was involved," Maggie adds, enjoying Gil's closeness.

"I thought lettuce, too,'" Selah muses.

"Wait, maybe you're right," Quinn admits. "It all had to do with migrant workers and apartheid."

"Kind of a stretch, don't you think?" Ben asks.

"Everything in 1989 was about apartheid and Free Nelson Mandela," Quinn explains.

"First, the Berlin Wall came down, and a few months later, Nelson Mandela being freed, those were heady times," Ben adds.

"Don't forget Bush 41 in office, setting up for the Bush dynasty, and W," Gil says.

"Such a history professor," Quinn comments.

"Politics have never been my area of research or teaching."

"Politics are everyone's area," Selah interjects.

"Let's not have the politics conversation." Maggie attempts to keep the peace.

"Oh, Maggie, we're not going to remind Ben about his love for Bob Dole in '92." Gil teases.

"Not really 'love' for Dole. I can admit Clinton was great for the economy with all the banking deregulation he passed." Ben looks smug.

"The young Republicans were the hottest guys on campus. Must have been the suits," Jo muses.

"All ten of them," Gil reminds her.

"Were there even ten? Counting Ben?" Quinn asks. "Evergreen is a capital 'L' Liberal college."

"Ha ha." Ben fake laughs. "Yes, more than ten of us. Lots of people who wished they could have voted for Reagan. Curse us for being born too late."

"You must have been devastated when he died," Quinn says with a straight face. "Ryan and I threw a big party. It was like a scene from *Point Break* or a Dead Presidents show with all the Reagan masks."

Jo laughs. "Ben was depressed for a week, walking around moaning about the glory days of the Republican Party. You'll be shocked to know we both voted for Obama in '08."

Everyone, but Jo and Ben, sits with their mouths agape. His college nickname, Alex P. Keaton, suits him to this day. Fiscal conservative to his core, Maggie still can't figure out how he chose such a hippie school as Evergreen.

"Thanks, Jo. My reputation is ruined. I just couldn't vote for Palin on the ticket. Her supersonic, long distance vision super-power

scared me. Who can see Russia from Anchorage? She must be a cyborg."
Ben shudders.

The waitress interrupts Ben. They order a pitcher of Toby's
Parrot Red Ale along with a couple pots of mussels in white wine broth
with crusty bread.

"Anyone want some oysters?" Maggie offers. "They're good
here."

"Oysters, eh?" Gil looks at her and smirks.

Maggie smirks back at him.

"Sure. I love oysters. Let's get a dozen," Jo speaks up.

"None for me," Selah says.

"No? I'd have thought you would love swallowing the briny
goodness." Quinn pokes her side.

"You would think. It's a texture thing as much as a taste thing."

"Interesting. The queen of pirate smut doesn't like to swallow."

Thankfully the waitress walks out of hearing range during Quinn
and Selah's conversation.

Maggie rolls her eyes. "Somehow we all get together and we
revert to being adolescents again," she comments, shaking her head.

"Speak for yourselves, I'm the mother of adolescents," Jo points
out.

"Eek!" Selah says, and they all laugh.

Their pitcher and food arrive. The cold beer and icy oysters are
the perfect thing to cool down with after the hike and time in the sun.

When nothing is left but bowls of empty mussel shells and small
puddles of broth at the bottom of the pots, they roll themselves out of
the booth, and walk out into the sun.

Beer at lunch makes Maggie sleepy, so she rests her head on Gil's
shoulder in the back of the SUV and falls asleep almost instantly.

Feeling Maggie sag against him, Gil gently extends his arm
behind her along the seat back, and she snuggles further into his side in
her sleep.

Selah turns in her seat to say something and sees Maggie
sleeping. "You two make a cozy pair."

At her words, Jo also turns to face Gil and Maggie.

"Are you going to dance around her all weekend or tell her
you've been pining for her for ages?" Jo asks.

Gil gazes down at sleeping Maggie. "I just got back into her life, I
don't want to scare her away with some grand gesture."

Selah and Jo look at each other and roll their eyes. "You know she'll never make the first move," Selah states as fact. "She has her walls up. You'll need to break them down, Gil. She's firmly ensconced here in her hidey-hole like a clam."

Gil strokes Maggie's golden-copper hair. Soft curls have come out of her braid and frame her face. Sleeping, she looks exactly like the girl who got away all those years ago. Her soft snoring is endearing.

"Maybe you should start by telling her the truth about how you waited for her to come back from France," Jo softly suggests.

"And how when she showed up with Le Frenchman, it broke your heart," Selah adds.

"How do you know my heart was broken?" Gil asks. He didn't realize how much he wore his heart on his sleeve back then.

"Oh, sweet Gil. We all knew you were in love with her. I think on some level even Maggie knew and maybe that's why she went to France. She didn't want to risk losing her best friend. She was in love with you, too, you know?" Selah pats his arm.

For years Gil has thought his feelings were one-sided, so Selah's words sting. If she's right, why did Maggie put both a continent and an ocean of distance between them?

"You think she loved me? I thought she figured out my feelings changed and didn't return them. That's why she never wrote to me from France. When she came back with Julien the next summer, her attention wasn't on me."

"Hmmm, Julien—The French Incident," Jo muses. "The reason we call him that is because he was an anomaly in her life. I think all the sex did something to her brain." Selah pushes her sunglasses up on her head. "Sexual awakenings can be powerful things. The brain releases all sorts of happy chemicals, which can easily be confused with love."

"Sexual awakening? Great. That makes me feel better," Gil scoffs, her statement bruising his ego, though he isn't going to confess this to Selah and Jo.

"We're trying to give you a pep talk here." Jo gives him her mom face. "You and Maggie were a couple in all ways, but one back in college. You were great together."

"The universe is setting you up for another chance. Don't waste it," Selah says, giving him a pointed look before turning around and telling Ben to stop at a liquor store.

"What this situation needs is more alcohol to loosen things up. I say we drink Jameson tonight." Selah turns back again, winks at Gil, then puts on her sunglasses.

A night drinking Jameson changed everything between Gil and Maggie one summer night twenty-two years before.

"The thought of Jameson makes my head hurt." Jo scowls. "I think I'll stick with wine."

Maggie stirs against Gil's shoulder. "What's all this talk of Jameson?" She mumbles, realizing she fell asleep on Gil. Wiping her mouth to check for drool, she straightens up. "Sorry if I drooled on you." She studies at Gil's shirt for wet spots.

"No drooling. But you did call out my name." He winks at her.

"I did?" She flushes. *Was she dreaming of Gil?*

"I'm teasing," he clarifies.

Maggie straightens her shirt and tries to contain the crazy on her head with her fingers.

"What's with the Jameson talk?"

"I had a hankering for some tonight. For old-time's sake," Selah says, petting Biscuit, who sits on a towel between her and Jo.

Maggie's mind drifts back to the last summer night when they all drank too much Jameson. It was the night before she left for France and the year that changed her life for better and worse.

"We should stop in Freeland. Maybe stock up on dinner stuff while we're there."

* * *

They go the liquor store first. A few bottles of whiskey are loaded into the back of the SUV before they drive over to the grocery store.

Maggie feels refreshed after her short nap. She grabs a cart as they head into the store. "Let's divide and conquer. Meet up front in ten minutes?" she asks before heading toward produce with Gil following her.

Green Day plays over the speakers. Maggie starts singing along as she wanders past a man examining watermelons. Gil harmonizes on the chorus.

Maggie meets his eye and laughs. "Can you believe Green Day is playing in a grocery store?"

"These are sentimental times," Gil says.

"When did you get to be so sentimental?" She places a few peaches into the cart.

"Aren't all people?"

"I don't think sociopaths and Cossacks are." She pushes the cart down the aisle.

"No comment on the sociopaths, but I'm going to go out on a limb and defend the sentimental nature of Cossacks. They probably believe in love, too, otherwise there wouldn't be small Cossacks."

"I figured the Cossack armies raped and pillaged to create smaller Cossacks." Maggie smiles at her deliberate misinterpretation of history to bait Gil.

"I'm being sentimental and you're talking about raping and pillaging. You have a cold black heart, Maggie May. " He fakes a grimace.

"I do not." She pouts. "I'm pointing out historical facts. The fact you choose to sugarcoat and rose-tint history, professor, isn't my fault."

Gil laughs at her as they wander down the cereal aisle.

Maggie grabs a box of Captain Crunch from the shelf. "I used to love this stuff, but it cut the roof of my mouth."

Gil puts the cereal in the cart. "That's cause you shoved handfuls in your mouth straight from the box instead of eating cereal with milk, in a bowl, like a civilized person."

Maggie sticks her tongue out at him. "Fine, then we need more milk, Mr. Civilized. I don't remember you being so refined the time we got stoned and found all the subliminal sex images on the box of Cracker Jacks."

Gil laughs. "It wasn't me drawing circles around imaginary cocks on the box. That was Selah. I was busy trying to the write down all the cultural references in 'Shake Your Rump' on *Paul's Boutique*."

"Right, makes more sense that was Selah. She's always been obsessed with naked people. Remember when she made us all go to that life drawing class?" Maggie and Gil both shudder.

"I swear that model was an STD poster waiting to happen." Gil shudders.

They continue to reminisce and laugh as they make their way through the store, tossing random things in the cart. Turning a corner, they run into Connie.

"Oh, hello Maggie!" Connie air kisses Maggie's cheek while keeping her eyes on Gil. "Is this your new fella? I thought I heard you were seeing John Day. Hi, I'm Connie." She sticks her hand out for Gil to shake.

"Gilliam Morrow," he introduces himself, shaking her hand.

"Very nice to meet you." Connie is practically purring. "Where has Maggie been hiding you?"

She cringes over Connie inferring she's dating John. Where does this woman get her information? She probably has all the phone lines tapped on South Whidbey.

Quinn walks up and says, "In her bed. Where else?"

Maggie wants to kick him. "Connie, this is my other friend, Quinn Dayton. My college friends are up visiting for the weekend. A few more of them are scattered around here somewhere."

"Oh, well, my mistake." Connie is still holding Gil's hand and releases it. "The way you two were smiling and carrying on seemed like you were an item."

Wanting to cut off any potential gossip, Maggie assures her they are all just friends before steering them away from Connie.

"Great. Of course we run into the biggest gossip on the island. Our engagement will be announced in the paper."

"I should get a box of Cracker Jacks for a ring." Gil chuckles.

Maggie snorts. "Classy."

"Would you rather have a candy ring? I'm pretty certain they have those here somewhere." Gil teases.

"Mrs. and Dr. Morrow—I like the sound," Quinn congratulates them. "Can I be the best man and maid of honor?"

They both ignore him and go to find Selah, Ben and Jo at the front of the store.

"Get everything you need?" Maggie asks.

"Who knows? Ben found Olympia beer and I got some things for appetizers." Jo points at their cart.

"We're buying Captain Crunch. Figured it would go with whiskey." Gil gestures at the box.

Maggie and Gil crack up when they see Selah holding a box of Cracker Jacks.

"What? I like the surprise." She looks at them both like they are crazy.

"Surprises," Maggie stutters before laughing again. Gil joins her with his own barely contained laughter.

"You two are nuts." Selah tosses the box in the cart.

Gil wheezes with laughter.

Maggie's still laughing as they check out. "You know the whole Cracker Jack thing isn't even at all funny. It really isn't." She starts giggling again.

"Come on, Chuckles." Gil throws his arm around her shoulders.

She sees Connie watching them from the next check out line. Turning her head, she catches Gil's wink at Connie when they pass by her. Let her gossip about my new fella, Maggie thinks. That should stir up things.

Sixteen

Everyone wanders off in their own direction when they get back to the house. With a mumbled explanation about fresh air and forced marches, Selah drags herself upstairs to take what Maggie assumes is a nap. Ben and Jo walk down the beach holding hands.

Maggie sees the dirty Scrabble game contains a few more words. She is able to play 'KISS' to add to the board's array of dirtier actions.

Gil flops down on the sofa, pulls out his phone, and taps away on the screen.

She doesn't want to pry, but can't help herself. Curious who he's texting, she sits next to him, and asks, "Texting a lady friend?"

"Lady friend?" Gil smirks. "No, not a lady friend."

"Is there a lady friend in the picture?" She pushes, trying to keep things light by using the silly description.

"Are you asking if I'm seeing someone? If so, the answer is no. Not dating at the moment."

"Selah told me you've had a girlfriend for a while now." She's embarrassed at her obvious lack of subtlety, but delighted he isn't dating.

"Oh, that." His hand goes to the back of his neck. "Selah was trying to set me up with every single and not-so-single woman she knew in Portland. I maybe let her believe I was seeing someone to get her to back off." He avoids her eyes. "Selah was pretty mad on the drive up when I confessed. I didn't realize she had told you that." His gaze drifts toward John's house. "I could ask the same about you. Dating?"

"Are you asking if I have a lady friend? The answer is no. Selah and I tried the 'lady friends with benefits' thing sophomore year. Wasn't for me."

"I remember that night. You two are lucky we went to college before camera phones. By the way, I think Ben kept that Polaroid. Don't tell Jo. And you didn't answer my question about dating anyone. What about the lumberjack?"

The thought of dating John makes her laugh. "John? No, no we are not dating."

"Are you sleeping with him?" he asks, bluntly.

It's a good thing she isn't drinking something or she would do a spit-take. "No, not sleeping with him either. Might make things awkward if it didn't work out." Cringing over her words, she avoids his eyes.

"Good. I mean that you're not sleeping with him. Not the awkward after part. That part sucks." He catches her eye, leaving the meaning of his words hanging between them.

Maggie knows he is no longer talking about John. The need to avoid any more talk of awkwardness makes her to deflect the topic away from herself, like she always does. Embarrassed to admit to Gil how long low ago she dated anyone, she brings the conversation back to him.

"Do you date? I mean since the divorce. Do you go on lots of dates? Out there dating?"

So much for avoiding awkwardness.

Gil laughs. Curious, are you? I've dated since Judith, nothing serious. It isn't as easy to date these days. I refused to do any more online dating, especially after Selah's Mr. Rochester incident."

"You know about Mr. Rochester?" Maggie leans back into the sofa, tucking her feet underneath her. The tension of Gil bringing up their past is forgotten.

"Selah showed everyone that email. I told her she should ask about his crazy first wife in the attic. I mean, if you are going to go with a romantic hero, the blind, burned guy who is almost killed by his crazy wife isn't going to bring in the ladies."

"No, not the best role model. Although, he truly loves Jane. He was a victim of fate and circumstances out of his control. They find love in the end, despite their roadblocks, that's what matters."

"You've always been such a romantic." Gil looks at her softly. The tension and awkwardness of the 'are you single?' conversation dissipates.

"Literature and French. I was doomed from the start." Maggie sighs.

"Before we get overly melancholy and take arsenic to end it all, maybe we should go for a walk on the beach. See if we can find Ben and Jo." Gil stretches his back.

"Walking on beach is very *French Lieutenant's Woman* waiting for her love to return to her."

"Beware of moors and beaches." He gets up and offers his hand to pull her up off the couch.

"And cliffs. Don't forget the cliffs." She smiles as she stands.

"Can't forget the cliffs. You must have some place to throw yourself when love ends."

"We sound like we are writing one of Selah's smut books."

"Have you read them?" Gil asks.

"I have." She lowers her voice and whispers, "They are very dirty."

Gil laughs at her.

"Have you?" she asks.

"I've skimmed one. I think the title was *The Pink Pearl*. Who knew there were so many ways to sheath a scabbard?" He mock cringes.

"Or the many ways to shiver timbers." She walks toward the door. "Makes me wonder if Selah keeps a trunk full of pirate costumes in her bedroom."

They walk out on the deck and down to the beach, pirate euphemisms flying between them.

* * *

After their walk, they find Selah opening a bottle of wine in the kitchen. Maggie hops up on the counter, opens the Captain Crunch, and grabs a handful, chewing a big mouthful of cereal, then wincing.

"It still hurts," she says with her mouth full.

Selah and Gil chuckle.

"Did you think it changed?" Selah asks.

"Gil and I were talking about it at the grocery store. I thought they would change the formula due to lawsuits and irate parents. Guess not." She closes the box and pats the top.

"As good as you remembered?" Gil stands in front of her and taps her knees.

"It's delicious. My teeth hurt and I think I cut my cheek." She pouts.

"Here, wash it down with some wine." Selah hands her a glass of white wine.

"Sauvignon Blanc?" Maggie asks, tasting it.

"It is indeed."

"It's tasty. Want some?" She offers the glass to Gil.

He takes a sip. "That's good. Selah, pour me some, if you don't mind."

The three of them are hanging around in the kitchen when Quinn wanders through with his iPod and puts it in the wireless speaker dock.

"I made us a playlist: *Songs to Remember What You Forgot.*" He turns up the volume. Lenny Kravitz's voice fills the room.

Quinn shuffles over to Maggie, bows, and extends his hand. "Dance with me?"

Gil steps aside and she hops off the counter to dance with Quinn.

"Dancing in the kitchen again?" Jo walks in and then pours herself a glass of wine while Ben takes out a bottle of Alaskan Amber from the fridge.

Quinn sings a few lines of "Always on the Run" in falsetto. Maggie turns her back to him and sways her hips. He spanks her, making her laugh.

"Okay, big boy, save the dirty stuff for Ryan."

"What time does Ryan get here?" Gil asks, staring at Maggie's swaying hips.

"His plane arrives early morning and he'll take a car service to the ferry. I figured I could borrow Bessie to go pick him up." Quinn winks at Maggie.

"Nice try. You can drive the Subaru."

"Boring. You're no fun."

"Bessie is too old to have her gears ground by the likes of you, Mr. Dayton." She jokes and pats his chest. "Who's hungry? And more importantly, who's up for killing some crabs?"

Selah, Ben, Jo and Quinn make faces.

"Wusses. Okay, I'll deal with it myself." Maggie grabs a large pot from the lower cupboard and fills it with water. "Can someone bring the cooler in from the garage?"

"I'll set the table," Quinn volunteers.

"I'll help." Selah joins him in gathering napkins and silverware.

"Cowards," Maggie says.

"I'll make a salad," Jo offers.

"I'll get the crabs." Gil heads toward the garage.

"My hero!" Maggie exclaims and dramatically clutches her

clasped hands to her chest. Feeling playful, she kisses him on the cheek as he passes by her.

"I'll never wash this cheek again." He plays along, touching his face.

"Watching you and Gil right now, it doesn't seem like any time has passed at all," Ben comments.

"That's a good thing, right?" Maggie asks.

"Tonight, it's a very good thing. It's nice not to be Benton Grant, VP, father, homeowner, blah blah blah, and just be Ben."

"There's a lot on your shoulders. I'm always impressed by all you've accomplished. You're a real grown up." Maggie compliments him.

"Yeah, but being a grown up all the time is tedious. Trust me on this. I envy your simple life here on the island. Feeding off the land and all."

Jo takes lettuce and cucumbers out of the fridge. "Ben has these fantasies of leaving it all behind and going to live off the land like Thoreau," Jo scoffs. "He'd last a week, tops. And only with a real bed, not a sleeping bag."

"The Grants are not campers." Maggie chuckles at the image of Ben in a tent, sleeping on the ground.

"Getting out of the rat race would be wonderful, for a bit. I couldn't walk away from it all, though. Kids need to go to college. I need to retire. Jo needs her upkeep." His words are light, but have an edge to them.

"Not to mention the giant alimony you'd be forced to pay me if I divorced you," Jo says as she starts chopping tomatoes from the basket on the counter.

"Divorce?" Maggie asks, sensing the change in the air between Ben and Jo. "Are you guys having problems?"

Ben takes a big swig of his beer. "Nah. Just the usual stuff."

"He's stuck with me. I can always have an affair with the tennis pro if I get bored." Jo smirks.

Maggie assumes she is joking. "You two are one of the few couples I always thought would make it the long haul. You must to stay together or I'll lose all faith in marriage." Maggie hugs Jo.

"Okay, we'll stay together for you." Jo pets Maggie's head as if she's a child.

"Plus, the tennis pro isn't good looking at all," Ben says.

"True. He has an extremely hairy back. My matrimonial vows of fidelity are safe as long as he's at the club."

"Do women still have affairs with tennis pros at clubs?" Selah asks, rejoining the conversation.

"They do in Connecticut." Jo nods.

"Such a cliché. I love it. So very *Stepford Wives*."

"You have no idea, Selah, no idea at all. Sometimes I forget what year it is."

"Fascinating. People like their roles and gilded cages," Selah muses.

"You should get out of Portland more," Ben says. "Come see how the rest of the country lives."

"Darien is hardly middle America," Jo chides.

"Remember when we wanted to take a road trip to Graceland after graduation? Why didn't we do that?" Quinn steals a cut tomato from Jo's pile.

"Yeah, why didn't we ever go to Graceland?" Jo asks.

"French Incident," Selah says, killing the conversation.

"Oh, right. Someone had to run off to France to be with her lover." Ben teases.

Gil walks in with the cooler and Maggie diverts the topic to the crabs.

"Should we say a prayer or a blessing before we boil them?" she suggests.

"I'd rather not be witness to the death, but I will melt the butter," Jo says before tossing two sticks in a bowl and putting it in the microwave. "I'll be outside with my wine." She grabs the bottle and chiller, and heads to the deck.

Selah, Quinn, and Ben follow Jo.

"Guess you and I will do the deed. Unless you want to hide outside with the rest of the cowards." Maggie opens the cooler next to the pot of boiling water.

"Nah, I'll go down in a blaze of gunfire with you."

"I knew I loved you, Clyde." She jokes. She holds her breath for his reaction to her accidental declaration and slowly exhales when he smiles.

"And I love you, Bonnie. Let's do this thing."

* * *

After dinner, Quinn rubs his belly and surveys the carnage of empty butter bowls and crab shells littering the newspaper-covered table. "Ryan is going to be bummed he missed this. The good doctor loves himself some shellfish."

"Isn't he Jewish?" Jo asks.

"Yes, but he's a High Holidays kind of Jew who enjoys a delicious pork belly or lobster."

"I still can't believe you married a dermatologist," Jo says with a slight pout in her voice.

"You can get the friends and family discount, sweetie. Come down to the city sometime."

"Really?" Jo perks up. Her face is smooth and nearly line-free as it is.

"Sure, sure. Have a painting aging in a closet like me and Dorian Gray." He points to his forehead.

"You get Botox?" Gil asks, not able to hide the surprise in his voice.

"Sure, why not? The youthful appearance of a cutting-edge artist must be maintained."

"I've been trying to convince Ben to get rid of the eleven between his brows, but he refuses."

"Wrinkles make me look more serious and threatening. I'm keeping them."

"It's so not fair men get distinguished," Selah comments while filling up everyone's wine glass.

The sun is starting to set and the twinkle lights, along with the candles on the table, cast a soft, flattering glow on everyone.

"I think you are all more beautiful now than you were in college," Gil says, looking at Maggie. "Your face tells the story of your life —revealing a depth that youth doesn't have."

"Lies! But I'll take them. Candlelight is my friend," Jo says.

"I mean it. You've all come into your own now." Gil continues. "The women sitting around this table are each gorgeous in their own way."

"Go on." Maggie flirts. The wine and good company make her more relaxed than she's been in ages. The house is full of laughter and love again. She smiles, looking at her friends.

Jo is still as beautiful as she was at nineteen, even if her looks today are helped with injections and a talented colorist. Ben has the swagger of his Most-Likely-to-Succeed title, only now he has gray at his temples along with more than a few frown and laugh lines. Maggie laughs to herself over the thought he is indeed what you could call 'distinguished.' Quinn looks exactly the same as he did in college without the ponytail. *Thank God.* Selah no longer sports her black, short, spiky cut, but otherwise she hasn't change much at all, except for bigger curves, which suit her larger than life personality.

Sweet, gorgeous Gil sits directly across from Maggie. He has gray in his brown hair now, but in the low light of the candles and twinkle lights, looks like he did when they first met freshman year. It also could be the flannel shirt he's wearing over a gray thermal.

Why has she kept him at arm's length all these years? Right now Maggie can't imagine not having him back in her life.

Snapping herself out of her musings, Maggie realizes she's no longer following the conversation. She glances around and sees expectant faces.

"Dessert?" Selah repeats.

"Oops. I almost forgot dessert. Frozen berries with warm white chocolate sauce. I'll go make the sauce and we'll be all set." Maggie gets up from the table.

"Marry me?" She hears Quinn call from the deck as she starts the stove. At least she thinks it's Quinn.

The quickest dessert ever is assembled before all the dishes are in the sink and the crab detritus disappears.

"I know Quinn already proposed, but if you are up for the whole sister-wives thing, I'd marry you for this dessert alone." Selah scrapes her spoon around her glass dish.

Quinn moans and uses his finger to get the last of the berry-infused chocolate sauce out of his bowl.

Ben claps his hands together. "Before this turns into some sort of food induced orgy, should we build a beach fire?"

"Right, beach fire orgy would be much hotter," Selah deadpans.

Ben rolls his eyes and groans.

"Punny, Dr. Elmore." Quinn chuckles.

Gil once again offers to handle washing dishes while the rest grab drinks, cups and blankets, and then head down to the beach.

"Are you sure I can't help?" Maggie asks before following the others outside. "I am a bad hostess making one of my guests do the dishes. My mother wouldn't approve."

"I'm sure. Washing dishes is the least I can do. I'll be down to the beach in a few minutes."

"If you're sure, then okay."

"I'm sure. Now off with you." Gil waves his soap covered hands in her direction. "Scoot."

"Aye, aye, captain." Maggie salutes him.

Seventeen

Once everyone is settled by the fire, Quinn suggests playing I Never. Along with the game of Three Huts, this is one of his favorite games from college. Road trips, boring Monday nights, parents' weekend, dinner parties—Quinn loves a good game of I Never.

Sitting by a fire on the beach with a bottle of Jameson reminds Maggie of college. Looking around at everyone, she realizes they've known each other more than half their lives. Decades. Their friendships now measured in blocks of years instead of weeks, months or even days. The fact they are drinking cans of 'Oly' might be adding to the nostalgia. She can't believe Ben bought a case of the stuff in honor of old times.

Selah flops down beside Maggie and tosses her a blanket. "Brr. I forgot how cold the nights are here even in summer."

Quinn claps and lifts the bottle of Jameson. "Everyone remember the rules? If you are guilty, you drink. If you're an innocent babe in the woods, you abstain. And if some scandalous revelation occurs, even better. I'll go first. I never saw Nirvana play live."

Everyone else drinks.

"How's it possible you never saw them live?" Ben asks. "We all went to their show at the Paramount in '91."

"Not me. I was in San Francisco that weekend for Halloween. Like I was going to miss the Castro on Halloween."

They all stare at him, mouths open.

"Shut your mouths. I know. Greatest band of our generation, not to mention practically local, and I never saw them play live."

"At least you saw Hootie live," Ben teases.

"Yay for Hootie." Quinn raises his cup and drinks.

A few rounds of 'I've never voted Republican' (Selah) and 'I've never eaten veal' (Gil) later, it's Quinn's turn again. He looks at Maggie with a glint in his eye that means he's definitely feeling the effects of the whiskey, and says, "I've never had sex with Maggie."

No. He didn't. He really didn't. Maggie stares at Quinn with her best bitch face.

He has the audacity to wink.

Out of the corner of her eye, she sees Gil slowly raise his cup and drain the contents.

Maggie is clearly not the only one to notice, because Quinn emits a sound that can best be described as a triumphant snort. He is bouncing.

Selah elbows Maggie, who stares at Gil, who is staring back at her now. Maggie can barely meet his eyes.

Gil gives Maggie his shy, sweet smile that melted her heart in college, and raises his empty cup in a toast.

"At least we've finally cleared up the big mystery." Ben sighs. "Anyone here have any money in the pool that Gil and Maggie didn't sleep together?" He looks around. "No? Okay, then. My turn. I've never kissed Maggie."

Everyone but Ben drinks. Ben's mouth drops open when he sees Jo toast to Maggie and take a sip. Jo smiles at her husband and pats his arm.

Maggie drains her glass and changes the topic. "I've never been to Nepal."

The only person to drink is Gil. He smiles. "Three weeks of hiking the Annapurna Circuit was the perfect thing before starting a doctoral program."

Quinn refills everyone's cup while Gil gets up to stoke the fire. Selah moves over to the seat abandoned by Gil, muttering "white rabbits," and complaining about the smoke.

Maggie doesn't buy Selah's excuse.

Since his old seat is now occupied, Gil sits next to Maggie on the sand. Reclining against the driftwood, he stretches his long legs out toward the fire.

"Sorry about that. But you know Quinn and the absolute truth of I Never. Are you mad?" he asks her in a low voice.

Maggie thinks for a few seconds. Her first reaction is she's mad and embarrassed over their silly secret being revealed after all these years. There might be a little shame in there, too. Mostly she is relieved, she's always suspected everyone has known since she left for France—or at least by senior year.

"No, not mad. Seems silly to be mad over a skeleton being dragged out of the closet after twenty-two years. Plus, it was only one time."

"Yeah, only one night twenty-two years ago. Nothing life changing or anything."

Maggie glances at Gil. Something in the way he says 'life changing' makes her think he's being sarcastic.

Gil continues: "It's not like finally sleeping with the girl you had a crush on since she showed up in the library wearing Kermit slippers during winter finals would be any big deal."

Maggie snorts. "I forgot about those stupid slippers. God, I lived in those things."

"I know. We all know how much you loved those monstrosities," Gil says.

"Monstrosities? Those were über cool back in the day."

"Oh, sure. Maybe if the day was 1982 and you were twelve." Jo laughs.

"Hey now, don't dis the lovers, the dreamers and me."

"Quinn, was it your idea to burn the Kermit slippers after finals sophomore year? Gil asks.

"Nope, that was all Ben. He declared them a bio-hazard when the last eyeball fell off."

"So much hate for Kermit. Jim Henson, rest his soul, would be appalled." Maggie crosses her arms.

Gil takes his beer and pours a little out on the sand. "To Henson and all the Muppet slippers who have died."

They all crack up, and pour some of their drinks on the sand.

Ben frowns and says, "And to all our friends who are no longer here."

The mood becomes somber.

"To Lizzy." Gil raises his cup.

"To Lizzy," everyone repeats in hushed voices. A quiet settles over them.

"Fucking cancer," Ben says.

"Fucking cancer," Selah echoes.

Although it has been five years, Lizzy's losing battle against ovarian cancer at thirty-seven still doesn't seem real to Maggie. Maybe because they don't all see each other on a regular basis to miss her presence in the group. Maybe it's difficult to accept the loss of one of your best friends when you are really starting to live your life.

"Before this gets all *Big Chill* and Selah asks Ben to impregnate her, let's get back to the game. Or we can play Hut Island. Lizzy would hate being the party pooper." Quinn changes the subject.

They all groan at his movie reference.

"My money is more on Gil and Maggie having sex in the boathouse," Jo says.

"We don't have a boathouse." Maggie realizes too late she hasn't objected to the idea of fooling around with Gil.

Gil arches an eyebrow. "So it's the lack of boathouse you object to? I can work with this." He waggles his eyebrows at her in a cheesy Lothario kind of way. He leans closer to her against the driftwood and she can feel the heat from his body along her side. It is familiar and not unwelcome.

Quinn raises his beer and toasts, "To Maggie and her brilliant family for buying this beach house all those years ago, but not having the foresight to build a boathouse. Hindsight's twenty-twenty."

Maggie sticks her tongue out at Quinn. She senses herself becoming overwhelmed by the big revelations and everyone's not-so-subtle hints. Following her instinct to escape situations that make her uncomfortable, she gets up and dusts the sand off her butt. "I'm going to put my feet in the water."

"Getting too hot and heavy for you already?" Selah asks. She's almost as bad as Quinn this weekend with her blatant attempts to push Gil and Maggie together.

Maggie ignores her as she walks down the beach to the water's edge. The cold waves lap at her ankles. She knows Gil follows her by Quinn's wolf whistle.

"Hey, you know we are mostly teasing you, right? It's easy to fall into the same old patterns when we all get together again," Gil says, reaching her side.

Maggie nods in response. This weekend is different. For the first time in decades, she and Gil are both single. If she ever had a chance, a second shot at something... she stops herself. She isn't ready for something with anyone until she sorts out herself first.

Gil drapes his arm around her shoulders.

His presence has always been a comfort. She might be feeling the Jameson more than she thought as she sighs and leans into his side.

"I know. It seems all so long ago. We're forty. How did we get to be forty? Where did the past two decades go? I mean, it's been five years since Lizzy died. Half a decade. Fuck." She breathes deeply, trying to squelch her rising emotions.

"Who's forty? Some of us are forty-two and others..." He nudges her. "...are forty-one."

"Reminding me of my age isn't making me feel any better, you know." She tries to break away from his embrace, but he pulls her in tighter.

"We are older, Maggie May. Fact of life. Can't change it. But that doesn't change how much we all still care about each other. How much we care about you."

His words seem weighted with more than group affection and nostalgia. She turns and gazes up at him. In the dark with a sliver of moon and the fire, he's the same twenty-year-old boy she loved, but never told. Her heart flutters at the thought the same way it did back then.

Gil rubs her shoulder as he returns her gaze. "What are you thinking about? Or should I ask what are you overthinking?"

"It's been a very long time since you called me Maggie May."

"I called you that at the fire and I'm pretty sure I used it yesterday and the day before."

"I meant in the grander scheme of time. You stopped calling me Maggie May after the summer we all lived together."

"This is true. I wish I never had stopped, but it didn't seem right anymore." He pulls her closer to him. "But now it feels right. Something about us all being together again." He tilts his head down, trying to catch her eye. "Do you agree?"

She looks up at him, their faces close together. She nods. Her old nickname does feel right. Being in Gil's arms feels right. She wraps her arm around his waist, and turns her body to face him.

He pulls her into a hug, wrapping his other arm around her back. They stay still a moment or two.

Laughter coming from the fire brings them out of the past and back to the present, and their potential audience on the beach.

"We should probably head back," Gil suggests.

Maggie is reluctant to leave their little bubble. "Can we continue this later?"

"I'd like nothing better." Gil takes her hand and squeezes, before leading her over to the fire.

They are greeted with cheers.

"At least this time you caught Maggie before she got too far away," Quinn says, handing them their plastic cups refilled with Jameson.

Maggie gives Quinn the stink eye.

Quinn ignores her. "Who wants to play the hut game?"

Everyone groans.

Gil and Maggie settle on the sand in front of the driftwood log. He has his arm around her shoulders and gently strokes her hair. Turning her knees, she curls into his side. She looks at the faces of the people who know her best, the people she loves. The warmth of the fire and Gil's soothing touch anchor her to the moment.

* * *

After the group majority manages to talk Quinn out of another one of his party games, they share stories and memories from college as the fire burns down.

"Remember the time Maggie almost burned down the kitchen trying to make biscuits?" Selah asks.

"The whole house was filled with smoke. It looked like she was trying to make hockey pucks," Jo adds.

"Where do you think Biscuit got his name? It was a tribute to my inability to make biscuits that summer. Or ever."

"True, but we discovered your gift for scones, so I can at least forgive you for the hockey pucks." Gil tousles her hair.

"It was a great summer. Everything changed after that," Ben says, innocently.

"It did change after that summer. Lizzy and Maggie left for study abroad. Leaving us all behind," Jo says. Grimacing at the implications of her words, Jo frowns and mouths, "Oops, sorry."

Maggie sighs. *And here we are.*

"Right, Maggie ran away to France and fell in love." Quinn can't leave it alone.

"I didn't run away. My focus was French Literature, Q, you know this." Maggie bristles. "Plus, Lizzy went to France with me."

"But Lizzy didn't fall in love. Or lust as it were," Selah points out.

"Ah, the French Incident discussed at last," Jo says. "Now that we know Maggie and Gil slept together, it all makes sense."

"It does?" Gil asks. He pulls his arm away from Maggie.

The cool night air replaces his comforting warmth.

"Sure. You and Maggie were inseparable. She left and you moped for the year. Hence the bet on whether or not you slept with each other," Jo explains.

"I didn't mope." Gil wraps his arms around his bent knees.

"Mope, pine, long, whatever verb you want to use, you did it." Jo looks at him as she continues, "This was back before sim cards, email, Skype, and Facetime. Once Maggie was in Europe, it really was being on the other side of the world. Then she returned with the Frenchman in tow, and that was that."

"I'm right here you know," Maggie huffs. "This is the most awkward way to have this whole conversation. This is something between Gil and me, not the whole class."

"We all had to suffer, Mags, so it does involve all of us." Selah gives her and Gil a sympathetic look.

"Life happens, people move on, things change. We've all changed," Maggie says. "Sometimes we make decisions that can't be undone and send us down a different path." She looks at Gil, who meets her gaze.

"Sometimes everything works out as it should," Gil says with a mix of hope and regret in his voice. The easy, familiar comfort between them from their talk down at the water fades.

Selah joins the conversation. "We can't undo the past. Think of all those strange twists and turns which led us to all be together again. If Maggie hadn't met and married Julien, she might not have discovered her love of food, if those burned biscuits were any indication. Gil might not have his career if Judith hadn't been such a hard-ass about him finishing his dissertation," Selah says.

"Who knows what would have happened if we did all take a road trip to Graceland," Ben says. "Maybe I would have discovered my inner wanderer, and taken to the road to follow the Dead or Phish around the country instead of going to Harvard."

"If you became a Dead Head, we would've broken up for sure. No kids, no big house, nothing." Jo frowns.

"See?" Selah sounds more positive. "It all happens for a reason. Each choice made us who we are today, for better or worse."

"I'm going to go with the better option," Jo agrees.

Maggie is quiet during this conversation, lost in her own thoughts of past choices bringing them to this point.

"I guess I can see your point, Selah," Maggie agrees. "If my mother didn't get sick, I never would have moved to the beach. I'd still be toiling away in a one bedroom apartment in New York. This is much better." She gestures around the bay, then glances at Gil's profile as he stares the fire. "The company is much better here. I'm very blessed to have you all in my life." She begins to get emotional again.

Gil turns to look at Maggie, and pulls her to his side.

"We're all blessed to have you in our lives, too, sweet girl." He kisses the top of her head.

Maggie rests her head on Gil's shoulder again. "Gah, sorry guys." She wipes a few tears from her cheeks. "Way to pull down the conversation with the emo."

Gil strokes her hair. "Don't worry about it. Digging up the past always brings things to the surface."

Everyone voices their agreement.

Ben yawns, which causes Quinn to yawn.

"What time is it? It has to be one o'clock at least," Jo asks.

"It's midnight. Are you turning into a pumpkin?" Ben nudges Jo, who yawns.

"I can't remember the last time I stayed up until midnight." Jo stretches. "God, I'm old." She laughs. In her black yoga pants and North Face fleece she looks like a college student, not a forty-something mother of three.

"We're all old," Maggie agrees.

"Speak for yourself. You are only as old as you feel," Selah says, stretching out her legs under her blanket. "Most days I am about twenty-seven."

"My mother once told me when she was in her early sixties she still felt thirty-four," Maggie says. "I guess age is relative."

"It's easy to forget how old you are until you see someone who's twenty-one or even thirty, and you realize how young they seem," Ben says. "New hires look like teenagers to me. They act like ones sometimes."

"Well, this teenager is going to bed." Jo gets up and stretches.

"Let me know if you need anything," Maggie offers, but doesn't move from her spot next to Gil. His arm feels good around her.

"I'm going to bed, too. I want to be bright-eyed and bushy-tailed for Ryan tomorrow morning." Quinn stands up and then gathers plastic cups and the empty bottle of Jameson.

"Me too." Ben follows Jo up to the house, carrying some blankets.

"Then there were three," Selah declares. "You two don't need a chaperone, so I think I'll go in and maybe write some smut." Selah kisses the top of Maggie's head as she passes by. "Live in the moment," she whispers to Maggie.

"And then there were two," Gil says as he sits up to poke the dying fire. "Do we need to stay until it's out?"

"We can spread out the logs and pour seawater on them when we want to go to bed."

"I don't mind hanging out a little longer. It's such a gorgeous night." Gil lies down next to Maggie and tilts his head back on the log to look at the stars.

"Sometimes we can see the Northern Lights here in the winter. They're amazing." She follows his lead to keep the conversation neutral. She scoots down so she is lying next to him, her hands clasped on her stomach.

"Must be beautiful. I missed seeing them in Alaska since I went during the summer solstice. Twenty-four hours of sunlight and all that."

"When did you go to Alaska?"

"I went with Judith and her parents on a cruise."

"A cruise doesn't sound like something you would choose." Maggie acknowledges to herself she doesn't know everything about this Gil.

"Not really, no." Gil laughs, but it's a dry laugh. "There was a lot about our relationship I wouldn't have chosen. But Selah is right. It was something I did which lead me to be who I am now. To be with who I am with now."

Maggie turns her head to face him. "I'm glad you're here. Even if it has taken us too long to come back together." She reaches out and interlaces her fingers with his. They stay that way for a while as the fire dies out and the stars slowly move across the sky. Neither breaks the comfortable silence as no more words are needed.

Eighteen

Maggie wakes up cold, with something hard under her cheek. It takes a moment or two for her to remember she fell asleep on Gil, on the beach. Gazing up at the stars and the thin wisps of wood smoke, she stretches, and glances over at a sleeping Gil. Her movement causes him to stir.

Blinking open his eyes, he scrubs his face with his hands, and looks at her.

"Hi."

"We fell asleep." She yawns, sitting up.

"Any idea how long we've been asleep?" He glances around. "The sky isn't getting light, so it can't be that late. Or early."

"No idea, but the fire is almost completely out." She yawns again. The embers glow and flicker under the accumulated ashes.

"Where's the bucket?" His own yawn echoes hers. "Let's put this thing out and go to bed." He slowly stands and grabs the bucket from behind the log where she points.

While he walks down to the water, Maggie gathers a few stray cups and blankets.

A cloud of steam rises into the air when he tosses the water on the embers, obscuring him for a moment.

After shaking the sand out of the blankets and folding them, she sits on the log and waits for him to get another bucketful of water. Watching the last embers, she is reminded of her conversation earlier with Jo. One small ember could reignite a fire given the right kindling. Her mind drifts to Gil. What they have now is an ember. Fragile and easily extinguished. She frowns at the thought of extinguishing that ember forever.

When he returns, she uses a stick to spread out the dampened wood, checking for any remaining hot spots.

"I think we're good," she declares and turns to look at Gil.

He's standing at her side and watching her. Darker now the firelight is gone, his eyes twinkle in the light reflecting from the slim moon over the water.

She wants to kiss him. Standing here in the dark on a quiet beach, sleepy, and chilled by the night, she wants nothing more than to curl back into his warmth and kiss him.

Gil watches her face.

She licks her lips and tilts her head up to him.

He takes a step closer to her, then leans down to brush his lips against hers. With their lips a breath apart, he waits.

Her breathing pauses when she feels his lips on hers. Before she can process they've kissed, he pulls away. Going on instinct, she kisses him back. Her body melts with his as she pulls herself closer to him.

Gil moans when she presses against him. He deepens the kiss and she responds by brushing her tongue against his. She fists the back of his shirt.

When he reaches a hand into her hair and tilts her head, Maggie's head begins to spin. Needing to take a deep breath, she pulls her mouth from his.

He kisses along her jaw, nibbling behind her ear. "God, you are as amazing as I remembered," he whispers.

"Memory doesn't do you justice." She sighs as he trails kisses down her neck.

He kisses her again, cradling her face in one of his hands. She reaches under his thermal to stroke his back.

Leaning back to meet her eyes, he softly says, "I'd be lying if I said I haven't dreamt of doing that for the past twenty years."

"I'd be lying if I said it hadn't crossed my mind several times since Wednesday." Her joke falls flat.

"Wednesday? Always out of sight, out of mind with you?"

She hears the hurt in his voice and flinches.

"Gil..." she pauses. *What can she say?* She's ruining the moment. "Wednesday of this week and many Wednesdays between now and then, I've thought about kissing you, being with you."

"Nice backtracking. My ego thanks you." He kisses her forehead.

"I'm sorry, Gil." She looks at him. "For so many things."

"Apology accepted," he says, before gently kissing her again.

Kissing Gil is amazing, and she definitely wants more. Selah might be right about this living in the moment stuff.

"We should go to bed."

"I thought you'd never offer." He teases.

"I didn't mean it that way." She knows she didn't mean to invite Gil into her bed, but the idea of Gil sleeping beside her is something she likes.

"I know, I know. I'm not going to push my luck." He holds her hands and squeezes.

They turn and walk back to the house. When they drop the blankets in the basket by the door, Biscuit gets up from his bed next to the wood stove and walks upstairs.

"What time is it?" Gil asks, walking over to the kitchen. "2:30," he reads the time on the kitchen clock.

"Wow. We were asleep out for a while." Maggie takes a glass out of the cupboard. "Water?"

"Sure. I have Jameson and sand breath."

"Sand breath?" She laughs.

"Mmm hmm," he hums, drinking his water, and then setting his glass back on the counter. "You didn't seem to mind my sand breath." He leans into her and gently kisses by her ear.

"I didn't even notice your sand breath." Her heart races. Somehow kissing Gil outside in the dark was different than standing close to him in her own kitchen. This feels more real, bigger than a few kisses.

He pauses and pushes her hair behind her shoulders. "We should go to bed," he repeats her words from earlier.

Maggie hums and finishes her water. While turning out the downstairs lights, she tries to organize the jumble of mixed thoughts and emotions inside her. A big part of her wants to invite him to sleep in her bed—this part sounds a lot like Selah.

He follows her up the stairs and Biscuit trails behind him. Pausing at the door to the room he's now sharing with Selah, he waits while she deliberates. After a moment, he moves to turn the knob on the door.

"I think the door is locked," he whispers.

"That's weird." She tries the lock herself. "Well, it appears Selah is meddling again."

"Guess I'll find out just how comfortable that couch is after all."

Making up her mind, she grabs his hand, and pulls him down the hall to her room. "I have the couch in my room. Plus, all the extra linens are locked in that room," she whispers as she opens her door.

Gil smiles and allows himself to be lead.

Once in her room, with the door closed behind them, she continues to whisper, "You can sleep in here tonight."

"Why are you whispering?" He chuckles.

"I don't know," she whispers again, then laughs.

"Isn't it only fair to wake up Selah since she's the one to lock the door to my room?" He teases her. "Or you can admit you want a co-ed sleepover for old time's sake."

"One of us can sleep on the love seat." Maggie ignores his teasing and points to the small sofa.

"Okay…" He sounds confused. "Sounds like a lot of subterfuge to get me into your room. You could just ask. I would say yes."

She tries not to get flustered. She wants to have Gil close, but isn't going to have sex with him tonight. Sleep, yes. Sex, no. This is what she tells herself. She pulls a pillow off the bed and then removes the back cushions from the love seat. Unfolding the throw from the arm, she makes a cozy, but very small bed.

"I don't think you are going to fit." She glances over her shoulder at him, taking in his long legs and broad shoulders. "Maybe you should take the bed."

"I'm not kicking you out of your bed," he says, walking over and sitting on the love seat. It looks tiny beneath him. He lies down, stretching his legs over the arm, his calves and feet dangling in the air.

Maggie laughs at him looking so uncomfortable.

"Quit laughing at me. I'll be fine. "Let me grab my toothbrush in the hall bath and I'll be right back. I'm warning you, I have nothing to sleep in but my boxers."

"You can get your toothbrush. I'm fine if you sleep in your boxers." She nods to show how fine she is.

After he steps out of the room, she goes through her nightly routine before changing into her navy cotton nightgown that falls a few inches above her knees. Not sexy, she thinks, but she isn't trying to seduce Gil. *Is she?* Her mind drifts to sleeping, or not sleeping, on a twin futon with Gil. She smiles at the memory.

When she leaves the bathroom, Gil goes in to brush his teeth. He walks out and heads over to love seat. She watches him toss and turn into a semblance of a comfortable position.

"Night, Maggie May," he tells her, turning his head to face her.

Looking at how uncomfortable he looks, she realizes she is being ridiculous. She might not be ready to have sex with him, but she can't torture the sweet man by making him sleep on what is essentially a large dog bed.

Deciding to be honest, she dramatically sighs. "Okay, you can share the bed. I liked sleeping next to you on the beach. Reminded me of all those times in college we'd fall asleep watching movies or reading." She hopes she sounds casual.

He unfolds himself from the love seat and approaches the bed. "I see how things work around here. The dog gets the prime spot," he says, nodding at Biscuit curled up in the middle of the bed.

"Biscuit, get down," she says, patting the dog's back. Biscuit gives her what can only be a dirty look as he jumps down, then lies on his cushion in the corner.

"It's a big bed," she adds to remind herself of the boundaries she's created.

He flops on the bed, stretching out his limbs. "This bed isn't all that big. I'm just sayin'." He smirks at her.

She pokes his leg where he is starfished across her. "If you're going to hog the whole thing, you can go back to the love seat or wake up Selah to sleep in your designated twin bed."

He smiles at her and rolls to one side. "We both slept in the same twin bed a few times in college." He notices her arched eyebrow. "Fine. I'll behave. But I can't promise there won't be cuddling."

She smiles back. "There better be cuddling. I fully expect cuddling. Thoughts on spoon size? Big or little?"

"Oh, I get to be the big spoon. No doubt." He gives her a playful, but wolfish grin.

Gil climbs under the covers and turns toward her. "This isn't awkward. See?"

"Shh," she hushes him. "Less talking or I'll make you sleep on the couch." She smiles and curls into his side

"I won't say another word." He pulls her close, but doesn't make a further move. "Goodnight." He kisses the top of her head. "Oops."

Tilting her head up, she gives him a soft kiss on the lips.

"Goodnight." Snuggling into his side, she drifts off to sleep, feeling a long-forgotten sense of peace.

He takes a few minutes longer to fall asleep, mulling over his impossible luck to be sharing a bed with Maggie again. He thinks about his wishing rock. Maybe those rocks are magical.

Biscuit jumps back on the bed and curls up behind Maggie. He swears the dog winks at him.

"Feels like home," he whispers before closing his eyes.

* * *

Maggie stretches and feels a warm body against her back. An arm wraps around her middle and she freezes. *Arm?*

Gil stirs and pulls himself closer to her.

"Morning," he whispers.

It takes a minute for the events of last night to drop into place. She remembers the game of I Never and a few rounds of Jameson. Blurry images of falling asleep on the beach with Gil filter through her mind, followed by kissing, lots of kissing. She vaguely remembers something about locked doors and him sleeping in here with her rather than with Selah. Must have seemed like a good idea at the time.

"Morning," she says, turning her head to face him.

Yep, Gil is snuggled in her bed. She kissed him last night. It wasn't a dream. She smiles at the memory.

As she's fully waking up, a quick knock at the door and Quinn's cheerful morning voice break the silence. Before she can tell him to go away or hold on a second, Quinn walks into the room holding two coffees.

She's impressed he doesn't drop the cups when he realizes she and Gil are in bed together.

"Well, well well, well," Quinn tuts. "I should have brought another cup this morning." He sets a mug down on the nightstand closest to Gil before joining them on the bed. Not awkward at all.

"Morning, Q," she greets him, tucking the sheet around her waist as she sits up.

Gil is clearly less shy, and sits up bare-chested.

"Do you ever wait for a 'come in' after you knock?" Gil asks, rubbing his hand through his hair and down his face. His scruff has grown in overnight, casting a dark shadow on his jaw.

"Where's the fun in that?" Quinn hands Maggie the other mug of coffee. "Plus, why would I ever think Maggie would have company?"

She gratefully accepts the mug, giving her hands something to do while she waits for Quinn's inquisition. She isn't ashamed Gil is in her bed, far from it. Quinn's appearance has burst their bubble sooner than she hoped.

"So?" Quinn asks, looking between them. "This is interesting."

"It isn't what it looks like, Q." She gestures between herself and Gil. "We fell asleep on the beach, and it was late. Then, Selah locked Gil out of their room."

"I see." Quinn scratches Biscuit's belly. "Just like old times when you two would have co-ed sleepovers and actually sleep?"

"Exactly," Gil agrees. "Nothing to see here. That's our story and we're sticking to it." He drinks Quinn's coffee.

Quinn pretends to lift up the sheet. "I'll be the one to make that decision."

Gil bats his hand away.

"Okay, boys. Behave," Maggie scolds.

"Behaving is so boring. I keep telling you this, Magpie, when are you going to listen to me?" Quinn lies along the bottom of the bed.

"What time is it anyway?" Gil looks around for a clock. He stretches over her to glance at the alarm clock. "8:00? Ugh." He falls back into the pillows.

Maggie thinks she should be entirely uncomfortable with Gil in her bed and Quinn finding them entangled, but she isn't. Instead, she feels happy and invigorated.

Quinn takes his coffee back from Gil and sips it. "So, are you two going to go public with the rest of the house?"

"There's nothing to go public about." Maggie stiffens. She can sense Gil's eyes on her, so she turns to face him. "What? There's nothing to tell."

"Okay," Gil says and drinks her coffee.

Quinn watches the unspoken exchange between the two of them. "More going on here than sharing a bed, but it's clear Maggie doesn't want to admit anything."

Maggie yawns and ignores him. "Jeezy-pete, so early. Why are you awake?"

"I'm excited to see a man about a clam this morning." Quinn hands her his mug.

"Ryan won't be arriving on the island for a few more hours. And that's if his plane isn't delayed." Maggie yawns again.

"Sounds like someone didn't get enough sleep." Quinn gives her a pointed look.

"Q, stop. Gil, tell him nothing happened."

"Q, nothing happened," Gil says without conviction. "Not in bed anyway."

Quinn's eyes sparkle. "I knew it!"

"You know nothing. Hush." Maggie laughs, finishing the mug of coffee. "Now if you two will excuse me, I'm going to take a hot shower and try to remind myself all the reasons I don't drink whiskey until the wee hours any more."

She manages to untangle herself from the covers without flashing anyone. "There's a key on the hooks by the front door for the all the room locks, Gil. Will one of you let Biscuit out for his morning constitutional? I'll feed him when I get downstairs," she says as she walks into the bathroom.

Nineteen

"Sounds like we've been dismissed from the queen's chambers," Quinn says.

"Yeah, it does kind of feel that way." Gil rubs his face.

Maggie's insistence that nothing happened last night confuses Gil. Does she not remember the kissing? Does she regret having him sleep in her bed? Or is history repeating itself?

"Hey, I'm not going to pry... much, but whatever is going on with you two, give her some time. She's got a hard, but thin, shell around her these days."

Gil looks at Quinn, seeing nothing but support in his eyes. "Thanks Q."

"I'll let Biscuit out and get more coffee. You do your thing. I won't say a word to anyone else."

"Thanks."

Gil waits for Quinn to leave, then gets dressed in his jeans from last night. After grabbing the key, he quietly walks down the hall to his room and unlocks the door. He smiles, thinking how Maggie could have easily unlocked the door last night. While Selah softly snores on her back, he grabs a change of clothes from his bag and heads to the hall bath.

Gil takes a long shower. His head is cloudy with memories of the night before and the similarities to what happened in college. Maggie was open and willing to his advances last night, yet this morning, she denied everything. Just like before. Shaking off his bruised ego, he resolves he isn't going to let Maggie go this time without some sort of declaration and fight, if needed.

He isn't a twenty-year-old boy anymore. At forty-two, he knows there aren't many second chances in life and he decides he won't give up on this one yet.

* * *

Maggie stands under the hot water replaying the events of last night and this morning in her head. Gil and she kissed. It was amazing. And this morning she denied him like Peter did Jesus.

What is wrong with her?

Gil is great, kissing him is great.

She rests her head on the cool tiles. She has no idea what she's doing with Gil or why she reacts to him the same way. *Is it the memories of the past making her nostalgic? Or is there still a connection with him now?* He makes her laugh and smile, things she hasn't done in ages. The easy comfort of old friends is one thing, the draw she feels to Gil is more.

A thousand thoughts run through her head as she turns off the water and gets out. After dressing in a denim skirt and a plum tank top, she throws on her favorite gray wrap cardigan.

Stepping into the hall, Maggie notices the door to Gil's room is closed and hears someone in the guest shower. It must be him. She hurries downstairs, where she finds Q sitting at the counter with a fresh cup of coffee.

She feeds the dog before filling her coffee cup.

"Thanks for the wake-up cup," she tells him.

"Thanks for the show. I love a good surprise first thing in the morning." He winks.

"Morning surprises?" Jo asks, walking into the kitchen. She heads over to the coffee machine and pours herself a cup. "Do tell."

"Morning, Jo. No surprises. Q was teasing," Maggie says, giving Quinn a look that asks him to keep quiet.

Jo sips her coffee, glancing suspiciously between them. "So who's up?"

"You, me, Q, obviously. I heard the upstairs shower going, so I guess either Selah or Gil is awake," Maggie lies.

"Ben's still sacked out. He never sleeps in this late. Then again he rarely stays up past ten either."

"So old and boring." Quinn teases.

"Yes, boring. Kids do that to you."

"So you like to tell me." His voice holds an edge.

Freshly showered, Gil walks into the kitchen. "Morning," he greets everyone.

"Coffee?" Maggie offers, dumping out the old grounds to make a fresh pot.

"Sure," he says, moving to stand close to her. "We haven't finished what we started last night," he whispers to her. "Don't think you're getting away so easily this time. We have another day and a half together. And I'm a man with a plan."

A shiver runs down Maggie's back and she glances over her shoulder at him.

His eyes twinkle and he gives her his charming smirk.

She is speechless.

* * *

"Buy, buy, sell, sell." Maggie jokes when Ben joins them at the table outside, his cell phone still permanently attached to his hand.

"It's Saturday, Ben. What work are you going to do on Saturday?" Quinn asks.

"The five day week is a myth, Q. Working on Saturdays is the norm. At least in my world." Ben starts typing away on his phone.

"Why am I the last to wake up every day?" Selah asks, dressed in her red kimono again, as she walks outside with an empty coffee cup.

"Because you're lazy?" Quinn teases.

"Maybe. Or I need the most beauty sleep."

"How did you sleep?" Maggie asks, filling Selah's cup with coffee.

"Fantastic. I expected Gil's snoring to keep me up, but it didn't. It was like sleeping with the dead." Selah gives Gil a knowing look.

"I don't snore," he defends.

"Who wants granola, yogurt, and berries? I couldn't face a big breakfast myself this morning, but there are eggs and other stuff in the fridge, if anyone needs something more hearty." She picks up a bowl and gestures to the offerings with her spoon.

Gil notes she quickly changed the subject away from his snoring last night.

"I'm surprised I'm not more hungover." Jo fills a bowl with berries and yogurt.

"I'm surprised too. We put a serious dent in the whiskey supply last night," Gil says.

"We have plenty of wood leftover, thanks to John. We can go another round tonight if anyone is up for it." Maggie suggests.

"I'm up for another round," Gil says with a wink. He observes Maggie fighting to suppress her smirk.

"No more Quinn games." Jo cringes. "I'm not sure I can handle more revelations from I Never."

"We haven't even played my hut game." Quinn pouts.

"Maybe save the huts for the reunion." Maggie pats his arm.

"Good idea." Quinn brightens.

"What's the plan for today, other than fetching Dr. Goodstuff from the ferry?" Selah asks.

"I wasn't sure what everyone wanted to do, so I haven't made plans," Maggie says.

"I'd love to do nothing but bask in the sun," Jo declares, stretching out her arms in the sunlight.

"Depending on when Ryan catches the ferry, we can eat a late lunch in Langley, or drive up the island and go to the driftwood beach by Ft. Casey. Or even go over to Port Townsend for the day. Shop. Hang out at the Red Cat—up to you guys."

"So many suggestions, Magpie. We don't have to do anything. No agendas." Jo stretches her legs into the sun.

"No more hiking." Quinn moans. "All that fresh air and natural perfection can't be good for the soul."

"You have some color on your cheeks. You look healthy, Q. Embrace the island." Maggie taps his nose.

"Embracing the island sounds like *Lost*. No thank you, smoke monster." Quinn swats her hand away.

Gil watches the easy exchange between Maggie and Quinn. He wants that lighthearted, effortless banter with Maggie. He realizes he wants it all with her, not the girl from his memory. This Maggie, who still has the same constellation of freckles on her nose as she did at nineteen, is amazing in the way she cares for and loves the people in her life, including him.

"Whidbey is kind of like that island. You get here and never want to leave. Well, some people don't." Maggie gazes out at the retreating tide and the wet sand sparkling in the sun. "We can poke around here if you want. No pressure."

"Hanging out would be completely fne with me," Gil says casually.

"Maybe John will be around and he'll schlepp some wood, without a shirt or something," Selah says, looking over her shoulder at John's house.

"You should ask him to pose for one of your covers," Jo suggests.

"That's a great idea. He'd make the perfect pirate. I wonder what his thoughts are about guy-liner." Selah thinks aloud.

"He just pulled up in his truck, so you here's your chance." Quinn points to the road where John and Babe are getting out of the cab of his Ford truck. He wears a plaid shirt and dark wash jeans over worn work boots.

"Does he always wear plaid?" Jo asks.

"Pretty much," Maggie answers. "That's where the lumberjack name comes from."

Gil watches all three women silently turn and watch John walk up the lawn between the two houses.

"Morning," John calls over. He changes direction to join them.

"Morning, John," Selah practically purrs.

"Putting it on a little thick, Elmore?" Gil grumbles.

"Never." She tightens the belt on her kimono and runs her fingers through her hair.

Maggie laughs at her.

"Cup of coffee, John?" Maggie holds up the carafe.

"Sure. Never going to say no to your coffee." John walks up the stairs, and joins them on the deck.

"I think you've met everyone here," Maggie says as she pours a cup of coffee for him.

"Yep. You all enjoying the island? You even get sun for the weekend. Don't tell anyone it didn't rain the entire time. We have a reputation to protect." He winks at Selah.

"Oh, I bet you have a reputation." She flirts back.

Gil and Maggie roll their eyes at her obviousness.

"What's on the agenda for today? Sightseeing?" John asks.

"Nah, I think we're going to hang around the beach and be lazy. Late night."

"Yeah, I saw the fire going pretty late. Almost came over, but didn't want to interrupt."

"You wouldn't have been interrupting," Selah says. "In fact, we're thinking of having another fire tonight. You should join us."

"Sure. That'd be cool. You have enough wood?" John looks at Maggie.

"Plenty of firewood. Not sure what the plan is, but if the fire is going, come on down."

Gil observes their silent exchange. While he's jealous of the lumberjack's desirable location, he realizes Maggie isn't flirting with the guy. He smiles at the thought he might be the reason why.

"Crabs okay last night?" John asks the group.

"They were amazing—so juicy and sweet," Selah answers, the purring comes back.

"Well, let me know if you need any salmon to grill tonight. I put the rest of that King in the freezer. Might go out later this evening." He squints out at the water, as if he is visualizing the salmon beneath the surface.

"You really are a man of the earth, aren't you?" Selah asks.

"I suppose. I do all right." He gives Selah his devastating, flirty smile. "I have to get some stuff done today since I'm heading off island all week. I'll stop by later if I'm around. Have a good time whatever you do." He puts his cup on the table, and heads over to his house.

"Oh, we will," Selah calls after him. Once he is gone she flops back in her seat. "I need to switch genres and write some lumberjack erotica. I'm thinking an entire series set in Alaska or British Columbia." She fans herself with her hands.

"You are too much. You put Quinn to shame with your flirting," Jo scolds.

"That is really saying something!" Quinn puffs out his chest in pride. His phone chirps with a text.

"The doctor has landed and is heading north. T minus 1 hour until he gets here."

"I'll help clear the dishes," Gil offers.

"You know what your dish washing does to me." Maggie sighs.

"I do." He smirks at her before walking into the house with the breakfast dishes.

Maggie feels her cheeks heat.

"A man willing to do the dishes is a good man to keep around," Jo says. "I can't remember the last time Ben did the dishes."

"It's the little things, isn't it?" Maggie says. "When we are younger we want the grand gestures—the roses, the candlelight. Now it's a man who does the dishes."

"I still want candlelight. Or even better, complete darkness. He can imagine my younger body better in the dark," Jo says.

"Who says romance isn't dead?" Ben pipes into the conversation. "Men need to know these things. Would save us a lot of money on jewelry."

"Oh, we still want jewelry. Always, honey." Jo kisses him on the cheek.

"Romance isn't dead. Romance books are billion-plus dollar a year part of the publishing industry. Dirty little secret is smutty books outsell most every other genre and keep the houses afloat so they can publish the crown jewels that win the awards," Selah explains.

"I had no idea," Ben says. "Do you actually make money writing naughty things about wooden legs and wenches?" He looks genuinely intrigued.

"I do. Not more than my tenured professor position, but you'd be surprised. I'm not doing this for my own shits and giggles."

"Interesting, very interesting." Ben goes back to tapping away on his phone as he walks down the stairs trying to find the best signal.

"Speaking of interesting," Quinn interjects. "I'm going to shower. Who's going with me to pick up Ryan at the ferry? Or should I take Bessie, since she's a two-seater?" He winks at Maggie.

"Nice try. You can drive the wagon. Unless you want company, I think you can find your way to the ferry landing and back home on your own."

"You are no fun at all. None." Quinn pouts.

"No sex in the Subaru, either!" Maggie yells after him as he walks toward the house.

"Seriously, you really need to get laid and lighten up." He turns and winks at her before going inside.

"You do need to get laid. He's right," Selah agrees.

"Thanks, I think you said that already. Like a thousand times." Maggie sticks her tongue out at Selah.

"Yet, you still don't listen to me." She gestures at Maggie's lap. "You probably have cobwebs. Things need to be aired out."

"Why does this conversation make me think of Miss Havisham in *Great Expectations?*" Jo laughs. "Yellowed lace and cobwebs everywhere."

"Hey, my…." Maggie gestures to her lap. "…is not covered in old lace and cobwebs. I'm not a virgin, you know. Thank you very much."

"Your what? I didn't catch what you said." Selah smiles.

"You know what I mean," Maggie says.

"Not sure that I do." Selah eggs her on.

"Let's put this in terms you probably understand—my lady garden, my pearl, my treasure chest, my x-marks-the-spot…" Maggie can hardly get the words out without giggling.

"Your x-marks-the-spot?" Selah cackles. "Oh sweetie, if he needs a map, he isn't doing it right."

"No one is using any map."

"And that, my dear, is precisely the issue."

"And we're back to the beginning of this conversation. I'm going to go put on my suit and sit in the sun before the good doctor gets here, and tells me how bad tanning is for my skin." Jo wanders into the house leaving Selah and Maggie alone at the table.

"I had the strangest dream last night. I dreamed I had the whole room to myself and didn't have to share with Gil." Selah stares over her sunglasses at Maggie.

"Odd dream considering you locked the door."

"Maybe a ghost locked the door?" Selah arches her brow.

"Very strange a ghost could do that." Maggie stares into her empty coffee cup, thinking about Selah's meddling. A soft smile forms as she thinks of how right it felt to have Gil in her bed.

"So, where did Gil sleep last night? Sofa downstairs? Love seat in your room?"

"Neither." Maggie looks at Selah.

"Uh huh."

"Nothing happened."

"Nothing? The way Gil and you were looking at each other this morning didn't look like nothing."

"How was Gil looking at me?" Maggie flushes a little, thinking of his words in the kitchen earlier.

"Like a man who didn't sleep on the sofa, and won't be sharing a room with me tonight either."

"Fine. He slept in my bed." Maggie tells Selah the same version she told Quinn earlier.

"Aha! There was kissing." Selah smiles. "Kissing is good."

"Mmm hmm. Kissing is very good." Maggie can't help but smile.

"You heeded my advice? Lived in the moment? Good girl." Selah pats her arm.

"Thanks, mom."

"Now what?"

"I'm not sure. Quinn woke us up this morning, so we haven't talked about anything."

"Less talking and more kissing is what I would do," Selah advises.

"Why am I not surprised? Nothing is going to happen with a house full of nosy guests."

"Don't let us stand in your way. I'm sure you two can find a quiet corner or broom closet to sneak off to, if you need."

"Making out in the broom closet?" Maggie laughs. "I don't see that happening. Plus, we're friends. That's what is most important."

"*Deja vu*, Maggie." Selah furrows her brows. "We didn't care what happened then, we wouldn't now. We all want you two to be happy."

"What? We are friends. Friends who kiss every twenty years."

Selah sighs. "Live, Maggie. Don't play safe. Live while you're still young enough to enjoy it!" She throws her arms wide. "*Carpe vir!*"

"Isn't the saying '*carpe diem*'?"

"Pfft. 'Seize the man' is so much better. And more appropriate for this situation."

Maggie laughs, but feels torn as conflicting thoughts and feelings about Gil swirl in her head.

"Don't overthink this." Selah taps Maggie's forehead. "Go with the flow. Have some faith."

Maggie nods in agreement, mostly to get Selah to stop spouting clichés. "Got it."

Jo returns and sprawls out on a towel on one of the chaise lounges.

"That looks like a brilliant idea," Selah says, getting up. "I think I'll put some clothes on and join you."

Maggie follows Selah into the house.

Gil puts the last of the dishes in the dishwasher, wipes his hands on a tea towel, and smiles at Maggie.

"Thank you for the dishes."

"Anytime. What's next on the non-agenda? Is everyone doing their own thing?"

"Quinn's driving to the ferry to get Ryan, the girls are sunbathing, and Ben is wandering around making people work on a Saturday. That's about it."

"The tide is almost out. Want to take a walk?" he suggests.

"Sure. Biscuit would love it. Can I bring him?"

"Of course. Gives us an excuse to escape everyone." He smirks at her and squeezes her hip as he walks by her.

"I'm on to you, Mr. Morrow." She squints at him.

"Good. Cause I'm looking forward to more of the nothing that didn't take place last night." He smiles. "Let me go grab some shoes."

Maggie leans against the counter. One way or another this man will be the death of her.

Quinn comes downstairs showered and wearing navy shorts and a striped polo.

"You are very preppy in this outfit. Like the husband of a doctor," Maggie teases.

"You like?" Quinn turns around. "I can't wait for Ryan to see this place. He'll love it." He kisses Maggie on the cheek.

"Car keys are on the hook. You know how to get there?"

"Yep, yep. Up the hill, left, right, hit the main road and keep going until you run out of land. I got this."

"We'll decide on lunch when you get back." Maggie waves to him as he heads out the front door.

Gil comes back down as the door closes. "Ready, Maggie May?" He holds out his hand.

As I'll ever be, Maggie thinks.

Twenty

The tide isn't at its lowest, but there is enough dry sand for a walk far beyond the sight of the house.

Maggie and Gil walk in silence for a bit, watching Biscuit run through the shallow pools of water dotted with sand dollars, moon snail shells, and kelp.

"Ever wonder if there are any geoducks out here?" he asks.

"There might be some further out where the water is deeper in a high tide. Did you know once a geoduck reaches maturity and digs itself down into the sand, it never leaves the spot? They can live for over a hundred years in the same hole."

"Talk about being stuck in the mud." He pokes the wet sand with his shoe.

"Isn't the saying 'a stick in the mud'?" She bumps his side with her elbow.

"I'd rather be a stick in the mud, than burrowed in the same spot for a hundred years with no eyes."

"Sticks don't have eyes either. You're weird." She laughs, but Jo's words echo in her head about hiding out. Maybe she is a geoduck, living in her same, comfortable spot, unwilling to ever stick her neck out, and retreating at the first sign of contact. Has she subconsciously buried herself away from life's risks all together?

Gil's splashing through a shallow pool brings her out of her contemplation. "How do you go about hunting geoducks anyway? Gathering? Harvesting? Picking?" he asks, ignoring her silence.

She snorts at the innocent question. "Are you asking if I want to go geoduck hunting, Morrow? In the bright light of day?"

"Hey, are you having impure thoughts about a bi-valve again?" He walks backward to face her.

"You've seen a geoduck. How can you not have impure thoughts?"

"We did go to the same college, so yes, I am familiar with geoducks. You're fourteen, you know this, right?"

"I am not. Not my fault this particular bivalve resembles an uncircumcised penis." She laughs.

"You would know more than I would," Gil says, sounding snarky.

"Yeah, I suppose I do. Unless you've been hanging around Turkish bath houses." Shielding her eyes from the bright sun, she peers at him over her sunglasses.

"No, no Turkish bathhouses. I was scarred by watching *Midnight Express*." Gil shudders.

When he steps in a big pool of water and almost loses his footing, she laughs at him. He takes up his spot beside her again.

"On the train back to Paris, Lizzy and I realized we had a small joint leftover from our weekend in Amsterdam. We spent the entire time wondering what French prisons for women were like. We decided if you had to be incarcerated, at least in France the food would be good."

"I doubt they serve *pain au chocolat* in prison, Maggie." He laughs.

"Probably not, but I could live off of baguettes and butter, maybe a little *jambon* on occasion. Plus, we theorized, they probably serve you wine."

"Doesn't sound like a bad set up." He smiles at her. "And you could master your French."

"Right?" She sighs, thinking about it.

"Marriage was probably a better choice in the end, though."

"Shorter sentence at least. I think. I'm not sure how long you'd go to prison for a joint in France."

"I have no idea. Probably only pay a fine."

"Easier than divorce."

"You and Lizzy had lots of adventures that year."

Maggie smiles her thanks for his sidestepping of the Julien topic. "We did. I can't believe we both survived with all the crazy things we did." She jumps over a shallow stream of water, while Biscuit splashes right through it.

"I bet." Gil's long legs mean he doesn't have to jump, instead clearing the stream in a single stride.

"Lots of adventures with everyone who came to visit. You were the only one who didn't come over and visit us. Why was that?"

"You know why, Maggie."

His words sting even though she does know why. "I wish you had come to visit. Things might have been different. I really missed you that fall." She gives him a small smile.

"You did? You never wrote or called. I assumed you regretted sleeping together and were putting literal and figurative distance between us."

She can see the surprise and lingering hurt on his face.

"I did miss you. I didn't know what to say in a letter or on the phone. I missed you, but Lizzy kept telling me not to pine. Something about *che serà, serà*. She was always saying if you and I were meant to be, you'd wait for me."

"Sounds like Lizzy. I did wait for you. It was you who didn't wait for me." He looks down and gives her a small, sad smile.

"I should have waited. I did wait, but when I never heard from you, I figured you'd moved on. I asked Selah about you during her visit over winter break. When she wouldn't give me any details, I assumed you were dating and in love, and she didn't want to be the one to tell me."

"I was in love. With a girl on the other side of the world."

"You were?" His words surprise her.

"I was. Very much. But I was a nerd, and scared, and stupid. So I didn't do anything." He runs his hands through his hair. "I guess I was of the same mind as Lizzy. If we were meant to be, you'd realize you loved me, and come back to me."

He stops walking and picks up a sand dollar, wiping off the wet sand. "But then the French Incident happened, and well, life went in another direction."

She frowns. "You never told me."

"You came home with Julien attached to your hip. I didn't really see the point." He tosses the sand dollar into the water.

"I'm sorry I was so blind, Gil."

"*Che serà, serà*. You seemed really happy with him. I wasn't going to ruin what was left of our friendship by making you choose."

"I probably would've chosen Julien at that point. I think my head was spinning with lust more than love."

He cringes. "Ouch."

Waving her arms around, she attempts to backtrack. "No, no, I mean it as a positive in your column. You were my best friend for years. Julien was French, and all about the seduction and romance. I was so caught up in the idea of him, I didn't really pay attention to the man behind the romantic ideal."

"I blame all the nineteenth century French romances you read in college." Gil half-smiles. "Listen, I get it. He seduced you. I was a geeky boy from Colorado. No sexy accent, bad haircut, and always wore socks with my shoes."

"You were never a geek." Maggie grabs his hand. "You were always cute. Don't forget grunge rock star who made all the girls swoon."

"Clearly you are forgetting my horrible Sally Jesse Raphael-style glasses freshman year." His smile widens.

She bursts out laughing and swings their hands between them. "I did forget those! Those were horrible. But you got rid of them before sophomore year."

"Amazing what contacts can do for a guy's image." Gil laughs with her.

She squints at him. "I like you in glasses. They suit your whole 'hot professor' thing. You should wear them more often."

He kisses her hand and laughs, saying, "My ego thanks you for saying that. How funny life is. After The French Incident, I never imagined you and I would be walking on a beach, holding hands, and talking like this again. I'm glad we finally addressed the elephant in our lives. I've missed you."

She grins at him and squeezes his hand. "Me too. Maybe Selah is right about everything happening like puzzle pieces fitting into place. It's possible if we hooked up in college and dated, it would've been a disaster. The whole group dynamic would have changed for the worse, and we wouldn't be here today."

"True, but two decades is a long ass time to wait to do this again…"

He surprises her by spinning her toward him and kissing her. Her shock wears off, and she kisses him back. She wraps an arm around his back, and tugs at the hair at the nape of his neck. He responds by pulling her closer and weaving a hand through her hair.

After a few minutes of kissing, she pulls back to breathe. "Definitely too long."

He kisses her again.

"Way too long."

She brings her body flush with his. Where their hips meet, she can feel him.

Maggie hums into his mouth. Gil smiles against her lips. He breaks the kiss and smiles down at her.

This moment seems more than just kissing. She strokes his jaw. Wanting to see his eyes clearly, she lifts up her sunglasses, and then his aviators. She wants tell Gil she felt the same way in college.

As she steps back to meet his eyes, a big squirt of water splashes Gil on the leg.

"What the hell was that?" He jumps back in surprise as cold water drips down his leg.

"Speaking of geoducks… that my dear friend, was a geoduck." She laughs.

He is laughing now, too. "Wow. That was impressive."

Maggie looks down. Not only is there a splash of water, she notices a distinctive bulge.

"Speaking of impressive." She points at his shorts. Looking up, she notices his cheeks redden.

"Don't tease me. It's been a while for me. I feel like a teenager for sporting after a few kisses."

"I wouldn't tease you." She steps forward until their bodies are flush again and rolls her hips a little.

"You are teasing me." He swats her arm playfully. "I don't want to meet Quinn's husband with a tent in my shorts."

"Probably not a good idea. He isn't that kind of doctor." She teases.

Thinking of Ryan, Maggie turns and squints back at the beach. She can barely pick out a cluster of people on her deck. "Speaking of the good doctor, looks like Quinn and Ryan are back from the ferry."

Gil groans a little. "We should probably head back. Is it wrong I don't want to rejoin the others?" He grabs her hip, and looks down at her body. "You look amazing in this top. The color brings out the green in your eyes."

"Funny you can see my eye color given where you are staring. You know that staring at my boobs isn't going to help the situation in your shorts, mister." She jokingly chides him.

"True. We'll have to stay out here all day, then." He kisses her again.

"We'd be underwater when the tide comes in, silly." She points out their location.

"Fine, we'll steal a boat or a raft, and head out to sea." He glances around as if looking for a boat.

"We can go to sea another day. Come on, you'll love Ryan." She grabs his hand and turns to head back to the house.

As they walk toward the beach, Biscuit jumps around, biting water from any clams or geoducks that squirt at him. When they get closer to the cabin's beach, Maggie drops Gil's hand.

He gives her a questioning look. "What's up?"

"Do you mind if we keep this between us? Just for now? I don't want Quinn to tease or Selah to smirk. I'd like to keep whatever this is ours for now."

"Sure," Gil agrees, but shakes his head. "No problem." He squeezes her hand before letting it go. "I'll follow your lead."

He waves his arm to follow her back to the cabin.

"Thank you. You're so good to me." She smiles at him and strokes his arm.

"I could be so good for you too," he whispers, so softly she barely hears him.

Twenty-one

Maggie introduces Gil to Ryan. In flat-front khakis and tucked-in white linen shirt and lobster decorated canvas belt, Ryan looks every bit the successful East Coast doctor. His brown hair is buzzed short to disguise his impending baldness. Warm brown eyes behind wireless glasses are framed by deep laugh lines. He's about the same height as Quinn but heavier.

"I'm surprised you aren't wearing your Nantucket reds, Dr. Gooding." She teases him after kissing both his cheeks.

"Didn't think you Left Coasters would get the historical meaning of pink pants." He teases back.

"Pink pants?" Gil asks. "On guys? This is a thing?"

"You buy them red and let them fade to pink. The more pink they are, the cooler you are." Ryan rolls his eyes. "Or something like that."

"East Coasters are strange," Gil comments.

"We are a rare breed. Was it Fitzgerald who said, "Go West, young man?""

"No idea, but his narrator in *The Great Gatsby* did make a speedy exit back west after the shit hit the fan," Quinn answers.

"Can't say that I blame him." Maggie sighs.

"You always were a Left Coast girl even when you lived back East," Selah says from her lounger next to Jo. "You can try to take the girl out of the Pacific Northwest, but you can't take the... you know..." she fades out with a wave of her hand.

"Ryan, how was your flight? Do you want a shower? A nap? Food? Coffee?" Maggie slips into hostess mode.

"I'd love a giant glass of water and maybe some coffee," Ryan says.

"Done," Maggie says, as she heads into the house where Ben is pacing by the windows, still on his phone.

When she comes back with a large glass of water and a full carafe of coffee, the guys are sitting around the table.

"We never decided on lunch plans." She mentions to the group. "We got distracted by the sun and our hangovers from last night."

"Hangovers, huh? Sounds like I missed all the fun," Ryan says.

"Oh, you did, my husband, you did. We solved the age old mystery of whether or not Maggie and Gil slept together in college. The answer is yes. I'd say it was a very productive evening."

Ryan glances between Maggie and Gil. "I'm guessing Quinn suggested a game of I Never. It's his favorite way to create drama and expose secrets at dinner parties."

"Remember when Dr. and Mrs. Fishcakes drank on 'I've never been to a key party?' That was the best!" Quinn claps his hands.

"Q, they were in their sixties. The probability that they went to a key party in the '70s was pretty high."

"Oh, I know, but it was so like the movie *Ice Storm*." Quinn looks delighted at the memory.

Maggie and Gil exchange glances. "At least there wasn't a key party involved," he says.

"Nope, no keys." Holding Gil's gaze, she blushes.

"Why Maggie, I forgot you could still blush. It's that fair Irish skin of yours," Ryan says, looking over his shoulder at Jo and Selah lying on their chaises in the sun.

"I see you looking over here, Dr. Judgey," Selah says without turning their direction. "I'm getting vitamin D, so I don't get scurvy."

"I think you mean rickets. Scurvy is what sailors got," Ryan corrects.

"Right, right. Rickets. Sailors and pirates got scurvy. Poor scurvy ravished pirates." Selah sighs.

"So as I was saying, lunch?" Maggie repeats, ignoring Selah and her pirates.

"Before I can decide on lunch, I need to know the menu for dinner," Quinn says. "I don't want to repeat."

Ben walks out through the door, the phone still in his hand, but apparently his conversation is over for now. "I was thinking of getting some steaks and grilling them. I'm a little seafooded out to be honest," he says as he sits down at the table.

"Grilling is easy. I have veggies from the farmers' market we can grill, too. Salad, bread, done. Sound good?" Maggie looks around the group, and gets consensus from everyone.

"Okay, now that's settled, lunch?" She feels like a broken record.

"Why don't we head into Langley and grab some sandwiches or something? They have that sort of thing here, don't they? Food not involving fish, mussels or crabs, right?" Quinn asks.

"I'm sure we can find you something that had hooves or feathers, Q." Maggie gets up from the table. "Whoever wants to come, let's leave in a half hour. If you want to stay, we can bring you something back."

"I'll stay here," Jo says without lifting her head from the chaise. "It's rare I can lie around and not do anything. I might even nap." She turns her head and sighs.

"I'll come with you. I want to check out that funky antique store by the pizza place," Selah says, putting down her iPad, and dragging herself off the chaise.

"I'm in," Gil says.

"Ben?"

"Yeah, sure. When do I get to hang out with you guys?" He stares down at his phone, typing away.

After getting ready, everyone meets up in the kitchen to head out.

Maggie notices Jo appears to be asleep already on her lounge chair. "Wow, she passed out fast," she observes.

"She's been run ragged by summer break. I think she's counting the days until the kids are back in school," Ben says.

Selah visibly shudders. "Ugh, I can't imagine."

Ben laughs at her obvious horror. "You really don't have the mother gene."

"I don't 'hate' kids. I just have no desire to 'raise' one." She frowns.

"We could always send ours to visit Aunt Selah next summer, and you can examine the half-formed minds of human adolescents."

Selah gives him a blank stare. "You wouldn't dare."

Ben is still laughing as they follow Maggie outside and pile into his SUV.

* * *

Langley is busier on Saturday afternoon than it was late Thursday night. Ben makes a loop around the block before finding a place to park in the public lot on Second.

Hopping out of the car with the help of Gil's hand, Maggie lists the options for lunch. Everyone votes for Village Pizzeria and sitting outside.

"As long as we don't get the pesto or anything with fresh garlic," Maggie agrees. "Those combinations are deadly."

"Only if you plan on kissing someone." Selah teases. "You'll be fine if Gil eats it, too," she says more quietly so only Maggie can hear.

"Hush." Maggie pinches her arm lightly.

"Ouch! Woman, quit pinching my arm!" Selah causes a stir.

"Why are you pinching Selah?" Gil eyes them both.

"No other reason than she probably deserved it for something." Maggie smirks at Selah.

Selah huffs and rubs her arm as they enter the garden of the pizzeria. Located at the edge of the bluff, it has a fantastic view of Saratoga Passage and Camano Island beyond. The smell of garlic and baking dough wafts out from the open kitchen windows.

Despite the crowded garden, they grab a table being vacated by a family. Pizza and salads are ordered along with a pitcher of beer and two white wine spritzers.

"This is a gorgeous place to live, Maggie," Ryan says. "I can understand why you ran away here, never to return. You seem lighter now. Dare I say, happier?"

"I didn't exactly run away. But thank you, I do love it here." Smiling at his observation about her mood, she admits, "And I am feeling happier this weekend."

"It doesn't quite feel real. I didn't see a single familiar sign or business on the drive from the ferry to the cabin, except the Dairy Queen," Ryan continues.

"That's because there aren't any chains or franchises on the south end of the island," Maggie explains. "There's a Walmart and all the chain fast food places up in Oak Harbor, but down here, we keep things local as much as we can."

"Wow. I knew there was something odd about not passing at least one Starbucks," Ryan says.

"Speaking of coffee, they have these coffee huts here manned by hot guys instead," Quinn excitedly tells Ryan. "Maggie was telling me all about Jack and his hut the other day."

She laughs at Quinn's exuberance. "First, his name is Jonah. Second, not sure he's hot or your type. Third, we can stop on our way home and get a coffee so everyone can experience the joy of the hut."

"Jonah, Jack. Same thing. Maggie was trying to throw us together, but I told her I only have eyes for you." Quinn grabs Ryan's forearm.

"Q, I've met you before." Ryan squeezes Quinn's hand on his arm. "You have eyes. We're married, not dead. And, maybe Jonah is my type."

"You two seem really good together. It's a little weird to think of crazy Quinn as married, but I can see this relationship works. It's nice to see Quinn settled down and happy," Gil says, smiling at the men.

"Thanks, G. I'm glad you're finally getting to meet each other." Quinn returns Gil's smile.

Their drinks arrive and after pouring the beers, Gil raises his glass in a toast. "To Q and Ryan."

"To happiness," Ryan adds.

"To old friends." Quinn raises his glass

"To good friends." Maggie toasts, looking at Gil, who winks at her.

"To good sex." Selah finishes the round of toasts.

"To good sex," they repeat as Maggie keeps her eyes locked with Gil's.

* * *

Bellies full of pizza and beer, the guys head into the Star Store to buy steak and other supplies for the night's dinner. Waving them off, Selah and Maggie wander toward the antique store.

Inside the store, Selah points to a stuffed squirrel on a high shelf. "You should get that for your desk to keep you company."

"A stuffed squirrel? Are you out of your mind?" Maggie snickers. "First, Biscuit would probably eat it, and second, yuck. Dead animal."

"But he is so charming and lifelike." Selah teases as she wanders further into the narrow aisles of the shop.

"Keyword being the like after life. No and no." Maggie shakes her head.

Selah finds a box of old, yellowed, frayed laces. "Remind you of our conversation from earlier?" She laughs, holding up a particularly old looking piece of lace in front of her waist.

Maggie laughs with her. "Such a lovely image. Miss Havisham would be an excellent, yet tragically sad, Halloween costume for me."

"Perfect for you. I usually go as Frida Kahlo, as you know." Selah puts the lace back in its box.

"Yes, I love the variations and accessories you wear. Rib cage or monkey this year?"

"I thought I might mix it up and go as something Victorian. Is steampunk passé?" Selah holds up a top hat.

"If I know about it, it probably has reached mass market status." Maggie puts the top hat back on its shelf.

"True. Like mustaches. I saw a toddler in a coffeehouse with a mustache and a monocle last week." Selah rolls her eyes.

"You do live in Portland."

"At least I think it was a fake mustache. Maybe he was a very short man." Selah taps her fingers on her chin.

"Like I said, you do live in Portland. You could always go as a pirate wench—a classic."

"True. Such a cliché. An author of pirate smut going as a smutty pirate is very meta." Selah seems pleased by this idea.

"You academics with your meta this and that. The rest of the world dresses as a sexy pirate, sexy nurse or a sexy cat."

"The sexualization of Halloween is fascinating, that's for sure. Think about it. What is scarier than women taking charge of their sexuality and sexual desires?" Selah steeples her fingers and taps them together like an evil mastermind.

Maggie shakes her head at her friend. "For some men, nothing scarier. Let's be thankful we don't have those men in our lives. Speaking of men in our lives, we should probably go meet the guys before they buy half a cow and ten pounds of bacon."

"Men do love bacon," Selah follows her out of the store.

"Who doesn't love bacon?" Maggie asks as they cross the street.

"Orthodox Jews? Vegans? Pig worshipers?"

"It was a rhetorical question. Pig worshipers?" Maggie chuckles.

"Sure, if the Hindu honor the cow as sacred, odds are there is probably some culture that worships the pig."

"Okay," Maggie agrees, pulling open the door to the market.

They find Gil and Ben with several steaks, and sure enough, bacon. Ryan and Quinn come over with another cart containing bottles of wine and a box of cling wrap.

"We have meat for the whole beach." Maggie looks at Gil and Ben behind their cart o'meat.

"We're growing men," Ben declares, rubbing his stomach.

"Wine for everyone," Quinn explains with a flourish, pointing at his cart.

"And growing alcoholics." Selah rifles through the mix of red and white wines. "Nice selection of Washington wines there, Doc."

"Can't find most of these back home, so I thought it would be fun to taste several."

"Speaking of not having things back home, I found Fat Tire." Quinn holds up a six pack decorated with a red bicycle.

"That's a Colorado beer, Q," Gil comments.

"I know, but it's still one of my faves, and you can't get it in the Northeast, or some nonsense like that."

"Weird. I don't know how you think you're the more civilized side of the country." Gil frowns.

"We have rotaries," Ryan says, as if rotaries explain everything.

Maggie eyes the cling wrap, and then Quinn. "What's with the cling wrap?"

"I noticed you were out. Thought I'd pick up more, being a good guest and all."

Gil picks up the box. "This is staying in the kitchen this time, right? I still don't want to know why you had cling wrap in your bedroom in Olympia."

"Don't ask, don't tell." Quinn tosses the box back in the cart.

Maggie leaves the guys in line for a few minutes before returning with her arms full with bags of marshmallows and a box of graham crackers. A jar of Nutella is wedged under her arm along with several bars of dark chocolate.

"S'mores," she explains when she sees Gil arch his brow.

"With Nutella?" He takes the jar and the chocolate from her.

"Yes, you haven't lived until you eat them with Nutella. The chocolate goes with a raspberry puree."

"I'll have to trust you on this one for now." Gil sounds doubtful.

"What doesn't go with Nutella?" She pokes Gil with her elbow.

"Bacon?" He holds up a pack from the cart.

Maggie thinks it over. "Nah. I bet Nutella and bacon sandwiches on brioche would be delicious for breakfast. Maybe done in a panini press so the bread is all toasty and the Nutella kind of melts."

"Earth to Maggie." Gil waves his hand in front of her face.

"Sorry. Got lost in some food porn there for a second." She sighs.

"Don't you ever get sick of thinking, writing, and talking about food?" Ryan asks.

Maggie gapes at him for a moment.

"Never. I love my job. I love food."

"I can appreciate good food, but I'm more of a fuel to survive kind of guy." Ryan shrugs.

"Men are weird about food," Selah comments.

Gil bags up their groceries as Ryan reaches for his wallet. Maggie tries to block him by insisting she's the host. Ryan wrestles his card free from her flailing hand blocks and hands it to the teenage cashier, who is watching them like they're crazy senior citizens on day release from the home.

"Hey now." Maggie pouts.

"Maggie, you are letting us take over your home for the weekend. Least we can do is pay for some supplies."

"He makes about a gazillion dollars a year, let the good doctor pay," Quinn says, as he loads the cart with the case of wine. "I married very well."

"I'm the one who married well." Ryan gazes at him.

Quinn gives Ryan a quick peck on the mouth.

The cashier's eyes widen in surprise. His 'have a good day' comes out as a cough.

"Guess they don't get a lot of mister and misters around here," Selah comments as they head out the back door to the parking lot.

"Not many, but times they are a changing. We're pretty open minded for redneck, country folk." Maggie jokes.

"I wonder how open-minded the lumberjack is," Selah says.

"Oh, do you think he's 'open-minded'?" Quinn winks.

"No, Q. Plus, I'm calling dibs." Selah reminds him.

"Fine. I still have Jack."

"Speaking of Jonah, let's grab a coffee before we head back to the beach. Jonah's hut is on the way," Maggie suggests.

* * *

There are two cars ahead of them at the Fellowship of the Bean when they pull into line. Maggie sits shotgun next to Ben. Quinn fidgets in the seat behind Ben, his window already down, and he cranes his neck to see the elusive Jonah.

Gil and Selah sit in the very back, clearly trying to pretend they don't know Quinn.

"Quinn, chill. He's not even your type." Maggie turns and shoots Quinn a look.

"There is no living with him at times like these," Ryan explains from his spot next to Quinn.

"What does everyone want? I don't want to sit around like an idiot once we get to the window," Ben says, sounding very much like the dad he is.

"I want a half caff, half pump—" Quinn starts to say.

Ben cuts him off. "Do not make me order those crazy coffees. You want half pumps, half foam, you order it yourself."

"Okay, Mr. Grumpy." Quinn laughs and pats the top of Ben's head.

Everyone else tells Ben their simple orders. When they pull up to the window, a man with a long goatee, wearing a black T-shirt, and what appear to be full tattoo sleeves, greets them.

"Hey folks, what can I get you?"

Maggie leans over the console and greets him, "Hi, Jonah."

"Hey Maggie! Didn't see you. What's up with the jumbo sized vehicle?"

"Friends visiting. Friends, this is Jonah. Jonah, these are the friends."

Jonah gives a friendly half wave. "Hey."

From his vantage point in the back of the SUV, Gil can't really see the coffee guy other than the tattoos and a stretched earlobe. "Hipster," he mutters quietly.

Selah gives him a nudge. "Your retroactive, possessive caveman attitude is so charming."

"Thanks for your sarcasm."

"First, the lumberjack, now the guy who stands around all day in a little box selling coffee? You can't be jealous or threatened by these guys."

"They have location desirability." He grumbles.

"And you have history on your side. Shut it, Morrow. Or Maggie will think you're crazy."

"I'm beginning to believe I am crazy." He rolls his head, before turning his attention to Quinn, who orders his coffee while leaning halfway out his window.

"Can you do a half pump of sugar free vanilla, too?"

Ben grumbles in the driver's seat while Quinn talks with Jonah.

"I think he's got the order, Quinn. Put it back in your pants," Ben scolds.

Ryan and Maggie crack up.

"Ben, there's no stopping him. You have to let him work it out of his system," Ryan advises.

Jonah passes their coffees through the window. Quinn's is last and has a large dome filled with whipped cream.

"Thanks, Jonah. If I lived here, I'd visit your hut every day," Quinn says, waving good-bye while Ben rolls up his window from the driver's controls.

Maggie turns around in her seat. "Was he everything you'd hoped?" She winks at Ryan.

Quinn takes a long sip of his iced concoction. "And more. I need a hut boy to call my own. Or maybe Ryan will role-play hot barista with me when we get home." He dramatically sucks his drink, and winces.

"Frozen headache." He cringes and rubs his forehead.

"Quinn, never ever change." Maggie faces forward, giving Ben directions back to the beach.

Gil thinks the same about Maggie.

Twenty-two

Biscuit runs to greet them when they walk up to the deck with bags of groceries and wine. Jo lies on her stomach on the chaise, but stirs when their footsteps sound on the deck.

"Hey, sleepyhead." Ben walks over to her, bends, and kisses her head.

"Mmmm," is all that comes from Jo.

"I hope she put on sunscreen," Ryan tuts.

"I heard you," Jo mumbles as she turns, shielding her eyes so she can see them. "You'll be happy to know I did."

"Good girl."

Inside, Maggie puts the bags on the counter and glances over at the Scrabble board.

Someone played "HUMP" and a few other words.

"Is that how you spell jizm? Is jizm even a word?" Gil asks, looking over her shoulder.

"I honestly don't know. You're a guy, shouldn't you know these things?" She turns her head. He's standing right behind her and their faces are only inches apart. Her breath hitches. She wants to kiss him, but doesn't want an audience.

"I don't think I've ever used the word 'jizm' before this conversation." Gil blinks.

"Jizm isn't a sexy word. You should probably avoid saying it." Maggie's voice drops to a whisper.

"I agree. Jizm is a terrible word." He gazes down at her lips.

"Can we agree to stop saying jizm? Make some sort of pact?"

"Done. I'll never say jizm again." He sticks out his hand to shake on it.

Maggie grabs his hand.

"Say what again?" Quinn interrupts. "Ew, who played jizm? Is that how you spell it?" He grabs some tiles and spells "TWAT," and then walks away.

"Twat? Really, Q?" Gil asks. "Whose idea was this game anyway?" He strokes Maggie's palm with his thumb.

Her eyes flutter briefly. The feel of his touch runs down her spine. "What?" she asks, realizing she hasn't been paying attention since Gil took her hand.

"I asked whose idea was this anyway."

"What idea?" Maggie furrows her brows. Is he talking about them holding hands?

He squeezes her hand. "I was talking about the debauched Scrabble game. Not this." He squeezes again.

Her Gil-induced fog clears and she looks at the board.

"Oh, right. Dirty Scrabble was much more hysterical in college."

"I agree. Nothing shocks us anymore."

"You still surprise me," she says softly.

"I do?"

She glances down at their joined hands. "You do."

He brings their joined hands up to his lips and kisses the back of her hand.

"That's a good thing. I'll take it." He lets go, walks over to the counter, and begins unpacking the meat, putting it into the fridge.

Maggie stands at the table, staring at the board, and trying to calm her heart. She sees a word and plays it.

* * *

A few hours later people are spread around the house and out on the deck. Jo has given up her sunbathing for a shower and proper clothes. Selah sits outside with her iPad, scrolling through lumberjack sites. Ben takes out his phone on the sofa. Jo takes the phone and threatens to remove the battery if he doesn't stay off of it for the rest of the evening. Gil and Ryan sit at the table outside while Quinn stacks rocks on the beach.

Maggie looks outside from where she makes sangria in the kitchen. She smiles seeing all her favorite people in one place. A contented sigh escapes and she realizes she hasn't felt this happy in a long time. She adds a few blackberries and green apple slices into the pitcher of Rosé sangria, and puts it in the fridge to chill.

Cranking up the volume, she blasts Alicia Keyes on the wireless speakers for her iPod. Looking out to the deck, she sees Gil turn around and signal for louder.

She grabs the speakers and brings them out to the deck with her, placing them on the railing

"Better?" She sits down next to Gil.

"Definitely better." He squeezes her knee.

"What are you two talking about? I didn't mean to interrupt." She puts her own hand on Gil's.

"Patagonia," Ryan answers.

"The clothing company?"

"No, the place. I'd love to take a trip down there."

Maggie stares at Gil. "You went to Patagonia?" She's amazed by all his travels.

"I did. I went about three years ago. I needed to escape myself and the furthest end of the earth sounded like the right place to do it."

"Did it work? Did you escape yourself?" Ryan asks.

"Not really." Gil chuckles. "Turns out you can't run away from yourself. Life? Yes. Yourself? No. It was an enlightening trip."

Maggie does the math in her head. Three years ago would have been after Lizzy's death, and after things fell apart in Gil's marriage. She reminds herself he hasn't been her best friend in a long time. There is a lot to learn about this Gil.

"Wherever you go, there you are." Ryan quips. "Such a clichéd statement but true."

"Absolutely." Gil nods.

"Patagonia. Wow. I've never even been to South America," Maggie says.

"I went to a dermatology conference in Sao Paolo once, but barely left the hotel," Ryan says. "That's the thing with medical conferences and traveling for work. You might as well be in any conference center in the world."

"Medical conference in Brazil sounds like a cushy trip," Maggie comments.

"It was interesting. Not in the same way as hiking around Patagonia or a visit to the Galapagos would be. Different natural, or unnatural wonders, as it were."

"If you want glaciers, you could always hike to the Blue Glacier over in the Olympics." Maggie gestures to the mountains looming to the west.

"Glacier? Really? Aren't those disappearing?" Ryan asks.

"I think they are. Glacier Park will be glacierless in a few decades," Gil answers.

"What will they call it then?"

"The Park Formerly Known as Glacier? Or maybe a symbol?" Gil quips.

"Even more reason for you to come back out west, and hike the Blue Glacier while it still exists," Maggie says.

"Can you imagine Quinn hiking a glacier?" Ryan asks, looking over the railing at Quinn on the beach.

"I'd do the trip with you. It's pretty short. Thirteen miles up to the glacier, you can camp on the way up or on top. Three day round trip starting in the Hoh rainforest. Pretty cool." Gil sounds excited about the prospect of the trip with Ryan. Maggie smiles, thinking another connection has been made in the group.

"Maybe you and Quinn can come back next summer and we'll do a trip out to the Olympic Peninsula," Gil offers.

"As long as Maggie is out here, I'd love to make an annual trip. I know Quinn misses her." Ryan winks at Maggie.

"It's nice to be missed. Sounds like a great plan and I might even join you on your mountain trek."

"Maggie May mountain climbing?" Gil gives her an exaggerated look of disbelief. "Where is the beret-wearing, red-wine-drinking, pale girl from college?"

"It was my idea to hike the bluff the other day, remember? I hiked in college, at least down to the beach on campus and occasionally through the thousand acre woods."

"You had a thousand acre wood on campus?" Ryan asks. "That's one big campus."

"Technically, they have a thousand and ten acres. The tree huggers live in their tree houses deep in the forest."

"People live in tree houses on campus? What kind of hippie school did you all go to?" Ryan asks sounding more curious. "Quinn failed to mention tree dwellers."

"Not everyone lived in a tree house. I don't think anyone lived in them—had sex, smoked pot, and pretended to be Thoreau for a while, and then it would rain or get cold so they'd abandon the tree house for the next hugger," Gil explains.

"Evergreen is the ultimate Liberal Arts college, though most of us Greeners turn out okay," Maggie says.

Ryan shakes his head. "We had dining clubs and ties. No tree houses or nude beaches for me."

"Quinn told you about the nude beach?" Gil cringes.

"Wasn't a nude beach by the time we got there. Sadly," Selah says from her lounge chair, joining the conversation.

"Not fully nude, but I do remember some topless activity." Gil waggles his eyebrows.

"Perverts in the woods is the reason campus cops shut down the nudity." Maggie elbows Gil. "Perv," she says, looking at him.

"Who needed the nude pervert beach when our apartment in Olympia had the roof deck?" Selah asks.

Gil smiles. "That was a good summer. I'm still grateful it was one of the sunniest ones on record."

It's Selah's turn to say, "Perv."

"I think even the doctor would back me up on being a healthy twenty-year-old boy."

"Sorry, Gil, but breasts have never been my thing. Unless Quinn was naked sunbathing, you are on your own."

Maggie glances at Selah. They both look at Ryan and giggle.

"Was there ever any doubt? Quinn was all about no tan lines," Maggie says.

Gil groans. "I was not expecting to witness that. Ever."

On cue, Quinn walks up the stairs from the beach. "Whatcha talking about?"

"Your naked ass, as a matter of fact," Ryan answers.

Quinn chuckles. "Summer of '90? *Omnia Extares,* and all that school spirit."

Gil scrubs his face as if trying to erase the memory and the conversation. "I don't think the college's founders meant 'let it all hang out' literally. Then again, maybe they did."

"No tan lines." Quinn sighs.

"Don't remind me." Gil groans again.

Quinn plops down on the arm of Ryan's chair. "Any reason we're talking about that summer in particular?" He studies Maggie, and then Gil.

"No, we were talking about Ryan and Gil hiking the Blue Glacier next summer. Not sure how the topic turned to your ass," Maggie says.

"Are you sure you weren't talking about blue balls?" Quinn throws a look at Maggie.

"Glacier, not balls, Q." She stares back at him.

Quinn shrugs. "Speaking of cold things, what about the rumor of sangria?"

"Oh, right! I forgot I put it in the fridge to chill." Maggie gets up. "Who wants sangria?"

She fetches the pitcher and a stack of vintage iced tea glasses. When she returns, the sun moves behind the clouds and the air cools. Maggie pulls her sweater tighter around herself.

"Chilly?" Gil asks, rubbing down her arm.

"A little. I don't think we'll get rain, but it might be colder tonight."

"We definitely should make another beach fire. Or a fire in the house," Gil says.

Ben and Jo join them out on the deck.

"Speaking of tonight, will you manly men handle the grill? We can do the prep and dessert," Maggie suggests.

"What's for dessert?" Jo asks.

"I was thinking we could make s'mores around the fire," Maggie says.

"Classic. Good choice." Jo nods.

"Oh, you'll never go back to plain bar chocolate and marshmallows after Maggie's s'mores." Quinn practically drools.

"There's Nutella involved," Maggie simply states.

"Nutella? I'm in." Jo smiles.

"What is it with women and Nutella?" Ben ponders aloud. "Jo keeps it in the cupboard and eats it with a spoon. I've never seen her put it on anything."

"That's not true. I made Nutella pizza once," Jo explains.

"Nutella pizza?" Gil and Ryan ask at the same time.

"Like with pepperoni and sausage?" Gil looks horrified.

"No, no, no." Jo makes a face. "Dessert pizza with only chocolate."

"Phew. Thought you were talking about weird pregnancy food stuff." Gil sounds relieved.

Ryan and Quinn exchange looks. Maggie watches them have a silent conversation, and then Quinn nods.

"So, speaking of pregnancy foods…" Quinn begins.

"You're pregnant!" Maggie starts laughing.

"Um, Maggie, hate to point out the obvious, but Quinn lacks a uterus to be pregnant," Ben argues.

Maggie's eyes grow wide and she gapes at Quinn. Her mouth opens and hangs there.

"Q? Are you really?"

"Wait, what are you talking about?" Gil glances between Maggie, Ryan, and Quinn.

Maggie's eyes fill with tears. "Really? This is your news?" she asks Quinn, then places her hand over her mouth.

Quinn's eyes are getting glassy. He nods and grabs Ryan's hand. "We're having a baby."

"Oh, Q," Maggie cries and launches herself around the table to hug Quinn. She's full out crying now. She hugs Ryan, too. While the three of them hug and cry, the rest of the table sits in stunned silence.

"How's Quinn pregnant? He doesn't even look it. I mean, I know there have been advances and all, but I'm still pretty sure you still need eggs and a uterus," he says, sarcastically.

"Oh, Ben." Maggie laughs, wiping her tears. "Shut up."

Ryan wipes his own eyes. "We have a surrogate, Ben. She's carrying the baby for us. Donor egg, but our sperm."

Ben nods in understanding. Jo and Selah both join in the hugging of Quinn and Ryan.

"Congrats, guys," Gil says. "I didn't even know you wanted kids."

"We never thought kids were an option for us. We knew we might be able to adopt, but it wasn't something we wanted to do. Hell, we never thought we'd be able to get married, let alone have kids of our own," Quinn says, wiping away tears with the heels of his palms.

"So when is the baby due?" Maggie asks, using her sleeve to wipe her cheeks.

"January. We're past the first trimester. That's why we both wanted to be here this weekend—to share the news in person." Ryan beams with happiness.

"Quinn's having a baby." Jo smiles with motherly pride.

"Our Quinn is going to be a father," Selah says, sounding a little stunned, and a tiny bit betrayed.

"Selah, you will be the coolest Auntie ever. We promise never to make you change a diaper, or babysit until the kid can tell Monet from Manet." Quinn attempts to comfort her.

Maggie raises her glass of sangria. "To Quinn and Ryan, the coolest dads any kid will ever have."

Everyone clinks glasses and Maggie covertly rubs her nose on the cuff of her sleeve.

Gil hands her a bandana from his pocket.

She takes it, wipes her eyes, and blows her nose, then tries to hand it back to him. Realizing she is trying to give him his bandana covered in her snot, she laughs.

"Ew. I'll wash it and give it back to you clean."

"Keep it. I have plenty of them." He wraps his arm around her shoulder. "Wow. Quinn's going to be a dad."

"Wow indeed."

"You okay?" He softly asks in her ear.

"Yeah. I think so. It's funny to think of our group still having babies. Kind of a miracle and miracles are always good." Maggie reaches up and links her hand with his.

Gil squeezes her tighter against his side. "Life is full of surprises and unexpected joy."

Nodding, Maggie observes Quinn and Jo, who are deep in conversation about names. Ryan and Ben shake hands, and do a weird man shoulder pat hug.

"On that note, we should have some champagne and a proper toast." Maggie offers.

"Any excuse to drink champagne is a good thing in my book." Selah walks into the house with Maggie.

"I can't believe those bastards didn't tell me before," Selah says to her as they grab flutes and a chilled bottle of Veuve Cliquot she keeps in the fridge in case of an emergency celebration.

"They probably wanted to make sure everything was okay. These things can go wrong."

"I get it, I do. It's just the gays were my ally in the fight against the breeders. Traitors." Selah smiles.

"You have me. And Gil. We still live in the land of the childless."

"Oh, Mags." Selah hugs her. "Fucking Julien."

This makes her laugh. "He isn't the reason I didn't have kids, Selah."

"Yeah, maybe. He was still an asshole, though." Hugging Maggie, she continues, "I do like you saying 'me and Gil' like you're a team. It makes me happy."

"I like it, too." She nods as she skillfully opens the champagne—it barely emits a pop.

"Good. My work here is done. No more from me. I promise." After crossing her heart, Selah pretends to seal her lips and then tosses an invisible key over her shoulder. "Let's go toast to the gay breeders."

Twenty-three

Shivering, Maggie pulls down the sleeves of her black long sleeved T-shirt, wishing she grabbed her vest from the house before coming down to the beach for the fire. Grateful she changed into jeans before dinner, Maggie notices it's definitely cooler tonight than last night.

Gil takes off his flannel shirt, revealing a gray thermal underneath, and hands it to her.

"I can't take your shirt. You'll be cold." Maggie tries to refuse.

"I'll be fine once the fire gets going. Take it or you'll have to walk back up to the house to get something."

"Thanks." Maggie pulls on the green plaid shirt, which swims on her, so she cuffs the sleeves. She inhales the Gil scent that surrounds her: sun, salt, and summer. Happiness.

Warmer already, Maggie grabs some thin pieces of kindling and stacks them in between the firewood.

"We forgot the newspaper." Ben searches for it around the logs.

"Don't need it. Selah, give me your lighter." Gil sticks his hand out. He uses Selah's lighter to light the small kindling. Soon the bigger pieces of wood ignite and the fire takes off.

"Impressive work, Morrow and Marrion." Ben admires their handiwork.

"You guys make a good team," Jo says, sitting on a log and stretching her legs out toward the fire, taking a sip of her wine. She's wearing black yoga pants and her blue North Face fleece again.

With her back against another log and knees bent, Maggie sits opposite Jo. Gil flops down next to her. Maggie observes a few bellies being rubbed and hears the sounds of satisfied post-dinner moaning.

"What is it about meat grilled over open flame?" Selah asks.

"Do you want the scientific explanation?" Maggie takes a sip of her wine.

"Rhetorical question, but I'm sure you know the answer." Selah lights a post-meal cigarette.

"I'm not moving ever again." Gil stretches his arms out behind Maggie. He rubs circles on Maggie's arm with his thumb.

"I haven't eaten this much meat in a long time," Selah declares.

Ben snorts.

"Shut it, Ben. I honestly think the pile of grilled veggies did me in. What sort of hocus-pocus did you do to them to make them so delicious, Magpie?" Selah says.

"Nothing. Some sea salt, olive oil, love," Maggie explains. "The magic of local grown, fresh, and seasonal."

"It's a delicious magic." Gil leans over and kisses her shoulder.

She notices he's having a harder time keeping his hands off of her after everyone is relaxed from wine and food. Maggie turns and smiles at him. "Thank you."

"Mmm... anytime."

She gets lost in his eyes for a moment. Maggie can feel her face begin to heat, and she isn't sure if it is the wine or Gil's attention.

"I could definitely get used to this lifestyle." Smiling, he turns away from her, poking the fire with a long stick.

"Oh, could you? Island living agreeing with you?" Maggie nudges his leg with her shoe.

"Definitely agreeing." He gives her a grin.

"Maybe you'll be invited again." She grins back.

"Maybe? Only maybe?" He nudges her shoulder with his own.

Biting her lip, she peeks at him through the corner of her eye. "We'll see how the night goes."

"Is that a challenge, Maggie May?" He leans forward and catches her eye, then puts his hand on her leg above her knee, and squeezes.

The heat of his hand warms her and her muscles clench.

"Maybe."

Gil licks the corner of his mouth. "Good to know." Leaning back, he keeps his hand on her thigh.

Mentally, Maggie fans herself. The fire in front of her isn't the only one she's playing with tonight.

Quinn and Ryan eventually make their way out to join the group after their turn doing dishes. They carry the s'mores supplies along with metal skewers from the kitchen.

"I can't believe I'm offering this after the meat feast, but who wants dessert?" Ryan gestures the platter of goodies.

"I'll never turn down chocolate or Nutella." Selah gets up to grab a skewer and marshmallow.

"I need to taste Maggie's Nutella s'more," Gil says, squeezing her leg. "Mind making me one?"

"If I can stand, sure." She pushes off the sand, using Gil's leg to prop herself up.

"Charred or not charred?" She waves a marshmallow in front of Gil.

"Charred, of course." He grins.

"Heathen." She teases and sticks the marshmallow directly into the flames. Pulling the flaming ball of goo out of the fire, she blows on it before handing the skewer to Gil. 'Hold this, and no eating it."

Carefully grabbing a graham cracker, she smears on a dollop of Nutella, then places the charred marshmallow on top before adding another cracker.

She licks a big dollop of Nutella off the side, getting some of the warm chocolate on the corner of her mouth.

"Here." She hands him the sticky mess.

"You missed a spot." He gestures to her lips before biting the s'more.

Maggie licks her lips, trying to get the smear of Nutella. She glances at Gil, who closes his eyes and moans.

"Good?"

"Mmmm.... mmm... mmm" is all that comes out of him. Still with his eyes closed he reaches up to swipe off the Nutella from his chin with his thumb. It's Maggie's turn to quietly moan as she watches him lick his thumb.

"Food porn as foreplay?" Quinn asks as he sticks his own marshmallow into the flames next to Maggie.

"What?" she asks, completely unaware of where she is.

"You have it so bad." Selah chimes in from behind her. "Move out of the way or toast another marshmallow." She bumps Maggie with her hip.

"More," Gil says, opening one eye as he pops the last of the s'more into his mouth.

"Best s'more ever?" Maggie asks, grabbing another marshmallow.

"Best ever." Gil winks. "More."

"Greedy." She chars another marshmallow.

The rest of the gang is likewise toasting and moaning over their creations.

"Where was this when I used to smoke pot?" Quinn asks.

"I'm grateful Nutella wasn't around back then. I would have been as big as a house," Jo comments, eating a perfectly toasted but not charred marshmallow.

Maggie hands Gil another s'more, which he snatches from her like a starving man.

"You okay there, big guy? Can I make one for myself now?"

Gil gives her a stink eye but nods his head, his mouth too full to respond verbally.

Maggie sits back down next to Gil with her own s'more. She takes a bite, closes her eyes and moans.

When she opens her eyes, she catches Gil licking the s'more right before biting it.

"What the fuck?" She tries to save her s'more from his greedy mouth, but he is too quick.

"It was dripping and going to land on my shirt. I was trying to be a gentleman and protect you from molten hot sugar."

Maggie stares at him.

"Not buying it?"

"No." She licks her lips where the melted marshmallow makes them sticky. She watches Gil staring at her lips.

"Can I help you with that?" He offers, his eyes flicking to her mouth, and back up to her eyes.

"I think I've got it."

"I'm not sure about that." He reaches out his index finger and swipes under her bottom lip. He shows her the chocolate. She grabs his finger, sucking it into her mouth.

"Mine," she declares after she licks his finger clean.

Gil whispers, "That's the sexiest thing I've seen."

Maggie gives him a small smile. "Good to know." She pops the last bit of s'more into her mouth.

"Talk about food porn," Selah comments from her spot at the fire.

Maggie realizes her little show with Gil's finger had an audience. She's grateful the firelight hides her blush.

Gil leans over to her and brushes her hair over her shoulder. "I love that you still blush."

His whispered words brush against her ear with his breath, sending a shiver down her back. Gil quickly nips her ear and retreats.

The soft moan that escapes her this time has nothing to do with Nutella. She crosses her legs and squeezes as familiar warmth spreads through her body before leaning into Gil a bit more. As he extends his arm behind her she realizes they've tuned out the rest of the conversations around them.

"If the baby is a girl, what would you name her?" Jo asks Ryan and Quinn.

"Lizzy," Quinn answers. Ryan nods.

"Oh, Q, that's so sweet," Jo approves. Maggie smiles and her eyes tear up. Gil squeezes her shoulder.

"And for a boy?" Maggie asks.

"Not as sure. We want to avoid any places or things. Logan, Austin, Cooper, Brooklyn, and those sorts of names are out," Ryan says.

"We also want to avoid any pop culture trends," Quinn adds.

"No television characters or vampire names?" Selah teases.

"I still can't believe there's a girl named Quinn." Quinn huffs. "I mean come on. Clearly, it's a masculine name."

"Maybe the television writers are familiar with your work," Ryan says. "Could be a tribute to you."

Quinn quirks an eyebrow at his husband. "Nice try. I'll buy it, cause I love you."

"What about Aslan?" Maggie teases.

"No pop culture, Magpie."

"I kind of like Aslan. It suited you in college."

"They called you Aslan in college?" Ryan looks intrigued.

"The long wavy mane of blond hair drove everyone wild."

"I bet." Ryan ruffles Quinn's short hair.

"I'm sure you'll find the perfect name," Jo says. "This is going to be the most spoiled baby ever."

"I doubt it," Selah disagrees. "I remember seeing pictures of your nurseries. Wasn't there a life-size stuffed sheep involved?"

Ben laughs. "The kids loved the sheep. So did the dog, unfortunately. And not in a brotherly-love kind of way."

"Ew. Your dog humped the sheep?" Selah asks.

"Yes. It was even more horrifying when he did it in front of the nanny." Jo cringes.

Everyone cracks up.

"I can't imagine." Ryan laughs. "Okay, no life-size stuffed sheep around dogs."

"I can't believe our Peter Pan is growing up." Selah sighs.

"Oh, this doesn't mean I'm going to be a grown up, Elmore. I'll still be the most immature, fun forty something you know." Quinn nods.

"I don't doubt it," Ben agrees. "But life changes, Q. You'll be surprised how your priorities change."

"Like going to bed at 10 pm." Jo looks at Ben's watch and yawns.

"Okay, old lady." Quinn tries to stifle a yawn, too.

"How come you feed kids sugar and they go crazy, but we eat it and crash?" Selah asks before succumbing to a yawn.

"Could be the multiple bottles of wine and the huge meat feast have had something to do with it." Jo yawns again. "It's almost eleven. That's a respectable time to go to bed." She stands to dust sand off her legs as Ben heads toward the house.

"Night all," they call as they walk up the steps to the deck, holding hands.

Maggie doesn't feel tired and turns to face Gil.

He strokes her arm. "Should we let the old folks go to bed while the fire burns itself out?"

"Sounds like a plan to me," she agrees. She turns to Quinn and nods toward the house. He stares at her for a second before realization dawns he's being dismissed.

"Come on Big Daddy, let's go to bed and sleep while we can." Quinn grabs the platter with the remainder of the sugar fest.

"Selah, you coming?" he asks.

Selah glances from Quinn to Maggie. Maggie tilts her head to the side. "Sure, since the sexy lumberjack stood me up, I'm frustrated and inspired to write some smut." She glances over at the dark windows of John's place. "Night, kids. Don't do anything I wouldn't."

"That doesn't leave out much." Gil laughs.

"Exactly," Selah says with a wink, and heads up to the house with Quinn and Ryan.

Gil stretches out more on the sand, extending his legs and rolling Maggie into his side. "Alone at last."

"You say it like you were tortured by the company of your dearest friends all night." She pats his chest where her hand rests.

"Tortured yes, but not by our friends."

"No? Then by what?" Maggie turns her head to look up at him.

"Oh, I think you know. What was with the finger sucking and lip licking? Were you trying to kill me?" He stares at her mouth. His eyes lift up to meet hers before he leans down and kisses her. The kiss isn't gentle or cautious.

Maggie takes a second or two to respond before shifting so she can kiss him more deeply. She swings her leg over his hips to straddle his lap.

"I thought they'd never leave," she mumbles into his mouth.

"Me neither." He kisses her neck and moves his hands up higher so they rest slightly below her breasts.

She softly moans.

"I've wanted to kiss you all afternoon. Why weren't we doing this all day?"

"I have no idea." She breaks away from his lips to kiss his neck.

"It was your idea to fly under the radar." Tilting his head, he gives her more access. Her hands wander down his chest.

"It was a terrible, terrible idea."

"Horrible." He kisses her again and rolls them on their sides.

"We're going to have sand everywhere." She giggles.

"Right now I don't care." He shifts his leg between hers, so she moves her leg up to align their hips.

They make out like teenagers on the sand as the fire slowly burns down. Coming up for air, Maggie notices embers have replaced flames.

"Maybe we should put the fire out and head inside." She pokes Gil's side to get his attention from where he's nuzzling her neck.

"Fire? Oh, yeah." He looks over at the embers. "You aren't going to send me to my room with Snoring Selah, are you?"

Maggie realizes she hasn't thought of where this is heading. She does know she doesn't want to stop and let her brain take over the what-ifs and what-does-this-means.

"No, you are definitely not sharing a room with Selah tonight."

"Thank god." He kisses her again. This kiss is different. This is a kiss of more than making out on the beach.

It makes her head swoon.

"Let's put out this fire." She breaks away from him. When she stands she feels sands shift out of her shirt. She ruffles her hair and the grit of sand is there as well.

Gil chuckles at her.

"Let's hope everyone's in bed. Or we'll have some explaining to do with you looking like that. You look thoroughly kissed. Lips swollen and your cheeks are extra pink from my scruff." He kisses her nose when he stands up.

"You have sex hair, mister. I wouldn't be gloaty if I were you." She tosses the bucket of sea water on the fire, causing it to steam and sizzle.

"Gloaty isn't a word. Sex hair? Really?" He looks pleased at the idea.

"Mmm hmm." She pulls her fingers through his hair. "Sex hair." She tugs a lock.

"Come on, let's see if I can sneak you into my room without the chaperons realizing." She takes his hand and pulls him willingly toward the house.

"Have you ever snuck a boy into your room before?"

"You'll be my first." She turns and winks at him as they walk up the steps to the deck.

"I'm honored," he says, formally bowing to her before walking across the deck.

The house is quiet and dark when they enter. Biscuit lifts his head from his bed, then flops back down with a sigh.

"Coast is clear. Lucky boy." She kisses Gil as she turns off the lone kitchen light.

"Oh, I'm a very lucky boy." He follows her upstairs to her room.

Twenty-four

Maggie reaches behind Gil to turn the lock.

"This door locks, too? Why didn't you lock it last night?" He grabs her hand as she brushes past him.

"I didn't even think about it. Not in the habit of locking my bedroom door or having men in my bed."

"Men? Plural?" He teases as she pulls him further into the room.

"A man. You. I'm not used to having you. Better?"

"Much better." He leans down and kisses her when they reach the bed.

Maggie gazes up at him, vaguely nervous about having him in her room behind a locked door and what that means. Before she can list all the cons in this situation, Gil lifts her chin with his fingers.

"Hey, don't overthink this. It's me. We don't have to do anything more than sleep." He bends to softly kiss her lips.

"What if I don't want to sleep?" She pouts.

"Ever? Not sure I'm up for an all-nighter." He teases, grabbing her other hand before kissing her pout. Stepping closer, their bodies meld together.

She pulls back a fraction. "You feel like you're up for something, though." Leaning forward again, she feels him against her stomach.

His laugh is nervous. "Oh, Maggie, what do you do to me? I feel like I'm twenty and you really have snuck me into your room."

She giggles. "It's kind of funny that we're sneaking around twenty-two years later."

"All we need is an *Annie Hall* poster on the wall and the Cocteau Twins on the stereo."

"That poster was so pretentious. You remember what was playing that night?" She studies him.

"I remember everything about that night. And the next morning." Kissing along her jaw, he gently pushes her back on the bed before crawling up next to her. His hand trails a path exposed by the open buttons of the flannel shirt over her T-shirt.

Maggie closes her eyes as memories flicker behind her lids. His touch, familiar and new, is a combination of memory and the unknown.

"What are you thinking about?" He whispers, brushing her hair back from her face, fanning it over the quilt.

"I was thinking of how nervous and excited I was to be with you. Everything was overwhelming." She turns her head toward him, and touches his face with her fingers, drawing them down his cheek and along his scruff-covered jaw.

"I was nervous, too. I couldn't believe it was happening. Even now it doesn't seem real. Maybe because you disappeared the next day."

She blinks at him. Butterflies flutter and her pulse quickens. "You were so intense and attentive. That was the single most sensual night of my life."

He gazes down at her face. "Up until that point, you mean?"

Maggie scrunches her brow. "Actually, ever." She rubs her thumb over his cheekbone, then leans up and kisses him.

"Ever?" He asks, intertwining their fingers and kissing her knuckles. "I had no idea what I was doing back then."

"You made me feel adored and worshiped. What could be better than that?"

"Nothing." He kisses her and the time for talking ends. He rolls so he's over her.

She wraps her arms around him, pulling him down to her. Their legs entwine and bodies align from memory.

His breath quickens when she reaches between them to palm him through his jeans. His moan makes Maggie giggle in her throat.

"I told you it's been a while. Laughing at me isn't helping things." He nips at her jaw.

"Sorry. It's been a long time for me. I love when I make you moan." She gently squeezes him, causing him to moan again.

He stifles any more of her potential giggles by kissing her. He rolls them, so she is on top.

"These shirts need to go." He tugs at the green flannel.

She pulls it off her shoulders, and lifts the hem of her black T-shirt. She's thankful she put on a nice bra instead of one of her usual beige. When her shirt comes off, she looks down at him.

He stares at her chest, looking infinitely pleased by what he sees. "Hello girls. It's been awhile."

This causes her to laugh again and his eyes flicker to her face. He grins. "What?"

"You're talking to my boobs. What do you mean what?"

"Shh, I'm saying hello to some old friends." He gives her a look before reaching behind her and unhooking her bra.

She holds the front in place as he pulls the straps down. "Stop being shy. It's me."

"I know, but your memory is of my twenty-year-old body. Not this one."

He sits up a bit and lightly bites her shoulder. "It's me. I think it is pretty evident I'm more than thrilled to be seeing you naked." He gently thrusts his hips, reminding her of her affect on him.

"This," he gestures at his own frame, "isn't the body of a college guy either. I know I've filled out over the years and am not the same lanky guy I was.

Feeling silly for being shy, she peels off the bra, and drops it on the floor.

"Beautiful," he whispers before gently kissing her chest.

Maggie hums at the touch of his warm lips on her flushed skin.

She tugs on the hem of his thermal. "Off."

He breaks away to pull off his shirt before tossing it somewhere in the direction of the floor.

"This is new," she says, dragging her fingers down his chest where he has more hair than he did at twenty.

"Not so new. Welcome to Gil, the man." He lifts her hand and kisses the inside of her wrist.

She wonders if he can feel the thrum of her racing pulse with his lips.

Skin to skin, they roll over on the bed, legs entwining and hips grinding. Hands stroke, cup, and touch. A familiar heat builds deep and low inside her.

Gil gathers her hair into a lose ponytail in his hand, and tugs her head back to kiss her neck. She squirms as his stubble drags down her neck, making her skin pebble.

She reaches down to his jeans, but pauses, and he looks at her. They stare at each other for a beat before he nods. She pops open the top button and notices he's wearing button flies. Some things never change.

He reaches for the button on her jeans and lowers the zipper.

"We don't have to do anything, you know this, right?" He catches her eye.

"I know. I need more skin, and it seems silly to be topless wearing jeans."

She rolls to her side to take off her jeans, kicking them off and to the floor, leaving her only in a pair of black boy shorts.

He lifts his pelvis and pushes down his own jeans, watching her the entire time.

"We match," she laughs, eyeing his black boxer briefs. She pulls him into a kiss before he has a chance to reply.

With nothing but thin cotton between them, she can feel all of him as they continue to kiss and explore each other.

She is exposed but not vulnerable. This Gil has the same emotion in his eyes as his younger self. She knows she's nothing less than adored in this moment. The entire night she's tried to turn her mind off and just be, but now she makes a conscious decision about what she wants.

With her fingers under his chin, she tips his face up to hers.

His eyes meet hers and he sees her determination. No hesitation lurks in her eyes as she reaches for him under his boxers. The feeling of her hand around his length causes him to close his eyes and hum in pleasure.

He feels her other hand pull and push his underwear down his hips. Opening his eyes, he watches her hand on him as she struggles to strip off the last remaining bit of clothing.

He sits up on his knees and she releases him. He attempts to remove his boxers, getting caught as he turns to get them off his legs. Flopping on the bed as he struggles, he laughs at himself.

"Yep, I still have the smooth moves." He finally gets his boxers off and kicks them off his leg.

Maggie giggles at his fish-flopping and then kisses his nose and cheeks. "Your smooth moves are one of the thing I love about you."

His eyes widen at her non-confession confession. She doesn't react, so he plays it off like she didn't just say she loves him. *She loves him.*

"Now what about you?" He looks down at her boy shorts still in place.

She lifts up her hips and slowly pulls off her underwear.

"Gorgeous," he says as he trails a hand down over her hip and cups her ass.

Kissing her shoulder, he gently rolls her on to her back. He props himself up on one elbow while his hand wanders down her body, charting a map of her curves. Reacquainting himself with her body, he watches his hand move over the swell of her thigh, moving toward her center. She gently parts her legs, creating space for his hand.

He explores her with his fingers, opening and caressing her. When she closes her eyes, he studies her face as he feels her body respond. He's in awe of her beauty, more so tonight than ever before. Her curves are more pronounced, but this is still the body he worshiped from afar all those years ago. Emotions bubble to the surface as memories combine with the new.

Slow exploration turns into more frenzied movements as the tension builds between them. Their kisses become sloppy with teeth bumping and lips being bitten. He shifts her so her head is cushioned in the pillows while he kisses down her body, dragging his scruff over her sensitive skin before pausing to kiss her hipbone.

She softly moans as his kisses become intimate caresses. When her body tenses, she lifts her hips off the bed, grinding into him while her eyes flutter and close.

He is gazing at her face when she opens her eyes again, his hand tracing her breast.

She turns on her side, facing him, and they lie there quietly, taking each other in, and feeling the warmth of skin on skin.

She brushes her hands over her breasts, and then reaches for him, stroking his length.

After a moment, she pulls away, and attempts to reach her nightstand.

"Condom?" he asks as she opens her drawer, producing a foil packet. "I never though to bring them and I don't carry one on me."

"No condom in the wallet anymore?"

"You remember that? I was so eager."

"You were a Boy Scout—always prepared."

"I was never a Boy Scout." He takes the condom from her and opens it. "Are we really doing this?"

"I hope so." She tugs him down over her.

"I want you, I've always wanted you." He kisses her as they join together. She moans as familiar feelings ignite.

"Maggie," he whispers, overcome with the sensation of being inside her again. He closes his eyes, absorbing the reality of being in her arms again.

She tilts her hips and wraps her legs around him.

"You feel amazing," she whispers in his ear, before swiping her tongue along his earlobe.

He groans louder and begins to move.

"You're amazing," he breathes out.

He falls into a rhythm, sensing her needs without words being spoken. Unlike his twenty-something self, he knows a few more tricks to pleasure her.

He watches as she tenses, keeping his rhythm steady. He reaches up and rolls her nipple between his fingers, and she comes undone. It's a beautiful sight. Her body's response pushes him over the edge.

He blinks his eyes as he comes down. Her arms are wrapped tightly around him, holding him to her, even though his weight must be crushing her.

"Amazing," she whispers, kissing his shoulder.

He lifts up and brushes her sweaty hair from her face. "How did I get so lucky?"

"I was thinking the same thing."

He wants to stay like this for as long as possible, but there is reality to be dealt with. He kisses her before pulling away from her to move off the bed toward the bathroom.

* * *

His absence exposes her overheated skin to the air, causing her to be chilled. Musing about how twenty-year-old Gil rocked her world, but how he has nothing on forty-something Gil, she snuggles under the covers and props herself up on her pillows. Her bliss is short lived as her mind jumps into hyper-speed. She slept with Gil. They just had sex. They had amazing sex. After three days together. Fuck. *Literally.*

Gil crawls back into bed beside her.

"Hi," he says, reaching out for her, and tucking her into his side.

"Hi. We had the sex."

"Yes, yes we did. You okay?"

"I think so. Maybe. I'm kind of freaked out. But it was good sex."

"'Amazing' was your exact wording." He smiles and kisses her head.

"It was pretty amazing. I'll be right back."

She gets off the bed and heads into the bathroom. She doesn't

186

turn on the light, not sure if she is ready to face herself and her "I've been properly shagged" face. She slept with Gil. Again. He's leaving tomorrow. What does this mean? She exhales, then takes a deep breath, attempting to quiet her mind. It's fine, she tells herself. *I'm an adult. We're adults.* Adults do this sort of thing. Friends with benefits. This won't change anything. *We'll be friends. We'll be fine.*

Finishing in the bathroom, she throws on her nightgown, and walks back into the moonlit room.

She climbs on her side of the bed and faces the edge. Gil spoons her.

"We okay?" he asks quietly.

"I think so. We're adults. We can handle this."

"Mmm, we can handle anything. Together." He dips his head to kiss her neck.

Her eyes are heavy and she snuggles into his warmth. "No Cocteau Twins this time," she mumbles.

"Are you falling asleep on me?"

"Sorry."

"Sleep, beautiful." He leans down, and she lifts her head to kiss him.

After a moment, he whispers, "I love you, Maggie."

She tries to keep her breath steady and even as if she is asleep.

He loves her.

He loves her.

He loves her.

Twenty-five

Gil's soft snoring breaks the quiet as Maggie tries to fall asleep. Sleep eludes her while her thoughts spin with images of their lovemaking, past and present.

He shifts away from her on the bed, but his leg still touches hers after he rolls on his stomach. She curls up and watches him before her eyelids get heavy.

A soft scratching at the door wakes her up. She stares at the ceiling as the pale light of predawn slowly brightens the day. Curled on his side facing her, his arm is draped over her belly as she lies on her back. She carefully moves his arm and gets out of bed to let Biscuit into the room.

Biscuit jumps up and curls by Gil's feet. She scratches the dog's head before getting back into bed. Gil's eyes open when she settles beside him. He blinks a few times.

"Hey," he says, reaching out for her.

"Hey." She moves into his arms. Whatever chaos is inside her head and heart, she's going to enjoy this quiet moment with him before reality sets in.

"So last night wasn't a dream?"

"No. You're naked in my bed."

"Hmm. Good. What time is it?"

"Six," she answers after looking at her clock.

"Way too early to get up."

He leans down to kiss her, keeping his mouth closed, and his morning breath to himself. She responds and wraps her arms around him. Curving into one another, his arousal brushes her leg.

"Sorry about that." He rolls his hips back.

"No apologies. Glad to know some things don't change."

Kissing by her ear, he whispers, "Shame to let something like that go to waste given my advanced age." He nips her earlobe.

Playful Gil is her favorite. Looking into his eyes, she sees no apprehension about his declaration as she drifted off to sleep. She kisses him more thoroughly—morning breath be damned.

Their movement disturbs Biscuit, who sighs and gets off the bed, curling up on his cushion by the window before turning his face to the wall.

"I think the dog judged us." Gil laughs, leaning up to see Biscuit.

"He did," she agrees, rolling on her side.

"Dog judgment kind of kills the mood, doesn't it?" His arm covers his eyes.

"Does it? It's not like he's staring at us."

"There's that. Come here." He pulls her back into him. She yawns and tries to hide it behind her hand.

"Sorry."

"More sleep?"

"More sleep." She kisses the side of his mouth and lays her head on his chest. Stroking her hair, he lulls her back to sleep.

* * *

She opens her eyes again and the room is brighter.

"Morning," she says, as Gil stirs beside her.

"Morning part deux."

It's still early, but no longer dawn. She stretches out, catches him watching her, and yawns.

"Doesn't seem right to be up this early on a Sunday." He looks over at the clock: 8:00.

"It doesn't. But we don't need to get up because we are awake." He moves toward her. She blinks at him, chasing the sleep cobwebs from her mind, and yawns again, covering her mouth with the back of her hand to avoid blowing morning breath in his face.

"Be right back." She crawls out of bed and goes into the bathroom. Doubt, insecurity, and confusion are creeping back in as the day brightens outside.

When she returns, Gil is stretched out on his stomach across most of the bed, rubbing Biscuit's belly.

"Want me to leave you two alone?"

"I'd prefer you and Biscuit switching places."

"You want to rub my belly?"

"Sure. I was more thinking I'd like you back in bed, but if a belly rub is what you want, I'm happy to oblige." He pats the bed.

"I should let him out." At the word "out" Biscuit's ears perk up.

"Why do I have the feeling if I let you leave this room, whatever enchantment we were under last night will be broken?"

She looks at him without answering and senses her shell reforming. Wanting to avoid any talk of last night, or confessions, or what next, she moves toward the door, giving him a soft smile.

"I'll come back, I promise." She grabs a short, striped, gray robe from a hook on her door. Biscuit jumps off the bed.

True to her word, she returns a few minutes later without Biscuit.

"Looks like we are the first ones awake. The house is still quiet." She gets back on the bed, but leaves on her robe.

Stretching his body, he reaches out and touches her leg—the only thing he can touch of her as she perches on the edge of the bed.

"I guess more sleep is off the table."

"I'm wide awake now," she mumbles, another small yawn escaping.

"I can tell," he says, laughing.

A quiet falls over them as he strokes her leg and she gazes out the window at the water.

Turning to face him, she opens her mouth to speak at the same time he does.

"About last night—"

"So—"

They laugh.

"Go first."

"No, you go first," she says, putting her hand over his.

"This feels awkward." Brushing his other hand through his hair, he meets her eyes, and gives her a small smile.

"What is it about the bright light of day?" Her laugh is full of nervous energy.

His nervous laugh mirrors hers. "Okay, I'll go first." Sitting up, he turns toward her, so she can see his face more clearly.

"What happened last night wasn't a one-off thing for me. This weekend has been more than I could've hoped for. You need to know this.

This wasn't about sex for me. Not after all this time. Not now, not twenty-two years ago."

Maggie watches his face while playing with her hands in her lap. She shifts her legs, tucking one leg under the other. Her silence encourages him to continue.

"I didn't come here to win you over or back or anything. There was no winning on my mind. I wanted to see you again. Then I saw you and everything came into focus."

Maggie reminds herself to stay calm and listen to him. Should she tell him she heard his whispered words last night? Can she pretend she didn't and hope this isn't going where she thinks it is? She isn't ready and feels her anxiety rising at the thought of facing her feelings.

"Gil..." she says, touching his hand.

He continues, "I need to say these things and you need to hear them. I'm not waiting another twenty-two years."

She braces herself, remembering to breathe in, breathe out.

"Maggie, I couldn't tell you when I fell in love with you, but this weekend has reminded me that I can't remember a time when I haven't loved you."

A breath catches in her throat as she listens to his words.

"I think you know I love you. Not past tense, not friendly love. Love. Love that lassoes the moon and lays it at your feet." His heart beats a steady, but nervous cadence.

Staring at him, she can only blink as his words wash over her.

"I've loved other women and nothing compares to my love for you. Maybe we were meant to go off and love other people. Maybe now we realize what a gift we've been given. I love you, Maggie."

He sits quietly, watching her face.

"You love me," is all she manages. Her vocabulary and ability to string words together abandon her. Thankfully, nothing pithy or joking comes out either.

"I do love you."

More silence fills the space between them.

"You've always loved me," she continues.

"Pretty much. Yes."

"You're telling me this now."

"I am."

Her chest feels too small for the heart beating inside it. Controlling her breath, she tries to think of what she should say. Does she love Gil? Of course she does.

"You know you love me, too," he says, reaching out for her hand while looking in her eyes.

It's overwhelming. She turns from his look, focusing on the small waves in the water beyond her windows.

She does love him.

"You know I love you, Gil. You were one of my best friends at a very intense point in our lives." It sounds lame even to her own ears. She is too scared to admit more.

"Yes, we were best friends. This is a different kind of love, though, and you know it."

She nods.

"Maggie, be open. That's all I ask. It's a big thing to ask of you, I know."

Conscious she is anything but open right now, she pulls her robe tighter and curls into herself. Her physical self mirrors her emotions.

"Open?"

"Yeah, the exact opposite of what you are right now." Tugging on her robe sash, he leans in toward her. "Let me in, Maggie."

"You've been in, if I remember correctly." She blushes at the double meaning.

"Yes, I have. But I was talking about your heart, not your body."

"My head is spinning. I just… I never expected all this."

He still holds the tie to her robe. They both look down to where he is tethered to her.

"I need coffee. I need a shower. I need to think."

"Coffee and shower sound good. It's the thinking I'm worried about." He releases the tie of her robe. "Hop in the shower and I'll go start the coffee." Getting up, he kisses her forehead and she leans into his touch.

* * *

Mind spinning, heart clenching, she walks into the bathroom and starts the shower. Facing the mirror, she reminds herself she is not a fickle twenty-something. She is a grown woman. She is wise. Hear her roar.

Gil loves her.

Hot water pours over her, steam rises and fogs the mirror. She contemplates staying in the shower forever. It's safe here, nothing has changed. Same soap, same shampoo, and the same pouf, which should have been replaced three months ago. Everything is same as it was yesterday, last week, last month. Safe.

Her fingers are beginning to prune while she stands under the water.

Gil.

His name repeats on a loop in her head along with memories of his touch, his smell, and his taste.

Gil loves her.

Foggy memories from college flicker in between the clear memories of last night. They weren't drunk last night. There is no excuse she can blame. She simply wanted him in her bed again.

When she remembers her house full of guests who might want showers, she turns off the faucet before she depletes all the hot water. She's going to have to face Gil. She can do this. As long as he supports her plan to play it cool and not discuss it, she'll be fine. She won't freak out. She nods. Fine. Cool. Got it.

Fine.

Cool.

Gil.

Gil loves her.

* * *

Maggie finds a quiet kitchen when she walks downstairs. Biscuit basks in the sun out on the deck. The water is running in the outdoor shower. It must be Gil.

Grabbing two cups for coffee, she makes one for herself and takes a long sip. The sound of the water shutting off alerts her to Gil finishing. She faces out the window above the sink, feeling shy, and wanting to give him some privacy. Yet she peeks when she hears him open the door.

"I wasn't sure you were ever going to get out of the shower, so I figured I should bathe while there was hot water." Walking into the kitchen, he dries his hair with the towel wrapped around his neck. He's wearing his jeans from last night, but no shirt.

Her eyes wander the paths of water drops on his chest.

"Eyes up here, sweetheart." Breaking her trance, the realization she's been sighing and staring at his chest flames her cheeks. "Not that I mind the staring. Just wasn't sure where things stood this morning." He ducks his head to catch her eye, smiling.

"Hi."

Taking the mug she offers, he makes a cup for himself then leans against the counter, crossing his legs at the ankle—the picture of relaxed.

"Hi. Good shower?"

"Yeah. Sorry about the hot water. Was there enough?"

"There was, but if you weren't downstairs when I finished I was going to break down the door to make sure you hadn't fallen, and couldn't get up."

Attempting a laugh, she makes an off sound that is a cough crossed with a snort.

"So, this is awkward. Yes?" He stares at her over his cup as he drinks his coffee.

"It doesn't have to be. I mean it shouldn't be. It isn't. Not really. Okay, maybe a little. Or a lot. Why is this awkward?" She babbles on for a bit before he stops her.

"It doesn't have to be. You were right the first time. I like you, you like me. We both liked what happened last night. We almost had a repeat of last night this morning. None of that was awkward. What changed?"

I love you, Maggie.

That's what happened. How does she tell him she's overwhelmed, and her head is too full, and her heart is scared?

Walking around to the other side of the island, she puts some distance between them, while drinking her coffee buys her a minute.

"So?" he asks.

Exhaling a deep breath, she meets his eyes.

"You did hear me last night, Fakey Fakesleeper. I can see it in your eyes. You have that scared rabbit look you get."

Caught. She nods.

"I did. I woke up this morning and thought maybe it was a dream, maybe I misheard you."

"Okay, Ms. Fakesleeper, don't add liar to your name. I thought you were still awake. That's why I said it. I shouldn't have said it last night."

"It was nice you said it. Don't take it back." Shifting on the stool, she stares into her coffee cup.

"Oh, I'm not taking it back. There are no do overs, Maggie. I meant it. I. Mean. It. Past and present tense. Then and now. I'm not talking about last night and this morning. I mean the first night we slept together."

"You didn't tell me you loved me back then. I would remember."

"I did say it. Only I was scared to say it when you were awake, and made absolutely sure you were asleep. I guess I hoped it somehow sunk in subconsciously, so when you woke you'd know I loved you. Bad plan."

This confession surprises her. She never heard his words that night. *Would things have been different if she had?*

"So?"

"What do you mean 'so'? You drop the bomb that you confessed your love to me then. You tell me you love me last night, and repeated it this morning. All this love is a lot to process. Two days ago, I still believed you were in a relationship." Her heart races.

"So?"

"So?"

"So now my feelings are out in the open, are you going to return the favor? What's going on in that mind of yours this morning?"

"I can't. I don't know. I just..." her words fade away as she acknowledges Gil loves her and he isn't playing it cool. All his cards are on the table, so she asks, "Do you want us to be a couple or date or whatever?"

"Maybe. It seems a little silly to date someone who you've known and loved for years, but sure we can date. I'll call you up and ask you out for three days later. Dinner, entertainment, kisses at your door." Gil jumps up on the counter next to the stove. Swinging his legs, his bare feet bump against the lower cabinets. She's staring at his chest again and she can tell he is barely hiding his smug amusement. His swinging legs and the grin behind his twitching lips give him away.

"We don't even live in the same place. You are going to drive all the way up here for 'dinner and entertainment'?"

"I'd very much be willing to drive up here to take you out. I'm serious. Take a chance on me."

Blood rushes in her ears. Love? Dating? Gil? All of this is not part of her plan—her quiet life and 'Maggie on the Island' plan. Her defend and protect instincts kick in as she tries to process his happy declarations and teasing.

"What do you want me to say? We haven't seen or spoken to each other in how many years? Five? It's not exactly like we've kept in close touch. This all seems a little out of nowhere and convenient to tell me the morning after we sleep together. Honestly, what do you want from me?" Maggie begins pacing around the kitchen, her anxiety bubbling.

"I want you to be open to the possibility. Of us. Of us being together. It isn't out of the blue for me. This is something I thought about for decades. Decades. I fucked up by not telling you ages ago. I get it. I think us all coming together here, now, isn't a coincidence. We wasted years. Decades. God, how can it be decades? I don't want to waste more time."

"I can't process this now. I can't."

"Don't shut down, don't shut me out again. Please." From his perch on the counter, he grabs her hand to stop her pacing.

She stares at Gil. His eyes are pleading and what appears to be genuine emotion is all over his face. *Is it love? Lust? Guilt? Hope?*

Quinn with his perfect timing walks into the kitchen wearing an ancient Inflammable Flannel band T-shirt and boxers. Maggie pulls her hand from Gil's and walks over to the window. Gil groans and hits the back of his head against the cupboard a few times. Quinn moves between them to the coffee maker, shaking his ass for Gil. "You can look at the pretty, but you can't touch this."

"Did you quote M C Hammer? Before noon? In the 21st century?" Gil asks.

"Yep," Quinn says, filling two cups with the last of the coffee in the carafe.

"Hey, you finish the coffee, you make more. House rules," Maggie tells him.

"Fine, fine." Quinn grabs the bag and begins feeding the beans into the coffee grinder on the machine. When he goes to the sink to rinse out the carafe and fill it with water, he looks at Maggie, and then glances between Gil and Maggie a few times.

"Oh wait. Did I interrupt something between you two?"

"No!" they both say at the same time.

"Jinx." Quinn eyes them with suspicion.

"Hey, what are you two doing up this early anyway? Maggie never gets up early on the weekends and it's barely past 8:30." He notices her wet hair. "Up and showered. Wait a second, wait a sweet second..." He looks at Gil. "...did you two finally consummate?"

Maggie blushes. *Damnit. Who blushes this much?*

"Why, Maid Marrion, I do believe you are blushing." Quinn teases.

"Shut up." Maggie can't look at either of them, but hears Quinn humming as he pours the water into the coffee machine. If they were eight, she would swear he was humming "sitting in a tree."

Maggie senses Gil jump off the counter and move toward her. She pretends she's looking out the window, but all she's really doing is trying to peer his reflection in the glass.

Her shoulders tense. Worried he is going to touch her. Afraid he won't. She's completely confused about what she wants and what she is too scared to admit.

She catches Quinn's eye and he gives her a questioning look.

He clears his throat dramatically, and mumbling something about seeing a man about a geoduck, he heads back upstairs.

Once Quinn makes his exit, Gil closes the distance between them, trapping her against the counter. She can smell everything that is good and Gil.

"Please."

"Please what?" she asks.

"Please don't let this all be nothing once we leave the beach. Please say we have a chance to make this more."

She closes her eyes, breathing in Gil, soap, and freshly brewing coffee. What is she afraid of? She has a job she can do anywhere, she doesn't have anything tying her down. Can she do this? Can she risk passing up a second chance?

She remains quiet and still, avoiding giving an answer she isn't ready to give.

Behind her, she hears Gil sigh and walk outside. Her own sigh echoes his.

What is wrong with her?

Maggie does the only thing that makes sense right now. She runs upstairs, puts on her running gear, whistles for Biscuit, and runs out the door.

Twenty-six

Maggie's calves burn as she sprints up the hill, pushing herself past her normal pace. Her breathing becomes ragged, and her head starts to spin. Turning up the volume on her iPod, angry music blasts in her earbuds.

Running on little sleep and only coffee is not the smartest idea she's had. *Neither is sleeping with Gil.* Her body aches in places that have nothing to do with running and her mind flashes back to his hands skimming down her back and hitching her leg over his hip. She remembers the way his scruff dragged along her skin, sending shivers down her spine.

Stop!

She tries to clear her thoughts and focus on her breathing. Sleeping with Gil isn't the issue. He isn't a real thing. He's nostalgic because of the upcoming reunion. There is no way he has loved her since college. *Who says things like that? He married Judith, didn't he?*

Maggie nods.

How dare he put everything on her. Her anger begins to simmer. She didn't run away to France. Her year abroad was a done deal before they even lived together for the summer. She doesn't run away from confrontation.

Except now.

She's literally running away from Gil and her house to avoid him. The irony isn't lost on Maggie and she begins to laugh. Biscuit gives her an odd look.

"Listen mister, don't judge me. I'm not losing my mind."

Realizing she is talking to the dog, Maggie adds, "Talking to you doesn't prove I'm a nutter." She sticks her tongue out at the dog. Biscuit looks away in what she interprets as doubt. "Okay, you're right. I am a nutter."

She accepts she can't literally run away right now. A house full of friends who are probably wondering where she's gone.

Turning for home, Maggie slows her pace, thinking about her ability to avoid what she doesn't want to face and what she's going to do about Gil. *Does she pretend nothing happened again?* That's not possible since Quinn sussed them out this morning. He's probably filled in the others already.

Avoid Gil? Maybe she'll play it cool and act like last night wasn't a big deal. Selah would do that. Sleeping, or fucking someone, isn't a big deal. Right. Right, not a big deal. Sex is sex. Love is an entirely different beast. She's experienced sex without love. This, whatever this is, is not that. Gil's words echo in her head.

But what to do about Gil's morning declarations? What about his actions and words all weekend? Selah and Quinn both seem to think she and Gil are meant to be. *Are they?* Even Jo seems to be on their team. *Is there a team?*

Have they wasted two decades over a silly miscommunication and comedy of errors?

It's too early in the day for all these deep thoughts. Maybe she can keep running.

After another grueling mile, the adrenaline from her flight leaves her. This isn't college. She can't collect her clothes, run home, and hide before her trip. This is her house and her life. Gil will be leaving in a few hours. He's the one leaving this time—leaving her behind.

All the fight goes out of Maggie. She's not the same girl she was twenty years ago. She isn't going to run. She'll face Gil, and talk this out like adults. Nodding her head, she turns toward home.

* * *

When Maggie approaches the cabin from the road, she sees Quinn sitting on the front steps.

"Walk with me, Ms. Marrion." After walking down the drive way to meet her, he turns left up the beach road.

"Ms. Marrion? Last name only? Am I in trouble?" She feels like she's about to get scolded by her father.

"Should you be in trouble? You ran out of the house like a banshee this morning."

"I went for my normal morning run," she lies.

"Bullshit. You were running away from Gil, like you did twenty years ago. No flight to France this time to save you. What are you going to do?"

"My first plan was to keep running. It didn't work out so well—I got tired."

Quinn links his arm with hers as they walk down the road to where the lagoon dyke separates the two halves of the beach.

"Why do you always want to run away from Gil?"

Maggie shakes her head. "I don't know. I just knew I had to get away before I made a bigger mess of things. Like I did in college. Did you know he was in love with me back then? Did everyone?"

"Unlike you, Magpie, we weren't blind. Or choosing to be blind. I think deep down you knew Gil loved you. And it freaked you out. Maybe you were too young to get yourself tied down. Maybe you were a chicken shit."

She scrunches up her face. "Probably both. I didn't want to rock the boat. We'd all gotten close. I didn't want to lose what we all had together."

"But Ben and Jo had gotten together, and they managed not to rock the boat. Why couldn't you have done the same with Gil?"

"I don't know! I didn't have the best track record with guys up until that point. No one stuck around for long or I lost interest. Gil was too important to lose."

"But you did lose him. You put him in a box and kept him there. He waited for you and you broke his heart, Maggie."

"He told me as much this weekend, but I didn't believe him."

"My point exactly. You don't believe what you see with your own eyes."

"I assumed he regretted what happened. I thought I threw myself at him at my study abroad going away party. I believed my feelings were all one sided."

"He was hurt. There was pining. He became a mopey bastard for a while. Of course, we all suspected something had happened between you two before you left, but he wasn't talking and you were in France."

"I was blind. How could I have missed all that?"

"You have a habit of rewriting the narrative to fit what goes on inside your head."

"This is true. I think that's why I married Julien. In my head, everything was perfectly romantic. The reality wasn't nearly as rosy."

Quinn begins humming an Edith Piaf song. "I think you fell in love with France more than him. Then you fell in love with sex. Sex can be a heady drug."

Feeling the familiar ache in her body that has nothing to do with her recent run, Maggie silently agrees.

Quinn lets go of her arm and turns to face her. "We aren't getting any younger." He taps the side of her eye where her laugh lines are. "You're single, he's single. You've dealt with a lot of shit in the past few years. Time to fly home from Neverland, Wendy. Look at me, I'm going to be someone's father. You can't hide out here on the island forever."

"You'll be an amazing father. You know I love this island. Don't be dissing the glory of island living."

"I get the love, I do. But you're hiding out. As fun as flirting with John is, do you want anything to happen with him?"

"No. Not really. And both Selah and Jo beat you to the hiding out speech." She reluctantly admits.

"You're becoming a geoduck, and I don't mean the euphemism for a dick."

"I did behave like a dick in the kitchen this morning. You're right about that part." Cringing, she remembers avoiding answering Gil's heartfelt question.

"You were. You don't have to die a spinster, alone with your cats and *Twilight* posters, because you are a single divorcee at forty-two."

"I don't even own a cat." She rolls her eyes.

"I see you don't deny the *Twilight* posters." He chuckles.

"I get your point, Q. I like my life. I'm finally feeling a little bit like myself again. I've been a wife, a divorcee, a doting daughter, a caretaker, and a grieving orphan. It's been a long time since I've been truly Maggie. I don't think I'm ready to be any title besides friend right now."

When they run out of road, they turn and head back to the cabin, this time walking along the beach. She unhooks Biscuit's leash and he runs ahead of them. As they get closer to her house, she can see Gil sitting on one of the sand mountains being built by a group of kids.

"Magpie, you know I love you. Always. But there is a man out there who loves you, too. You owe it to yourself and to him to tell him where you're at. Embrace the love or cut him loose. Don't leave him hanging like you did in college."

At the thought of admitting her feelings to Gil, her heart clenches. She can't, she can't do it yet.

"Hey Gil," Quinn shouts, and waves to get Gil's attention.

Gil turns toward Quinn and Maggie and gives a small wave before going back to instructing his minions on building his tower.

"No hiding now. Be a big girl and go talk to that man." Quinn gives her a shove toward the one man island.

"I hate you right now."

"No you don't."

"You're right. I hate that you're right, and wise, and pushy. The last part most of all."

"Shoo." Quinn waves her toward Gil before taking the leash and heading up the stairs to the deck. "Be brave."

Maggie watches the mountain builders running down the beach, leaving Gil alone.

* * *

She picks her way across the sand, side stepping the deeper pools.

"Hi," she greets Gil when she stands at the foot of the mound.

"Hi."

"Mind some company?"

"When the company is you? Never." He extends a hand to help her climb up his mountain.

"Thanks." She sounds awkward and unsure, reflecting her feelings.

Biscuit runs closer to them, stops and vomits up seawater.

"Looks like someone has been chasing geoducks." He laughs.

"Or he's hungover again." She attempts a joke. They fall into a silence that settles somewhere between uncomfortable and awkward, and lasts longer than a pause.

"I love how far out the water goes on this bay. The ever changing landscape is amazing. You don't get views like this in Portland," he says, not looking at her.

Okay, we're going with non-sequiturs and casual conversation. "You can see Seattle. It's sparkling.

"Like the Emerald City."

"We're not in Kansas anymore, are we Gil?" She looks at him, shielding her eyes from the strong glare off the water. The faded blue oxford would make his eyes stand out, if he weren't wearing sunglasses.

He shakes his head and continues to stare out over the water.

"I'm sorry—"

"I'm sorry—"

They both say at the same time and awkwardly laugh.

"What are you sorry about?" she asks. "I'm the one who freaked out and ran out of the house like a freak."

"Yeah, I noticed. I don't think I've ever had a woman physically run away from me before."

"Sorry. I kind of freaked out."

"You think?"

"A little." She pinches her index finger and thumb together. "Okay, maybe more than a little."

"I'm sorry for pushing things in the kitchen. I should have guessed you'd be skittish. If the past is anything to go by, I shouldn't have been surprised you ran away either."

"I'm not proud of the running, Gil. Or the freaking. Somehow when I'm around you this weekend, I feel nineteen again—in good and bad ways."

"At least there are some good ways. I thought there were lots of good ways last night."

"There were." She sighs.

"I hear a 'but' in your sigh."

She laughs. "You know me well."

"I do. It's nice to know someone, to have a history together, and a past full of memories."

"But we don't know each other anymore. Not like we did in college. We've changed. We've lived lives apart. Been married to other people. We're different now."

"True. We are different, but some things don't change. The part of me loved you twenty-plus years ago still loves you. I'm not going to regret last night. I never regretted our night together twenty-two years ago. But I'm also not going to let you run away again without knowing how I feel."

"It freaks me out."

"Gee, thanks." He faces out toward the water again.

Maggie cringes at the hurt in his voice. She reaches out to touch his arm. "I didn't mean it like that. I didn't mean it was a bad thing. I'm... Argh! Freaked out," she grumbles. "I'm freaked out by you walking back into my life and feeling like no time at all has passed. I'm freaked out we had sex. I'm freaked out by what this all means or doesn't mean, and what happens next." She takes a breath. "Mostly I'm freaked out by the thought of messing up again and not seeing you for years. Can

I overuse the word 'freaked' more?" She rolls her eyes at her lack of vocabulary.

Gil looks at her face. She's wearing sunglasses like he is, but she knows he can see the anxiety in her expression when he puts his arm around her shoulder.

"Hey now. Breathe."

"I'm starting to be myself again after all the shit with mom. I love my little life and my cabin, my island family of friends, and my dog. I don't have to worry what crisis awaits me when I wake up or someone else's needs taking precedent over my own. I realize I sound selfish."

"I get it. I didn't come up here this weekend with plans to seduce you and tear you away from the life you clearly love here. I was thrilled to see you again. It's been a long time since we have both been single and unencumbered."

"This wasn't 'Operation Get in Maggie's Pants' organized by you and Selah? She's devious."

"No. I will tell you Selah has been championing for me to reach out to you for years. There may have been a drunken night of shuffleboard right after the divorce, where I asked a few too many questions about you and it made her suspicious. Hidden beneath her smut-loving exterior is the heart of a romantic."

"I think that's why her books are so good. In between the pillaging and throbbing manhoods, there's always a love story."

"Please don't ever say throbbing manhoods again."

"What if it's about your throbbing manhood?" She grins.

"Are you flirting with me again? Cause if the answer is yes, I'll take it as a good sign we're getting past the awkward morning after." He smiles back at her.

"Maybe."

"I hope that's a good thing. I couldn't handle another French Incident." He rubs circles on her back.

"Gil, I'm sorry I'm a freak. I'm sorry I told you no about having a chance for more. I wish I could take that back. I wish I could be the woman you think I am, the woman you deserve."

"You are. You always have been. You need to trust yourself and your heart more than your head." He knocks on her head with his knuckles.

"This," she gestures between them, "this stuff, this banter and comfort isn't worth gambling. I got my Gil back and I'm afraid of losing you before I even get to know this new you. I'm afraid to fuck things up."

"You wouldn't."

"I might."

"Maggie, you can't mess this up. I understand you aren't ready to hear it, but I do love you. Not in the old friends way I love Selah, Quinn, or Jo. After this morning, I'm not going to push you. You know my feelings."

"I noticed you didn't include Ben in the love." She pokes him.

"Yeah, Ben is more of a deep like. Quit changing the subject."

Maggie nods her head and stays quiet. Her heart is racing at his declaration.

"I won't try to talk you into anything you're not ready for because the last thing I want is for you to feel uncomfortable around me. Just know I'm here."

She sighs. "It's a lot to take in."

"Do you regret having sex with me?" He cringes.

"No, no. Well, maybe a little. It complicates things. I don't want things to be awkward." She suddenly finds the sand on her feet fascinating. "But the actual sex was good. Great." She feels herself fighting a smile.

"Great? I can live with great." Gil grabs her hand. "We won't let this be awkward. We're not unsure, insecure college students. We're adults. We can handle this better than we did before."

She weaves her fingers through his. "You have so much faith in me, more than I have in myself."

"I have enough faith for both of us." He strokes the back of her hand with his thumb.

"I know it sounds lame, but can we be friends for now?"

He stares at her a beat or two. "Sure. Friends for now."

"Will this make the reunion awkward?"

"Why would it be awkward? Are you planning on bringing a date?" Gil jokes, but his voice lacks humor.

"Who would I bring?"

"I'm sure Paul Bunyan would be happy to be your date. For the reunion or anything else."

She shouldn't enjoy seeing Gil's jealousy but she does. "I told you, John is a friend. He's too much of a flirt to be serious about."

He grumbles.

She laughs at him.

"I'm glad you find my caveman emotions funny. I didn't get jealous over Judith. You're the only one who brings it out in me."

"I like that."

"I'm sure you do." He winks at her. "So, we're good here, Betty?"

"We are, Al." She feels slightly let down, but brushes it aside. "Now what do we do about the goon squad back at the cabin?"

"My guess is Quinn has already updated them." He gestures behind them to the peanut gallery sitting on the cabin's deck.

"They aren't so subtle, are they?"

"Nope. We should head back before the tide changes." Gil looks down at the wet sand surrounding their perch. "Though that doesn't seem to be for a few more hours."

"True, but eventually we'd have to swim back. I don't own a row boat to take us out to sea." She stands and pulls him up by their still clasped hands.

"Would one of those be a pea green boat?" He quotes one of her favorite poems, making her laugh. "Thanks for the chat. When you ran out this morning, I thought you might avoid me—and the elephant in the room—for the rest of the day." He wraps his other arm around her and brings her closer for a semi-awkward hug.

"I should be the one thanking you for not thinking I'm a freak."

"I never said I don't think you're a freak. I'm owning that some things will never change. Your freakiness being one of those."

"Gee, thanks," she says, pushing away from him. Maggie takes off her shoes and socks to descend their mountain.

After climbing down, he grabs her shoes to carry them for her.

She splashes through the refreshing chill of a small tidal stream between their oasis and the beach.

When they reach dry land, he spies a wishing rock. He picks it up and pockets it as she watches him.

"Hoarding wishes now?" she asks.

"You never know when you are going to need a little extra hope and faith."

Twenty-seven

Everyone appears occupied when Gil and Maggie step on the deck. Selah and Ryan seem to be having an in-depth discussion of bacteria on public transportation while Ben taps away on his phone, facing south toward Seattle as if the good cell reception will reach him from there. Maggie spots Jo inside at the dining table and wonders if she's playing another dirty word.

"You can't make this sort of down home charm shit up, can you? Did you know two llamas escaped on Campbell road? Only to be found grazing in someone's kale patch?" Quinn sits with the local paper spread on the table.

"Is the down home charm part the llamas or the kale patch?" Selah asks, not acknowledging the Gil-Maggie elephant on the deck.

"Hello?" Maggie asks, glancing at Gil. "Can they not see us? Are we invisible?"

Gil walks over and stands a hair's distance behind Ben.

Ben jumps. "What was that for?"

"Ben can see us."

"He might have super powers," Maggie stage whispers.

"We can all see you, Magpie. We're giving you some space. So are you two all settled?" Quinn peers over the paper.

"When's the wedding?" Selah asks, smirking.

Maggie blanches at the thought of marriage and a wedding.

"Kidding. Sheesh. You should see your face right now. You know I don't think everyone should get married." Selah looks at Ryan. "The gays can get married. I do support marriage equality. You all might do a better job than the straight breeders. Go for it."

"Thanks for your blessing, Selah." Ryan pats her shoulder. "I hate to bring up the end to this fine weekend, but what time do we need to catch the ferry to get back to civilization?"

"What time is your flight? Given today's a summer Sunday, the ferry line might be bad. We should have left a car on the other side last night," Maggie says.

"Quinn booked us an early flight tomorrow and a hotel downtown. We have no agenda as long as we get to SeaTac by morning."

"I figured Selah and Gil could give us a ride into town since they'll be driving through Seattle on their way south," Quinn says.

"Of course," Selah agrees. "Then we can spend the long wait in the ferry line grilling Gil about his weekend." She gives Gil a wicked grin.

"Great. Really looking forward to it." Gil rubs the back of his neck. The gesture almost makes Maggie feel sorry for him, but she is secretly happy it's him and not her.

"What about you and Jo?" Maggie asks Ben.

"We're the same. We're on the red eye tonight out of Vancouver. We'll avoid the ferry line and drive up the island. At least we can sleep in first class."

Jo joins them outside. "Speak for yourself. I can never sleep on planes. Well, not true sleep."

"Take a sleep aid. You'll be fine. I have to go into the office tomorrow at some point to check on the chaos created during my absence." Ben sighs.

Sitting on the arm of his chair, Jo wraps her arm around his shoulders. "It'll be fine."

"Everything okay at the office?" Gil asks. "You've been glued to your phone all weekend with the same sour expression on your face."

Ben sighs, again. "Yeah. Sure. Probably." After placing his phone on the table, he swipes his hands down his face. Jo squeezes his shoulder. "We might need to do a round of layoffs if the quarterly projections don't hold. Finance isn't what it was before '08. Fucking derivatives."

Gil and Maggie exchange looks that say this doesn't sound good.

"'We' as in you'd be the one doing the layoffs or 'we the powers that be' slashing jobs, including yours?" Gil asks.

"Both. Who knows? That's why working Saturdays is no big deal any more. Six day work weeks, twelve hour days are the norm, not the

For instance, counterhegemonic groups like KIWA that pushed the community to engage in open dialogue about internal inequities came into their own primarily through the support of labor unions and progressive groups outside the Koreatown community. The influx of mainstream resources after the 1992 civil unrest clearly provided an opening for female leaders and staff members and financed various programs focused on the needs of subgroup populations like workers, women, and youth. The likelihood of organizations serving and collaborating with other racial and ethnic communities also hinges on the amount of resources and organizational support they receive from mainstream American society. Bridging organizations like KYCC and KIWA were able to employ key non–Korean American staff members and service otherwise neglected minority populations in Koreatown with the assistance of government contracts, private funders, and ties with other racial/ethnic organizations.

Conversely, budget constraints and lack of outside support function only to preserve the more isolating and hegemonic features of ethnic political structures. The declining state of the economy and major cutbacks in social services under the current Bush administration will most likely shorten the range of organizational activities in Koreatown, with more severe repercussions for peripheral ethnic nonprofit organizations like KIWA. In recent years, KIWA has been forced to downsize its already-small full-time staff membership, although they are still mobilizing strong campaigns against supermarket owners in Koreatown. Conversely, KYCC has experienced a notable growth in its staff membership and service programs. In fact, during my last meeting with the executive director, he noted that they were fortunate to have the new office space in KOA because the organization had grown so large.

Crossing Boundaries in the New Century

While ethnicity is viewed as an important base for political empowerment in the present, it is not my contention that it is the most feasible path to political empowerment in the future. In particular, two aspects of American society warrant a more nuanced approach to political empowerment: first, the way political discourse and opportunity structures are partly organized around historically entrenched racial divides and second, the practicality of using larger bodies to address concerns that transcend neighborhood boundaries. Despite its multicultural population, the undercurrents of national conformity run relatively strong in the United States. This nationalistic framework, however, is based not on the restrictive model of Anglo-conformity forced upon Southern and Eastern European immigrants in the early twentieth century, but rather, a more diverse interpretation of societal relations based on artificially conceived notions of "race" and "culture." However, the con-struction of race among African Americans has taken a divergent path from that of Asians, primarily because the former group's subjugation has come to rest heavily on the color of their skin and a historical legacy stemming from slavery, whereas the latter has become increasingly centered on the foreign-ness of their physical features and questions about their cultural and political loyalties. The September 11 terrorist attacks on the World Trade Center and the Pentagon have cast widespread suspicion on immigrants and "foreign-looking" groups and reinforced the stigma of racialized citizenship for the Asian American population. The government has done little to ameliorate the situation by promoting aggressive anti-immigrant legislation; these include the USA Patriot Act (HR 3162), which broadens the government's powers of surveillance and investigation in the war against terrorism, and more recent congressional efforts to heighten border control measures and impose restric-tions on the rights of both documented and undocumented immigrants (for example, HR 4437).

Challenging claims that Asian Americans have been incorporated into American society as "honorary" or "token" Whites, this research highlights the adaptive strategies that Asian American organizations such as the ones in this study have taken to acknowledge the diverse experiences of their constit-uents. While mainstream America continues to categorize groups as "Black" or "White," Asian American organizations have taken their own diverse path toward collective empowerment in a manner that adapts well to the racial and ethnic mosaic of Los Angeles politics. By creating bridges to other racial and ethnic groups, these organizations are not dissolving the bonds of ethnic-ity so much as broadening the meaning of "Asian Americanness" within the framework of mainstream politics. In so doing, they hope to create a medium through which to articulate their political voice and ensure better representa-tion for their constituents in mainstream society, without undermining the shared values and interests that bring them together.

In the end, some organizations are expected to give way to non-ethnic-based organizations, some will retain their ethnic focus, while still oth-ers will become subsumed under other pan-Asian and umbrella organiza-tions. Yet among the various political streams that make up Asian America, the larger organizations offer the most potential for pursuing ethnic-based exception. Do more with less—the mantra of the post-recession world. It's fucking stressful."

"It must be stressful you're dropping f-bombs left and right," Maggie comments.

"With one income, we're screwed if things go tits up. Private school tuition for three, mortgage, lifestyle. Not that we're overextended. We're fine. Better than most." Ben glances up at Jo. Her perfectly smooth forehead disguises all but the smallest furrow of worry.

"All of it can go away. We could always hide away on an island and live off the land, like Maggie," Jo suggests.

"Ouch." Maggie cringes.

"That was rude. I'm sorry. This doesn't feel like the real world. You live a life completely about you and your desires. It's a good life. We fret about school tuition and building the right resume for our fourteen-year-old kids, so they can get into the right university, so their degree will mean something."

Jo's apology still stings Maggie. "I didn't exactly choose to move out here. Someone had to take care of my mother. Being single and childless meant I would move home."

"Hey now, no one is attacking you, Mags." Ben looks at her. "We all have our struggles and choices. Ditching the shackles of success and the money chase sounds appealing when you are sitting on a beach."

Bristling with the urge to defend herself, Maggie walks away and sits on a chaise next to Selah.

"We all make choices and live with those decisions. Even the choices out of our control lead us down the path," Selah comments and reaches over the space between the chairs to squeeze Maggie's hand.

"If anything, I envy your life, Maggie." Jo walks over and sits on the foot of the lounge chair. "My life hasn't been my own for over a decade. Rarely is a day about what I want to do or what I accomplish outside of the kids and not killing my husband."

Half smiling, Maggie squeezes Jo's arm.

"Fuck. Life is shit, it's tough, and not at all what we promised ourselves." Selah pulls her friends into a group hug.

"Great. Now they are hugging it out." Ben glances at the other men. "Does this mean we should hug?"

"Nah, I'm good," Quinn says, holding up his hands. "Life isn't all career and stuff."

"Says the man who has made a career about stuff," Gil says.

"Right, then." Ryan appears decidedly uncomfortable at the turn of the conversation. "With your experience, whatever happens, you'll land on your feet, Ben. I'm sure of it."

"I love it when you sound so assured and fatherly." Quinn glances at Ryan and smiles.

"I have exactly the life I always wanted. The career I imagined when I was in high school, the woman I fell in love with in college, the two-point-five children… it's all as I imagined it," Ben says.

"Who of our kids is the half child?" Jo asks.

Looking at his wife, Ben says, "Theo" at the same time she does. Laughing, they both nod.

"We've been very lucky." Jo smiles at Ben.

"You two have always been a good team. Even in college, as soon as you started dating, you were a team," Gil observes. "That's why you work. There was no team in Judith." He laughs at himself. "It made more sense in my head."

"I don't think I ever had things planned out. 'Be creative' was as far as I got. Marriage and kids weren't even on my radar. Or gaydar, as it were," Quinn says.

"Me neither," Maggie agrees. "To no one's surprise, I'm sure. You all have advanced degrees. I let my heart lead me. Good that it did. I'm just starting to put my career first again."

"You've had an interesting, adventure of a life. Don't sell yourself short," Jo tells her. "Conventional success isn't the only measure of a good life."

"I thought once you hit this age, life gets easier. You've established your career, the home, the spouse, the kids, and enjoy the comforts of a good income." Ben turns his phone over and over on the table. "Now it seems it can all go away at any time. When you get your own shit figured out, you're dealing with parents or kids, or both. Control is an illusion."

"Control *is* an illusion. Maybe our parents' generation was better at the smoke and mirrors of being real adults," Gil comments.

"The smoking probably helped, and the drinking at lunch." Ryan chuckles.

"I think my parents self-medicated with pot," Selah adds. "I'm pretty sure Mom has a medical marijuana prescription now. Anyone in California can get one."

"You sound a little jealous, Selah," Jo says.

"Completely. We were the first Prozac generation. Now we're the Xanax and Lexapro generation. Maybe pharmaceuticals aren't the answer."

"What was the question?" Quinn asks.

"The last time I felt totally in control of my life, and also the first time I felt like I was a real adult, was at twenty-seven." Maggie muses. "I had a husband, a career, a NYC life. Recent grads were young and silly. Anyone over thirty was stuck. Forty was ancient. Little did I realize how fleeting the feeling would be. How fleeting that life would be."

"Would you go back?" Selah asks.

"Me?" Maggie confirms. Taking a minute to think about it, she shakes her head. "No, I don't think I would. Would any of you?" She notices everyone shaking their heads.

"No do overs, even if we could go back," Gil says, catching Maggie's eye.

"I'd tell myself to worry less and put money into an IRA before thirty," Quinn says. "But change things, or hope for a do over? No. All of the noise and chaos in my twenties lead me here." He winks at Ryan.

"Wow. Philosophical discussion and Quinn comes in with sound financial advice." Ben turns his phone face down and pushes back from the table. "I wouldn't change my life with Jo. Change any one thing and none of us would be sitting here together today. It all fits together."

Gil and Quinn look at each other, and then at Ben.

"Ben is wise. Like Yoda," Quinn says, with a laugh.

"Wise like Yoda, Ben is," Gil adds in his best accent.

Everyone chuckles.

"I'm going to need to get more cats if I plan to die a lonely cat woman," Selah declares, mostly joking.

"You'll be an eccentric. Like Beatrice Woods, the ceramicist. Or Georgia O'Keefe. I think they both took young lovers well into their old age," Maggie suggests.

Selah tosses a look over shoulder toward John's house. "Yes, there is something to be said for younger lovers. I'll wear caftans and big chunky necklaces."

"You've already started on the chunky necklaces." Jo points at Selah's chest.

"And the younger lovers." Selah winks with pride. "Old age, here I come!"

"Didn't Mrs. Roper wear caftans and big necklaces, too?" Quinn comments and receives a glare from Selah.

"Is it too early for a drink?" Ben gets up from his chair.

"What time is it? I have no sense of the time." Maggie realizes she's still in her smelly running clothes, but the events and freak out this morning are a distant memory.

"Time for a Bloody Mary. Or since you have clam juice, Bloody Caesars. That's what time it is." Ben steps through the door. "Who is joining me?"

"Tomato juice in the cupboard. Pickled asparagus in the fridge," Maggie calls out to him.

"More clam juice. Joy." Selah deadpans. "Add double the vodka in mine."

"I need another shower," Maggie mentions to no one in particular.

"Outdoor shower right over there," Gil states out the obvious.

"What happened to friends?" Maggie asks, getting up to walk inside.

"Friends who have outdoor showers should use their outdoor showers."

"Oh, what the hell. It's not like you can see me in there. I'll take a quick shower while the Bloody Caesars are being made." She disappears inside to grab a towel and a change of clothes.

Gil cheers her easy agreement, noting she put up little resistance. Maybe, just maybe, her shell hasn't completely reformed.

"Ahem," Selah says, standing beside him. "I see your cocky smile, Mister."

"Not cocky. Happy. Maybe a little optimistic."

"Optimism works. No do overs, but you two are finally where you're meant to be."

"Couldn't agree more. Plus, I have a few of these as insurance." He pulls out the wishing rock from his pocket to show her. Selah moves to grab it out of his hand, but he closes his fist and returns it to his shorts for safekeeping.

* * *

Brunch is but a memory as Maggie stares at the piles of luggage filling her hallway. Bags are packed and the ferry line is being checked again from her laptop.

A lump forms in Maggie's throat as she thinks about everyone's departure. The cabin has been full of life and laughter this weekend. She's been full of life and laughter, too, and returning to her beloved quiet seems less desirable.

From the corner of her eye, she spots Jo struggling down the stairs with a tangle of linens and towels. "Here, you didn't have to bring those downstairs," she says, grabbing the mess from Jo. "You could've left the beds. I'll deal with everything this week."

"Oh, please. I can strip beds and gather used towels. It's practically my job," Jo says, handing off the massive pile to Maggie, and following her into the laundry room tucked off the kitchen.

Maggie holds back a snarky comment about a housekeeper and nanny doing the laundry.

"I can see you not commenting on the housekeeper and babysitter. Yes, it's rare I do all the laundry, but I can strip a bed. You wouldn't be able to imagine how many towels and clothes teenagers and tweens can generate in a week."

After stuffing the laundry on top of the washer, Maggie spontaneously hugs Jo.

"I know you, Jo. I know the girl you were and the woman you've become. Don't ever think I don't see you. Not mom, not wife, not Junior League member. Not Mrs. Benton Grant II. Not Josephine Asotin-Grant. Just you." She pulls back, and sees Jo has tears in her eyes.

"What brought that on?" Jo swipes at her eyes.

"I felt you needed the reminder. So much of everything we talk about when we talk about you is really about the kids and Ben, and Ben's job, and the kids' stuff. Sometimes the real Jo gets lost in everything else."

Jo gives her the once over. "Thanks. I think."

"You're welcome. The comments outside about me hiding out on the island and being selfish have me thinking. Yes, my life is all about me right now. Yours is the opposite. Right now. But it doesn't always need to be that way. For either of us."

Sighing, Jo hugs her again, then kisses her on the cheek. "Thanks for saying those words. I love my life. I do. I'm blessed in many ways and I feel terrible for ever wanting it all to go away sometimes. It would be nice to switch places for a day, or two, maybe a week. Or a month in the summer." Jo wipes away the dampness around her eyes. "We all have our challenges and paths. I chose mine a long time ago. It's what I know. It's what I love."

Maggie stares at her friend. "I believe you. Know I'm here if you ever want to vent or visit. Or do a *Freaky Friday* switcheroo. But rest assured, I have no intention of sleeping with your husband."

"Good to know about Ben." Jo giggles.

"What about me?" Ben stands in the door to the laundry room.

"Maggie is not going to sleep with you if she and I ever switch bodies," Jo says with authority.

He glances between them, shakes his head, and walks away.

"Poor Ben. He never did get my humor." Maggie giggles. Walking out of the laundry room, she sees Gil standing by the windows, looking out over the water. Footsteps echo in the hall as the last of the gang disappears through the open front door, the luggage pile greatly decreased.

She takes a deep breath before joining Gil. "Hi."

"Hi."

"Hi," she repeats.

"Isn't this how we started out this weekend?" He squeezes her fingers.

"Was that only a few days ago? It's hard to believe."

"It was. Four days ago. Under a hundred hours."

"A hundred hours? You counted the hours?"

He nods, then lets go of her hand, and wraps an arm around her shoulders. Thinking he's going to make another romantic declaration, she leans closer to him.

Leaning down he whispers into her ear, "I did the math in my head."

"That's not romantic."

"You didn't want romance, remember? You want friendship. Friends admit they've got no game." He grins at her as she pretends to pull away from his embrace.

She doesn't want romance because she doesn't want the complications. She wants friends with no game and comfortable embraces. She nods.

"Right. I chose the blue pill."

"*The Matrix* it is, then. We stay in the world of friends."

"Nice catch on the pill comment. I made some Agent Smith reference the other day to John and he didn't get it. He thought I meant *Mr. and Mrs. Smith.*"

"That proves he isn't the man for you, Maggie May."

Her old nickname makes her smile. "I'm still Maggie May?"

"You always have been, even when I didn't say it out loud. Once a Maggie May, always a Maggie May."

"Once and always," she echoes him.

Turning so he can gaze into her eyes, he repeats the words again, "Once and always."

Tears prick at her eyes and she hugs him to hide her watery eyes. *Gah*, she is going to miss him.

"I'm going to miss you, too." He rubs circles on her back.

She smiles, knowing he read her mind. He knows her so well.

A cough from behind them breaks their bubble.

"Um, yeah, sorry to interrupt, but the others sent me in here to remind you we need to, um, get down to the ferry line." Ryan couldn't sound more awkward.

Maggie wipes her cheeks and notices Gil's eyes are glistening.

"Sweet of the cowards to make the new guy come in and do their dirty work," Gil calls out, loud enough to carry outside. There is a shuffling sound as multiple pairs of feet move away from the front door.

"Again, sorry." Ryan turns and walks out the door, grabbing the last of the luggage.

Inhaling deeply, Maggie faces Gil.

"I really will miss you."

"You say this like we won't ever be in touch. It's not 1990. We have cell phones and the internet, and freeways and ferries. I know where you live." He rambles on a bit before she places her index finger on his lips.

"I promise I won't disappear. I owe Selah a trip to Portland and can probably do some restaurant reviews while I'm there. I'll make a week of it."

"Okay, my ego is not happy to be the add-on to work and Selah, but since we are doing the friend thing, I'll nod and say give me a call when you're in town."

Seeing his frown, Maggie attempts to backtrack. "I didn't mean it that way. I didn't want to give you mixed messages and... fuck. I don't know what I'm doing."

"Neither do I." He begins walking out the front door, her following behind him. "We've never had the awkward morning after goodbye. Let's say goodbye, wave, and pretend we'll see each other next weekend. We know we'll all be together in six weeks at the reunion. We'll chat in between and hopefully be cool when we see each other again."

Chewing on her thumbnail, Maggie listens to him, trying to agree with him. It sounds like a good, logical plan, but her mind and her heart are anything but logical right now. She wants to be cool. She wants to beg him to stay. A tug of war rages between her head and her heart so she says nothing.

"Nod if you agree," Gil breaks into her thoughts.

Nodding, she follows him outside where the others are gathered around the cars, waiting to say good-bye. Anxiety makes her heart race. "I hate goodbyes. I'm going to say that now." She stands up straight and squares her shoulders as she faces her friends.

Selah comes over first and hugs her. "Sweet girl, I know. Be kind to yourself. Nothing has to be figured out today," she whispers in Maggie's ear before stepping back.

Hugging everyone and thanking them for coming is almost more than she can handle. Promises are made to see each other at the reunion. Even knowing she'll be with them in a few weeks doesn't help. She doesn't want them to go.

The last person not in a car is Gil. He steps forward and kisses her at the corner of her mouth. Opening her palm, he places something warm and hard in her hand before closing her fingers around it.

"In case you forget and need a reminder."

Glancing down, she sees a perfect wishing rock. When she looks back up, Gil is getting in the car and everyone waves their goodbyes as they depart.

After closing his door, Gil sees her bring the rock up to her mouth and kiss it before closing her eyes. He wonders if she made a wish and what her wish might be.

"What did you give Maggie from your pocket?" Selah asks as she turns toward the main road.

"What she needs most. Hope and faith."

Twenty-eight

Walking back into the house, Maggie expects to enjoy the quiet and return to normal. Instead, she looks around, seeing emptiness and hearing the overwhelming silence. She whistles for Biscuit and grabs her keys. Coffee, she needs coffee.

When she gets into the car, she realizes she's still holding Gil's wishing rock, so she places it on the dashboard. Seeing it makes her smile, and her heart clenches in a sweet, but painful way. Sweet Gil.

No one is in line at Fellowship of the Bean as she pulls up in Bessie. Biscuit barks a greeting to Jonah from his position as co-pilot.

"Hey guys," Jonah greets them while handing Maggie a squirrel-shaped dog cookie.

"Hiya. Can I get an iced mocha, light on the syrup?"

Jonah gives her a look. "I know how you take your mochas, Maggie."

"Right, of course." She smiles at him.

"Distracted? Where's the merry band of fools you were with yesterday?"

"Sitting in the ferry line probably. They all left a little while ago."

"House too quiet for you?" Inside the tiny building, Jonah focuses on the espresso machine in front of him.

Maggie scrunches up her face. *Does everyone read her so well?* "Yeah, I guess. Plus, we had a pitcher of Bloody Caesars with brunch. If I drink alcohol early in the day, I need a nap. I'm hoping the caffeine will tide me over for a bit."

"I hear you. Was over in town last night to see a steampunk band and missed the last boat. Had to drive around and didn't get home until three o'clock. My ass is dragging today." He finishes her drink. "Whip?"

"Yes, please."

"Whip kind of mood. Sure you only needed the caffeine?" He winks at her.

"Maybe. Maybe not. The house is quiet. My life is quiet. Being around old friends made me think about stuff, you know?"

"I do. You know where to find me if you ever need an ear. Or to think about stuff out loud. I've learned a lot about people and human nature standing in this hut."

"I can only imagine. You must have all the dirt on everyone. You're practically a drive-up gossip booth."

"You don't want to know." Jonah laughs, and then shudders. "Here's your mocha. You and Biscuit should take a drive, enjoy the sun. Heard the rain is coming back this week."

Maggie hasn't paid attention to the news or weather report this weekend. She groans. "It is? Already?"

"Yeah, for a couple of days. Or so they say. Don't want to freak people out that summer is almost over."

"Hush. We have another month of summer, according to the ferry schedule and the calendar."

"Oh, I'm not wanting the season to be over. I'll cut my hours come November. Thinking about heading down to Mexico for a few weeks over winter."

"Eek. No coffee hut coffee? You're my salvation." Maggie frowns.

"Never fear, you won't be cut off from coffee entirely. Red Cat will be open and I won't be gone forever. You can survive a few weeks without me."

Jonah's "few weeks" comment reminds Maggie of the upcoming reunion. *Reunion. Gil.* She bites her lip thinking about him and his parting words.

"Earth to Maggie." Jonah waves his hand outside the hut.

"Hey, sorry." She reaches for her purse and realizes she doesn't have it. Or her wallet. "Um, oops. I don't have any money on me."

"You're out of it. No problem. Pay me tomorrow. Or this week. Or whenever. You're good for it." After making a note on a pad next to the register, he smiles at her. "Maybe you need a nap more than you think."

"Sorry. Thinking about the weekend. I'll get you the money this week."

Looking in her rear-view mirror, she spots a car waiting behind her. "I'm holding up the line. I'll catch you later. Thanks for the coffee." She waves and puts Bessie into gear.

"Drive or a walk with Babe?" She asks Biscuit. He barks his excitement, but she isn't sure to which part. "Babe?" Biscuit barks again and lifts his paw.

"Babe it is. You must be pining."

Driving past the fields on the way to the beach road, Maggie can see clouds gathering beyond the sun dappled water. It's been so dry and sunny here, she actually misses the rain. A good rainy day will suit her mood.

* * *

The ferry line slowly edges down the hill to the dock. Based on their location, Gil figures they should be waiting two more boats. Once they come to another stop and Selah turns off the engine again, Quinn gets out of the car to investigate an ice cream slash coffee shop.

"How does he stay slim?" Selah asks the car in general.

"Freakish metabolism," Ryan answers from the back seat of her Explorer. "Bastard."

She laughs. "Bastard is right. He eats nothing but crap."

"I swear he burns it all off with creative thinking. Or something." He winks.

Gil zones out in the front passenger seat, holding his phone. He has a full signal, and knows he should check voicemail and his texts. Instead he scrolls through some of the pictures he took this weekend—casual snapshots taken when no one was paying attention. There are a few of Quinn's Trojan dog and the Lost Boys, but his favorites are of Maggie laughing—the red in her hair flaming in the sunlight. She is a glorious thing to behold with her head thrown back and her eyes shut in full laughter.

Selah leans over and taps his screen. "That's a great shot. You should print that, maybe even frame it. You know what they say about lasting longer." Poking him in the shoulder, she teases him.

His thumb hovers over the image for a second longer before he swipes it across the screen, revealing a picture of Selah sucking on a crab claw. It's more than a little pornographic.

"I was thinking of this one for a collage for the reunion." Turning the phone so she can see it fully, he arches his eyebrow.

"You wouldn't dare. I am a respected professor!" Her indignation is a front.

"Yes, but the people at the reunion know the truth about you, and your past."

"You do have a point. Can you do something about the double chin?" Patting her chin, she stretches out her neck, and looks into the rear-view mirror, examining herself.

"Your neck is fine," Ryan observes. "Nothing a few collagen injections and a small bit of liposuction couldn't fix. Then again some men find waddles sexy." His smile gives him away.

"Hey, you, Mister New Guy, no talking about women's waddles."

"Doctor New Guy, thank you."

Quinn comes back to the car, carrying a tray of ice cream and a giant, frothy, frozen drink.

"You scream, I scream…" He hands out cups of ice cream.

"Um, thanks Quinn. No sprinkles?" Gil takes a cup of chocolate.

"No sprinkles or for Ryan, Jimmies." Quinn finishes handing out ice cream to everyone.

Cars begin to head up the hill as the ferry unloads. Selah starts the car when the line moves down the hill after the next boat is loaded. They stop short of the ticket booth and she turns off the engine. "Who wants to take bets on whether or not our island recluse friend will show at the reunion?"

No one raises their hand at first.

Thinking about his parting words to Maggie at the cabin, Gil slowly raises his hand.

"Sweet man." Selah pats his arm. "So, that's one yes, and three noes?"

"Not great odds, but better than no chance at all. I think progress was made this weekend." Nodding more to himself than anyone else, Gil goes back to eating his ice cream.

"By progress, you mean the fucking, right?" Quinn asks.

"Nice, Q, nice." Gil tosses his spoon at Quinn.

"Sorry. The lovemaking? Better?"

"Sex. How about sex?" Gil offers.

"I'd thought you'd never ask, but I'm sitting here with my husband, so this is a little awkward," Quinn says.

Rolling his eyes, Gil addresses the elephant in the car. "Yes, we slept together, had sex, whatever you want to call it. No regrets."

"'No regrets' doesn't sound like a grand plan to get the girl to me," Ryan comments.

"Oh, but you don't know this girl. She has to think it was all her idea."

"It's true," Selah adds. "Maggie will rebel if she thinks she is being pushed into anything. She's more stubborn than you can imagine. Just a matter of laying out the pieces, and then letting her figure everything out."

"Interesting. What's the legal term for that? Leading the witness?" Quinn asks.

"I think so, but I'm not a lawyer. Doctor, remember?" Ryan answers.

"Speaking of pieces, who started the dirty Scrabble game?" Gil asks. "It couldn't have been Ben or Jo since it was going before they arrived."

No one answers right away.

"Like I said, it's a matter of laying out the pieces." Selah smirks.

"Are you saying it was you?" Gil asks. "I swore that had Quinn written all over it."

"Why me?" Quinn attempts to sound innocent. "I am a gentleman, and like Maggie, would never use the C word in polite company."

They respond to his declaration with laughter. "Uh huh, Q. I remember a certain Warhol-inspired project."

"Damn you all and your long memories. Clearly you didn't do college the right way. Everything should be all fuzzy and vague." He crosses his arms.

"Since there are no do overs, we'll have to live with the memories we have. Or agree to the new versions. No reason why we can't follow in the grand tradition of historians before us and rewrite things to favor the victors," Gil says.

"I wonder how history will write this weekend," Selah ponders out loud.

"I'm thinking of Waterloo," Quinn says.

"The battle between Wellington and Napoleon? Who is who?" Gil furrows his brow.

"No, *ABBA*. Silly man." Quinn shakes his head.

"Oh, Q, so stereotypical," Gil admonishes. "That song is about surrendering… so I guess it does fit."

"I, for one, hate *ABBA*," Ryan replies.

"How can you hate *ABBA*?" Selah asks, the judgment clear in her voice.

"I do. Liking *ABBA* is not mandatory to be a fag."

"I like your husband, Q. He's a man of convictions." Gil smiles.

"Back off the hot husband. You've got a woman to woo."

"What's the plan, Gil?" Selah pushes.

"Now we, I, wait. I have faith," Gil says.

"Gil, I have faith in the both of you finally pulling your heads from your asses and figuring this out once and for all." Selah tosses her empty ice cream on the tray sitting on the console. "Sugar high in five, four, three…."

"I should have asked if anyone is lactose intolerant before getting the ice cream. This could be a long drive to Seattle," Quinn says.

"Little late." Gil rolls down his window. The horrified look on Quinn's face makes him laugh. "Kidding. Totally kidding."

The ferry pulls into the dock and the cycle of unloading and loading repeats, as a seemingly endless line of cars streams up the hill behind them.

"I can see why islanders stay put over here. This ferry wait is an exercise in patience." Ryan yawns and stretches.

"Many things in life are," Gil muses. "We don't realize it most of the time. We're busy rushing to get to the next thing, hit a milestone, or whatever. We're always pushing to get to the next stage, counting down to the next zero birthday, or being able to mark decade anniversaries. Being patient is a virtue for a reason."

Selah looks over at him. "Wise man is wise. When did this happen?"

"Not sure. Maybe five years ago at Lizzy's funeral. Maybe this weekend. Hard to say for sure. I'm not saying everything happens for a reason, only there are things that happen which fit together in ways we don't see until later." He rubs the back of his neck.

"You sound like a history professor," Quinn says.

"There's a quote about knowing history and not repeating history I could recite, but I won't. Let's say I've learned a lot in the past twenty years. I pray I'm not making the same mistakes now I made then."

* * *

Made the ferry. Thanks for everything.

Maggie reads the text from Quinn and smiles.

Miss you already. Safe travels. Tell everyone the same.

Another text pings from a Portland number that isn't Selah's. Smiling, Maggie opens it.

Quinn says he won't be our go between. Miss you.

She sighs and clutches her phone before responding.

Who is this?

A new text sounds right away.

Gil. Who is this?

Giggling, she types: *You texted me. Shouldn't you know? ;) *

A beat or two later there is a new text.

Funny girl. Take care of yourself. See you soon.

She smiles again. *You too. x*

Laying her phone down on the counter, she walks over to the dining table where the Scrabble game lays discarded. Many more words have been added and it's now an impressive array of swear words and body parts. She notices there is an "H" tile abandoned next to the board. Where it used to find a home is now "TRUST". This simple change causes her to smile. Did Gil do this? Or was it one of the matchmakers? Rather than sweep the tiles back into the bag, she decides to leave the board on the table for a little while longer.

She contemplates working on some articles or checking her email for new assignments, but the idea of work doesn't appeal. Not even as a distraction. Instead, she grabs one of her mother's romances from the bookcase and her coffee, before going out on the deck to catch the last of the sun before the rains come back. A simple, happily-ever-after riding off into the sunset is the perfect thing she needs.

Twenty-nine

Rain hitting the windows wakes Maggie the next morning. The gray sky gives little indication of the time. Stretching, she tries to remember what day it is. Biscuit yawns and looks at her, then tucks his head back down. It must be early. Craning her neck she can see 8:14 on the bedside clock. Early, but not atrocious.

She shifts to stare out at the monotone gray landscape where the water is lighter than the sky. This is a real rain, not a passing summer afternoon thunderstorm. Checking the weather forecast might be a good idea, she notes.

Mentally she goes through her day and then week, trying to figure out if she can stay in bed all day. Biscuit gets up and shakes, jingling his tags and collar.

"No run today, sweet boy." She snuggles further under the covers.

A wet dog nose pokes at her forehead.

"Don't make me get out of bed, please?"

Dog tongue licks her head.

"Fine. You and your tiny bladder. I should've gotten a cat."

She shuffles over to put on her robe. The room is chilly and she shudders when her feet hit the bare wood between the rugs.

She lets Biscuit out and he makes his way across the deck to the lawn. Wrapping her robe tighter around herself against the damp air, she wanders into the kitchen to start the coffee maker. The neatly-stacked plates in the drainer next to the sink make her smile. Something so simple is the sweetest gesture. Who knew a man who washes dishes, who loves to do the dishes, was such a turn on? She smiles at the image of Gil, hands and forearms soapy, standing at her sink.

She waits for the coffee to finish, pondering what to eat for breakfast. Setting a single bowl on the counter, she makes some yogurt. One cup, one bowl. Sighing, she looks out to the deck and sees a wet and muddy Biscuit standing by the door.

"How did you get this muddy so fast?" After grabbing his towel, she dries him off, before letting him in the house. He shakes off the last of the water, leaving sprinkles of sand and water on the floor. He trots over to his bowl and devours his breakfast before curling up on his dog bed, sighing in resignation.

Maggie hops up on the counter to eat her yogurt. There's nothing she must get done for the day, but she doesn't want to wallow, if that is what she is doing. She might be wallowing.

Dumping her empty bowl in the sink, she wanders into the den and turns on the television. It's early, but surely she will find something mindless on to watch—some housewives or dentally challenged people with interesting ways of making money.

Snuggled under a throw on the couch, Maggie wastes the morning watching TV. Finally grabbing her computer in the afternoon, she opens her email and finds her inbox bursting with new messages. She scans the typical blog notices, flash sales, and work related emails she can deal with later. Gil's name stands out amongst the usual suspects.

An email from Gil. She feels nervous. Silly but true. She puts off opening it, telling herself she needs to deal with a few work things, which are important but could be done later.

His unopened email teases and tempts her like a note passed in class in middle school that she wants to save to read until she is alone in a bathroom stall or home in her room with the door securely locked. A nervous fluttering settles in her chest.

She texts Selah for information on what happened on the ride back to Portland.

Everyone make it to their destinations last night?

Selah's response arrives a few minutes later.

Sorry. Getting coffee. Yes, we all made it. Fascinating conversations. Gotta run.

Typical of Selah to taunt her but not spill the dirt.

Tease. x

No response. It's Monday. People work. Maggie wonders what Gil is doing today. Her mind insists on drifting toward thoughts of him.

Finally unable to stand it any longer, she opens his email. The message is short—a thank you for the weekend and how great it was to see her again. Casual. Friendly. The postscript says he probably should create a password for his phone. There's an attachment.

She clicks to open it, and sees a picture of the two of them, sitting on a driftwood log. Taken from behind, they are turned, slightly facing one another, knees touching, heads close together. Beyond them is Quinn's dog sculpture and kids running on the beach, but they are in a bubble. The only two people on the planet. The afternoon sun gives them a glow and blurs their faces. If she didn't know better, the picture could be from college. They look ageless.

Maggie stares at the image, and blinks back tears. This is love. Not silly French accents and over the top seductions—a quiet, comfortable bubble.

"Oh, sweet Gil." His email was casual, but this picture says more than chatty words. It says everything.

Uncertain of what to reply, she saves the file to her desktop before closing the email. She tries not to think about all that happened over the weekend. Knowing she'll need time to process, she attempts to push his face from her thoughts.

"What am I going to do about you, Gil?" She dries her cheeks on the sleeve of her robe. Doing her best Scarlet O'Hara, she tells herself, "I'll think about it tomorrow."

* * *

Gray clouds allow fleeting patches of sunlight to brighten the days, but it rains every day the rest of the week. The rain isn't heavy—more of a mist—perfect for cool morning runs, enough to stay inside in the afternoons, working and watching TV.

It dawns on Maggie she's now caught up with every TV show that features housewives. Maybe she *is* wallowing. She tries to remember the last time she showered after taking two showers on Sunday. It's Saturday. Certainly she's bathed since Sunday. She vaguely remembers a particularly muddy run on Wednesday and showering after that. She sniffs herself.

"Shower," she declares. "Maybe time to get out of the house. Go visit Sally at the market." She nods. Having a plan is good; bathing is good.

The rain stops as she pulls into the parking area of the farmers' market. Mud puddles, where the dry earth was only a week ago, squish under the tires of the Subaru.

Her wellies protect her feet from the mud and wet grass in the field. Sally stays dry under a large white tent with all but one side closed. Looking around, Maggie notices she's the only other car in the lot besides Sally's.

"Slow going today?"

"Hi, sweetie. Been slow and soggy all morning. You show up and the sun comes out." Smiling, she hands a biscuit to Biscuit, who offers his paw.

"Where is everyone? I don't think I passed more than a few cars on the way over here. It feels like November already."

"It isn't that bad. Raining and the tourists stay away. Missed you on Tuesday. I see you've switched back to Saturday pick-ups again."

"Sorry. I've been working." She makes an excuse for her flaky behavior.

"Don't worry about it, sweetheart. You okay? You seem…" Sally pauses. "…not quite yourself. Did you have a bad time with your friends last weekend? Connie mentioned she ran into you at the store and you looked like a young girl in love. Handsome guy was with you, she said."

Connie.

"I knew she wouldn't be able to stay quiet after seeing us."

"You were topic number one when she stopped by this morning. In fact, you probably only missed her by ten minutes. She's concerned about you."

"Sally, we both know Connie's a gossip. It's her life."

Sally laughs. "Okay, that's true. But we're old and boring, and have lived here a long time. You're young and exciting to us old birds."

"Young? I don't feel young."

"Age is relative. Wait 'til you're my age. You'll realize forty is the beginning of really living."

"What have I been doing for the past twenty years?" She watches Biscuit wander around the tent, nose to the ground, snuffling for more treats.

"You've been figuring things out. Well, hopefully you have. Most of us don't even begin to know who we are until long after we're married and done raising our kids."

"I don't have either of those." Maggie frowns.

"Look at me putting my foot in my mouth."

"It's fine. You're stating the facts. No need to apologize. I've been pretty happy with my life."

"You have a good life. Maybe not the past few years. We all grow up by facing our own challenges. Your path is a little different. Typical or not, your mom was always proud of you and the life you created."

A smile spreads over Maggie's face. "Thanks for saying that. You always know the right thing to say."

"I don't have a daughter of my own, so you're the closest thing I have." Sally walks around to Maggie's side of the table to hug her. "You've got your island family. Never forget."

"Is Connie my gossipy aunt?"

"She is." With one last squeeze, Sally releases her. "Now tell me about this handsome guy."

"Gil. His name is Gil. We went to college together. Not much to tell," she fibs. Her face gives her away.

"Not much to tell? I don't believe that for a second. Connie was convinced you've been dating John Day, but I never saw that happening. He's not complex enough for you. What does this Gil do? Is he local?"

She is surprised at how much these women talk about her. Not sure what she should divulge to Sally, she keeps it simple.

"He's a professor. Lives in Portland."

Sally watches her face. "Simply the facts. Okay. I get it. Be quiet and stop prying." She walks over to where the weekly CSA boxes are stacked, attempting to hide her grin. "I promise, I won't tell Connie a thing about the sparkle you get in your eye."

"Sparkle?"

"Oh yes, when you think about that professor friend of yours."

Maggie's cheeks heat up.

"The blush explains a lot more than the sparkle. Oh dear, this might be serious." Chuckling, Sally hands her the box full of veggies.

She sighs and takes her box. "It's nothing. We're old friends who reconnected after not seeing each other for a long time. That's all."

"You know, I heard there is a zombie doughnut place down in Portland. Sounds like an interesting post for your blog."

"Voodoo Doughnut?"

Sally smiles at her, and gives her a knowing, motherly look. "Zombies. Voodoo. Same thing. Weird doughnuts, that's all I know. I'm just saying is Portland has lots of restaurants and curious food. Good chocolates, too. Be sure to have your friend take you to Alma Chocolate."

Confused by the talk of chocolates and undead baked goods, she tells Sally good-bye and whistles for Biscuit, who is wandering outside the tent. He trots over to the car, dragging his leash through the puddles and mud. Placing the box on the bumper, Maggie opens the back. Biscuit jumps on his blanket and she puts the veggies down next to him, it hits her. Sally thinks she's going to run off to Portland to be with Gil. What would give her that idea? She turns to wave good-bye to Sally, and sees her smiling.

"You can think I'm crazy, but sometimes us old birds know a thing or two," Sally calls out from the tent.

She shakes her head and replies, "You are a crazy old bird. Love you."

"Love you. Keep me posted. Let me know how things work out. Portland's an easy drive for the weekend. Don't ever sell the cabin."

She smiles as she drives away. They might be crazy old birds who gossip, but they are the only family she has here, and she's lucky to have them. Sell the cabin? Never.

Thirty

The sun returns, appropriately, on Sunday. Squinting, Maggie stretches and yawns as she gazes out the window to see blue skies once again. Biscuit's ears perk up when they hear barking from outside.

"Sounds like Babe and John are back." At the word Babe, Biscuit's starts bouncing his tail on the bed.

Inspired by the sun's return after her week of sloth, she throws on her running clothes before heading downstairs.

When she lets Biscuit outside, he runs next door, pouncing on Babe like long lost lovers. She notices John standing on his deck watching the dogs, and waves. He waves back, so she pantomimes drinking coffee. He laughs and holds up his cup, gesturing for her to come over.

After walking barefoot over the dew-covered grass, she joins him. "Morning."

"Morning. Already made a pot of coffee. You want some?"

"Looks like the tables are turned. Sure. Milk, please." While he goes inside to get her coffee, she sits on the built-in bench along the deck railing. Tilting her head back, she closes her eyes, absorbing the warmth of the sun.

"Here you go."

"Thanks. How was your trip?" She takes the coffee from him.

"Boring. Meetings. At least it was raining, so being trapped indoors wasn't inhumane."

"I love being inside, but you weren't cut out for a cubicle job. "

"Says the woman who doesn't work a nine-to-five desk job either. Working in your pajamas is an office worker's dream."

"True. I'm blessed."

"How was the rest of the weekend? Sorry I didn't stop by Saturday night. Ran into old friends and we ended up hanging out in Coupeville."

"Seems like it was the weekend for old friends. You have a good time?"

"Yeah, sure. Seems like everyone is married, settled. Kids or planning on having kids."

"I remember those days. Everyone turns thirty and freaks out that they should be married and procreating."

"That happened with you and your friends?"

Maggie thinks about it. "No, not really. Some of us were already married, some of us never wanted to get married. I spent my late twenties and early thirties getting divorced and dealing with my dad's death, so I was a decade ahead of everyone else."

"Shit. That's heavy. I feel like everyone has a timeline in their heads except me."

"I say don't worry about it. Live your life. Fall in love when you find the one and figure out your life together as you go. Schedules are for ferries."

"Sounds like good advice." He sips his coffee. "You going to take it?"

"Me?"

"Yeah, you," he says, smiling.

"I'm great at meeting deadlines and following a routine, so I'm assuming you aren't talking about schedules. It must be the part about falling in love. There's a long line of people ahead of you giving me advice about love, just so you know."

"Are you listening to any of them?"

"Was your work thing this week some sort of personal development retreat or something?" She eyes him suspiciously.

"Hell no. I would've called out 'fishing' if that were the case. Nah, I noticed how happy you seemed with your friends. Was good to see you laughing and being carefree."

His words settle as she remembers he isn't the only one to comment on how light and happy she seems recently.

"Am I really dour?" Drinking her coffee she waits for his answer.

"Dour? Not dour. Although, I'm not exactly sure what that means, but if it means you're a downer, no, not really. More like you've been in a fog."

"Hmm. You aren't the first to mention it. Sally was saying something about a spark in my eye yesterday."

"Yeah, I wasn't going to comment on that." He frowns into his cup.

Watching his face as he struggles with what to say, she knows it's about Gil so she prompts him. "Sally thought it was about Gil."

"That's obvious. You two seemed close. Plus, he looked like he wanted to invite me outside every time I saw him."

"Pistols at dawn?"

"Yeah. What's up with him?"

She answers him with her now standard, "just old friends."

"Bullshit," John swears, and then drains his cup. "Just friends? We're just friends. You don't look at me like you look at him."

"You and I have only known each other for a few years. We're different, less history."

John stares at her. "Are you telling me this or yourself?"

"Back to the cryptic remarks?"

"Okay, I'll be blunt. Why aren't you two together?"

"Wow. That came out of nowhere." She avoids eye contact.

"Cut the bullshit, Maggie. I have eyes. I've been flirting with you for months, and have never gotten a quarter of the reaction you gave him."

"But that's what we do, flirt. It's what you do. You flirt with me, Selah, the married summer women, and from the way she purrs around you, Connie at the bank."

"Yes, king of flirts. But I flirt with you because I like you. You're an amazing woman. I'm jealous of this Gil guy showing up out of nowhere and getting you."

"No one is getting me. Gil and I are friends. That's all."

"That doesn't make any sense. Not with the way you two act around each other." Exasperated, he puts down his mug and walks to the opposite side of the deck. Leaning up against the railing, he stares at the bay.

She can hear him mumble something about "women" and "crazy".

"I'm definitely crazy."

"Nah, not crazy. Stubborn," he says, and smiles.

"So I should take my own advice, then?"

"You'll figure it out eventually. That's all I'm saying."

"Gotcha. Can we change the subject now?"

"Sure. Want to catch a movie at the Clyde and grab a beer at the Doghouse after?"

She nods. Needing to clarify, she asks, "Not a date, right? Just friends, hanging out?"

John shakes his head. "After this conversation, nothing but friends. I promise."

Instead of a sense of relief, Maggie is met with guilt for hurting his feelings. Or at least she thinks she's hurt his feelings.

"I'm an asshole. I've been off all week." Gesturing at her clothes, she says, "I'm going to go running until I turn back into a normal human being who isn't an asshole."

"Good luck with that." John laughs and she joins him.

"Yeah, thanks for the encouragement. Mind if I leave Biscuit with you. He and Babe seem to be having their own reunion of sorts."

Glancing at the dogs tugging on the same piece of driftwood, he agrees. 'Yeah, those two are like long lost lovers, reunited after years apart, not buddies who haven't seen each other in a week."

"Point taken. Truce? I admitted I'm crazy and an asshole. What more can I say?" She sighs, rolling her eyes at herself.

"Nothing to me. You don't owe me anything. Promise me you'll be truthful to yourself. Deal?"

Digesting his words, she nods. "Deal."

"Okay, then I'll come by later and pick you up. Now go running. I'd like to hang out with Normal Maggie."

"Got it. Thanks for the coffee." She salutes him and walks back to her own house.

* * *

After her unsettling and awkward conversation with John this morning, her run feels good, even though her lungs burn after days of sloth. She waits for the endorphins of a runner's high to kick in, but once again she doesn't achieve the elusive bliss. Still, the repetitive pounding of feet against pavement sets a cadence for her thoughts. John, Sally, and Selah. Breathe. Gil. All of their words swim in her head as she deepens her breathing and slows her pace to work out a stitch in her side.

She breathes in the fresh air of the woods around her and exhales. So much can change so quickly, yet the view is the same as ever —same stoic trees, same fenced fields, and same mountains in the distance. Actors come and go, but the scenery of this stage remains the same. She remains the same. After years of uncertainty and upheaval, her own stoic life is a comfort. Nothing wrong with quiet, comfort.

Thoreau had his cabin by Walden Pond. Annie Dillard had hers at Tinker Creek. Maggie has the beach.

The Unabomber had his in Montana, a soft voice whispers in her head—a voice who sounds a little like Selah. The Donner Party had their cabins in the Sierra Nevada, says Gil's voice in her head. Nice, cannibals she thinks. Okay, so a cabin of isolation may not be the best thing for everyone.

Fine Young Cannibals' "She Drives Me Crazy" comes on her running playlist.

"Ha! Speaking of crazy women and cannibals." Looking up at the sky she shouts, "Someone has a sense of humor!" Laughing, she turns for home. She sprints down the hill, smiling as she remembers racing Gil back to the house on their run.

* * *

On track after her week of moping, Maggie faces her upcoming calendar of work and potential projects. After opening her laptop on the dining table, she scrolls through her inbox.

There is an email from her editor outlining a choice of travel assignments in September. Glancing at the calendar on the fridge, she reminds herself it is still August. The get-together has thrown off her sense of time and even what day of the week it is. Her typical life of singular company is unmoored after a few days spent with friends.

Her editor is offering her an assignment to cover a big farm-to-table dinner in Vancouver mid-month being hosted by one of the top chefs in British Columbia. The article will appear in one of the most prestigious print food magazines, now headed by her former editor. This could be the opportunity she's been waiting for to get noticed for bigger national and international projects. Her blog name in her byline couldn't hurt ad income either. Without checking her calendar, she immediately accepts the assignment. A chef's dinner with a world renowned restauranteur and getting paid to eat is why she loves her job.

"Who gets paid to eat amazing food?" Gesturing to herself with her thumbs, she says, "This girl right here."

The big assignment eases the discomfort she's been having over the past week. International travel, well, crossing the Canadian border in her car, but it does require her passport—she'll have to find it—is not something spinster, shut-in recluses do. Nodding her agreement, she clicks through the rest of her work related emails, feeling pretty good about herself. Better at least. September is shaping up to be a busy month. The last final burst of late summer produce means lots of fodder for the local food movement blogs and farm-to-table restaurants.

Her editor emails back a few minutes later, confirming the assignment. With a note saying hotel and the photographer information will follow, she gently reminds Maggie to put it on her calendar so there isn't a conflict. Rolling her eyes, she sighs. Once, one time, she double booked two restaurants on the same evening.

Oh, shit.

After flipping to her calendar for September, she sees 'REUNION' in bold letters across the weekend she agreed to go to Vancouver.

"Fuck."

"Crap."

She paces around the house, doing a figure eight around the kitchen island, back to the dining table and then looping through the living room, before returning to the kitchen. Pinned to the bulletin board on the fridge is a copy of the summer ferry schedule, a calendar from the bank, and the reunion Save-the-Date postcard. How could she forget? *Fuck.*

She can't back out on Vancouver because of a conflict. She'll look like an idiot to her editor and flaky to her former boss. Chomping on the side of her thumb, she makes another lap around the open room. Biscuit sits up and watches from his bed.

"Shit."

She never curses this much. Maybe she's developed Tourette's? Maybe she really is losing her mind. Was Miss Havisham crazy to begin with? Or, did all those years alone push her over the edge?

"Great, now I'm Miss Havisham. I'm talking to myself."

Of course, the dinner is on Saturday night. If it was Friday, she could do both the reunion and Vancouver. She fears the wrath of her friends, but she did spend a long weekend with them. They can't be mad if she misses the weekend for work. Work, career, all that stuff is important. Especially to Ben. He'll be supportive and take her side. Quinn and Selah will give her a hard time, but they'll understand. She nods.

What about Gil? Fuck. She hasn't responded to his email. Ugh.

"I am a terrible person. This is why I'm single."

Her pacing slows and she realizes maybe this conflict is a good thing. It buys her time and delays seeing Gil again. Gives her more time to digest everything that happened between them and wrap her head around her emotions. Relief spreads through her. This is the universe stepping in and making the decision for her. She isn't backing out because she is scared to move forward with Gil, she can't go to the reunion, and it's out of her hands.

Relieved she justified everything in her head, she sits back down at her laptop to email Selah and the gang that she won't be seeing them in Olympia after all. She'll keep it light, no big deal.

After she writes to everyone but Gil, she opens his email again. Studying the thumbnail of the two of them, her resolve falters slightly. She stares at the blank page of her reply, tapping her fingers on the keys, but not typing, and wonders what to say. She does miss him. Is it normal to miss someone so much you haven't seen in five years, haven't spent time with in twenty years, and saw for less than an hundred hours?

Thirty-one

Maggie hits send on her email to Gil. She bites the nail of her index finger knowing he won't reply instantly, but still fretting over his reaction.

Glancing at the time, she realizes she hasn't eaten lunch. The box of Captain Crunch calls to her from its place on the counter. It might make a fine lunch. In a bowl. With milk.

Emails answered, jobs booked, she feels productive thinking about the day so far. Time for a break.

After bringing her bowl of cereal and laptop into the den, she flops on the sofa. With the bowl carefully balanced on her stomach, she stretches her legs on the ottoman and flips on the TV to one of the food channels, which is on a commercial. As a food writer, she considers this research, which is part of work. Technically, she's being productive. Checking the guide, she learns the program is a hybrid travel-food show where the host visits local restaurants and has the chef show off their signature dish. This episode appears to be about Philadelphia. When the show comes back on, she pauses... on the TV is the French Incident.

"Holy crap." Her breath catches in her throat.

She knows Julien is successful, but what is he doing on TV? And since when is he in Philadelphia? What happened to New York? It appears to be the second segment of the show, so there's no mention of the restaurant name or what his signature dish is.

Not paying attention to the food prep, but the man on the screen, Maggie takes inventory. She's resisted searching online for him over the years. He's rounder and his hair is thinner, decidedly more gray than brown now. All salt, no pepper. His accent is overly thick. He's flirting with the young, thin hostess of the show. The accent always thickens when he flirts. The woman on screen appears fascinated and keenly interested in whatever he is making.

Maggie leans forward and puts her bowl on the ottoman. The soggy cereal is forgotten for the moment. After finishing a mirepoix, Julien continues with the layers of ingredients. He is making cassoulet— his mother's recipe, which she could never stand. Maggie makes a face thinking about it.

A flash of gold on his left hand catches her eye. "He's remarried. Of course he's remarried."

She tries to remember the last time she spoke to Julien. After the divorce, but before she left New York. It was one of those odd NYC run-ins. After going for years without seeing him, they bumped into each other at a tiny wine bar a few weeks after Lizzy's funeral. He was single then. She remembers being surprised he wasn't remarried. He was, and apparently still is, one of those serial monogamy guys. He loved being married and the idea of a wife.

Maggie makes a sour face.

What surprises her most as she watches him is how little she feels for the stranger on the screen. His face is familiar and his voice sounds the same, but this is not the man who swept her off her feet at twenty.

Gone is the special sparkle he would get in his eyes when he looked at her. Gone is the feeling in her chest when he whispered something dirty in French only she could hear. Gone is the loneliness of her marriage and the pain of ending their marriage.

She smiles, watching him present his finished dish and talk about his new restaurant. He is a stranger to her. Nothing more now than a box full of memories. She discovered her career thanks to him. Being married to an up-and-coming French chef opened some doors for her at food magazines. Her three years living with him in France perfected her French. Thankful for both those things, she wishes him well.

"Good luck, Julien." Raising her cereal bowl, she toasts him.

He would be horrified by her bowl of Captain Crunch for lunch. She eats a big bite and smiles. Soggy cereal is disgusting, so she brings the bowl to the kitchen to dump it in the garbage.

After finding her phone on the counter, she texts Selah about what happened and settles back on the sofa. She changes the channel to an old movie before any other ghosts pop up on the screen.

Her phone chirps with a message.

Julien. Ugh. Glad you didn't freak out. Is he fat?

Maybe. Married apparently.

Good luck to her.

Maggie chuckles. Selah knows exactly what to say to her.

Her ex-husband is remarried and she wonders if he has kids. Eyeing her computer, she decides to look him up online.

The first page of results is all about his new restaurant. Given her career in food, she probably should know this already. Thankfully focusing on the local foodie culture keeps her away from the drama and egos of the East Coast restaurant scene.

She amends her search and adds 'wedding.' Aha. Success. Looks like he got remarried four years ago. New wife is in her late twenties, one kid. A son. Madam Armand must be thrilled. Good for them. She can't find any information on what the wife does for a living. If Julien has had his way, she's probably a housewife. Nothing wrong with that. Nothing at all, unless you are Maggie. She realizes she has never pined for her marriage or missed the traditional expectations of his family. Not once. Her current life makes her happier now than she was back then, especially with the return of Gil. Smiling with her new knowledge, and the reminder she is better off without Julien, Maggie closes the search window as her email pings.

After switching to her inbox, she sees the email is from Gil. Perfect timing. First, the Fine Young Cannibals and crazy people living in cabins, now Gil popping up after the ghost of husbands past. Maggie looks at the ceiling and winks before opening Gil's email.

From: Gilliam Morrow <gmorrow@psc.edu>
To: Maggie Marrion <maggie@marrion.com>
RE: Weekend

Sounds like I lost the pool. Damn. I'm out $20. Yes, Selah had a pool going about whether or not you'd make the reunion. The odds were 3 to 1 you'd skip. I had faith in you, let the record show.

Can't say I'm not disappointed. Was looking forward to seeing you again.

We'll have to find another time to get together. I'll be busy with beginning of the year stuff for the next few weeks, but maybe October? We have a mid-semester break around Columbus Day. Let me lure you to Portland.

Glad you like the picture. I have no idea who took it either. Reminded me of college.

You'll be missed in Olympia.

What are your thoughts on the telephone? I hear you can use them for voice

conversations, not only texting. Thought I'd put it out there.
Take care of yourself, Maggie May.

They made bets? Damn them. They know her so well. She wishes she hadn't sent the other email letting them all know she wasn't going.

She quickly types a response to him.

From: Maggie Marrion <maggie@marrion.com>
To: Gilliam Morrow <gmorrow@psc.edu>
RE: Weekend
Damn. I'm sorry you are out the $20. I'll pay you back. I can't believe I'm missing the reunion. I agreed to Vancouver without checking my schedule. Completely spaced. Can I blame old age? ;)
Phone? What is this telephone talking thing you speak of? It sounds familiar, and very 20th century.
You have my number. I think I remember something from the dark ages about boys calling girls being the proper way of doing the talking thing.
Take care, Dr. Morrow. Good luck with those students.
X

Hitting send, she smiles. When thinking about Gil, she finds herself smiling a lot. Friends or whatever happens, she feels better for having him around again. Maybe she'll take Sally's advice and do a weekend trip to Portland. Check out the undead donuts and see Gil. Maybe even Selah, too.

* * *

Tuesday and Wednesday pass in a blur of writing, editing, and research, aka watching cooking shows. The rain gives way to long days of sunshine, so Maggie resumes her daily runs and walks on the tide flat with John. After their not-a-date movie and beer night on Sunday, things seem a little off between them, not strained but different. At least he still agrees to watch Biscuit when she goes to Vancouver.

Maggie works outside in the late afternoon sun on Thursday. Looking out on the beach from her spot at the table, Maggie watches John step out on his deck. He glances in her direction and she waves. He smiles and waves back, but doesn't come over. A few minutes later, a woman with long dark hair joins him. She squints, trying to see the woman's face, but the sun is behind them. Curious, she wonders if this is one of the old friends he ran into a few weekends ago. John didn't mention a woman, but then again, he wouldn't. She'll have to ask him about it tomorrow when he comes over for coffee.

Her ringing phone startles her out of her musings on John's imaginary love life. Almost knocking the phone off the table in her attempt to grab it, she barely glances at the name on the screen before answering. It's Gil. She lets out a breath.

"Hi."

"It's Gil." His smooth, bass voice greets her.

"I know. My phone told me."

Deep laughter comes over the phone. "I really do feel like I'm calling a girl in high school. At least your dad didn't answer the phone."

"That's the good thing about dead parents. You don't have to worry about them listening in on conversations with boys."

"Oh, shit. I'm sorry, Maggie. Not even a minute into the call and I've stuck my foot in my mouth."

"Stop. I was kidding. Seriously. Laughing about them being dead doesn't bother them. They're dead."

"Wow. Wasn't expecting the call to turn to death so quickly."

"At what point during this call did you think the conversation would work its way around to death?"

"You're laughing at me."

"I am."

"I'm nervous. I don't know why, but I am. Can we have a do over?"

"I believe it was my friend Dr. Morrow who told me there are no do overs in life. Sorry, no phone do overs either."

"This doctor sounds wise."

"He is. When he isn't continually bringing up my dead parents." Giggling, she tucks the phone under her ear and picks up her computer to bring it inside. She's not sure she wants John overhearing her conversation with Gil. Not that John is listening. She imagines he is distracted by his guest.

"Sounds like you are on the move. Is this a good time to talk? Should I have texted first?"

"No, it's fine. I'm out on the deck and moving inside. Do people do that? Text to talk?"

"Selah does it to me."

"Now you mention it, she does it to me too. Why not just call?"

"Were you working outside? In the sun? With the water behind you?"

"Jealous?" She teases.

"Damn. I have a window in my office but it faces north and looks straight into another building on campus. No view and no direct sunlight."

"Dreary. Are you at work?"

"It is and I am. Getting some prep work done for the semester. No students back on campus yet. Boring academic stuff and meetings."

"Not the glamorous academic life we're led to believe from television and the movies?"

"Ha! No." He laughs. "Not at all. Speaking of college, you're definitely out of the reunion?"

"Unfortunately, I am. I got an earful from Selah via text and email. Jo sent me all the info on the house rental, just in case. Quinn's giving me the silent treatment after a one word email."

"What was the word?"

"Fine."

"Ouch. You are in the doghouse now. Are you looking forward to the big assignment?"

"I know. I'm on a list somewhere where he's crossed out my name and maybe drawn a skull and crossbones next to it. I am looking forward to the dinner in Vancouver. Farm-to-table can be sea-to-table, so who knows what we'll be served."

"Geoducks perhaps? That would be fitting. You sitting at a fancy dinner, eating the carcass of your college mascot instead of attending the dreaded reunion."

"That's a macabre image. Fits nicely with the start of this conversation." She jibes him. Hearing a banging sound, she asks, "Are you hammering something?"

"No, that was my head hitting my desk."

"You were banging your head on your desk? Literally? Or figuratively, like in emoticon speak?"

"Literally. Next I'll bring up your dead puppy."

"Dead puppy? Biscuit is in fine health, mind you."

"Good to hear."

"He misses all of you. He's been in a funk for a week."

"Oh he is, is he? Just Biscuit?"

"No," she pauses, "not just Biscuit. I miss you all more than I thought I would. Cabin seems quiet and still now."

"I miss you too. Portland isn't far. Good for a weekend trip. The I-5 goes in either direction."

"Yes, I remember in your email you were going to lure me to Portland."

"I will. You wait and see. There will be luring."

She can hear more knocking. "Are you hitting your head on your desk again?"

Laughing, Gil replies, "No, not again. Someone is at my office door. Listen, I've got to run to a meeting, but let's do this phone talking thing again. I promise I won't bring up death next time."

"I like the phone talking thing." She's bummed he has to cut their conversation short.

"Sorry to go, but I've got to run. Your turn to call me."

"So forward and demanding."

"I've seen you naked. The least you can do is call me."

"Interesting logic. Okay, go. I'll call soon."

"Bye," he says as the phone disconnects.

Putting her phone down, Maggie sighs. As silly and odd as the conversation with Gil was, she smiles. The man can make her smile and laugh like no other. She does miss him. More than she imagined.

Her phone chirps with a text alert.

Bad timing on my part. Should've waited to call. Call me later. Or tomorrow. Soon.

I will. :)

Not feeling like writing any more for the day, she wanders over to the stereo. *Blue* still lays next to the turntable, so she plays it, turning the volume up loud.

When she notices the Scrabble board at the end of the table, she picks up the box to put it away. Before she folds the board to pour the tiles back in their bag, a thought occurs to her. Clicking the shutter button on her phone, she captures the layout for posterity. She texts Selah, Quinn, and Gil the image.

Selah responds first. *Trust is not a dirty word.*

The next response is from Quinn.

Still mad at you.

She doesn't hear back from Gil right away.

Glancing around the downstairs, she decides to dust. Something about listening to music her mother loved makes her feel domestic.

Duster in hand, she dances around, singing along to "California," the music too loud to hear herself.

The gentle scratching, skipping sound alerts her to the record finishing. Downstairs has been dusted and straightened. She turns the record over and heads upstairs to continue cleaning.

She enters the guest rooms and realizes she hasn't been in them since everyone left. Jo stripped the beds and the linens went back in the closet. Looking around Gil and Selah's room—really only Selah's—she spots a heart shaped wishing rock laying squarely in the middle of the pillow Gil used.

After picking it up, she closes her eyes and kisses the rock. Making her wish out loud, since no one is here to hear her, she says, "I wish for trust in myself and all things love."

She opens her eyes and tucks the rock in the pocket of her hoodie to throw in the water later.

By the time she goes back downstairs with her duster, the record has finished playing. Nothing but a soft hiss and a few pops come from the speakers.

The solitude she enjoyed during her year of mourning is now stifling. Maybe she is ready to return to the living.

Gil responds to her text later in the evening. *Trust. ;)*

His winking emoticon is so not like him, making her giggle.

* * *

Maggie calls Gil back the next day and they start a routine of talking almost every day for the next several weeks. Not texting and emails, but real voice conversations. Her little world is less quiet and less solitary. If she were honest with herself, she'd admit she was growing more and more disappointed she isn't going to Olympia in two weeks.

As their calls become daily, and on occasion, multiple times a day, she begins to think she should cross over the imaginary border she drew between friends and more to protect her heart. Gil doesn't raise the issue, nor does he shy away from flirting with her. He plays the game her way, no pressure from him. She shouldn't be disappointed he respects her boundaries even if sometimes she is. Maybe she is beginning to have faith when it comes to all things love and Gil.

Thirty-two

Another week of writing, running, and island living passes by in a flash. Labor Day comes and goes, taking away the majority of summer people, and a few of the Snow Birds. Long ferry lines disappear as August becomes a memory, and the second week of September begins.

Maggie finally receives a text from Quinn. She hasn't heard from him since his curt replies to her email and text. Reading his text, she chuckles.

You are the very worst kind of friend. Can't believe you are not coming this weekend. Geoduck hater.

Geoduck hater? Really?

Clearly. I hope the universe or karma or Buddha cancels your plans and shows you the path of righteousness.

Righteousness is a big word for a txt msg.

I've called in favors with the universe. Beware of Buddha's army.

Not being able to control her amusement, she snorts over his peevish tone.

Don't gloat, but I hope your favors work. I'll miss you guys.

You mean you'll miss Gil. I have spies. I know all about the talking.

She rolls her eyes.

Benedict Selah.

You should know better than to trust her.

She gets another text from Quinn before she can reply.

JSYK, we are all THRILLED about you two.

Um, thanks. I think.

Let's Skype this weekend when we are all in Olympia, and you are not.

Let's. Gotta run. Have fun.

We will. And I'll rub it in.

Would expect nothing else. X

XXXX

Oh, Quinn. She feels terrible for missing the reunion. Every day she talks to Gil her guilt increases. Their conversations remain just on the border between friend and more, straying across the line once in a while into flirting and sexual tension.

Shaking her head over Quinn's texts, she opens her laptop and tries to focus on finishing her research for the dinner in Vancouver.

An hour later, she wraps up her background research and decides to check her inbox. There is an email from her former magazine editor, with request for her to cover the new Portland food festival next weekend. In fact, it starts a week from today. This is short notice, but Maggie thinks she can do it. Quickly checking her calendar, after learning her lesson last time, she realizes she has the weekend open. Her excitement over going to Portland builds, and it has nothing to do with a food festival. This is the perfect excuse to visit Gil.

She picks up her phone and hits call.

"Why are you calling me?" Gil answers.

"Do I need an excuse?" She laughs.

"No, never. Just surprised at the timing. Two minutes ago I got a text from Quinn saying I lack conviction and proper motivation."

She snorts.

"Did you snort or are you near swine?"

"I snorted. Quinn texted me he's sending Buddha's army after me."

It's Gil's turn to snort. "Buddha's army is an oxymoron. Does Quinn realize this? And why is he sending fake armies after you?"

"He's pouting about me not going to Olympia this weekend."

"We're all pouting. I know I am. I've been writing your name all over my notebook and everything."

She laughs at the image. "I hope you don't do that in front of your students."

"I might. They need to know mooning over girls doesn't stop when you grow up."

"Speaking of mooning and girls, I think I have a job in Portland next weekend."

Silence greets her.

"Hello?" She checks the call hasn't been dropped. "Hello?"

"I'm here. I'm trying to get the picture of your naked ass out of my head, and come up with something appropriate to say."

"Why are you thinking of my naked ass?" She asks, confused by the jump in topic.

"You said, and I quote, 'speaking of mooning and girls.' I got distracted."

"Such a guy. Next weekend there's a new food festival in Portland, which my old editor wants me to cover. Last minute assignment."

"Any other reason you'd be coming to Portland?" He baits her.

"There's this guy I've been talking to on the phone a lot lately, and I was thinking it might be nice to spend some time with him. Maybe hang out, or go on a date, or something."

"Date? Will there be mooning on this potential date?" Gil laughs.

"On what date is mooning considered appropriate? Is that the fourth date? It's been a while since I've had an official mooning date. I'm pretty certain mooning is not first date material."

"We've known each other almost twenty-five years, I don't think we could ever have a first date at this point. I held your hair when you threw up on your shoes. You sat through my terrible band gigs where the band outnumbered the audience. These are things you only do well into an established relationship. Or never."

"True. Mr. Rochester would be appalled by shoe vomit. He'd probably never call back or stick around long enough for the mooning date."

"He'd be missing out. The good stuff, the very best stuff comes after you get past the mooning date. What are we even talking about?"

"I have no idea. I'm coming to Portland in a week and you brought up vomiting."

"I did. We have the weirdest conversations. Let's go back to talking about the good-looking guy you've been talking on the phone with."

"Who said anything about him being good looking?"

"Ouch."

"Don't tell him, but he is very good looking in a hot, older guy way. And if he plays his cards right, there could be potential nudity and mooning. Maybe. More likely yes."

"Maggie, don't tease."

"I'm not teasing. I do think you're hot in an older guy way. Kind of like how Dave Grohl gets better looking with time. In fact, you remind me a lot of him."

"Maggie."

Giggling, then sighing dramatically, she admits, "I want to see you. I want to spend time with you. And if things happen and paths are taken, I'm happy with that."

Silence.

"Hello?"

"I'm here. Are you serious? This doesn't sound like friend territory. This sounds like taking the red pill."

"It isn't friend territory. I realize how bummed I am about missing Olympia this weekend and it really has nothing to do with the reunion, or staying in a house with Ben and Jo and the rest of the gang. It has to do with not seeing you. Columbus Day weekend is so far away. Quinn was talking about pulling strings with the universe and maybe it worked."

"Does Quinn have those kind of connections? Cause if so, I'd like to put in a few requests."

"You know what I mean. I'm taking this assignment as a sign we've spent enough time on the phone talking. Time to be in the same place. See what comes." She surprises herself with how confident she feels about this.

"Wow. This is totally unexpected. So this is a done thing? You'll definitely be down here. No backing out or cold feet?" Gil smiles, but he can't quite believe her.

"If I have cold feet, I'll wear socks. Yeah, this is happening."

"Does Selah know?"

"No, I called you first. I wanted to find out if I should tell my editor I need a hotel room, or if I have a place to stay."

"You are staying with me. End of discussion. Don't tell Selah until next week. I don't want her co-opting all your time. Or better yet, don't mention it until after."

"I like this take charge Gil," she says, squirming on the sofa.

"I've waited long enough for you to come to your senses, I'm not going to sit back and let you slip away again."

"I won't. I promise."

"Good."

The conversation pauses.

"A week from tomorrow, then?" His voice sounds cautiously optimistic.

"Yes."

"I wish it was sooner."

"Me too."

"I can wait a week."

"Me too." She nods even though he can't see her.

"Then I guess I'll see you soon."

"You will."

"I look forward to the mooning." He teases.

"Glad to hear it." She laughs.

"I love your laugh."

Her breath pauses. He loves her, not only her laugh. This is a certainty, an absolute. No maybes. He loves her.

"Did you think I was going to say I love you?" Caution outweighs optimism in his voice now.

"I might have. And you know what?"

"What?"

"I am disappointed you didn't."

"Really. Well, then—"

"Wait!" She stops him from saying anything. "Don't say it now. A week from Friday." She wants the next time he tells her he loves her to be after she says it to him. He needs to see her face and her honesty.

"Okay. We're still playing this by your rules."

"Thank you. Listen, I'm going to go and leave this conversation on a good note before you bring up dead puppies."

"One time, I made everything about death. One time." He laughs.

"Once was enough."

"Once with you is never enough."

She groans.

"Too far?" He laughs at himself.

"And on that note, bye Gil."

"Bye, Maggie. See you next week."

"Bye," she whispers after the call disconnects.

Smiling, she bounces around her living room and does a shimmy dance. She's seeing Gil in a week. A week. What is a week when you've waited twenty-two years to say you love someone?

* * *

Despite the gray skies on Friday morning, Maggie grins when she wakes up. A week from yesterday she'll be catching the ferry to see Gil. Six more sleeps and she'll tell Gil she loves him too. She bounds out of bed, startling a still-snuggly Biscuit.

"Come on, sleepy head. We have a run to complete, beach to explore, and a bag to pack. You don't have any bags, but you are staying over at Babe's house this weekend."

At the sound of Babe's name, Biscuit gets up and stretches before bounding down the hall.

"Someone is excited to see his friend," she calls after the dog.

Dressed for her run, she lets Biscuit out, then makes his breakfast. While she waits for him to do his business, she starts a list of things to bring with her for the weekend. At the top of the list are her passport and power cord. She won't get far without either. The next thing she adds to the list is: find passport. Not quite sure where she put it, she guesses it's in the mini-safe in her closet. She pins her to-do list to the fridge and notices the ferry schedule is still the summer version.

"Now where did I put the fall schedule?" She taps her chin with the pen in her hand. "Did I get a fall ferry schedule?"

The schedule doesn't change much from season to season, but she knows a few of the early and late runs will be dropped with the dip in traffic.

Biscuit scratches at the door to be let inside, distracting her from the location of the new schedule.

"Eat up and let's go," she encourages him. She adds a few more things to her list on the fridge while she waits for him to finish eating.

They walk out the front door as John pulls into his driveway. He gives them a sheepish wave that makes her wonder if he is doing the drive of shame. It isn't too early for him to be running errands, but something in his look causes her think differently.

"Come by in forty-five and I'll make us some coffee. Looks like you could use it," she yells at him as she runs backwards up the road. Ear buds in place, she glances down at Biscuit. "Let's do this thing."

* * *

Forty-five minutes later, she is showered and making coffee in her kitchen when John knocks on the window.

"Come in, come in." She fills his cup with coffee and sets it on the counter.

"You're up and about early. Ready for the trip?"

"I'm getting there. Thanks for watching Biscuit this weekend. I'll happily return the favor any time you need."

"Sure." He drinks his coffee.

Hmm, someone is quiet this morning.

"Out running errands early?" She pries.

"No."

"Not telling?"

He looks at her and she can see his internal debate. "Getting home, in fact."

"That sounds much more interesting than errands. Name?"

"Kelly."

She goes through her mental file of names and faces on the island, and comes up blank.

"You don't know her. High school friend from Coupeville," he answers her unspoken question.

"One of the friends you ran into a few weeks ago?" She remembers him saying something about meeting up with old friends the weekend Gil was here.

"Yeah, that group."

"Wait!" She puts her coffee cup down with a thud. "Long dark hair, pretty face?"

He looks at her suspiciously. "Yeah, why?"

"She was over on your deck a few weeks ago."

"Are you spying on me?"

"No, I was outside doing work and you waved at me, but didn't come over. Saw the woman on the deck."

"Yeah, that was her. She's cool."

"My oh my, John Day sounds smitten. Old girlfriend?"

"Not at all. She didn't give me the time of day back in school."

"Good for you." She honestly means it.

"We'll see. I have no expectations." He shrugs.

"It's okay to have expectations and want more than flirting and flings, John."

"Are you giving me love advice?" His face shows he doubts the validity of any love advice she might give him.

"I am. I've had a change of heart. Trying to change my spinster ways."

"The Gil guy?"

"Yes, Gil. Seeing him next weekend in fact."

John frowns and nods. "He's coming back up here?"

"Actually, I have a writing gig in Portland and I'm going down there."

"Leaving the island and everything? Look at you go." There is a tinge of sarcasm to his words.

"I'm leaving this weekend. Remember?"

"True, but that's for work. As is next weekend. Technically."

"Yes, technically it's for work, but I'd like to see it as the universe is presenting the opportunity."

"It'd be different if you were going to Portland just for him. At least it would if it was me."

Maggie considers his words. The Portland food festival is a good excuse. If things with Gil are weird or awful, she has a safety net for the trip. And her heart.

"I hadn't considered that."

"Hey, he's probably fine with it. He still gets you for the weekend. I know if he was me, I'd wonder why there was a safety net." He shrugs his shoulders, and finishes the last of his coffee. "What time are you dropping off Biscuit's stuff? I might go fishing."

"I was planning to leave around five to head up island. If you aren't home, I'll use my key and drop his stuff by the door."

"Sounds good. Didn't mean to throw a bucket of water on your trip and Gil reunion. Like I said, he's probably fine with it. He's known you for years, so he knows you don't operate without a net."

Nodding, she partly agrees with him but isn't listening. Her thoughts are caught up in figuring out why she is holding on to her safety net when it comes to Gil. Seeing a hand waving in front of her face, she realizes she's zoned out.

"Hey."

"Sorry, was thinking about nets." She shakes her head to clear her thoughts.

"No problem. I'm going to take off and get some shit done. You'll be home Sunday afternoon?"

"Yeah, yeah, Sunday afternoon," she mumbles.

"I'll let myself out. Stop overthinking. Have fun in Canada. I'll catch you later." John dumps his cup in the sink and then lets himself out.

Her excitement for having an excuse to see Gil next weekend fizzles. If Gil were only coming to the island because of a work thing, she'd feel like an afterthought. Gil isn't an afterthought. Shaking her head, she realizes she doesn't need a reason to go to Portland other than to see Gil.

With a happy sigh, she turns back to her list on the fridge to start packing for this weekend's trip.

* * *

She finds her passport in the safe, right where she left it. Clothes packed, charger packed, and her bag set by the door, she has some time to kill. She washes the dishes from breakfast and lunch. Glancing over at the fridge again, she remembers she was going to find the new ferry schedule. Checking her purse and the pile of papers on the dining table, she isn't able to find it. She doesn't need it to drive to Vancouver, but knows it's somewhere in the house. She swears she got a new schedule the last time she took the ferry.

Quinn! Bessie! Aha!

After scampering out to the garage, she takes the cover off of Bessie. Finding the schedule in the glove compartment gives her a sense of triumph. She pats Bessie's dash and spies Gil's wishing rock. Trying to remember what he said when he found it, she picks up the rock, and strokes the smooth surface with her thumb.

"Hope and faith."

Taking it as a sign she isn't a terrible person for having a safety net, she places Gil's rock back on the dashboard before getting out of the car.

She decides to take Bessie to Portland if the nice weather holds, and calls Steve the mechanic to ensure the car can make the trip. He gives his approval, saying it would be good for the old girl to get off the island and stretch her legs. While talking to him on the phone, Maggie pins the new ferry schedule on the cork-board, and takes down the summer one.

Right after she ends the call, her phone rings again. Thinking Steve is calling her back, she answers without glancing at the screen.

"Maggie?" A female voice greets her.

"Yes, who is this?"

"It's Ruth, your editor. Did you not recognize the number?"

"Oh, hi, sorry. I didn't even look at the screen."

"You're not driving are you?"

"No, not driving."

"I'm glad I caught you before you're on the road to Vancouver."

"Why? What's going on?"

Ruth never calls her. Now that she thinks about it, she can't remember the last time they spoke on the phone.

"Everyone in Vancouver is sick or has food poisoning or something. The dinner is postponed."

"Postponed? Everyone is sick? In all of Vancouver?" Her mind tries to wrap itself around Ruth's words and what this means.

"No, don't be silly. The chef and her staff apparently had a bad mushroom, or clam, or it's a stomach bug, or something. I don't know. I was just told everyone is sick and the dinner is postponed."

"Until when?"

"I have no idea. I'm relieved I caught you before you were in Canada for no reason."

"Thanks for calling and letting me know."

"You're welcome. Listen, I've got other calls to make, and a photographer to reschedule. I'll email you with the new date. It'll probably be in a few weeks. Gotta run. Kisses."

No dinner this weekend.

Her weekend is free.

The ferry schedule falls to the floor.

Thirty-three

"I'm free this weekend," Maggie whispers. "Why am I whispering?"

She thinks about what she should do for about three seconds before making her decision. This isn't about relying on safety nets and excuses. This is about going after what her heart wants now.

Looking at the clock, she realizes it is seven after four. If she hurries, she can make the 4:30 boat. Ten minutes to repack and race down to the dock. No line, and she might make it.

Maggie snatches her already-packed bag, runs upstairs, and starts throwing work appropriate clothes on the bed. From her closet she grabs her favorite navy hoodie, a pair of jeans, and a stack of T-shirts. The little black dress and jacket for the dinner tomorrow night stays in the bag. She's wearing a white oxford, jeans and olive green Toms. She can travel in this. Clothes and shoes are tossed back into the canvas tote.

Biscuit sits in the hall watching the frenzy. She almost trips over him when she hurries back downstairs with her stuff. Shit. Biscuit.

She decides to bring him with her. Pulling another boat tote out of the closet, she stuffs his leash and food into the bag. Biscuit bounces around her feet in excitement.

"Yes, we're going someplace. Someplace we've never been before. Exciting stuff." He jumps up in front of her. "Ready?"

He barks.

She walks around checking doors and windows are locked. Satisfied the house is secure, she glances at the clock. 4:16. She still might make the next ferry.

Whistling for Biscuit, she opens the garage door. While she puts her bags and his folding travel crate in the trunk, Biscuit jumps into the passenger seat through the open door.

After securing his harness, she backs out of the driveway, barely missing John's truck.

He looks at her like she's gone insane.

"Change of plans. No Biscuit. Geoducks," she shouts, leaning out the window as she peels out and speeds down the beach road.

John has no idea what she said, but swears it was something about geoducks. He waves and shakes his head at his crazy neighbor.

The drive to the ferry dock is a blur. When she finally heads down the hill, she sees the last few cars on the dock being loaded on the ferry.

"Shit," she curses, knowing she'll have to wait at least a half hour for the next boat.

She tosses a ticket at the ticket booth operator just as the safety arm lowers at the end of the dock.

"Looks like you barely missed this one," the woman in the booth tells Maggie. "Lane one."

Sighing, Maggie grumbles her thanks and shifts Bessie into gear to pull into the first spot in line.

"When you finally make up your mind about doing something, you don't want to wait a minute longer than you have to," she explains to Biscuit, who sighs in agreement. She smiles at him and gives him a scratch on his head. After putting the car in neutral, she's about to turn the key off when movement on the dock catches her eye.

Turning her head forward, she sees the safety arm being lifted and Bert frantically waving her forward on to the ferry.

She puts Bessie back in gear and drives ahead. Biscuit barks his approval.

"Hiya," Bert greets her, walking alongside the car as she drives slowly down the ramp.

"Noticed a flash of green racing down the hill as we were loading up. Realized it was you and Bessie, and figured this was an important trip. You're lucky you have such a tiny car. Never could squeeze you on if you were in your other car." Bert smiles his gap-toothed grin at her.

"You have no idea, Bert. I owe you big time."

He guides Bessie into the smallest spot ever at the end of the deck—a regular size car would never fit. The engines roar to life as the lines holding the ferry to the dock are pulled in and coiled on the deck.

"Second time in about a month you're taking this car off the island. You becoming a commuter?" He teases.

"Nah, going on a very important trip, Bert. Most important trip ever. Did you know geoducks are for lovers?" Maggie grins at him.

Bert gapes at her.

She wonders what Connie will make of that gossip and hopes Sally figures out the code.

Feeling in her pocket, she pulls the heart shape wishing rock from her hoodie, and places it on the middle of Bessie's dashboard next to Gil's rock. Hope and faith. Trust.

Rather than go up on deck, she sits in the car on the short crossing. Biscuit curls up on his seat and snoozes.

She sends a text.

I believe in the power of Buddha's army.

Picking up the hope and faith rock, she decides the time for hoarding wishes is over. At the back of the boat, she kisses the rock one last time before throwing it as far as she can. It makes a small splash and is swallowed into the churning water behind the ferry. Smiling, she watches the island recede behind her as the wind off the water tangles her hair. The afternoon sun creates a halo over the far shore, casting it in shadow, while shining bright in her eyes.

Her phone chirps with a new text.

Confused.

She grins and sends a reply.

It will all make sense in a few hours.

When the ferry docks, she waves to Bert before pulling off the boat. She's the last car off this time. Better late than never she thinks, driving up the hill before catching the freeway heading south toward Olympia to meet up with her past, present and future.

* * *

A car pulls out of a parking spot right across from the Northern art space in downtown Olympia. Maggie maneuvers Bessie into the spot, congratulating herself on her talent for parallel parking. She'll take her own praise. She's not nervous to see Gil, no, nervous isn't the right word. Her heartbeat flutters. This is it. This is the moment.

After getting out of the car, she smooths down her black sheath dress and straightens her jacket. After swearing Jo to secrecy, Jo left her a key to the house. Biscuit set up, clothes changed, and pep talk given to herself, she is arriving only an hour behind everyone else to the party.

Better late than never.

The art and music space is teaming with hip and not-so-hip forty-somethings, who spill out the front door on the sidewalk. She notices a small cluster of people outside smoking, but no Selah. Good. The first person she wants to see is Gil.

After wandering inside, she checks out people's backs, tops of heads, and profiles while picking a careful path around clusters of people who look mostly unfamiliar.

Still no Gil.

She finds herself in front of a makeshift bar table and grabs a plastic glass of red wine. The crowd is thicker around the bar, so she moves to the opposite wall. From her new vantage point, she can view the back of the room. Standing in a group of men with his back to her is the man she loves.

Gil.

At first she doesn't recognize anyone in the group other than Gil. A bald man with a middle age paunch facing her looks somewhat familiar. Trying to place him, she realizes it is the lead singer from Gil's college band. Mark Jones has not aged well. Selah will be disappointed.

Maggie watches Gil look in her direction, then turn back to his conversation. Did he not see her? She realizes she's surrounded by taller men and women in teetering heels.

Now that she's spied Gil, Maggie has a clear path to him. The crowd parts, a few steps more, and Gil is standing in front of her, his mouth open, and his expression shocked.

Time slows and the room quiets as she takes the few final steps toward him.

"Hi," she says.

"Hi."

"Hi."

"Buddha's army?" He smiles at her.

"Buddha's army. Yep. I guess Quinn has some major pull with the universe."

"But what happened to your big dinner? Big dinner, big article? Vancouver?" He shakes his head.

"Turns out everyone has food poisoning. Bad mushroom or a bad clam. Terrible."

"Terrible," he says, looking into her eyes.

"So I had the weekend free. No plans. No one expecting me anywhere for anything. Thought I'd come find you."

"You found me." He stares at her. "I can't believe you're standing in front of me."

"I am and I have something I wanted to give you." She puts her glass down. Reaching into her jacket pocket, she pulls out the heart shaped wishing rock she found on his pillow. "You gave me hope and faith before you left the island. I wanted to return the favor." She hands him the rock.

"You're giving me a rock? One of your hoarded wishes?" He stares at the rock in his hand and smiles.

"I'm giving you my trust. I'm giving you my heart, Gil Morrow. I love you."

Gil blinks a few times.

She steps forward, laces their fingers together, then reaches up to place a soft kiss on his mouth.

He pulls back from her lips, staring in her eyes.

"You just told me you love me. Out loud and everything. You love me."

"I did. I do. I do love you. I loved you when you had long hair and all your clothes came from thrift stores. I loved you when you had no game and horrible glasses. I've loved you forever, Gil."

He smiles with watery eyes. "And it only took us twenty-two years to get to this moment." He lets go of her hands to pick her up and hug her. She squeals a little before finding his mouth with hers. She kisses him, forgetting everything but Gil.

A familiar scream breaks them out of their bubble.

"Sounds like Quinn has spotted you." Gil laughs, slowly returning her feet to the ground.

"I was hoping we'd be able to stay in our bubble for a little while longer." Maggie straightens her dress. "You have lipstick on your bottom lip." She gestures to his mouth.

He wipes it off with his thumb. "Thanks. Doesn't matter. I think everyone in the room saw our kiss." He turns her to face their friends.

Blushing, she smiles at the happy faces of the people she loves most in the world. Taking Gil's hand, she walks over to them and is engulfed in hugs.

She's exactly where she's supposed to be.

~The End~

Acknowledgements

I am grateful to all who have supported my writing. With special thanks:

To my mother, who instilled in me a love of reading, and my father, who is a natural storyteller. And to my husband, without whom this book would be just another idea stuck in my head.

For those who have been my friends for years and decades, your friendships inspired the close connections in this book.

To Becca, Dawn, Kellie, Kelly, Marla, Mary, Nicole, and Suzie, who were brave enough to beta-read early drafts of this, and gave me the honest feedback and the support I needed to make it better. And to Catherine, who polished my words and fixed my crimes against punctuation.

To the Lost Girls, who are the sisters I always wanted, and Jack, for being the ultimate fanboy.

For the women of the 'online book club' I stumbled upon nearly four years ago and who are the biggest cheerleaders for good writing and following your dreams. Thank you especially to the Bunker Babes for their friendship.

For my family, who may not always understand me, but love and support me.

To my island family and the people of Whidbey Island, for welcoming me into the fold years ago. Many of the places used in this book are real, others no longer exist, and some are made up because I wish they did.

To The Evergreen State College, an incredible, unique college that has the best motto and mascot ever.

Thanks to National Novel Writing Month for being the enemy of procrastination and giving me a goal to get this book off the ground.

Last, but certainly never least, thank you to the readers, bloggers, and reviewers who took a chance on this book. Thanks for reading!

About the Author

Before writing full time, Daisy Prescott worked in the world of art, auctions, antiques, and home decor. She earned a degree in Art History from Mills College and endured a brief stint as a film theory graduate student at Tisch School of the Arts at NYU. Baker, art educator, antiques dealer, blue ribbon pie-maker, fangirl, content manager, freelance writer, gardener, wife, and pet mom are a few of the other titles she's acquired over the years.

Born and raised in San Diego, Daisy and her husband currently live in a real life Stars Hollow in the Boston suburbs with their dog, Hubbell, and an imaginary house goat. She is working on her second novel.

To learn more about this author and her writing visit:

www.daisyprescott.com